KILKENNY BAY

On Halloween night, Curt MacPherson took a boat out into the Bristol Channel and has yet to return. Left with three children and another on the way, Angie decides the sensible thing is to move in with her mother-in-law Daisy, and help run the family store. Curt's brother Calum also returns home, following the end of a relationship. Twenty-year-old daughter Holly falls all too quickly for a local Italian boy, and Angie also finds herself the subject of male interest. But how can she think of looking at another man when her husband has not yet been found?

KILKENNY BAY

KILKENNY BAY

by

Avis Randall

Magna Large Print Books
Long Preston, North Yorkshire,
BD23 4ND, England.

British Library Cataloguing in Publication Data.

Randall, Avis
   Kilkenny Bay.

   A catalogue record of this book is
   available from the British Library

   ISBN   0-7505-1638-0

First published in Great Britain in 1999
by Judy Piatkus (Publishers) Ltd.

Copyright © 1999 by Avis Randall

Cover illustration © Melvyn Warren-Smith by arrangement with
P.W.A. International Ltd.

The moral right of the author has been asserted

Published in Large Print 2001 by arrangement with
Piatkus Books Ltd.

Magna Large Print is an imprint of Library Magna Books Ltd.

Printed and bound in Great Britain by
T.J. (International) Ltd., Cornwall, PL28 8RW

For my grandchildren, the apples of my eye
Nicola, Jessica and Joe
Daniel, Michael, Michael and Bill

As dark storm clouds ebb
promises of safe harbour,
stars silver rock pools.

Haiku by Margaret Holli

Acknowledgements

My sincere thanks for their contribution to *Kilkenny Bay* go

to Judy Piatkus for asking me to keep my head down – and my finances up – by writing another story in the same mould as *Different Kinds of Loving*

to Maeve Binchy for helping me to keep my head down – and my spirits up – with her generous words of encouragement when my pen slowed or my purpose faltered

to my fellow Ivywriters who at our monthly get-togethers accompanied their demand for a reading of the latest chapter with lots of helpful criticisms – and the occasional compliment. Special memories of Ivy McKnight who united us all in the first place

to my agent Serafina Clarke for nudging me in the right direction with her reviews of my draft and her overview of the story

to my editor Gillian Green for promoting, polishing and packaging *Kilkenny Bay* – perfectly

and last, but not least, to Mike – my constant!

Prologue

Hallowe'en night, cold and bleak. With the first frost wind of the season blowing up the Bristol Channel, it was time for the return of the cod after their seasonal break. A tingle of anticipation ran down Curtis MacPherson's spine, setting his heart racing. He was making ready to go fishing, even though his own boat was laid up and he'd asked his brother, Calum, for the use of his.

Collecting his gear from the upstairs bedroom of his council semi, he looked down to see his twin sons scaring the living daylights out of any unsuspecting neighbour walking along the back lane by pouncing out at them from behind the garden shed. Garbed in robes they'd made from wartime blackout curtains their grandmother had unearthed in a box in her loft, and with Hallowe'en masks covering their faces, they jumped and hopped around, making spooky, weird noises.

Holly MacPherson, nineteen years old and growing into an exceptionally attractive young lady, her father thought, strolled down to the end of the garden path to bring in the washing her mother had hung out earlier and hadn't yet had time to bring in.

'Yah ... hh – boo,' the boys yelled. Holly dropped the washing basket and rushed back indoors.

As Curtis descended the stairs, he heard Holly grumbling about the lads to her mother in the kitchen, and Angie's exasperated response. His wife, during the last month or so, seemed to have nowhere near her usual amount of patience with the children; neither did she show the same tolerance to his devotion to fishing, though she'd known from the start how important it was to him.

'I'm off now. Expect me when you see me, all right?' he announced, slipping into his thick all-weather jacket.

'Yeah, 'bye Dad,' answered Holly, opening the back door as she returned to the garden to pick up the scattered washing. She stopped to give him a peck on the cheek; it was friendly, but nothing at all like the tight hugs she'd given him when she was a little girl.

Angie was busy at the sink. Curtis came up behind her and wrapped his arms round her waist, nuzzling his face gently in her neck. 'OK, are you?' he asked.

'Yeah, OK now,' she replied. 'I don't really mind you going, you know that, don't you? It's just ... well ... sometimes it all gets a bit too much. I'm feeling kind of strange, physically. I could do with a holiday, I guess.'

'Angie-baby, I promise, *promise!* Next year somewhere fabulous, if things turn out the way I plan.'

He kissed her warmly. She turned round in his arms and kissed him back. 'Safe sailing,' she whispered. 'You know I love you, really.'

'I know, and I love *you,* too. You're my life,

Angeline MacPherson – you and our three nutty kids.'

He went out into the cold night. A myriad stars twinkled in the ebony sky as he headed for the cove where his brother's boat, *Solitude,* was moored, and where the evening tide, rising fast, was heavy with the secrets of the sea.

Chapter One

July – Nine Months Later
The scenes and thoughts racing round Calum's head were always the same whenever he went out in his brother's boat. He accepted the fact they always would be, at least until there was a resolution to the mystery.

Green Pepperoni ... a fanciful name. Calum wondered who'd chosen to call the boat that. It didn't sound like Curtis's choice; he would more likely have gone for the name of one of his kids, and yet you never knew.

It reminded Calum of a poem he'd learned at primary school. *The owl and the pussy cat went to sea in a beautiful pea green boat.* There – that was a blast from the past! He recalled how he'd shared a desk with Roxanne Cox, and once put a grass snake down her blouse. The commotion she'd caused had got him a caning, and a hundred-line detention after class.

At least it had for a few moments switched Calum's thinking away from the same old subject going round and round in his brain – his brother's sudden disappearance on that frosty October night almost nine long months ago.

'Bring 'er round – that's it, Rust,' he heard Figgis, the hobbler, call. Calum eased off the engine and steered his craft into the shallows of Lee Creek.

Hitching the boat to the mooring buoy, he boarded Figgis's dinghy for the short journey to shore. Reaching the harbour wall, Calum leapt across a narrow strip of mud, and grabbed the handrail of the iron steps leading to the quayside. With a wave of his hand, the hobbler cast away.

'See you in the shop later, Rusty!' Figgis called.

Calum paused halfway up the steps. 'Aah,' he confirmed. 'I'll be there for the next half an hour.'

'Can't make it then,' Figgis said. 'I'll be in for the two o'clock at Wincanton. I'll see thee *then*, mate.'

'Know something, do you?' asked Calum.

'Nothing I've heard of, but I fancies Bert Entwhistle myself.'

'Never in a month of Sundays,' Calum scoffed as he climbed on to the quayside wall. 'Bert Entwhistle's nothing but a milkman's hoss.'

'Well, that's what I'm a-gonna do. Maybe I'll have 'im each way, just to be on the safe side.'

'You'll bloody need to,' Calum called. 'He'll be still out there running when 'tis time for the next race.'

He shook his head as he crossed the green, heading for the betting shop. Bert bloody Entwhistle ... whatever did some blokes have in their noggins for brains?

'Tell your uncle his dinner's on the table,' Daisy told her granddaughter, Holly. 'If he's not back directly, he knows where it'll go – straight down the lulubelle, that's where. It won't be the first nor the *last* time he's had that happen to him, as

15

well you know, my treasure.'

She turned her attention to the simmering hotpot, while Holly slipped out the back door of the whitewashed stonebuilt cottage. The spacious two-storey cottage, with the front converted into a small general store, had been home to the MacPhersons since 1951, when Daisy and Cameron were married. Daisy had lived in the village all her life but her husband had come to Somerset as a soldier in the regular Army, from his home in Oban on the west coast of Scotland. After his discharge from the Army, Cameron had found a job with a local farmer and lodged at Mariner's Cottage for a while. A year or two later, when the owners decided to sell, he and Daisy, recently married, had bought the property from them.

Cameron's sister, Vinnie, lived in Oban still. It was a while since she and Daisy had met, though they'd kept in close contact over the years, and more especially the last few, since they were both widowed. Vinnie was on Daisy's mind this morning. She'd received a letter from her, stating that her son, Stuart's, wife had died quite suddenly at the age of forty-four. *Everyone* had their cross to bear, Daisy thought; she must give Vinnie a ring soon.

Setting a saucepan of green beans on to simmer, she went into the dining room to lay the table for six. Only a few months ago, she'd been on her own and thinking of selling up. It was sod's law, she knew, but it seemed no sooner had Angie and the children moved in, than Calum, her youngest, split up with his girlfriend, and

16

now he was back living at home again, too.

Holly, on her way to the betting shop, checked her watch; it was a quarter to one. The smell of her grandmother's hotpot had stimulated her tastebuds, and putting on a spurt, she hurried down the steep hill that led to the waterfront.

The village of Fuzzy Cove nestled at the end of Lee Creek. Fuzz-on-the-mud it was known as locally, though when the tide was in, as it was now, it didn't look half so bad, Holly thought. A flotilla of small boats bobbed at anchor. Most, with the exception of her father's *Green Pepperoni*, were painted white or blue and, in the main, looked fairly well cared for. If it wasn't for the murkiness of the water, they could have been moored in a picturesque Mediterranean port, or some little chocolate-box harbour on the Cornish coast. Even on a fine July day like today, the river was the colour of yesterday's stale tea. It wasn't until Holly had been taken on holiday to Polzeath, at the age of four, that she'd seen there was a nicer, more wholesome-looking, hue to the sea than the tidal water of the Severn and the Bristol Channel.

A Cornish fishing town would suit her mother, Angie, fine, of course. Angeline MacPherson had been born in Polzeath, and dreamed of going back there to live one day. It wasn't a completely impossible dream either, Holly reminded herself, now that her father was gone.

He had been missing for some while now. On the night of Hallowe'en, nearly nine months ago, he'd taken Calum's boat, *Solitude*, out into the Channel to fish, and was never seen or heard of

17

again. No wreckage had ever been sighted, and neither had his body been found. The whole family had been shocked to the core by his disappearance, and each was still adjusting to the loss in their own way.

Holly didn't share her mother's hankering to move away. She had lived in Fuzzy Cove all her life, and she wanted to stay; to be here on the day her father returned. Holly absolutely refused to entertain the notion that he was dead.

Holly pushed open the glass-panelled door of the betting shop, and a couple of locals barged past her on their way out, nearly knocking her down. They had the glazed, fixed stare of the serious gambler; the same look she saw daily in the dark sapphire eyes of her Uncle Calum.

She walked over to the counter where Roxanne Meredith, her best friend's mother, was working behind the counter. Honey-blonde hair teased into a beehive high on her head, Roxanne was flirting like crazy with the customer whose bet she was taking. She winked a heavily mascaraed eye at Holly.

'You girls going out tonight, I hear,' she chortled, handing the man his betting slip, and sliding the change across the top of the green vinyl counter.

'Yeah.' Holly nodded. 'Remind Erin to be ready prompt at a quarter to eight. Jasmine's brother's going to give us a lift into Bristol.'

'And you just mind what you'm up to,' Roxanne Meredith warned, her husky voice loaded with innuendo. 'Don't get doing nothink *I* wouldn't do. It's a big wicked world out there.'

'*Only* Bristol,' Holly reminded her.

'It all depends where you'm going to in Bristol,' Roxanne said. 'You'd best make sure you got your cast-iron knickers on – all of you.'

She indicated with her thumb towards a doorway, hung with a pair of swing wooden half-doors, like a Western saloon. 'Your Uncle Rusty's in the back, large as life, and twice as ugly.'

The dimly lit room, more like an alcove, was where Holly's uncle usually congregated with a group of his special cronies. She was well acquainted with the place; she'd been hauling him out of this den of iniquity for absolutely *ever.*

Through the slats in the swing doors, Holly watched her uncle for a while. Slim and wiry, he had the same vivid red hair as her own, though, at the age of forty-two, Calum's was receding fast, while hers was thick and bushy, cascading round her shoulders like a wild rosy cloud. His eyes were identical to hers, too – a dark, dense shade of blue – almost navy. Holly was reminded how very similar to her father he looked. He was nothing like her father in his ways, though. *Curtis* MacPherson was honest and straight as a die, steadfast and true to just one woman.

At the time of his brother's disappearance, Calum had been living with his long-time girlfriend, Suzi Glue, at her home at Portmills, in Bristol, on the far side of the river. Ever since Holly was old enough to remember, her uncle had been involved with a number of different women. As he continually boasted, none of them had managed to trap him into marriage, though Suzi, the mother of his two small daughters, had

19

come remarkably close to it. No one really knew what Calum had got up to, Holly told herself. There were probably a few other little redheaded MacPhersons out there somewhere, if anybody went to the trouble of looking.

She guessed that Roxanne Meredith knew more about Calum's affairs than almost anyone else; they had grown up together, and were still very close. Holly hoped to get up the nerve one day to ask Roxanne about her uncle's pursuits – both past and present. There seemed to be no one else in his life just now, although he continued to pop in and out of Suzi's house whenever it suited him. Holly knew he did, because she regularly babysat the girls for Suzi. He was living at home with his mother again now, sleeping on the bed-settee in the front parlour, with the three upstairs bedrooms being occupied by Holly and her family.

Calum looked up and, seeing Holly watching him, grinned a cheeky welcome and began to gather his bits and pieces together.

'Yere she is then – love of my heart, liver, and lights. Our mother sent you down to hustle me out, I've no doubt.'

Jumping to his feet, he picked up his *Daily Mirror,* cigarettes and lighter, and slipped a red and a green Biro into his Levi jacket pocket. 'Come on, my little rosebud ... let your favourite uncle escort you home.'

'My *least* favourite uncle,' Holly teased.

Calling goodbye to Roxanne and to the regular punters in the shop, Calum threw his arm round her shoulder and steered her through the door.

Linking arms companionably, they made their way up the steep incline that led to Mariner's Cottage.

Angie MacPherson tiptoed quietly round the bedroom, careful not to wake up eight-week-old Evie, whom she'd just put down for her afternoon nap. With three-quarters of an hour to go before opening up, she was able to push all thoughts of the shop to the back of her mind. Her twin sons were chatting to their grandmother in the dining room below. Angie guessed they were already at the table – starving hungry as usual.

When after several months Angie had given up hope of her husband's swift return, she had taken up Daisy's invitation to come and live with her at Mariner's Cottage. Ever since Curtis's disappearance, Daisy hadn't been sleeping well; she was looking and feeling increasingly tired. She had assured Angie she would much rather cook the family's meals and look after the baby than manage the shop. And Angie, after more than twenty years of *having* to go out to work while looking after a home and children, had jumped at the chance to change roles. She hated housework these days, and only cooked meals for the children for the same reason that she gardened and vacuumed – simply because it had to be done.

She sighed disconsolately, and sank down on the padded window seat. Contrary to what she'd thought when she was first married, life was seldom any *wonderful* voyage of discovery ... and, if it was, the experience usually didn't last long. Hardly anyone that she knew had it perfect – or even near-perfect. Since Curt's disappearance, Angie's own enjoyment of life had spiralled quite spectacularly downhill.

Since that day in October, almost nine months ago, when her strong healthy husband vanished, Angie had existed in a vortex, her mind in turmoil, her thoughts twisting and turning in all directions. A gigantic question mark hung over her life. She was unable to make any plans for the future, not knowing if he was alive or dead.

Angie picked up a blue cushion and buried her face in its soothing softness. Smoothing back her dark curly hair, she held the cushion tightly to her body while she pondered the mystery of her husband's disappearance, the way she'd done a thousand times before.

It was a horrible thought, she knew, and one best not contemplated in the middle of a long dark night, but he – or what was left of him – could be lying on a remote beach somewhere, murdered perhaps, or, most likely, drowned. The biggest puzzle of all, though, was what had happened to the boat? If *Solitude* had gone down in the Channel, it was astonishing that no wreckage had ever been found.

She supposed it *was* possible that her husband had taken off somewhere – a fake disappearance he'd been planning for a while. But *that* was completely foreign to the Curtis MacPherson that Angie knew. She could think of no good reason why he should go missing voluntarily. They'd been rubbing along quite satisfactorily, she had thought. Or was she merely kidding herself? Months of wishing and wondering could drive a person crackers ... persuade you into thinking just about *anything!*

Angie laid the cushion to one side, propping it into its usual corner position. Sitting upright, she rubbed a residue of pink window cleaner from the windowpane. It was important that she kept busy; the minute she found herself with time to think, the strangest thoughts came tumbling into her mind. Just a few moments longer, she told herself, and then she really must shake herself out of this mood of retrospection.

When she and Curt were first married, the physical attraction they'd felt for each other had been sufficient to patch up any incipient rift. And *what* a physical attraction it was, Angie thought now. No matter how serious their quarrels, making up had been a stupendous firework show, a wonderful, absolutely heavenly spontaneous combustion. Fiery red hair, and the passion to match. From the very first moment he chatted her up at the annual Pill Regatta, Angie had been putty in Curt MacPherson's hands.

In later years, although the passion had abated somewhat, they still sometimes had their moments. Not as frequently or perhaps as passionately as then, but neither were they at all *un*happy. Angie fiddled with a long loose thread at the hem of the blue cotton curtains, finally biting it off with her teeth. Her hazel green eyes clouded with uncertainty. Well, *she* wasn't unhappy, she reminded herself, and she didn't think that Curt had been, either. With not much

23

else in common except the three children, like many other couples who'd been married a good number of years they had drifted into a state of comfortable compromise, rubbing along together quite contentedly.

Angie could hear Holly talking downstairs in the kitchen. So – Holly had successfully tracked down the wicked one! Rusty MacPherson, as Calum was known by most people outside his own family, was in need of a minder, Angie thought. Always in trouble of some sort or other ... she hoped it was only *minor* trouble. He thrived on taking chances. Along with the rest of the gang he mixed with, he liked sailing close to the wind in more ways than one.

Daisy was most probably dishing up lunch now and, if Angie knew her, chary of calling her down for fear of disturbing the baby. Angie went over to the cot to look at her sleeping infant. Dear, sweet little Evie, pink and beautiful as a summer rose; and her father lost before she was even born. Angie wondered what Curt would think if he knew they had another child. She was certain when he saw this sweet little soul, he would love her as much as *she* did.

At the time of his disappearance Angie had been nearing her fortieth birthday, and a few weeks afterwards she'd discovered she was pregnant again. When she missed her first period, she had put it down to shock. However, by the time that Christmas came, she'd known for certain she was pregnant. Her pregnancy had seemed a mixed blessing at the time. Now, though, she couldn't imagine life without her baby girl.

Like Angie's other children, Evie bore no resemblance to Angie herself. Her baby blue eyes were dark as midnight sapphire, and her frizzy strawberry pink hair soft as fairground candyfloss. She looked, Angie thought, very much like Holly had looked at her age, though now Holly's hair was fiery red ... the MacPhersons' inheritance with a vengeance.

Angie went into the front bedroom which Holly shared with her grandmother; Holly had a small folding bed, and Daisy the high feather bed where she'd slept all her married life. Angie opened the drawer that had been allocated to Holly in the old-fashioned chest of drawers, and placed some clean underwear inside. It wasn't often that she had to bother with her daughter's laundry. She'd taken to doing her own washing now, and certainly all of her ironing.

During the time since her father had gone missing, Holly had changed from a young girl into a responsible, capable woman. Though her daughter still remained her close and valuable companion, Angie knew it was time to let her go – allow her to live her own life and, where necessary, make her own mistakes.

Holly had announced earlier that she was off to a nightclub in Bristol for the evening with her friends. Angie knew that she wouldn't get a wink of sleep until she heard her key in the lock – however late it might be. She thanked her lucky stars that the boys and Evie were still young enough to be tucked up safely in their beds at night. Their day would come soon enough and, with Jake and Luke, it wasn't too far away.

Perhaps Holly will be settled in a home of her own by then, Angie told herself. One down; three more to go.

It was nice to envisage having some time for herself, however far off it might be. Angie sighed, and rose to her feet. There was no point getting too excited. With a new baby to bring up, and her husband missing, the day of freedom seemed a lifetime away.

Gently closing the bedroom door, Angie went down to the kitchen where Calum was washing his hands under the cold water tap.

'How's your luck?' she enquired, patting his arm fondly in passing.

Calum screwed up his mouth, and shook his head dolefully. 'Down the pan, Ange, I'm afraid ... all down the pan.' He dried his hands on the roller towel and added cheerfully, 'We're all set to win the lotto tonight, though.'

'You're sure about that, are you?' asked Angie.

'Too right I am, mate. You'd best keep in with me: I'll be a roll-over millionaire in–' he consulted his watch '–exactly seven hours from now.'

'And pigs might sprout wings and fly,' said his mother, flapping a tea cloth at his head.

Daisy had already dished out the hotpot, Angie saw. Grabbing an oven glove, she picked up two brimming plates and carried them through to the dining room.

'He's mad,' remarked Holly, almost crashing into her in the doorway. She stepped back to allow her mother by. 'Oops – sorry,' she apologised. 'Are there any more to come?'

'No, that's the lot now, love – thanks,' Angie

26

replied. 'Only your uncle's left, and he'll bring in his own, I dare say.'

Calum touched the dish gingerly with his finger, 'Ouch, that's bloody hot,' he exclaimed.

'Always moaning,' Daisy said, pushing past him to reach into a cupboard for the low-sodium salt. 'Nothing to do, but eat what's put in front of him ... and he's *always* bloody moaning.'

'This time tomorrow, I shall have a butler doing this,' Calum told her, slipping his plate on to a small metal tray.

'And how long d'you think a butler would last with *you?*' Daisy asked.

'Like Anthony Hopkins,' Calum continued, disregarding her remark. 'In that film what our Angie had out the other day. It were filmed down yere in Clevedon; I recognised the pier.'

'*The Remains of the Day,*' called Holly from the next room.

'That's 'e,' said her uncle. 'The best butler I ever saw – perfect for when I've bought me mansion with the old lotto money.'

'Makes a change from racehorses; I'll give you that,' Daisy commented, following Calum into the dining room.

Chapter Two

Aware that she was forfeiting the last ten minutes of the Saturday omnibus of *Brookside*, her favourite soap, Erin Meredith was washing her long blonde hair. Her mother wouldn't be home from the betting shop for another fifteen minutes, so Erin had the bathroom to herself.

Every four weeks, on a Saturday, their local pub, the Smuggler's Retreat, put on a country and western show. Marty Riley, a small-time professional, was booked tonight to do his impersonation of Charley Pride. Roxanne had been going on about it all week. She raved over Charley Pride, and had done for as long as Erin could remember. She would be doing herself up to the nines, hoping to catch Marty's ageing eye.

Erin helped herself to a good measure of her mother's special shampoo for naturally blonde hair, followed by a large dollop of matching conditioner. That was a laugh ... Erin smiled quietly to herself. It was unlikely that her mother's hair had ever been naturally blonde. From what Erin remembered, it had *always* come out of a bottle. No doubt about it, though – Roxanne would have Erin's guts for garters if she knew she was nicking her best Beauty Parlour shampoo.

After she had showered, and wrapped a towel round her head, Erin went and stood in front of the full-length wall mirror where she proceeded to examine her body carefully. Ever critical of her physical defects – one or two real, though most of them imagined – she ran her hands over her slender hips and down her slim thighs. Her knees were too wide and too knobbly for her skinny legs, she thought, and the spot at the end of her nose felt as huge as a mountain. Her nose looked as long as Pinocchio's when he was telling those monstrous lies.

I'm a liar, too, Erin told herself. She lied to just about *everyone*, about simply *everything*, every day of her life. A plain ugly, useless, no-good lump of flesh, who no boy would ever want to take out, leave alone fall in love with and one day want to marry.

Her mother always told her she looked all right, and really had nothing to worry about, but how did Roxanne know how she felt? She'd never understood the slightest thing about Erin since she was born. And neither did the daft woman understand anything about the man she'd been married to for more than twenty-four years, Erin concluded sadly.

Her father, Henry, was the dearest, sweetest man alive, though – even she had to admit – he was a complete wimp where her mother was concerned. She and her father both knew that Roxanne loved him in her own way, but she certainly didn't deserve a husband as nice as him, not with *her* randy carryings on.

Erin's sympathy was with her father, to whom she was loyal with every scrap of her being. She often wondered how much he knew about her mother's philandering, for discretion wasn't a word that Roxanne understood. He was no fool, but the way he closed his eyes to her promiscuous behaviour Erin found difficult to understand. Her mother often made Erin ashamed to be a woman ... those bouncy great breasts, and the strutting Tina Turner walk was embarrassing to watch. God alone knew what her father thought. He couldn't not know the way she gallivanted off the moment his back was turned. When he worked nights on the hospital switchboard, she sometimes didn't come home until morning.

Forever wishing to please his wife, her father was probably, even now, dressing in the gaudily checked shirt Roxanne had bought him, the unsuitably tight blue jeans she'd chosen for him to wear on their Saturday nights out. Erin hadn't a clue if he actually enjoyed the entertainment; she strongly suspected he didn't. There was one thing about which she *was* certain, however; her mother didn't give a damn *either* way.

Roxanne always liked to go out on a Saturday night. 'Out on the razzle', as she called it. Karaoke night; a country and western special; even a humdrum quiz: anything of a social nature turned Erin's mother on.

Erin shivered apprehensively, feeling the goosebumps crawling up her arms and all the way down her back. She quickly plugged in the hair drier, anxious to be finished and out of the bathroom before her mother got back. She didn't want an interrogation about her own evening out, where she was going, and what she would be doing every minute of the time. Her mother was the sort of mother who liked to interfere in her daughter's business in the mistaken belief that she was fostering a lifetime friendship. Some hopes of that, Erin thought, unless her mother changed her ways drastically.

From time to time Erin suffered from a mild bout of bulimia, though she was no longer anorexic – thanks to her good friend Holly MacPherson, who'd given her no peace until she agreed to visit the school health counsellor. The rare instances of bulimia worried Erin, but she was certain she could conquer it completely, given time and a little less interference from her mother.

As Erin was returning to her bedroom, she heard her mother come into the house. Erin quickly slipped into her going-out gear, a long-sleeved white silk blouse and black miniskirt, with black Lycra tights and brown lace-up ankle-length boots.

Holly had phoned to say that their friend Jasmine's brother, Dominic, a newly qualified doctor, home on leave from his hospital in Gloucester for the weekend, had offered to take them in to Bristol in his mother's car. Erin's stomach turned a complete somersault at the thought. She wondered whether Dominic was coming to the club with them, and if not, where else he planned to spend his evening.

Although she hadn't told anyone else – not even Holly who was her dearest friend – Erin secretly hoped that Dominic would be joining them at the club. Dominic Stone was her idea of

31

an exceptionally dishy bloke; better even than Christian Slater, or Brad Pitt, whose pictures adorned her bedroom wall. He might have attended a posh boarding school, and then trained to become a doctor but from what Erin had seen he and his sister Jasmine had no 'edge' to them at all. In that respect, they were completely different from the rest of their toffee-nosed family.

Erin shivered again, this time with pleasurable anticipation. In one hour from now, she would be sitting in the back of Dominic Stone's mother's car while he drove her and her friends to the Night Owl nightclub on Whiteladies Road. She suddenly felt sick, and clapped her hand to her mouth. She would be unable to eat a thing for tea, and *that* would set her mother off, for sure. She'd have to say she'd already eaten, and hope and pray that her father kept his mouth shut. If not she might have to resort... Erin broke off the unthinkable thought midway.

Although it was still daylight, the floodlights were on at the rear of the big house on the top of the hill, illuminating the terrace and the blue-tiled octagonal swimming pool. Beyond the neatly clipped box hedge bordering the garden was a stunning view of the Bristol Channel where it washed the pebbled shoreline and hidden rock pools of Kilkenny Bay.

The front of the smart grey stucco residence overlooked a wooded valley, at the bottom of which nestled the village of Fuzzy Cove. The main street of Fuzzy Cove, comprising a row of stonebuilt cottages, interspersed with one or two shops, faced the west side of a small horseshoe-shaped harbour at the head of Lee Creek, a short, narrow inlet which flowed in from the Channel near where it merged with the River Severn.

Viewed from the Stones' mansion on a winter's night, Fuzzy Cove resembled a scene from some romantic movie. Shimmering neon street lights formed a half circle round the harbour, their yellowy orange glow mirrored in the water that lapped against the glistening green walls. Jasmine, as a child, looking down at the village from her mother's bedroom window, had thought it a fairytale place, inhabited by wondrous, fairy-like characters. Her childhood fantasies had altered abruptly at the age of eleven when she transferred from her private prep school to the local comprehensive.

'Bloody holy shit.'

Jasmine Stone, sitting in front of her gingham-draped, glass-topped dressing table, grumbled impatiently. Her pump-straight ebony hair had developed a kink, and she slapped on some water to straighten it, holding it in position with a short length of Sellotape. Dark brown eyes, almost black, stared back at her from the mirror; she applied a mascara wand to her thick black lashes, and smoothed grey eye shadow on to her lower lids, adding a dash of cinnamon pink above. Peeling off her jeans, and throwing them on to the cream lace duvet cover, she walked over to the walk-in wardrobe and selected the shortest miniskirt she could find – black – the same as

Holly and Erin would be wearing, she thought. Jazz normally liked to 'play it different' but tonight she wanted to look the same as her friends.

'Any chance you might be ready?' Dominic called to her from the top landing.

Tall and well built, with the same curly mid-brown hair and turquoise blue eyes as their mother, Mirabel, Jasmine had to agree that he wasn't bad-looking as brothers go. In her frequent clashes with other family members, Dominic was always her ally. He was *all right* – the opposite of their elder brother, Giles, a law graduate, who was training to be a barrister, like their father, Quentin C. Stone, the eminent West Country QC.

'Just can't get my bloody hair to lie straight, but apart from that, Dom, I'll be with you any minute,' she replied.

Jazz slipped into a close-fitting peony-pink knitted top, pulling it down to an inch above the waist of her miniskirt, leaving her navel exposed. Shiny beige Lycra tights and a pair of tan leather cowboy boots, which their father had bought on a lecturing tour in Arizona, completed the snazzy outfit.

'How d'you like this top?' she asked. 'Too tight, d'you reckon, is it, bruv?'

Dominic shrugged. He wasn't interested. Having shared digs with a couple of female students, and being surrounded at work by nurses of every shape and size, he was completely unbothered by women's apparel – sexy or unsexy.

'Do we pick up the blonde first, or the wild redhead?' he asked.

'Erin lives the nearest,' Jazz told him.

Resisting the urge to knot a pink-and-white spotted bandana round her neck, she dropped it back on the bed and slipped a tan leather shoulder purse over her head.

'Ready? Let's go,' she announced.

'Stefanie not going with you tonight?' her mother questioned, when she and Dominic had descended the thickly carpeted stairway.

'She hasn't been asked, and neither is she likely to be,' answered Jazz.

Her mother was matchmaking again, lining up a suitable partner for her brother and, at the same time, an acceptable girlfriend for herself, Jazz knew.

'God, Jasmine, I wish you would find someone else to go nightclubbing with,' Mirabel Stone wailed. 'I ran into that wretched common woman in the village post office this morning, and just because her daughter was being picked up by Dom tonight, she seemed to think she could converse with me on equal terms.' She shuddered as if she found the memory repellent.

'Lord alive, Mother, what a snob you are,' said Jazz. 'Erin Meredith is one of the nicest, sweetest girls you could ever hope to meet.'

Giles, Jasmine's elder brother, sauntered towards them from the direction of the drawing room. He cast Jasmine a supercilious glance before addressing their mother.

'That's what comes from having let her go to the comprehensive. I told you you'd live to regret it.' Staring his sister in the eye, he shook his head sadly. 'You have to admit, Ma – Georgia *never*

35

behaved like this.'

'Shut your trap, toad-features,' said Jazz. 'What would *you* know about it anyway? You wouldn't recognise a decent person if your life were to depend on it ... most especially a *girl.*'

Giles sniffed disparagingly. 'I recognise a middle-aged slut and a first-class wally when I see them ... like your friend's mother and dad. Don't forget, little sister, people will judge you by the company you keep. Georgia is a sister to be admired,' he added.

Jazz stared back into her brother's hard dark eyes, feeling a great distaste. Giles, like their father, was several inches shorter than Dominic; more heavily built, on the verge of becoming podgy.

'Our precious sister to be admired? You don't know her as well as I do, Gilesy dear,' she said.

'Let's be on our way,' interrupted Dominic. '*Who* did you say we ought to pick up first – the quiet Meredith girl or Holly, *whoa-ho,* Mac-Pherson?'

'God Dom – have you got cloth ears or something? Erin first, and then Holly, I said.'

Jasmine heaved a sigh, and shook her head. 'There's some brilliant country and western playing at the Smuggler's tonight ... I'd a million times rather be going there.'

She was into country and western music in a big way – very unusual for someone her age, she knew. It had started four years earlier, built on the strong attraction she'd felt – and still did – for the chunky fair-haired manager of the Smuggler's Retreat public house. Although Barry

36

Buckley hadn't succumbed since to Jasmine in a romantic way, he was still her good mate – her pal – her very best buddy of all time.

'Heaven preserve us,' groaned Giles. Leading his mother into the drawing room, he headed for the tall drinks cabinet and, while Mirabel Stone sank wearily into a comfortable armchair, he poured them each a large glass of port and Remy Martin.

Henry Meredith tapped his fingers in time to 'Stand by Your Man', sung by a woman the wrong side of fifty, all dolled up to look like a sixteen-year-old bimbo. Roxanne, in a shiny emerald green dress with plunging neckline, was leaning over talking to the couple at the next table, so that all Henry was left to look at was the sight of her plump rear. He didn't object to *that* in the least. His wife's size was the least of his worries. He only wished she wasn't quite so boisterous ... so into everything ... on the move, from morning till night.

Roxanne turned round and smoothed Henry's neck, planting a kiss on his receding hairline.

'Lillian yere says she once seen Tammy Wynette in the flesh,' she chirruped excitedly. 'Crystal Gayle and Box Car Willy was on the same programme, too.' She squeezed Henry's thigh. 'What about *we* going up to Wembley, next time there's a country and western show?'

'Sounds like a good idea,' Henry replied. 'You'll have to look out for when it's on.' With any luck, he thought, there wouldn't be one for the next twelve months. And if there was, it might be fully booked. Fingers crossed, and toes.

'A coach firm at Weston always sends Lil the details,' Roxanne informed him.

Jabbing her neighbour in the arm, she sought confirmation that this was so. She turned back to Henry. 'Lil says she'll give me a ring as soon as she knows summat,' she said.

'I see,' answered Henry, trying not to appear too unenthusiastic. The other woman was smiling and nodding in his direction. Her husband, a mortuary attendant whom Henry knew vaguely at the hospital, was nodding encouragingly too.

'Ooh,' Roxanne enthused, squirming happily as she reached for her cigarettes. 'Ooh, I can't wait for Marty Riley to come on. He'd beat all them other impersonators into a cocked hat.'

'I'd better get the drinks in then, before he starts,' Henry told her.

Getting to his feet, he pushed his way through the crush to the bar. He wondered why so many men liked to hog the bar stools, blocking the way and making it difficult for anyone else to be served.

'Excuse me,' Henry murmured, squeezing past an oversized golfing type. The man stared at him curiously before moving his beer an inch further along.

As Henry waited resignedly, the female singer left the makeshift stage. A great roar went up as the main attraction took her place. Henry wasn't averse to country and western, though given a choice he'd much rather listen to Pavarotti. But anything that made Roxanne happy was all right by him – a contented Roxanne was always his goal. She could make or break the Sabbath day of rest, all according to what she'd got up to the night before.

Henry wished his wife was more a stay-at-home sort of woman. Until recently, he'd had Erin to keep him company in the evenings. But now that she had started going out with a group of friends, he had no excuse to remain at home.

Brown boots, he thought, remembering his daughter's weird apparel tonight. The kids of today certainly wore some funny clothes! Brown boots, with thick black stockings... Henry couldn't fathom the thinking behind such a daft idea. His daughter had gone into town this evening wearing the same sort of hobnail boots that street urchins wore in the days that Charles Dickens wrote about. And they said that women were liberated now! Henry was baffled to know just what most of them *did* want.

He flapped a ten-pound note almost in front of the barmaid's face, but she hurried past, ignoring it as though it didn't exist. Henry sighed. It was all such a terrible waste of time. There was nothing he liked better than a Saturday night in; at this very moment he was missing *Casualty* on the box. Working in a hospital, Henry took a special interest in all the medical programmes. Thank goodness for video, was all he could say.

Still waiting to attract the bar staff's attention, Henry heard his wife call out to the singer. 'Marty, Marty – we love you, Marty.' A moment later Roxanne's exuberant cheers were lost in a wild burst of guitar music as her idol began his routine.

At last the barmaid turned Henry's way. 'Half of best and a lager and lime,' Henry said.

'Sorry I couldn't get to you before,' the woman apologised as she pumped his beer. 'We're ever so short-staffed. I've bin rushed off my flaming feet all night.'

She plonked the drinks in front of him, pushing away some damp strands of hair from her sweaty forehead with the underside of her forearm.

'This Saturday night caper's getting right on my tits, I don't mind telling you,' she complained, 'And there's two more hours of it to go yet.'

Henry smiled his commiseration. Only two more hours to go, and then – Roxanne permitting – he'd be tucked up in bed with the latest John Grisham bestseller that he'd taken out from the village library this morning.

Henry had a thing about whodunnits, especially American whodunnits. He liked the way American writers often highlighted their towns, making them seem familiar to the reader, and not just a name on a map. It was Memphis in Grisham's case. Similarly, scalpel-sharp Scarpetta had so acquainted Henry with Richmond, Virginia that he felt he knew the place intimately now.

When Henry was a young man, longer ago than he cared to remember, John Steinbeck had introduced him to Monterey, in his novel *Cannery Row*. The west coast of the USA was somewhere he planned to visit one day. He hadn't said much on the subject to Roxanne; mention America to *her*, and it would be

Nashville that sprang immediately to mind. In fifteen years' time, when Henry retired – before, if he could afford it – he intended to take the holiday of his dreams. He'd hire a car somewhere in Northern California and drive all the way down the coast road to Los Angeles, taking in Big Sur and Steinbeck country on the way.

Roxanne could please herself whether she went with him or not, he thought, weaving a path back to where she was sitting applauding the show. Henry was damn sure *he* was going, and nothing was going to stop him, other than his health failing or – God forbid – pegging out prematurely, before he had the time or money to put his plan into action.

Chapter Three

Bert Entwhistle *had* come in last at Wincanton, just as Calum predicted. He hadn't touched the nag himself, though a few of the silly buggers in the shop had stuck their shirts on it. They'd obviously been listening to the same source that Figgis had. Like a flock of bloody sheep following little Bo-Peep, Calum thought.

One in particular was a sad case known to everyone in the betting shop as Snooky. He must have a first name, Calum mused, but no one, to his knowledge, ever used it. Snooky had been in a right state this afternoon, pouncing on anyone and everyone who came in the door to see if they'd lend him a quid. Calum had been caught unawares; it was easier to slip the poor sod a pound than have to listen to his long tale of woe.

'I'll pay you back in the week,' Snooky had promised, but Calum had written the money off, and determined not to get caught again.

Dabbing a generous splash of Paco Rabanne on his neck and chest, thus avoiding his newly shaven face, which, because he was fair-skinned and freckled, was prone to develop a rash, Calum slipped into a clean blue shirt, all ready for his evening out. He was in with a promise, he hoped, later on, provided the bird he'd arranged to meet at the Gordano service station turned up.

It hadn't been a definite promise, he had to admit, but she'd looked fairly decent, and his mate, Kevin Buttercup, reckoned she was good for a laugh if nothing else. Whether or not Kev had been farther than that – a laugh – Calum hadn't the vaguest notion. He would be testing the water for himself, so long as his luck held out. It didn't do to rely on hearsay, even if the source of the gossip did happen to be a good mate. Calum believed in forming his own conclusions. You could be losing your shirt on a nag called Bert Entwhistle if you didn't watch out for yourself.

The bathroom doorknob rattled, interrupting his train of thought.

'Uncle Calum, can I come in?' he heard one of the twins shout.

'Which one is it?' he asked, looking in the mirror to check that his hair was lying straight. It needed a cut – perhaps he'd make it to Bob the barber's next week.

'It's Jake, and I'm busting ... *Uncle...*' His nephew's voice was growing desperate.

Calum threw open the door. 'Come on in, my cocker,' he said. 'We can't be doing with a pool on the floor. I'm on my way anyway.'

After exchanging a few words with his mother and sister-in-law, and instructing his dog, Gyp, to *stay*, Calum left by the front door and climbed into his twelve-year-old, rust-coloured Cavalier hatchback parked in the road outside.

He stopped for petrol at the Shell station, where he ran into two of his mates, Jacko Jackson and Dexy Glue, brother of his long-time girlfriend. It was through Dexy, whose real name was Desmond, that Calum had first met Suzi, now the mother of his two small girls. They had been pals since their teenage years, and had sworn long ago never to let any problems arising from women come between them.

Jacko and Dexy told Calum they were on their way to Watchet, where Kevin Buttercup was waiting with his boat. They would be sailing with the ten o'clock tide, all set for a night's fishing. In other circumstances Calum would have dropped what he was doing and gone with them. There was only one thing in the world, apart from a money-making deal, that could keep him away from fishing and that was the thought of getting laid. Not with any old scrubber, of course, he reminded himself. Rusty MacPherson had never had to stoop to *that* low level.

Bidding his friends goodbye, Calum made for the main road leading to the M5 motorway and the service station. He had arranged to meet Marlene there but where they would finish up was anyone's guess. Kevin had introduced him to her the previous Sunday morning at a car boot sale. It turned out he'd known her old man before she'd split from him. Perhaps Marlene would invite him back to her house, Calum thought. It would make a nice change to wind up in a comfortable bed, instead of performing the usual acrobatics in the back seat of his car.

He hardly dared admit it to himself, but deep inside Calum knew he was doing this mainly to get back at Suzi. In the five months since they'd broken up, he'd been content to take his mind off things with fishing, and perhaps a little bit of racing in the afternoons. He had sensed during the last couple of weeks that Suzi wasn't giving him quite the welcome that she used to and, recently, he'd heard snippets on the grapevine that she was seeing another man. If that was the case, he was darned sure he wasn't going to stay celibate simply because he couldn't do it with *her* any more.

While Calum drove, he cast his mind back to the betting shop and the sorry plight of Snooky. Not only had the little scrounger stung Calum for a further pound, he'd caught him again later for the price of a cup of tea and a currant bun from the cafe on the other side of the green. If you could believe a word Snooky said, it was all he'd had to eat since the previous evening, when his wife had chucked him out because he'd gambled away her housekeeping money. With two daughters still at school, and his missus working all the hours God sent, it was apparent to Calum that the poor cow had had enough. There weren't many women who would put up with that sort of behaviour, not in this modern day and age, he'd told the useless deadbeat.

Calum pressed down hard on the brake pedal as he approached the roundabout at the entrance to the service station. When he reached the parking area, he looked around to see if he could locate Marlene. A red Fiesta, she'd said – it seemed that half the population of Avon and Somerset were driving that particular model ... some old and clapped out as hell, others spanking brand new. Calum didn't know the year of Marlene's car, but he thought it more likely to be an oldish one. She hadn't looked all that flushed, financially.

It was in moments like this he wished he was still smoking. He'd given it up some time ago, when he was living with Suzi at her house in Portmills and she'd grumbled at him for polluting the air with two small children around. IIe was feeling decidedly edgy. He hoped Marlene wouldn't keep him waiting long – always assuming she did decide to turn up. He'd go ballistic if she didn't ... a whole night's fishing sacrificed for *nought*.

The sound of Oasis blocked the chance of any conversation Jazz might have had with any half interesting male. She knocked back the remnants of her sixth Black Velvet and headed for the dance area again. It was after eleven o'clock, the time Dominic had said he would try to get back.

45

He'd gone down to the city centre to meet some fellow doctors who were still working at Southmead Hospital, where he'd done his initial training. Jazz wished he'd arranged to meet them at the Night Owl instead: the place would benefit from the presence of a few husky males; there was absolutely *nothing* here that she fancied tonight.

'Hi, Erin.' She draped an arm fondly round her friend's shoulder. 'How're you doing my precious?'

Erin smiled sweetly and nodded her head, without pausing in her dancing.

How unassuming she was; how very different from her mother, Jazz thought. Flamboyant Roxanne Meredith was the mother from hell! As a woman, Jazz liked her fine ... but as a *mother* – that was a whole different matter. It was no wonder Erin was so diffident and shy. Lucky for her that her father was such a nice man, or she would have been absolutely *swamped*. Jazz didn't much care for her own mother, but she was certainly nowhere near as embarrassing as Erin's mum was.

'All right?' A male voice cut into Jazz's thoughts as the long, lanky rasher of wind who'd been pursuing her all night loomed over her shoulders and yanked her round to face him.

'Get your hands off me,' Jazz warned, but nevertheless she finished out the remainder of the dance with him. It was only a dance, she reminded herself, not an act of adultery to the accompaniment of a raunchy number played by the brothers Gallagher.

Holly MacPherson, rotating to the music, her red hair flying wildly, waved to Jazz from across the room. She was pleased to see that Jazz had taken to the dance floor, even though she knew she'd been trying to avoid the tall, thin specimen who'd been pestering her since they first arrived.

Holly loved to dance, and wasn't too fussy what the person she was dancing with looked like. Gregarious and friendly, Holly got on with almost everyone. There was no special man in her life, and that suited her just fine. She'd never yet met anyone who really turned her on.

Jazz's brother, Dominic, was all right ... but only *all right,* Holly thought. She wished she could think that was how he felt about *her,* and wasn't about to start coming on strong. It might have been only her imagination, but he seemed to have been paying her some special attention on the way in to town this evening. She'd been relieved when he'd driven away to the city centre to meet some friends.

Moving her body to a fast rhythm, Holly was enjoying every moment of the action. The black-haired Latin-looking boy she was dancing with was knock-out-gorgeous handsome; she strongly suspected he knew it, too. Not that she could blame him for that; he really was the Antonio Banderas type and, what was more, he had a great sense of humour – an important attribute in her book, after a lifetime of fencing jokes with her Uncle Calum.

'Has anyone ever told you you're the spitting image of the bird that's married to Tom Cruise?' he asked during a lull in the music. His eyes were lustrously black, but a warm and friendly black, like liquorice, and Holly had always had a terrible weakness for liquorice.

'Yeah, and when he's finished with her, I'm next on his list ... he's promised me that,' she quipped.

Although she had heard a similar chat-up line many times before, this boy wasn't the *usual* chat-up merchant, she decided. She fixed him with a penetrating look from her navy-blue eyes, and he stared right back at her, his dark chocolate gaze steady and unwavering. He looked a thoroughly decent sort – so different in appearance from the type Holly had always fancied – yet she found herself responding in a way she'd never have believed possible. He seemed far more interesting than any boy she'd met before, and she wanted to know more about him.

When the dance ended he found a bench where they could sit. She learned his parents were Italian, and he lived in Hotwells, not far from where she worked. Giuliano was his name, but his English friends all called him Guy.

Handsome as handsome comes; the thought popped into Holly's head. And more interesting to talk to than most men of his age. He went to the bar to order drinks, and Holly watched him detach himself politely from the group of boys he'd come with. The whole bunch of them swivelled their heads to look in her direction, then Guy came back to her and led her to a relatively quiet corner where they could continue their tête-à-tête.

The more time she spent with him, the more Holly realised how much she was enjoying his company. He told her about his family; his three sisters who weren't allowed out without a chaperone, someone from their own family. It seemed to her a stifling way to live but, from the way Guy described them, they sounded really nice. He asked if he could see her again and, after some false hesitancy, she agreed to meet him one evening after work. They settled for Wednesday, at a pub near her office, and he suggested they see a film afterwards.

So engrossed had she been in her conversation with Giuliano, Holly didn't notice Dominic come back. He noticed her, though – straight away. She was the main reason he'd persuaded his friends, Tom and Marcus, to put in an appearance at the Night Owl an hour before closing time. He made an immediate beeline for Holly to ask her to dance but, to his surprise, she declined, explaining that her feet were killing her, and she'd had to take off her shoes.

Dominic, though not entirely convinced, accepted her reasons and left her in conversation with the dark-haired stranger. His heart sank when he saw just how eagerly she was responding to the young man's attentions.

Erin Meredith had seen and noticed everything. Leaning against a divider screen, she watched as Dominic Stone – the man she lusted after ... the only man she'd *ever* lusted after – went over to Holly and, after chatting to her for a while, came away again, a desperately disappointed look on his rugged face, to rejoin his friends.

Jazz grabbed hold of his arm and led him to where Erin was standing. His friends were trailing behind; they looked as though they didn't know what they were doing here, she thought.

'What are you drinking?' Dominic asked, when he at last became aware of Erin's presence.

'A diet Coke, please,' she replied.

'Go on, daft – you want something stronger than that,' ordered Jasmine. 'How are we ever going to get you drunk?' She shook her head and, turning to the others, added, 'This girl *never* loosens up. Can't one of you lot do something about her, for pity's sake?'

'Don't let my sister corrupt you, Erin,' Dominic said. 'You stay exactly as you are. You're perfectly all right to me.'

I wish, thought Erin. God, how she wished.

Dominic and Tom went to fetch the drinks, and their friend Marcus asked Erin for a dance. He seemed fairly shy, she thought, especially for a doctor. She felt comfortable with him, more comfortable than she'd imagined she could be with someone she'd never met before – more particularly when that someone was a man, a professional man at that.

Returning from the bar, Dominic found a table for them all, where he sat while Jazz and Tom also went off to dance.

Erin, throwing herself into the action with Marcus, nonetheless kept an interested eye on Dominic Stone. How good-looking he is, she told herself. If only he would look at *her* the way he looked at Holly, she would never wish for anything more. Dr and Mrs Dominic Stone, she thought ... the basis of all her nighttime dreams – now, and for the rest of her life.

What a pity it wasn't him but Marcus who was pulling her into his warm embrace, now that the music had changed into a smoochy Take That number. But there he was, still taking glances at Holly; with eyes only for *her* ... those drop-dead, turquoise eyes, flecked with highlights of dancing jade, and the curly brown hair nestling into his white shirt collar at the nape of his strong manly neck. There was only one word for it: perfection. And her best friend, Holly – the object of this wonderman's affections – was completely blind to his charms. How unfair life was, Erin told herself. She wished she could weave a magic spell, like a wizard in the bedtime stories her father used to read to her when she was a child, and he'd called her his little Snow White. She would have Dominic Stone for her very own Prince Charming, and turn all the rest into dwarfs.

Later, seated in his mother's car on the way home to Fuzzy Cove, the girls discussed their evening out. Holly had nowhere near as much to say as usual, Erin thought. In fact, her red-haired friend was quieter than she'd ever known her.

'He was *different*,' Holly explained, in answer to Jasmine's probing. *'Interesting.* His parents came over from Italy in 1966, before he was born – and his three sisters sound ever so nice.'

'Interesting,' repeated Dominic. 'Interesting, eh? So will you be seeing him again – this very interesting guy? Pardon the pun on his name – a slip of the tongue, I fear.'

'I *am* seeing him again, as a matter of fact,' Holly said. 'And, ha-ha, I do excuse your terrible pun. We're going to the pictures on Wednesday night, to the new Bristol Centre.'

'Well, good for you. You've got a date. *I* should be so lucky,' exclaimed Jazz. 'I didn't set eyes on a single bloke who I would want to go out with.' She yawned, and stretched her arms sleepily. 'So good for *you*, Holly, I say! Eh, Erin? Eh, Dom?'

Dominic muttered a reluctant 'Mmmm,' and Erin, happy, yet sad because she felt sorry for him, nodded in agreement.

'Oh, well, there's always next week,' sighed Jazz.

When they arrived at Mariner's Cottage she brightened up suddenly. 'There's your Rusty getting out of his car,' she informed Holly, lowering the window of the BMW.

'Hi there, Rust,' she called, waving frantically at Calum.

'You look bloody miserable,' she told him as he strolled towards them.

'So would you look miserable if you'd missed a whole night's fishing for bugger all,' Calum said.

'You've got it wrong there, my old, love. I can't think of anything I'd hate more than to spend a whole night fishing out on the rotten river Severn.'

'The Bristol Channel,' Calum corrected her. 'I could have bin fishing off Watchet for pollack with me mates.'

Jazz's voice softened. 'I do know what you mean – I really do. Wasting good time that could have been spent more profitably doing something you really like to do.'

When the others drove away, Holly grabbed her uncle's arm and squeezed it exuberantly.

'Come on, sweetness,' she coaxed. 'Come and let your little Holly make it all better. Listen while I tell you all about the really great fish that *I* caught tonight. It wasn't at all the sort I usually go for but I think it's a tasty one, all the same.'

'I don't know what the hell you're talking about,' said Calum. 'I can only suppose it's a bloke.'

Holly laughed as she waited for him to open the front door. 'Could be, Nunky – you'll have to wait and see.'

'Take my advice, and make sure you tests the water for a while before you hauls 'un in,' Calum told her. 'You can take it from one who's bin there.'

'You sound thoroughly disillusioned, mate.'

'I *am*. Rush into summat, and you'll live to regret it for evermore; I'm telling thee that now.'

'My God, Calum – has Suzi upset you *that* much?'

'Suzi?' said Calum. 'Who's Suzi when she's at home?'

'The woman who wanted to marry you and have your kids. Who *did* have your kids, regardless.'

'That's all history now. There is no Suzi as far as I'm concerned.'

Calum called to his dog, and let himself out the back door to give the animal a last-minute run.

He's got the hump, well and truly, thought Holly, but nothing or no one could dampen *her* exuberant mood tonight.

'Roll on Wednesday,' she murmured happily as she made her way up the stairs to bed.

Angie heard her and, relieved, settled down to sleep. Another night in bed alone, not knowing if she was a widow or one of the vast army of single mothers ... free, if she wanted, to start a new relationship with another man. Fat chance of that, she thought. Tied to the house with a tiny baby; what hope did *she* have of finding someone else, even if she'd wanted to? She touched her body – tentatively, exploring – and felt the first faint stirrings of sexual desire. Now that Evie was three months old, she and Curt would have been making love again.

The thought was strangely disturbing. 'I miss you, Curtis,' she whispered. 'Touch me, here, and here and here...' She dug her fingers into her groin and, for the first time since her husband's disappearance, simulated his familiar touch, pretending he was with her still.

Chapter Four

Caitlin Sinclair, homesick for England and the West Country of her childhood, was sitting on a bench near the entrance to Pier 41 on the San Francisco waterfront, watching a stream of summer visitors making their way towards the booth to buy tickets for a boat trip to Alcatraz. The line, now winding back on itself, was more than a hundred yards long. She had been watching it lengthen since early morning, after she'd alighted from the Van Ness trolley car, and two boatloads had crossed to the island in the meantime.

The sea mists had shrouded the bay area beneath a dense, dripping curtain of dampness, and the sun was having great difficulty coming through, but at least it wasn't raining.

Caitlin thought back to the June day just over a year ago when she and Tyler, on their first visit to the city – still agog at all the wonders the Pacific coast of America had to offer – had boarded a Red and White tour boat to visit the half-derelict penitentiary. The rain had poured down relentlessly, forcing them to stop at the souvenir shop to buy yellow plastic capes to save being soaked to the skin as they climbed the steep uphill path that led to the forbidding grey concrete structure.

Caitlin had viewed the interior of the prison with a fearful, masochistic delight. Here lingered the ghosts of Robert Stroud, the birdman, and Al Capone, the gangster, whose notorious exploits she'd read about when she'd ransacked her grandparents' bookshelves, looking for something to while away the long summer evenings when she and her brother Gwyn stayed with them in Ilfracombe.

Caitlin got up from the bench and strolled away in the direction of Fisherman's Wharf. There was a McDonald's nearby where she could buy a cup of coffee ... or perhaps hot chocolate. Hot chocolate was even more comforting when you were feeling low.

As she walked, she savoured the glorious morning, a morning filled now with sunshine; the sea sparkling like tinsel beneath its reflected light. She took a deep breath and filled her lungs with the salt-laced air. Her lips tasted of it ... but clean, and pure – scouring all impurities from her insides, she hoped. *It had better be,* she told herself.

She was pregnant again; her own special secret. No one else knew about it, not even Tyler. She was determined not to take any chances this time. Seven months ago she'd had a miscarriage twelve weeks into the pregnancy and the twelfth week of this pregnancy was just four weeks away.

Arriving at Fisherman's Wharf, Caitlin paused for a while to watch the seals. The walkways between the mooring bays were packed solidly with them. They looked and sounded like sleepy brown dogs, she thought, and as defenceless as the precious baby she was carrying. Despite her own anxiety about all remaining well, her honey-gold eyes lit with pleasure as she watched the baby seals at play.

The miscarriage she'd had at Christmas wasn't an experience she wanted to repeat, not only for the baby's sake, but for her own, too. Physically, it had hurt like hell – though, as everyone said about labour pains, the memory of that was fading fast. Emotionally, it had been the most devastating thing to happen to Caitlin in all her twenty-eight years. She knew the memory would remain with her for the rest of her life.

For Christmas and New Year Tyler had rented a

small, Spanish-style bungalow in the San Fernando valley, on the outskirts of Los Angeles. Persimmon Sorbet, the five-piece rock group in which he was lead guitarist, were performing at a smart eating-place at Malibu Beach for the whole of the holiday period. With the extra money, renting the bungalow was an improvement on the shabby hotels and bleak motels where they usually stayed.

Caitlin looked past the seals out to sea, where the Golden Gate bridge spanned the water across to Marin County. The mists had lifted completely now; she unwound the scarf she'd wrapped round her head and let her wavy brown hair fall loose over her shoulders. Her face was nicely tanned from her daily walks along the shore and, when she smiled, the healthy pink glow of her cheeks emphasised the whiteness of her teeth. She looked and felt in really good shape, and that was the way she was determined to stay.

Leaving the waterfront, she made her way up a side street towards the fast food restaurant. Once inside, she abandoned her normal resolute control and ordered hot chocolate with a cinnamon-and-apple doughnut. She seldom allowed herself such treats, but was desperately in need of one today. *Comfort eating,* her Granny Hutchison had called it when Caitlin was a little girl. She was missing her grandmother and grandfather badly just now. If only they were still alive, she'd have been sure of a huge welcome from *them*.

Finding a corner table for one, Caitlin settled

down to enjoy her treats, licking her fingers like a child as she tucked into the sugary doughnut. She recalled how Marie-Carmen, the kindly Mexican lady who'd cared for her at the time of the miscarriage, had always indulged Caitlin's craving for certain foods. It had reminded her, she'd said, of her own pregnancies thirty years before.

Caitlin's thoughts skipped over the happenings of that fatal afternoon and picked up on the evening, after Tyler had left for Malibu. Battered and bruised, both mentally and physically, she had suddenly and without warning developed excruciating stomach pains. She'd started to bleed quite heavily and, in her panic, telephoned Lisa, the wife of the keyboard player who was staying in the bungalow next door. Lisa had come over immediately and, realising that events were moving fairly fast, had fetched Marie-Carmen, the warden at the holiday complex.

As it happened the plump Mexican woman, with her reassuring, motherly presence, arrived just a moment too late, for there, in a green plastic cooking bowl which Lisa had brought from the kitchen, was a tiny six-inch foetus. In her shocked state, almost passing out, Caitlin saw that it was a boy.

At the sight of the minute, perfectly formed body, Marie-Carmen had blessed herself and let out a sad, mournful wail as soulful as a seagull's cry, a sound so distressing, it haunted Caitlin's dreams to this day. She, too, had felt like wailing, and screaming, and tearing out her hair, and flailing around in the bed. Instead, with strong

English resolve – a resolve made easier by a feeling of total disbelief, she'd remained quite still, like a statue carved from stone, staring at the little thing in the bowl on the floor, all curled up, like an illustration in a childbirth manual she'd seen. It was real and precious to her, though ... *precious beyond belief.*

The paramedics had arrived soon afterwards to whisk her away to hospital in downtown L.A. There, with true American no-nonsense and, it seemed to Caitlin, a cool disregard for his patient, a gynaecological surgeon had performed a hasty D & C before despatching her back to the adobe bungalow and into Marie-Carmen's care.

When she cast her mind back, Caitlin vaguely remembered Tyler returning home the next morning to find her lying quietly on the sitting-room sofa, shaky and pale – minus the baby that was due to have been born a few weeks ago. Her present need to pamper herself with goodies was an attempt to buffer the pain of remembrance; her only consolation the new little life that was growing inside her right now.

She was determined there would be no repetition this time and, for that reason, had an airline ticket booked to leave for England in six days' time. She knew Tyler well enough to realise he wouldn't let her go without a fight, and Caitlin had had enough of fighting to last her a whole lifetime.

The group were due to begin a six-week gig in Las Vegas the following weekend. Caitlin had arranged it to the minute. As soon as they hit the road for Nevada, she'd be heading out to the airport and boarding an afternoon flight to London Heathrow.

Even her family in England didn't know she was coming. Caitlin didn't think it wise to tell them. Her parents would never agree with her decision to leave – not in a thousand years! In their opinion, she'd made her bed the day she married Tyler Sinclair from nearby Burnham-on-Sea. Never mind that he'd taken to drinking heavily in the last twelve months, and often beat her up. As far as her stick-in-the-mud parents were concerned, their wilful daughter was asking for all she'd got for ignoring their advice in the first place. Olive and Roland Hutchison, lost in their own little world – a world steeped in old-fashioned prejudice – could never, ever bend. It was the story of Caitlin's life.

Sipping her chocolate drink slowly, she reflected on her seven-year marriage to Tyler. Persimmon Sorbet was a moderately successful group and, although British, was better known in America, where they played regularly to large open-air audiences on the West Coast. During the two years since she and Tyler had come to California they had lived in relative wealth and splendour, in comparison with their former way of life. She was thankful now, though, that they hadn't sold their home in England, even though Tyler had suggested it at the time. A modern semi, it was situated at Worle, not far from her parents' home at Weston-super-Mare. Caitlin had made the decision to rent the property out so that they'd have somewhere to come back to, if and when the need arose. *And, boy, had the need arisen,* she reminded herself now.

She had heard from the estate agent that the house was now empty, the couple who'd rented it having moved on to France. Caitlin had kept this news from Tyler, and planned to stay there initially while she looked for a job and somewhere else to live. The baby wasn't due until February; she'd have plenty of time to get settled before then. She hoped Tyler would agree to a straightforward divorce, without too much fuss. She knew that he'd never admit it but, according to Lisa, he was sleeping with an American girl, and had been for some months.

'And he's probably had lots of other affairs when I wasn't around,' Caitlin muttered bitterly. How naive she was to have believed his assurances that he'd never want anyone else but her.

None of it mattered now. She wanted nothing more from Tyler. If needs be, she would fight him for the baby's custody; she fully intended to bring it up herself. She was sick to death of living the unsettled life of a rock wife and, more especially, being used as a punchbag whenever Tyler had had too much to drink. She wanted out and she had no intention of waiting around while he tried to persuade her otherwise, as he always had in the past.

She scooped the empty food containers on to a tray and into the trash chute, then, leaving the restaurant, made her way back to the crowded wharf to take a last look at the seals. Sad little faces, with big staring eyes. Today wasn't actually goodbye, though. She would be back to see them again before she left San Francisco for good.

While she waited for the trolley car to take her back to the motel, Caitlin again looked out over the bay. A faint haze at sea level made even the island of Alcatraz look attractive as it shimmered like an opal set in the greeny-blue sea. To the left of the island rose the rust-red span of the Golden Gate bridge, backdrop of countless movies she'd seen, while never dreaming for a moment she would one day be standing here looking at it for real.

As they had discovered, it quite often rained in the Bay Area, even in summer, bringing heavy mists to obscure the stupendous view. Today, however, the sky was purest azure – wide and vast – without a cloud in sight. It was a perfect day for gathering memories ... wonderful memories she knew she would cherish forever.

The air hung motionless, heavy with the scent of the jacaranda trees that lined the sidewalks. From where Caitlin stood the busy traffic, manoeuvring the ups and downs of the city streets, looked like painted coaches on a distant roller-coaster ride, disappearing without trace into the tall, pale skyscrapers that populated the business section.

San Francisco was a vibrant, exciting place and, in different circumstances, and with the right partner, Caitlin knew she would have been perfectly happy here. But, for all that Tony Bennett might sing how it captured his heart, it wasn't where she really wanted to be, not any more. The green hills of England and, in particular, the West Country where her roots were, was where *she* had left her heart.

She didn't doubt that Tyler would come looking for her as soon as he could. She was banking on the fact that he'd be tied to his contract for the next six weeks. Now wasn't the time to worry about it, she thought, hoisting herself on to an outside seat at the rear of the trolley car. There would be plenty of time for worrying when Tyler discovered that she'd left him for good, was pregnant again and planned to rear their child without any help from him.

The following Thursday, the day before Persimmon Sorbet was due to leave for Las Vegas, Tyler returned to the motel early after an afternoon's rehearsal. Caitlin knew he was looking for a fight as soon as he came into the bedroom, where she was busy ironing. Although he was smiling his voice was truculent and argumentative; she hurriedly shoved the suitcase she'd been packing into a closet, and picked up one of his shirts.

As always, when Tyler was sloshed, his powers of observation seemed more than usually acute. He couldn't know that she was planning to leave him – he hadn't even seen the suitcase – yet he latched on immediately to the fact that Caitlin seemed flustered, and dived straight into the attack.

'What's up with you?' he questioned, before Caitlin had time to gather her wits.

'What do you mean, what's up with me? Nothing's up with me,' she countered, pinning a cheerful smile on her face in the hopes of diverting a scene.

'You *are* bloody up to something – I can tell by your face,' Tyler persisted.

Caitlin decided to change the subject. 'Like something to eat?' she enquired and, switching off the iron, started to walk into the main room where she kept a supply of food in the small fridge.

He put out a hand to stop her, and she tried to wriggle past. His expression changed then; he grabbed her arm, pinning her back against the door jamb.

Caitlin sighed. She really ought to have read the signs, she knew, yet she always lived in hope. He always acted the same way ... giving the appearance of being affable, when, really, he was spoiling for a fight.

'No, I *don't* want something to eat,' he snarled and, cupping her chin in his hand, he pulled her round to face him.

'We're meeting up with the others presently. It's all been arranged,' he said. 'That new seafood restaurant down on North Point.'

'Fine,' Caitlin replied. 'That's all right – but we mustn't be late getting back. You're leaving for Vegas at ten in the morning, remember.'

'Don't you worry your head about that; you just worry about what you'll be doing in the six weeks I'm away. Your mate won't be here to keep you company. I hear she's coming on to Vegas herself in a day or two.'

Caitlin knew Lisa would be driving out to join Damian early next week; two of the other group members' girlfriends were travelling with her too.

They'd asked Caitlin to go with them but, knowing the tricky situation that existed between herself and Tyler, hadn't pushed the offer too hard.

She decided against asking why he wasn't insisting she accompany him, when, only a few months ago, he'd wanted her with him wherever he went. It would only give him another excuse to lie, she thought, and she knew the reason anyway. It was common knowledge among the rest of the group that he was having a red-hot affair with an American showgirl called Tammy, and Lisa had passed the news on to Caitlin.

Tyler suddenly released her and, rubbing her wrist to ease it, she went through to the main room where she filled the electric kettle. Tyler followed her, watching expectantly, waiting to hear what she had to say.

'The agency phoned,' Caitlin lied. 'They've got another job lined up. I'm to start work on Monday.'

She had no scruples about lying to Tyler; he'd been lying to her for months. And according to Lisa, his girlfriend was waiting for him in the desert town, strutting her stuff at Aladdin's Palace, the first of the exotic venues where Persimmon Sorbet were booked to play.

'Pushy damned Yank,' Lisa had said in disgust. 'Honestly, Cait – I don't know how you can take it so calmly.'

Caitlin could take it calmly because now she didn't care. For the first few years of their marriage, she'd never had cause to question their love for each other, but one or two things had happened during the past twelve months which had begun to undermine her confidence in his love for her. Now, all she asked was that he'd leave her in peace to live her life the way she wanted. Instead, he was acting as though he still owned her; it was *that* which was driving her crazy.

The sooner I'm gone, the better, she thought; then blushed, for fear that he could read her mind. He was looking at her closely – far too closely for her liking. He *had* noticed something different about her, she was sure.

'You'm bloody up to something,' he repeated. 'You wouldn't have that dumb-cow look on your face if you wasn't. Who's this bloke, down the agency? Hank, or Buddy – or some such goddamn stupid name like that?'

'It's Chuck – his real name's Charles, and he's as bent as a threepenny corkscrew; you've always known *that*, Ty.'

'Takes all sorts,' Tyler replied. 'I wouldn't mind betting there's *something* going on.'

'God give me strength.' Caitlin ran her hand across her forehead distractedly. 'Just because *you're* unable to stay faithful to me, please don't tar me with the same brush.'

'You're talking twaddle. You've got no bloody reason to say what you just said.' He paused, his tone becoming more threatening. 'I don't *have* to listen to this,' he growled.

Caitlin stared at him defiantly, her golden eyes blazing angrily. 'Why else wouldn't you want me coming with you this time, when you always have before?' she demanded to know.

'Shut your face; I've had enough.' Tyler came towards her, his fists raised. Instinctively, Caitlin huddled back against the fridge.

'You'd be better off in L.A. That fat cow could keep her eye on you then,' he said. 'I've already told you why I don't want you coming to Vegas. For a start, there'd be nothing for you to do all day. At least you've got your job here, such as it is, with *he...*'

He dangled his wrist limply, mocking the boss of the clerical agency where Caitlin had worked for the past three months, and who'd shown her nothing but kindness.

'I wish I *was* in L.A. I'd *love* to see Marie-Carmen again,' she snapped.

'Only because she takes your side against me. Loved it, didn't you, hearing *her* put me down? Just like old Olive and Roland back home.'

'Ty – let's forget it. We're eating out, you say?'

He took out a bottle of Scotch from the fridge and poured himself a large beakerful. '*If* I've got any appetite left,' he snarled. 'Your bloody miserable face is enough to put me right off.'

'I'm making tea,' Caitlin said, ignoring his remark.

'I'll want something bloody stronger than tea then, if I'm going out with *you*.' He glared at her angrily. 'God dammit, woman – *keep* your bloody tea.' He hit the kettle out of Caitlin's hand so that it fell into the pink porcelain washbasin.

'You idiot ... you could have scalded me,' she yelled angrily. Tears sprang into her eyes when she saw the drunken fury in his. He bore no resemblance to the Tyler she'd loved – the man she'd gladly and cheerfully come to America to be with.

'A pity I didn't. You could have me arrested. Put me in jail – I'd be safe out of harm's way then. All these crazy ideas you've got about me and other women ... I should be so lucky!'

'I'm not stupid, Tyler. I'm not imagining things!'

'You – you daft cow. If I *was* seeing somebody else, it 'ud be no more than you deserve. Boring, boring, boring. You're the most boring bitch in all the world.'

'And you, of course, are God's gift. It's gone to your head, all these cute little Californian girls. Don't you realise they'd go down on their backs for any bloke that plays in a band?'

'At least they know talent when they see it. That's more than I can say for you.'

'I *always* thought you had talent. I quarrelled with my mum and dad about that, if you remember.'

'That dozy pair of no-hopers. It's easy to see where you get it from.'

'Do not judge me by them – *please*. Out of my way; I want to get by. I'm going to get washed and changed.'

As Caitlin pushed past him he toppled drunkenly and held on to a table for support. His dark eyes flashing furiously, he went after her and punched her in the back.

She turned to face him in the bathroom doorway, and he kicked out at her, aiming for her stomach, the way he had at Christmas. Caitlin, forewarned this time, was able to partly shield her tummy with her hands. The kick was hard, though, and it shook her up. She sank to her knees and, half fainting, knelt over the lavatory bowl to be sick.

Swearing quietly to himself, Tyler walked away. Hearing the outer door slam, and the sound of his car starting up, she ran a bath. Lying in its gentle warmth, she prayed to be gone from here by the time he returned. Yet another part of her brain was telling her she should lie doggo, and wait for morning, when he would be leaving to go to Nevada as planned. If his pattern of behaviour ran true to form he would be back by breakfast-time, most likely sober, and remembering nothing at all about tonight.

Covering her stomach with a warm soft flannel, Caitlin thanked God that the only injuries she'd sustained this time were those to her right hand, where the knuckles were bruised and sore. By this time tomorrow evening, she thought, she would be halfway across the Atlantic, well on her way to England, and praying for the plane to notch up air miles faster than it ever had before.

'Halleluja – put out the flags, we'll soon be on our way,' she told her little lump as, squeezing out the flannel, she sprinkled warm bathwater all over it.

Chapter Five

The pain was insidious; crafty and sly. It came with no warning, and lasted only a few moments. Just when Daisy had forgotten all about it, it slid through her chest from right to left, halting her in her tracks. Daisy secured the brake on the baby's buggy and sat down on the low stone wall of the funeral parlour, just as a procession was emerging from the high wrought-iron gates a few yards away.

First, a hearse, carrying a coffin bedecked with brilliant flowers, followed by two matching limousines with white-faced occupants dressed in black, while other mourners clambered into several cars parked along the street. God, she thought, I've certainly picked a good spot if I am going to collapse. She had no intention of doing so, though. The moment the strange pain faded away, she'd be back on her feet again, heading for home up Maritime Way. Daisy believed in keeping up appearances at all costs. It was for the same reason she renewed her medium-brown hair colour every six weeks, and never went out without a dash of lipstick, and always with a smidgen of eye colour.

'OK baby?' Daisy smiled at her granddaughter Evie, who was staring at her as if to say, 'Well, what are we waiting for? What's this daft old woman doing, parked halfway up the hill?'

Daisy promised herself she would see the doctor the moment she could. Just because she had always been fit and hearty, it was foolhardy to ignore the pains and hope they'd go away. She was glad she'd made the decision to relinquish the running of the shop to Angie, though during the last week or so the cooking, and looking after Evie, which she'd formerly enjoyed, seemed more and more like hard work. Angie was in need of the mental stimulation the shop offered, Daisy knew – dealing with customers on a daily basis, and organising deliveries – all the responsibilities a retail business entailed. It was for her sake that Daisy was determined to stay strong. Daisy always tried to keep her grief and misery to herself, though since she'd been sharing her bedroom with Holly, even having a good old cry in bed wasn't always possible.

Daisy was sure in her own heart that Curtis hadn't disappeared deliberately. Not that she could afford to be too cocky, she reminded herself. She had seen other mothers on television saying exactly the same. 'Never in a million years ... my son would never disappear without letting his family know.' Yet, sometimes, their sons had done precisely that.

Arriving safely back at Mariner's Cottage, at the top of Maritime Way, Daisy wheeled the pram indoors. Evie had fallen asleep, and Daisy lifted her gently out and carried her upstairs to her cot. Then, after she'd finished preparing the vegetables for the midday meal, Daisy made coffee for herself and Angie, and took it into the adjoining shop, where her daughter-in-law was

71

expertly slicing a side of gammon, weighing the slices simultaneously on the electronic scales.

'Good morning, Bett,' Daisy greeted an elderly woman who was waiting at the counter. Betty Tinker, like most of their regular customers, had been buying her cold meats and cheeses from Daisy ever since she and Cameron opened the business shortly after their marriage in 1951. Daisy had been twenty-one the following year when Curtis was born and, thirteen months later, his brother Calum had put in an appearance. Two little redheads, mused Daisy, followed by a miscarriage when Calum was a year old. That was the sum total of her medical history to date. She had never had a serious illness and found it difficult to comprehend that – overnight – her body was telling her it wasn't anywhere near as fit as she'd thought.

When the customer had left, Angie went over to Daisy who was sitting on an upturned orange box.

'Thanks for the coffee,' she said, pulling over another box and plonking herself down. 'Where's Evie? Is she OK?'

'In her cot. Gone out like a light,' Daisy told her.

'You look tired,' observed Angie. 'Are you sure it's not too much, looking after a young baby, and all that cooking? it's enough to wear you out ... at...'

Daisy laughed. 'Go on, say it – at *my* age.'

'Well...' Angie answered cautiously.

'You're quite right. I *am* feeling a little jaded,' Daisy said. 'I shall make an appointment to see

72

the doctor presently.'

'You ought to pack it all up and let Josh take care of you, Mum. He's longing to have you move in with him – you know he is.'

'And what would become of you and the children? The way things are, we *have* to keep the shop going. It's your best chance for earning a decent living, Angie.'

'*I'll* keep it going, if you'll let me. I can get someone in to look after the kids ... that's if you...' Angie's voice trailed away.

'If I agree that it's high time I was turned out to grass?' joked Daisy.

'No, no, I didn't mean that,' Angie assured her. 'What I meant to say is – *if* you trust me to make a good job of it.'

'Of course I do.' Daisy was adamant. 'There's no one I'd trust with the business more than you.'

'Forget what I said about you moving in with Josh,' Angie continued. 'I only said it because I know how much he wants you to. Your home will always be here for as long as you want it to be. You know how much we all think of you – me and the kids.'

'I know, Angie love, but the place is getting a bit overcrowded, don't you think?'

'But it won't *always* be. The kids will grow up and leave home eventually. Holly can't wait to get a place of her own; she's always going on about it.'

'There's Calum to consider, too,' Daisy said. 'Who ever would have thought that *he'd* be living back home again at his age?' She sighed deeply. 'I wish that boy would sort himself out, and settle

73

down like any normal fellow.'

'You've no need to worry, Mum. I'd never chuck him out.'

Daisy frowned. 'I'm not so sure that wouldn't be a bad thing. Though, bless him, I suppose he does have his good points ... if you search hard enough.'

Angie fixed her mother-in-law with a solemn glance. 'Promise me you'll take no notice of what I said just now. You'll only go to live with Josh if it's something *you* really want to do.'

'I promise. I know you're only thinking of what's best for me,' Daisy said. 'Anyway, wherever I finally finish up living, I'm going to make the shop over to you right now. It's no use waiting until after I'm dead. I know you'll make a good job of running it – you're a worker, Ange, the same as me.'

Angie gasped. 'That's wonderful for me! I can't say I'm not grateful, but I hope you know what you're doing, Dais. You'll still need some income to live.'

'I've got my pension, and a bit put by, and...' Daisy chuckled. 'And ... I quite like the look of those new retirement bungalows North Somerset Council are putting up.'

Angie took Daisy's hand and squeezed it tightly. 'What *can* I say, Mum? Thank you's not enough.'

'You're worth it, love. Just give me long enough to fix everything up, and get myself settled.'

'I'll start looking now for someone to help take care of Evie. It's been in my mind for some while; I can't have you wearing yourself out like this.'

'Are you sure you won't miss seeing to her yourself? They're only babies for such a short time.'

'Uh, uh . . .' Angie shook her head firmly. 'I feel I *need* to work in the shop. After all, Evie and whoever's looking after her will only be on the other side of that wall.' Angie gave Daisy a warm smile. 'And I'll be banking on *you* popping in and out to keep an eye, on things, of course.'

'Just you try stopping me,' said Daisy.

Almost apologetically, Angie explained, 'I've had years of looking after a family, Mum. At long last I'll be doing something for *me*. If I make a go of it, expand the business as I'd like to, I'll be ever so, ever so proud.' Grinning saucily, she added, 'We're already looking up, now that I've clinched that permanent order for vegetables with Rex Carpenter.'

'As long as Adge Fletcher doesn't cut up rough. You'll be taking some of the trade away from his shop, you know that, and he won't like it – not one little bit.'

'Then he'll damn well have to lump it. He's been getting away with selling stale fruit and veg ever since I've known him. And Rex is pleased. It saves him having to drive miles and miles, selling his produce from the van.'

'My poor Josh is going to have his work cut out convincing the Fletchers that there's room in the village for more than one greengrocer's shop,' remarked Daisy.

Angie nodded. 'There is, though, with all the new houses they're building at the bottom of Upalong. Poor old Josh ... how awful to be married into that dreadful family. Not that his wife seemed as bad as the rest of them, I thought.'

'She wasn't a happy woman.' Daisy screwed up the corners of her mouth. 'A bit tricky to live with, by all accounts; but then, she was the sister of Minnie Fletcher.'

'Well let's hope Josh puts in a good word for me with his in-laws,' remarked Angie. 'Work your charm on him, and see what you can do, Dais.'

'My *ample* charms, you mean, only you're too polite to say so.'

'Josh is a sucker for them, whatever they are,' Angie said, laughing.

Daisy rose to her feet. 'The weather looks like it's brightening up. I'll get that washing pegged out before young madam wakes up.'

Two more customers came into the shop and, as Angie waited for them to make up their minds on what they wanted, she pondered the situation. It was high time Daisy took a break, she thought; she had been working nonstop ever since Angie had known her. The older children would have to learn to fend for themselves. First of all, Angie decided, I'll have to increase the variety of ready-prepared meals I fetch from the Cash-and-Carry, and provide more salads; that would start the ball rolling nicely.

That evening, Josh called to take Daisy for a drink. Their favourite place was the Albatross pub on the coast road, north of the village. It was quieter than the Smuggler's Retreat. You couldn't hear yourself think there for the noise the youngsters created.

From her seat beneath the rustic window, Daisy looked across at Josh Berry, standing by the bar. Six feet tall, at sixty-five he still had all his own hair – a nice shade of dark grey which made him look distinguished. Daisy fancied him no end.

She had been keeping company with Josh for the last eighteen months, and what had started off as a friendship had since turned to love. Daisy had known him for many years, though only from a distance when Cameron was alive. Josh was related to the Fletchers by marriage, and Cameron had treated him with exactly the same disdain he did them.

'There we go then – one red wine, and some plain crisps.'

Josh sat down next to her on the red velvet-padded bench and, taking a sip of light ale, murmured pleasurably, 'Mmm ... that's good; I really needed that.'

'Cheers,' said Daisy, clinking her glass against his.

'Cheers,' he echoed. He leaned away slightly and his concerned blue eyes peered hard into Daisy's misty grey ones.

'Angie tells me you've been having some chest pains,' he said quietly.

'Oh, my Lord, why on earth did she have to tell you *that?*' Daisy was miffed with Angie for telling him. He was the world's worst worrier and, as far as Daisy was concerned, the less he knew about her problems, the better.

'I particularly asked her not to say anything until I'd seen the doctor,' she grumbled. 'And in any case, it's only when I go uphill or hurry too much. I shall have to try and slow down a bit ... you know *me*.'

'I *do* know you,' replied Josh. 'You do much too much for your own good – I've been telling you that for some while. Looking after that big old house, and the baby – cooking for the whole family, as well.'

'Stop going on about it, love. I've already discussed it with Angie this afternoon.'

'Well, something's got to be done about it. We can't have you killing yourself, and that's what will be happening.'

'You're getting on my nerves, Josh. I said I'm going to see the doctor, so just let it go, will you?'

Daisy wished he would stop fussing. She wasn't an irresponsible fool, and that was what he was making her feel. Josh made no secret of the fact that he wanted her to live with him in his very comfortable bungalow on the outskirts of the village, but now all thoughts of that had flown from her mind; all she felt like doing now was dapping him over the head with her handbag.

The following morning Daisy called to see Dr Chadwick at the village medical centre. After testing her blood pressure, he wrote out a prescription for a strong beta blocker to be taken every morning. The pains almost certainly indicated angina, he said, and referred her to the Bristol Royal Infirmary for an immediate ECG. She decided to catch the bus into town: there was one due, and it would save searching for a parking space.

At the hospital she made her way to the third

floor and, to her great relief, in spite of Dr Chadwick's concern, the electro-cardiogram results showed there was no irregularity. Nevertheless, the nurse reiterated the GP's warning that if she was to avoid another attack, she would have to slow down, and try to avoid any source of stress.

Holly had taken the day off work to look after Evie while Daisy was at the doctor's and her mother was in the shop. She had arranged to meet the boy from the Night Owl that evening, and every time she thought about it, a deliciously warm sensation crept into the pit of her stomach. Yet he isn't at all the type I've always fancied, she told herself, hoping against hope she wasn't making a big mistake.

At midday she fed and changed the baby, then took her upstairs for her afternoon nap. It was Wednesday, half-day closing, and Holly hurried down to the kitchen to heat up the golden vegetable soup which her grandmother had prepared the previous day. Angie joined her at the dot of one, followed a few minutes afterwards by Daisy. When they were seated round the table, Angie announced that she'd placed an advert in tomorrow's *Bristol Evening Post* for a live-in mother's help.

'Are you sure we can afford it?' quizzed Holly.

'We'll jolly well have to,' answered Angie, 'even if I've got to keep the shop open evenings as well as weekends.'

'If you do, Mum, I'll help,' Holly promised. 'Let's think big, and try to build up a really successful business. There must be other things we can sell, besides food. Let's see what ideas we can come up with.'

'That's what I was hoping you'd say,' replied Angie.

Holly paused, frowning, and said, 'Just one other thing, Mum: where on earth will she sleep?'

'Over the shop next door,' Daisy chimed in. 'If we move out all the junk, it can be used for living quarters. There's a toilet and washbasin; even a tiny kitchen.'

'Umm...' Holly became silent, her brain hatching a plan to have the place for herself.

Daisy set down a home-baked apple and apricot pie on the table, and a jug of steaming custard.

'There, I know it's July, but it's really quite chilly today. I thought we could do with something to warm us up,' she said.

'This is gorgeous, Gran,' Holly told her, 'but we're really going to have to learn to cook for ourselves.'

'So *you're* quite happy to make me redundant, too,' replied Daisy, pretending to be upset. 'I don't know whether to be glad or sad.'

'*Daisy,*' said Angie, 'you need to take a rest. There'll be loads for you to do still – but not *everything,* the way you've been doing until now. If we can find the right girl, it will leave us free to put all our efforts into improving the business. We'll make it the success story of Fuzzy Cove.'

'To draw in all the summer tourists,' Holly added, laughing. 'The non-existent summer tourists.'

'I'm serious,' her mother said.

'So am I... Excuse me for laughing, but I had a sudden vision of them all queueing up for ice creams and fancy hats. The Council will have to import a beach.'

Angie tapped Holly's wrist. 'You might be laughing on the other side of your face next summer, my lady, if what I've got in mind comes off.'

'You *are* planning to ask the Council to bring in a beach!' Holly exclaimed. She added seriously, 'I notice Uncle Calum's not included in all of this.'

'You couldn't depend on our Calum to take the *shutters* down of a morning,' observed Daisy.

'That's exactly what he *does* do ... take the shutters down in the mornings,' Holly replied.

'So he might,' laughed Daisy. 'But that's only because I'll have already booted him out of bed. In the days when he slept upstairs it would take an earthquake to shift him'

Angie cast Daisy a quizzical glance. 'Did you mention anything to Josh last night?' she said. 'You know ... about moving in?'

'No.' Daisy's answer was firm. 'That's something I need to give a lot more thought to. I can't have him fussing over me as though I'm a complete invalid; it makes me feel so ... so incapable.'

'You're certainly not *that*, Gran,' Holly reminded her. 'You could have asked one of us to drive you into hospital this morning. Instead, you caught the blooming bus.'

'I knew there was one due any minute; there were several people waiting at the bus stop,' protested Daisy.

'Dear Gran,' said Holly, hugging her fondly.

Angie sliced up the fruit pie, and served it on to their plates. 'Eat up,' she told them. 'Let's get finished before Evie wakes from her nap. She's due to have her booster injection this afternoon.'

'Poor little lammykin; I'll come with you for moral support,' Holly said.

'OK ... if you've nothing else to do.'

Holly shook her head. 'Nothing more important than keeping my mum company in her hour of need.'

'Remember with the boys?' Daisy said. 'Curtis or myself always had to come with you, to give you a helping hand.'

'That was because they *both* needed a special cuddle after having their jabs.' Angie cocked an ear towards the door. 'There we go,' she said. A loud wail came from upstairs. 'I'll get her up,' she went on. 'It's the only time of the week I'm free to enjoy my little girl's company.'

The back door burst open, and Calum came in, his rough haired tan and white Irish terrier, Gyp, at his heels. He eyed them warily. 'What's this, a bloody pow-wow you're having in here?'

'You're late,' reproached Angie, getting up from the table and making her way upstairs. 'You know we always try and eat at one.'

'Just as well I *am*, by the look of things.' Calum looked at them curiously. 'A coven of bloody witches, plotting the downfall of all men, I shouldn't wonder.'

'Oh, yeah! We wouldn't waste our time,' Holly scoffed.

'And this redheaded one's the worst one of the

lot.' Calum ruffled her tangled curls. Placing his hands round her neck, he pretended to throttle her.

'Get off,' yelled Holly. 'Your hands are all dirty. Covered in newspaper print or something equally disgusting.'

'Angie's right. You can't walk in at a quarter to two and expect to find your dinner waiting on the table,' Daisy told him. 'Whatever have you been doing all this time?'

'Been busy ... seeing to a bit of business,' Calum replied. 'What's for grub?' he demanded to know.

'Too late. We've eaten it all,' Holly said. 'There's nothing left for you.'

Daisy grunted. 'That betting shop – it's your second home, Calum. You might as well move your bed down there.' Nonetheless, she produced some soup and sandwiches, and cleared a place for him at the table.

'Are we going to tell him, Gran?' Holly asked.

Calum looked up and, with his mouth full of bread, said, 'I knew it. I knew you was bloody plotting summat.'

'We're not plotting at all. If you'd been here, you would have heard it all,' his mother said. 'I've been to hospital this morning to have an ECG.'

Calum stopped eating. He looked startled as he asked, 'And what did they say?' Without waiting for her to answer, he went on, 'Good God, Mother. You never let on them pains you were having were anywhere near as serious as this.'

'I'll be all right ... the results were normal. I just have to take things more easy, that's all. I told

Angie yesterday I'm going to make the shop over to her.'

'But I thought Angie were already running the shop. I thought that was why you've bin looking after the babby – and seeing to the house, like.'

'Yes, well, I'm going to be easing off on all of *that*, too. Angie's going to get someone to live in; it will leave her free to do the job properly.'

Taking a swig from the can of beer he'd brought with him, Calum said philosophically, 'I'd always+ thought the business would come to Curt, anyway. Being the eldest, he would inherit the property, like.'

He burped quietly, and wiped his mouth with his fist. Fixing his mother with a questioning glance, he continued, 'It doesn't affect *me* either way, does it ... *or does it?*'

'No, it won't affect you, my son,' Daisy answered quietly. 'I just wanted you to know that I'm going to give it to Angie, legally. It'll give her and the children the security they need.'

Calum nodded, and Daisy continued, 'If God smiles on us, and Curtis does come back, it shouldn't make any difference. It'll just be in Angie's name, instead of their joint ones.'

Holly grinned at her uncle. 'If you're good, Uncle Cal, we'll still let you live with us,' she told him. 'But you must give us your promise that if you do win the lottery and buy that mansion, we can all move in with *you*.'

'Cheeky bloody cat,' Calum exclaimed. 'You'd best hope nobody decides to chuck you out ... you've got so much to say.'

Holly tossed her head proudly. 'Nobody would

do that. *I'm* worth my weight in gold.' She softened then, and looked at him fondly. 'Dear old love. He's neither useful, nor an ornament ... but I wouldn't swap him for all the jewels in the crown.'

'Take no notice of that young minx,' said Daisy. 'She's a darn sight too big for her boots these days.' She rose from the table and dumped some used crockery in the sink. 'You have to admit, though, Cal, you bring a lot of it on yourself. If only you would settle down and look for a decent job.' She shook her head, and sighed. 'However Suzi puts up with you calling in whenever it suits you, I really don't know. The girl's a saint, that's all I can say.'

'She's not quite the saint *you'd* have her to be,' mumbled Calum.

'And if she isn't, then it isn't any thanks to you,' retorted Daisy.

Angie came back into the room, soothing her half-awake baby over her shoulder.

'Sleepy girl ... come to Granny then.' Daisy reached up and took Evie into her arms, cuddling her in her lap.

'I've been telling Calum about our plans, Angie,' she said. *'My* plans for the shop, that is. You and Holly will no doubt have plenty of ideas of your own for expanding the business.'

'I hear you're advertising for an au pair, Ange,' remarked Calum. 'A nice Scandinavian girl, I hope – one of them page three lookalikes – keep us *all* happy.'

'You watch too much telly,' Angie told him. 'There aren't any girls like that in real life.'

85

'There damned well are,' said Holly, 'but they wouldn't be any good at looking after a baby and cooking food for two ravenous jackals like my brothers.'

'That's not what *I* had in mind for her,' Calum replied.

'We all know what *you* would have in mind for her,' retorted Holly. 'And I should think she'd take one look at you and head straight back to where she came from.'

'You'd do best sticking to the one you had,' Daisy reminded him. 'You wouldn't have gone far wrong, settling down with *her.*'

'I know – you just said. Play me the same old melody, Dais.'

Calum dipped a crust of bread into his vegetable soup and chewed it contentedly.

'You, my son, are going to come unstuck if you're not very careful,' warned Daisy. 'You live each day as though there's no tomorrow. Some day there'll come a sorry tomorrow, and when that happens, don't you come crying to me.'

'Mother, I know what I'm doing ... all right? No more lectures on how to live my life; understood?'

'I understand, Calum. I understand exactly. You carry on in your own sweet way; I'm only thinking of what's best for you – that's all.'

Calum got to his feet. He placed his soupbowl and plate in the sink and, calling to his dog, opened the back door.

'Don't be getting anything special in for tea,' he announced. 'I'm off to see a man over at Pilning. He's promised to let me have some of the cod he's caught this morning down in Bridgwater Bay. I helped him out with a bit of bait, so he owes me.'

'Well-*wicked*,' mocked Holly. 'So it's fresh cod and chips for supper tonight, always supposing our Granny feels up to making the batter. Full of wonderful surprises, he is – my bad, terrible Uncle Rust. Don't we all love him to little pieces?'

Chapter Six

Calum parked the Cavalier in the supermarket car park and made his way along the harbour-front towards the betting shop. He had some winnings to collect from the day before but had not picked them up that morning because Snooky was in the shop and on the cadge. He hoped to avoid him this afternoon by getting in earlier than usual.

There were only minutes to go before the start of the two fifteen race at York, but just enough time to stick a two-pound bet on Henry Cecil's only entry for the day. The little roan filly had a very good chance, Calum thought. He was a firm supporter of this particular trainer, and believed in backing British wherever possible. So many racehorses these days were owned by Arabs, it was a wonder the fillies weren't all wearing yashmaks, so that no one could see their faces.

For once the shop was a Snooky-free zone.

Calum walked over to the counter where the buxom Roxanne was plying her trade. Her voluptuous bosoms were bursting from her frock like dumplings boiling over in a pot. Calum had complimented her on the size of them once before, thinking it would please her. To his surprise, though, she'd plonked him one in the eye with the back of her hand. 'Just because you and me was at school together, Rusty Mac, you needn't think that gives you a licence to come in here and treat me like I was a flaming scrubber,' she'd yelled.

He eyed her warily now. *More than in school together, Rox*, he thought. 'Afternoon, Rox,' though, he said politely. 'I've come to collect me winnings.'

He handed her the ticket, and she paid him out in two crisp ten-pound notes, together with a handful of loose change.

'You'm in a hurry, ain't you, Rust? Somebody on yer tail for money as usual?' she commented.

Calum's hackles rose slightly. You weren't allowed to insult her, and yet she thought nothing of showing him up in public.

'Thought I'd better get in quick, before that little creep turns up,' he said.

Roxanne nodded. 'Umm ... I know exactly what you mean.'

'Now I can concentrate on what I came yere for. Two quid on the nose for this one, if you please.'

After she'd taken his betting slip, Calum hurried to the door, anxious to make his departure for Pilning where he would be meeting the man with the cod. Luck wasn't with him, though. Through the glass panel of the entrance door he saw the dreaded Snooky heading towards him. He pressed back hard against the wall, hoping he wouldn't be seen, but Snooky noticed him immediately.

'Ooh ... ah ... Rusty, me old son – just the bloke I wants to see!' said Snooky, diving in for the kill. 'Have you got five minutes to spare, only I've had *this* lot come in the second post. It's from some bloody solicitors. Looks like they'm trying to evict me from me own house. They can't do that, can they?'

Short of stature, and insignificant to look at, he gazed at Calum as though Calum was the fount of all knowledge. 'I was hoping you could give me a bit of advice,' he went on, 'only it's not summat I'd want to discuss with any old Tom, Dick or Harry.'

Dipping into his shabby raincoat pocket, Snooky produced a crumpled white envelope, folded between the pages of the *Sun* newspaper. 'I can't make top ner tail of this, Rust,' he said, taking out an official-looking letter which he spread out on the counter for Calum to read.

Calum saw that it was a divorce petition, and asked himself what he'd ever said or done to warrant anyone having such faith in his ability to advise on the whys and wherefores of a divorce action, especially as he himself had never been married, let alone gone through a divorce.

'I'm in a bit of a rush just now, old son,' he said, relieved to fend him off with a genuine excuse.

Snooky didn't bat an eyelid at the rejection.

'Just a little minute, Rusty, eh?' he pleaded.

'It will have to be only a minute then. I'm due to meet a bloke in Pilning at three o'clock.'

Keeping his flat cap on, Snooky shed his raincoat and hung it over the back of a chair before sidling up to Calum and jabbing at the epistle with a grubby forefinger. Calum saw it was addressed to a Mr *Leonard Stockingham Snook*. An important-sounding handle for such an insignificant bloke as Snooky, Calum thought, doing his best to suppress a smile.

'Looks like trouble to me,' he observed. 'Trouble with a capital *T*. You wants to get a solicitor on to that, or you'll be in danger of losing the bloody lot, my son.'

A hasty perusal of the letter revealed to Calum that Mrs Esmeralda Rita Snook had applied to the courts to have her husband permanently barred from ever setting foot in the house again – *the joint marital home,* as it was described in the letter. Typical bloody lawyer's jargon, Calum decided. He thought it hardly surprising that an ordinary geezer like Snooky had trouble understanding it; it would need another flaming lawyer to unravel that great load of gobbledygook!

'How the 'ell do I go about *that?*' whined Snooky, his beady brown eyes beseeching Calum's help. 'She says in there I'm a gambler. I likes a bet, as you well knows, but I don't lose *all* my money ... not like she says.' Snooky prodded the letter angrily. 'I tell you, I'm not standing for it, mate. I've paid for most of that bloody house meself!'

'I don't know ... I'll need to give it some thought,' Calum told him. 'Look – I've got to go now. I don't think it'll hurt to wait a day or two.'

He handed the letter back to Snooky who took it from him reluctantly, holding it between his fingers like an unexploded bomb.

'If you wouldn't mind them knowing, I could get my good mates Kevin and Jacko to cast their eyes over it for you,' Calum said. 'They've both bin divorced – Jacko three times – so they'll know the best way for you to go about it if you intends holding on to your gaff.'

'It ain't as if I've bin messing about with another woman. I've never looked at nobody else but 'er.'

Leonard Snook cast such a sad, imploring look that Calum was tempted to feel pity for him. It was obvious that the silly, daft bugger had brought most of his troubles on himself, but the hectoring tone of the solicitor's letter had really angered Calum. He hated the thought of all these jumped-up little Hitler lawyers riding roughshod over a person's life and hopes.

'It's a sod, but there's nothing I can do about it, mate,' he said. 'Your best bet is to get on into town, to the Citizens' Advice Bureau.'

Fifteen minutes later Calum was driving on the M5 over the Avonmouth Bridge, headed north. He slipped his Eric Clapton tape into the dashboard, and the sound of 'Lay Down Sally' filled the car. Listening to this particular number was sheer punishment for Calum. Always a special song, it reminded him of things he would rather forget: of the many nights he'd lain in Suzi's arms, all cuddled up to her curvy body, her legs entwined with his, their two hearts beating as one.

He wished he could leave the motorway at the next exit and surprise her with a visit, but that wasn't on the agenda any more. The last thing he wanted to do was bump into her new boyfriend; he knew he could not restrain himself from landing him one on the chin.

Those sweet little girls, he thought – Lucie and Emma; bright little redheaded moppets ... how could Suzi think of introducing another father figure into their lives? He decided he would have to do something about it soon. Take the bull by the horns, and thrash the matter out with her. *Him*, too, very likely, he thought.

Not today, though, Calum told himself; it was much too nice a day for that. He was pinning his hopes on seeing Marlene again this evening – same place, same time as before. He was on a promise; she'd hinted to him on Saturday night that her time of the month ought to be over and done with by then.

Glancing down at the river through the slatted railings, he saw that the tide was ebbing fast. He hoped the catch of conger had been a good one for Kevin and Dexy this morning, they'd promised him a couple of pounds if they had enough to spare. There was nothing like Daisy's oven-baked conger pie.

Above his sunroof, he saw a cluster of ragged white clouds sailing across a sky of speedwell blue. For once, Avonmouth's chimneys weren't belching out their usual gaseous stench, and to his left, the sun's blinding reflection bounced off endless rows of newly docked cars that filled the immediate hinterland. It was a rare day, and if only things had been right between him and Suzi, Calum's joy would have known no bounds.

He slid his window down to let the clean July air rush through. There was a curious odour to the interior of his car; a cloying, pungent scent that lingered constantly, despite all the doses of upholstery spray he'd given it, as well as opening the windows at every possible opportunity. The smell was highly suspect; an unwanted legacy of the secondhand car dealer from whom he'd bought the Cavalier, following his brother Curt's introduction to him a year ago.

'A drug dealer's car,' Holly had said, the very first moment she sat in it, her nose sniffing the aroma in instinctive reaction.

'How the hell do you know that?' Calum had asked her. Although he'd recognised the sweet odour instantly, he hadn't imagined that any of his nearest and dearest would. Whatever the Vauxhall's previous owner might have dabbled in in the past was definitely no business of *his*.

'Glory be, Uncle Cal,' Holly told him, 'that's grass, or I'm a Dutch girl.'

Calum refrained from mentioning that it was her father who'd originally introduced him to the dodgy car dealer – that both he and Curt had been of the opinion that cannabis was a different thing entirely from any hard drug. After all, it was now being used medicinally in many quarters, they both knew.

Dealing in hard drugs, and the consequent death and destruction they caused, didn't enter into Calum's code of practice in any way. His mode of operation broadly involved anything that came under the category of having fallen off the back of a lorry, or – he corrected himself – a passing ship, as the case might be, but he drew the line at going anywhere near the importation of heroin or cocaine.

His Clapton tape drew to a close as he was approaching the junction with the M4. He switched back to radio and turned down the slip road, heading for the Aust ferry and Pilning. His mate Starkey had arranged to meet him with the cod in the garden of a roadside pub. The place would probably be closed by now, Calum thought – if so, he hoped Starkey had thought to get him in a pint of Courage bitter.

Later that evening, Angie settled the baby in her cot and sat down to watch TV – alone, as she often was at this time of day. It was after nine o'clock, the twins' usual bedtime, but they had broken up for the school holidays, and they were in Clevedon with Jake's best friend's father, Frank Goodyear, who ran the local Scout patrol. He would be taking them camping in Swansea Bay next month, so tonight they were learning to light fires on which to cook their barbie-burgers. Angie didn't expect them home before ten.

It was in the evenings that she missed Curt most of all. Apart from his regular fishing trips, he hadn't been one for gallivanting far. When he wasn't out sailing – and that was usually only at weekends – they had spent a great deal of time in each other's company, perhaps watching television or, if there was nothing especially interesting on the box, sitting quietly reading.

The house was unusually quiet, though its ancient timbers produced creaks and groans that always caught Angie unawares if she happened to be engrossed in something else. After living for many years in a modern semi on a council estate, the sounds she was more used to hearing were very different from these – and altogether more irritating, she reminded herself.

Josh had called to pick up Daisy shortly after seven, an hour earlier than usual. Angie wondered if they were going somewhere special. She couldn't understand why Daisy didn't marry the poor fellow, and put him out of his misery. She ought at least to move into his comfortable bungalow on the outskirts of town, up beyond Upalong. It was spacious and bright, with sliding glass doors that opened from the living room on to a paved patio with a fantastic view of the valley; mile after mile of bright verdant meadows, bordered by hedges of darker green, and interspersed here and there by stands of tallest poplar or secret copses of oak and ash.

Angie could imagine herself sitting there now, instead of in front of her sad old television set trying to listen to the indistinct headlines of the BBC nine o'clock news. She thought of Daisy, who was most probably somewhere else – perhaps enjoying a drink with Josh at the Albatross, their favourite pub. Angie knew where *she* would rather be on a warm night like tonight:

on Josh Berry's spacious patio, sipping a nice cool vodka and lemon, admiring the panorama of the Gordano Valley and watching the sun slip out of sight beyond the faraway Welsh hills, like a scene from a Merchant Ivory movie.

There was only one thing missing ... the ocean. Angie missed the sight and sound, the exciting thrill, of the wild Atlantic rollers off the Cornish coast, where she was born. She dreamed of returning there to live one day. When she reached Daisy's age – especially if she was still alone – would be the time to do it. To renew old friendships, and visit the two maiden aunts – darlings both – who had helped to bring her up when, at the age of ten, her parents were killed in an horrendous car smash. It was only lack of money that stopped her from visiting them more often.

In fact, the acute shortage of money had been Angie's biggest problem ever since Curt disappeared, and she'd been glad to move in with Daisy to save the rent on her council house. Curt's employers had kept him on full pay for a while, but when, after three months, it was clear he wouldn't be returning in a hurry, they had made her a small compassionate grant but frozen all his pension rights, pending the outcome of police enquiries which were still going on.

These days she tried not to dwell too deeply on Curt's disappearance. In the beginning she had thought of nothing else, but having Evie to care for had helped take her mind off her worries. In those early months she had spent many desolate hours imagining what it was like to drown – to gulp in great mouthfuls of grey Channel water and then go down twice ... to come up for the third and final time ... hands and arms flailing wildly ... desperate for help. She never quite reached the ending, which was too dreadful to bear. Her strong, brave man, sinking below the surface – lost to everyone and everything he held dear.

Her children were the focal point of Angie's life now. Holly, in particular, was a great source of comfort and strength. Her thoughts turned back to a few hours earlier, when her twenty-year-old daughter, hyped up as Angie had never seen her before, had driven away in her grandmother's Metro for a date with a boy she'd met in a Bristol nightclub.

She was usually so upfront and honest about her friends and acquaintances but, with this particular lad, she'd retained an air of un-characteristic mystery. For the first time in her life, she'd been thrown off-balance by a member of the male sex, and the most Angie knew of him was that his name was Guy, and he had the blackest of black hair, and very, very dark eyes.

How lovely she looked tonight, Angie thought. She had swanned out of the house wearing a dark navy silk blouse and flowing, wraparound cotton skirt in swirling patterns of blue and white. Angie had refrained from asking too much about her date. She knew that Holly would tell her what she wanted her to know as soon as she was good and ready.

Mmm ... Angie mused, conjuring up a picture of the two of them together. A *black-haired boy, and my titian-haired girl. What a striking contrast they must make.*

The television news was drawing to an end, and another episode of the comedy programme she'd enjoyed last week was about to commence on HTV. Angie pressed the handset and switched channels, hoping for an uninterrupted thirty minutes' viewing before either the baby woke up, or her sons returned from Clevedon.

They burst into the house shortly after ten, as though an eruption had swept in.

'Eh, Mum,' yelled Luke, usually the quiet one, 'guess what Mr Goodyear let us do tonight?'

Angie was immediately alert. 'Nothing too dangerous, I hope?'

'No, Mum, it wasn't really dangerous at all,' chimed in Jake, the eldest by four and a half minutes.

'Come on then, let's have it,' challenged Angie.

'Well, he let us climb the cliff face at Ladye Bay...'

'It was all right ... we were roped up either to him or Mr Starling,' interrupted Jake.

'Roped up to Mr Starling?' exclaimed Angie. 'He's no bigger than a flipping starling himself. How in the world would *he* be able to stop you from falling?'

'We wouldn't fall. Mr Goodyear's teaching us properly, Mum, honest.'

'Yeah, honest,' echoed Jake.

'He'd blinking well better be,' said Angie, drawing both of them to her and hugging them tightly, one in each arm.

Their strong, sturdy bodies were sublimely

sweet to cuddle. Jake's was slightly broader, more muscled than his brother's; Angie could tell them apart in the dark. My soon-to-be-thirteen-year-old boys, she thought ... smelling a little bit sweaty after their long hard climb. It was still the same little-boy sweat, she reminded herself. Not yet the serious stuff, like Curt's when he exercised.

How precious they were, she thought, how utterly alive and full of abundant activity! Curt had enjoyed them, too. His two sporty little followers – game to tackle everything that life had to offer.

She checked herself silently. It's no good getting back on that old track, she thought. She must always treasure precious moments like these, because they sure as dammit weren't going to last forever.

'Off you go then – get ready for bed.'

Angie released her harum-scarum sons, patting their bottoms as they went.

'Your hair smells of bonfire – both of you,' she chided. 'Remember to wash it in the morning; it's much too late now.'

Delighted to escape the chore of hair-washing, the twins scuttled off to bed.

'I'll be up to tuck you in in exactly ten minutes,' Angie warned, 'So no mucking about up there – and I'll *kill* you if you dare to wake up Evie.'

'We won't,' they assured her, speaking together.

'No?' queried Angie. 'I've heard that promise before.'

'Where's Gran?' asked Luke, popping his head back round the door.

'Out with Josh, where d'you think?' Angie said.

Luke came back into the room quietly. Always more introspective than his brother, he asked worriedly, 'She isn't going to die, is she?'

Angie looked at him, startled. 'Why do you say that, Luke?'

'Because ... well ... Jake said Dr Chadwick sent her to hospital today. Something to do with her heart. She won't die, will she, Mum?' he repeated.

His clear blue eyes surveyed hers anxiously, awaiting the reassurance that all was well with his grandmother, and that he wasn't about to lose another close member of his family, the way he'd lost his father on the night of Hallowe'en.

'No, sweetie, nothing like that.' Angie drew him into her arms again, feeling his firm, skinny ribcage, his strong heart beating against her chest. 'Granny will be all right. It was only for tests, and she passed them all with flying colours, love.'

Luke's anxious expression lightened. 'Honest, Mum? Is that the honest truth?'

'Honest gospel, as true as I'm stood here,' Angie assured him. 'As true as I'm stood here, squeezing my Lukie tight.'

'So what was it made the doctor think she had a bad heart then?' he persisted.

'Oh, Lukie, Lukie, please stop worrying. Granny's going to be all right, I said. She isn't going to die – not before her time – and we're going to make sure of it by getting in someone else to take care of Evie while I concentrate on running the shop.'

His concerned gaze came back at her. His eyes were kind and gentle, somehow paler, more crystalline than Holly's or Jake's.

'You'd better get going now or we'll have Jake back, wanting to know where you are.' Angie kissed her son's smoky-smelling forehead. 'Come on, off with you. I'll tell Gran to explain it all properly to you in the morning. She's going to let me have the shop. That way, we'll always have somewhere safe to live.' She smiled at him lovingly. 'At least until my two handsome sons grow up, and your sister has sorted herself out permanently.'

'I'll always look after you, Mum,' Luke said.

'And me,' piped up Jake, who had come downstairs to see what was keeping his brother. She released Luke, and took him into her arms. 'We'll never leave you, not like...' Jake left the sentence unfinished. He was referring to his father, Angie knew.

'*Never?*' she laughed, touched by the depth of their love; their genuine concern for her wellbeing. '*Never?* Gosh, does that mean I'm to be saddled for the rest of my life with two odd bachelor sons?'

'Like Gran with Uncle Cal,' observed Jake seriously.

'Well, I wasn't thinking of Gran exactly,' Angie told him, 'But yes, perhaps you're right, Jake. Though don't go repeating what I said to Gran or Calum, will you,' she warned. 'We don't want either of them to get upset.'

'We won't,' Luke assured her from the doorway.

'Goodness, Luke, haven't you gone yet?' asked

101

Angie. 'I told *you ten minutes,* and that was at least eleven minutes ago. Off with you both, or I'll have to get out that cane, the one Grandad Cameron kept up on the dresser for Calum and your dad.'

They scurried away and, soon afterwards, the baby awoke for her late night feed. After Angie had settled her down, she flopped into her own bed, and turned off the bedside lamp. As usual her thoughts switched back to Curt where they lingered for a while. The lingerings were less ponderous, though, and happened a lot less often now.

If – as seemed likely – Curt was dead, Angie wished she could know it for certain. She had stopped clutching at straws some while ago, after the senior police officer investigating his disappearance had told her he believed her husband was almost certainly drowned.

She closed her eyes and tried to summon up a picture of Curt's face, but found it hard to do. His voice, too, had become a distant memory. There was only one thing left that Angie recalled with perfect clarity, and that was the sound of his cough. He had been a heavy smoker in their early days together, and it had left him with an irritating cough when he first awoke in the mornings.

Cough, cough... She remembered hearing him moving about downstairs and, a few minutes later, he would appear in their bedroom doorway, bringing her tea in bed. It was possibly the thing she missed most of all, she thought – that early morning cup of tea.

There were, however, compensations. It was good to know that her children were growing up relatively unscathed by their tragic loss. How proud Curt would have been if he could have heard the boys expressing their worry and concern for his mother tonight. Although she was lonely for one of his hugs, Angie felt extremely blessed to have the warmth of her children's love all around her – cosy and comforting, like a glowing coal fire on a cold winter's night.

Chapter Seven

It was quiet in Josh's bedroom; even the birds outside in the garden had settled down for the night, though they'd been making a merry racket earlier on. In the distance Daisy could hear a dog barking and the rushing sound of traffic on the motorway, but it was all very muted. She snuggled down further in the bed. Josh had gone to the bathroom to freshen up and, after that, he'd promised to bring some coffee to wake them both up before he took her home. As Holly had borrowed the Metro for the evening, Daisy was dependent on Josh for a lift anyway. There was no disguising the fact he liked it better that way. He didn't really want her to go home at all.

Holly had been walking around with her head in the clouds all week; Daisy hoped that the boy she was meeting tonight was worth all the fuss. Thinking of Holly, she smiled quietly to herself.

What the young ones didn't realise was that all these weird emotions weren't only applicable to them. Daisy blushed at what Holly would think if she knew what she and Josh had been up to barely an hour before ... and *barely* was the operative word.

She could hear the coffee percolator bubbling in the kitchen, and the sound of the fridge door opening and closing. Josh was the most domesticated man that Daisy had ever met. He was a paragon of virtue, cooking her nice meals, and always making her feel cherished and cosseted. And, what was more, he was still quite wonderful in bed ... imaginative, and surprisingly nimble with all the little tricks he liked to come up with. And *romantic*. Daisy's lovely man was romantic beyond belief!

Always, after they'd made love, it was the nicest thing in the world to be able to share with Josh her deepest thoughts. He was the only person she could really talk to about Curt; all the sweet, and sometimes not so sweet, memories she'd stored away over the years. Daisy sighed contentedly. Their conversation tonight had flitted here and there including just about everything under the sun. Josh was so easy to talk to, she thought – a rare attribute indeed, compared to most men she knew.

Her husband, Cameron, like the majority of his generation – and probably more so because he was Scottish and dour by nature – had never liked discussing anything of an intimate sort. He hadn't been a *bad* lover, Daisy realised now, but he'd never been as thoughtful and as anxious to ensure her participation in their lovemaking as Josh.

Because of Daisy's referral to hospital earlier that day, Josh had been wary of having sex tonight. For some strange reason, though, she'd needed him to make love to her. She'd especially wanted his reassurance that the pain that precipitated the trip to hospital was merely a minor interruption in her usual healthy state and nothing of any consequence.

She was reminded of a song that was in vogue some years ago about love, like youth, being wasted on the young. Unlike Josh, her husband had never taken the time to listen to the words of a love song, though Daisy had asked him to time and time again. It was disappointing, but she'd realised there was no point yearning for something better when, in every other way, she and Cameron had been perfectly well suited.

Working with him every day, and sharing the upbringing of their two boys, Daisy had, on the surface, been reasonably happy. It was only when she was listening to a song sung by Frank or Bing – some beautiful lyric, composed by Cole Porter or Sammy Cahn – that her emotions became charged with a dangerous, secret force; a deep-down basic desire stirring inside her, that she'd never really understood.

Daisy found it amazing that she'd never been unfaithful to Cameron, though she'd had no shortage of admirers in her time. People nowadays rushed into affairs of the heart willy-nilly, she thought. They paid no heed at all to other responsibilities they might have.

Perhaps the fact that Angie had never expressed an interest in another man said a good deal about her relationship with Curtis. It was early days yet, though, and it would be a sad thing if a girl as sweet as Angie went through the remainder of her life unloved.

Daisy had been widowed several years when she agreed to go out with Josh for a meal. During the time she was married to Cameron, she'd liked what she'd seen of Josh Berry. It was his close relationship with the Fletcher family that had rendered him strictly *persona non grata* in her husband's book and, although Daisy wasn't in agreement, she had gone along with it eventually for the sake of peace.

She rested her head on the pillow, meditating on the way it once had been. My Cameron was a right old tyrant in his own way, she told herself. He'd hated Adge Fletcher with a vengeance, and caused their families to be at loggerheads for as long as Daisy could remember. She had had many an argument with him about it during their forty years of marriage, but nothing had altered Cameron's opinion.

Their ancient rival was still a considerable thorn in the flesh where the business was concerned. There was a new row brewing over Angie's decision to supply the inhabitants of Fuzzy Cove with the super-fresh vegetables that Rex Carpenter grew in his market garden on the slopes of Hooper's Hill.

In contrast with her earlier life, Daisy's relationship with Josh Berry was peaceful and calm. He'd awakened in her all those long-buried

106

romantic notions that she'd learned over the years to suppress. At this moment, lying here in Josh's bed, she was seriously thinking of taking up his offer to move in with him. He still irritates the hell out of me, she thought, when he fusses too much, but since her panic-scare this morning, the idea was wonderfully tempting.

She glanced round his bedroom. The thought of living here permanently, in an atmosphere as peaceful as this, seemed more inviting by the minute. The glass-fronted, built-in wardrobes ... the attractive rosewood furniture he'd bought after Daisy told him she didn't feel truly comfortable amid his former wife's possessions. I'd be an absolute bloody idiot to turn it all down, Daisy mused. Josh Berry was offering her his heart, his love, and his life; only a fool would refuse all that – a wary, distrustful fool, something that Daisy never wanted to be.

Where on earth would she find another man to love her as much as Josh did, she asked herself. The answer was crystal clear in her mind: *nowhere*. She made up her mind she would tell him the minute he came back that she wanted to move in with him.

Josh returned a few minutes later, bearing a tray loaded with crackers and cheese, and two mugs of steaming coffee. Setting the tray down on a bedside table, he clambered back into bed.

'How's my sweetheart?' he said, nudging her bottom along a little way. 'Coo, what a great bulk,' he teased, 'it's a darn good job I like my women big.'

Daisy sat up and patted the pillows into shape.

107

'You didn't say that an hour ago when you were having your wicked way with me,' she said. 'I didn't hear any complaints from you then, you horrible pig.'

'Don't remind me, or I'll be wanting to ravish you again before you go.'

He reached over for the tray and rested it on the bed. 'Here ... you'd better get stuck into this or it'll be midnight before we get you home. I shall have some explaining to do to your daughter-in-law if I keep you out too late, you bad, wicked floozie, you.'

Daisy took the coffee Josh handed her and sipped it contentedly. She never minded his teasing; she almost always gave him back more than his fair share anyway.

'I've come to a big decision, Josh,' she said. 'I had a long chat with Angie, like I said, and she's going to take the business over completely.'

She fixed Josh a steady look with her slate-grey eyes. 'So – with that in mind – I'd like to take up your offer to move into Cedar Keys. That's if you haven't changed your mind since I almost didn't pass my MOT earlier today.'

Josh was taken by surprise. 'But you did,' he exclaimed. 'You passed it with scarcely a blip.'

He took the mug from her and, putting it back on the tray, wrapped his arms round her tightly.

'Oh, my sweetheart, I'm so pleased,' he breathed. 'Now I can look after you properly, instead of *you* being the one to look after everybody else under the sun.'

Daisy stroked his cheek tenderly. 'I'll have to call in the shop quite often to keep my eye on things, love,' she told him. 'Poor Angie will have her work cut out at first, seeing to the children as well as being responsible for the business.'

She smoothed Josh's furrowed brow and, with her fingertips, caressed his closed eyelids. 'It won't be like now,' she continued. 'You and I and our future together will have to come strictly first from now on. I love you, Josh Berry, and I'll *never* take for granted what you're offering me. It's much too special for that.'

'Nothing I'm offering you – as you put it – is worth anything to me, my sweetheart, without you here to share it. Oh, I'm so very, very pleased...' Josh eased his body a little way away, and stared at her earnestly. 'Daisy MacPherson, will you marry me?' he said.

Daisy was taken aback. She hadn't expected this.

'Oh, Lord, Josh, you'll have to give me a moment to think *that* one over. You've never mentioned such a thing before.'

Josh laughed. He leaned down and tickled her bare ribs. 'Don't look so worried,' he said. 'Take all the time in the world to give me your answer. But I'll tell you this much, I'm *never* going to give up. I want you wedded to me, Daisy dear – good and proper – so that we'll never be apart again.'

Daisy nodded. 'Perhaps,' she told him. 'Let's wait and see how it goes, eh?'

'OK,' he said slowly. 'But I'm saying that just to keep you quiet, you understand?' He kissed her full on the lips and, for a moment, Daisy relished the safe, peaceful, feeling it gave her. 'When you've finished your coffee, it'll be time to hit the road,' Josh went on.

She took another sip. 'So will it be all right if I start moving my stuff up here next Saturday, love?' she asked. 'The sooner, the better, I think,' she continued, 'so that when Angie starts interviewing housekeepers and sees one she likes, I'll be ready to skedaddle right away.'

Holly sat in the public bar of the Rat and Drainpipe feeling like a prize lemon. It was ten minutes past the time that Guy had arranged to meet her, and there was still no sign of him. On the far side of the room three young men were playing a game of pool, while a group of businessmen wearing smart city suits were propping up the bar, talking animatedly together. A mobile telephone suddenly bleeped; one of the group walked over to near where Holly was sitting and began gabbling into the handset. He winked at Holly cheerfully as he lied into the telephone. 'I'm stuck in a traffic jam – bored out of my mind. That's right ... down near the overpass, not far from Temple Meads Station.'

Holly coolly cast him a look of contempt. People with mobiles annoyed her; they very seldom seemed to hold conversations of any great importance. This one was no exception.

She turned her back on the whizz kid, and glanced at her wristwatch again. It was the first time she'd ever agreed to meet a comparative stranger in a strange pub in the middle of town. She was beginning to wish she hadn't, and then remembered how strongly the boy had affected her; how she hadn't been able to stop thinking about him all week. He was fifteen minutes late, though. Five more minutes and she would be on her way. She still just had time to join her friends at the Smuggler's Retreat before they moved on elsewhere.

Jazz, too, had a date with a boy she'd met at the Night Owl on Saturday night, Holly remembered. The difference was that canny old Jasmine had asked *him* to come out to the village to see *her*. She's not as daft as little old me, thought Holly. Jazz wouldn't set herself up to be humiliated in public like this.

She wondered why she hadn't thought to do the same as Jazz. She knew the answer though, only too well. It was because she liked Guy too much to want to share him with anyone else yet – to be seen by all and sundry meeting him at the village pub. She'd wanted to keep him special – and all to herself. Now it had rebounded on her. Guy, or Guy-liamo, whatever his damn stupid name was, had made a great big monkey out of her. Ignoring the persistent glances of one of the boys at the pool table – a boy who in other circumstances she would have thought pretty dishy – Holly picked up her purse and left the room.

Outside in the pub yard, the sun's glare caused her to blink, and she reached into her blue denim bag for her sunglasses. Inside the Metro, the heat was unbearable; she slid back the overhead glass and opened the windows wide. Disappointment swilled over her like a summer's deluge. She had never before in her whole life been so smitten, and now the object of her affection had let her

111

down in the worst possible way. Dominic Stone had hinted as much; she'd ignored him, and been taken for a fool. Swallowing hard, and fighting back the tears, Holly turned the key in the ignition. Then, shoving the gear stick into first, she was ready to start her journey home.

At that moment, a motorbike ridden by two black-leather-jacketed men swept into the yard and squealed to a halt some four or five cars away, completely blocking her exit. The passenger leapt off the back and sprinted away in the direction of the pub. As he disappeared inside, the driver climbed off the powerful motorbike and, resting it on the stand, lolled against the wall, his eyes fixed on the pub entrance.

Holly hesitated before sounding the horn. You never knew with these city types, she told herself. While she was still deciding what to do, the pillion passenger emerged from the brass-plated door of the Rat and Drainpipe. He was walking slowly now, his crash helmet dangled disconsolately from his hand.

Suddenly her heart stopped. For a split second, everything froze. It was as though she'd been dipped into a vat of icy cold water; her whole body seemed drained of warmth. And then it all started to race again – much faster than before. She could feel a pulse beating hard in her neck, so hard that it almost made her choke. It *was* him, and she couldn't speak ... she was quite unable to move, or even call his name. Any minute now he would leap on to the back of the motorbike and be gone from her life for ever. Desperate to move, Holly forced her leaden legs out of the car, only to find that her body wouldn't follow them. It felt as though she was fixed to the driver's seat by rivets, her hands stuck to the wheel by superglue.

And then she did it! Resting her size 34Bs on the steering wheel, she pressed the horn with the inner top of her arm. Glory be ... it worked! Just as he was about to mount pillion and drive into oblivion, Guy turned round and saw her. Shielding his eyes from the sun, he stared at Holly as if he couldn't believe who it was he saw.

Holly sounded the horn again. Then, climbing out of the car at last, she leaned on the door to steady herself.

'*Hey*... Hi.' Guy nudged his companion in the back and, taking off his helmet, hurried over to her. The pulse in Holly's neck was a solid thing now, choking her half to death.

'Hello,' she squeaked, her voice tiny, like that of a mouse. She licked her dry lips and the lump subsided back down where it belonged. She reached back into the Metro, and turned off the engine. 'I'd just about given you up,' she said.

'I guessed you would. I was afraid you would,' Guy said. They stared at each other for a moment, and then he added, 'Come over and meet my brother. He's had to give me a lift. My car broke down soon after I left home. I'm so sorry ... I can't apologise enough.'

Guy's brother was sitting astride the motorbike again, all ready for the off.

'Holly, meet Vincent. Vince, this is Holly,' Guy said.

Vince raised the face-shield of his helmet, and

113

nodded, 'Hi, Holly. Nice to meet you.'

His eyes, Holly saw, were the same dark liquorice-black as Guy's – and yet they were completely different. The eyes that she had been dreaming about for the past four nights belonged to him, and him alone. Still tongue-tied, she watched Vincent drive away, then Guy took her hand and led her back to the little lemon-yellow Metro.

'We're probably too late to catch the start of the movie now,' he said. 'What say we take a rain-check? We could go to see it next week.' He fixed her a searching look with his coal-dark eyes. *'This* week, if you like ... it's only Wednesday now.'

Holly nodded; her thoughts were no longer with the widely advertised Oscar-nominated film she'd so badly wanted to see only a few short days ago. I'll go *anywhere,* she wanted to say – anywhere, just as long as it's with *you.*

'Yes,' said Guy decisively. 'We could go on Friday night. That's if it suits you, of course.'

Holly nodded. 'Fine ... and if your car hasn't been fixed by then, I could always pick you up somewhere.'

'It *ought* to be,' Guy said. 'I'll get my garage mechanic friend to look at it first thing in the morning.'

He peered at her closely again, and Holly began to shake. She'd dreamed so often of those ebony eyes gazing into hers, and now she was afraid it might still only be a dream.

'In the meantime then,' Guy continued, 'shall we have a drink in here?' He inclined his head towards the recently revamped, completely characterless Rat and Drainpipe pub.

'I'd prefer somewhere else,' said Holly. 'Somewhere not too far, as I'm going to have to drive you home afterwards,' she hinted.

'We'll try the Sailing Ship then,' Guy said. 'It's down by the harbour, not far from where I live.'

Holly opened the passenger door, and he slid into the seat next to her. She had just about recovered her equilibrium and although her hands on the steering wheel were a little clammy, she was proud of herself for coping so well.

The Sailing Ship was also a modern pub, though totally different in character from the one they'd left. She and Guy sat down at a wooden picnic table where they could watch the ships ploughing to and fro in the harbour. Closer to them, a sailing lesson was in progress; a raw beginner was making an awful mess of hoisting a sail. The instructor hastily righted it and the hapless learner sped away – across to the far harbour wall. Holly sympathised with him; she was sure she would have got it wrong, too, with all these people looking on.

'Do you know anything about boats?' Guy asked suddenly, his question catching her by surprise.

A fleeting feeling of panic shot through her, and she didn't reply. Boats, and her menfolk's love of them, was a subject Holly tried to avoid.

'I'm afraid I don't,' Guy went on, 'A motorbike's more up my street.'

Taking a deep breath, Holly plunged in and began to tell him all about her father, his disappearance, and his love for *Green Pepperoni*.

And how she'd helped him to choose the name when he'd decided to keep the little cabin cruiser in its original green, and not paint her blue and white, or any other colour, just because everyone else said it signified bad luck.

She told Guy about her Uncle Calum, and how her father had borrowed *Solitude* from him because his own boat was awaiting an engine repair. Although he had never sailed in Calum's dinghy before, he was so well used to handling boats that no one had given it a second thought. As she recounted the story, her eyes misted over with tears, and Guy put his arm round her shoulder, holding her gently to him.

'Sorry about that,' Holly apologised. 'He's been gone a long time now ... Mum's had a baby since.'

'A baby?' Guy said, surprised. 'Your mother's had a baby since then, you say?'

'That's right.' Holly nodded. 'Dad went missing on the last day of October and, not long afterwards, Mum discovered she was pregnant. Now I have a little sister,' Holly continued. 'A sweet little ginger-haired girl. So how about that for a nice surprise, eh?'

'A wonderful surprise it must have been. I hope your mother didn't find it too difficult a time.'

'Not once she'd got over the initial shock. She couldn't afford to go to pieces – not carrying such precious cargo.' Holly smiled, remembering. 'That's what my Uncle Calum always used to say, "she was carrying precious cargo".'

She then told Guy about some of Calum's less colourful exploits, and other things about the rest of her family, too. Guy was equally forthcoming

116

and by the time she dropped him off at his home, they knew a fair bit about each other's immediate family, and their various friends. They made arrangements to meet at the cinema complex the evening after next, and Guy responded quite happily to Holly's invitation to come out to Fuzzy Cove the night after that, Saturday, to join her at the Smuggler's Retreat.

'We won't have to stay there all evening,' Holly assured him. 'We can go out for a drive, somewhere on our own, after that.'

Before Guy got out of the Metro he gave her a goodnight kiss. It wasn't a passionate kiss, like the ones she'd dreamed about, but a sweet, wonderful kiss that hovered over her lips, though barely touching them, like a butterfly skimming over a leaf.

All the way home to the village, she savoured Guy's kiss ... our very, very first kiss, she thought. She had a strong suspicion it was the first of many, *and,* she hoped, the first of lots of other equally delicious experiences too.

Angie was still listening out for Holly. She found it quite impossible to get off to sleep until she knew her daughter was home. Will it always be like this, she wondered – the anxiety I always suffer, every time any of my children are out late at night? Common sense told her that it was probably only a temporary thing; all tied up with the shock of losing Curt.

She had heard her mother-in-law come in half an hour earlier. She was most likely tucked up in bed and fast asleep by now. There was still no sign of Calum, but what *he* got up to on his nocturnal wanderings it didn't pay to dwell on too deeply, Angie knew ... even more so, since he'd broken up with Suzi Glue. That was something Angie and the rest of his family thought was a stupid move on Calum's part.

She turned to look at the bedside clock. It was past eleven thirty. All her senses were geared to listening out for Holly.

Just then, to her relief, the bedroom door opened, and she heard Holly whisper, 'Are you asleep, Mum? I'm just popping in to say goodnight.'

'I didn't hear you come in,' said Angie, keeping her voice low so as not to wake the baby. Holly's face was glowing radiantly, Angie saw. 'You look as though you've had a good evening,' she observed.

'Oh, Mum, I did. It was awful at first; I thought he wasn't going to turn up.' She squeezed Angie's hand, then smiled. 'And then he did, and it was great.'

She beamed her mother another radiant smile. 'Oh, Mum, he was just as lovely as I remembered him. Oh, dear, I'm keeping you awake! I'll tell you all about it tomorrow when I see you.'

She kissed Angie's cheek fondly. 'Night-night, God bless,' she said.

'Night, sweetheart,' whispered Angie and, when Holly turned to go out the door, she saw that her eyes were deep blue pools of enchantment. The boy had bewitched her; that was clear. Angie only hoped he was worthy of such strong and genuine emotion.

118

Chapter Eight

Caitlin alighted from the bus at the end of Magpie Way and took a left turn into Linnet Avenue. Anxious to be home, she walked briskly along the tree-lined avenue to number thirty-four, her own little two-bedroomed semi. At seven in the evening, the sun was just starting to fade. The sky over Worlebury Hill was a glorious mixture of red and gold, a sign of fine weather tomorrow. She chanted the words of a rhyme she remembered from her childhood.

'Red sky at night, shepherd's delight... Red sky in the morning, shepherd's warning.'

She had been back in England for almost a week; a particularly fruitful week it had been, too, but she was more than thankful now it was Friday. At last, a little time to myself, she thought.

She had arrived back at Heathrow in the early hours of Saturday morning and in only six days she'd first of all managed to find work –although only temporary – then acquired a small black cat. Now, today, she had found a tenant to live in her house, though it meant that Caitlin would have to move back in with her parents again. *That* proposition was definitely not what she'd had in mind when she'd decided to return.

Circumstances had dictated otherwise. Back in San Francisco, when she was making her plans, she hadn't given too much thought to what Tyler's reaction might be when he discovered she was gone. Although she knew full well what he was capable of, she had still underestimated his ability to try to destroy her. She had learned from her father that the first thing Tyler did on arriving in Las Vegas on Friday night was to put through a call to the motel, only to be told that Caitlin had checked out an hour or so after he left. He'd then made enquiries with the airlines, who confirmed that she'd taken a flight to Heathrow earlier that evening.

Since the previous Tuesday Caitlin had been working for her former boss, the manager of a busy travel agency in the main street at Weston-super-Mare. She had contacted him first thing on Monday and, to her delight, he'd told her that his personal assistant was away on holiday in the West Indies, and the temp from the secretarial agency was, in his words, next to bloody useless. He'd asked Caitlin if she would like to have her old job back for the next three weeks.

Since her previous tenants' departure to France, she hadn't had the telephone re-connected. It was a comfort to know that Tyler couldn't call her now, or whenever he felt like it. However, soon after she started work, Tyler had phoned her father to say the standing order to the building society would be cancelled unless Caitlin went back to live with him. Without Tyler's help with the mortgage, she knew she couldn't keep the house going, so when Julie Moon, a girl at her office, said she was looking for somewhere to rent, Caitlin invited her to move in with her and share the running costs. It turned out, though, that Julie had a boyfriend, and was actually looking for a house to rent for the two of them.

Caitlin couldn't afford to turn them away. Tyler had made it clear to her father that he intended to come to England to seek her out the moment his contract ended. She had exactly five weeks to establish herself elsewhere, she realised. She no longer doubted his talent for causing trouble; she'd been a fool to think he would ever let her go lightly.

Her house was in sight at the end of the road; she looked forward to getting inside and making herself a decent cup of tea. Her stomach was rumbling quietly, reminding her she'd had nothing to eat all day except a tuna-and-mayonnaise sandwich for lunch. She had declined her mother's offer of beans on toast when she called to see her on her way home from work, because she said she needed to get home to feed the cat.

This piece of news had gone down like a lead balloon with Olive and Roland Hutchison. Caitlin's mother was no animal lover; she only tolerated her husband keeping a dog because he lavished even more attention on herself than he did on the animal. In addition, the possession of a cat had put Caitlin at a positive disadvantage when she'd asked if she could stay at their house until she found a permanent job and, with luck, somewhere suitable to live. They had agreed – albeit reluctantly – leaving her in no doubt that the cat was even more unwelcome than herself.

121

Caitlin pushed open the front gate of number thirty-four and went into the small front garden. Halfway along the path, she paused to pinch out some dead flowerheads from the colourful profusion of petunias and busy lizzies her father had planted along the border earlier in the year. He liked to insist he was looking after her interests, but Caitlin knew he was merely being nosy. Tending her garden gave him the perfect excuse to find out not just that the house was being properly looked after, but what her tenants were up to in their private lives.

She turned the front door key in the lock, and stepped inside the cool hallway. Picking up some circulars which the postman had left, she carried them through to the kitchen and, depositing them on the table, threw open the back door. 'Here, kitty, kitty,' she called and the half-grown kitten/cat scampered past her feet, heading towards its food bowl in a corner by the washing machine.

'Well, I like that,' said Caitlin, giving him the remainder of a tin of Felix from the fridge. As the cat gobbled the food, she crouched down to stroke its soft neck.

'I don't know ... another little something for me to worry about,' she murmured.

She'd found the cat sitting on her back doorstep the day she got back from America, and although she'd tried to stop it coming indoors, it had slipped past her feet, the same as today, giving every impression of belonging here. It did belong here, of course, or at least it had belonged to the couple who'd been renting the house.

Caitlin's neighbour, Esme Snell, had later told her the full story. It appeared that Caitlin's tenants had arranged for the local animal refuge to find it a new home before they left for France but, when the time came to take it there, it was nowhere to be found. Scared off by the clattering of the removal men, Mrs Snell supposed. Sod's law being what it was, the old lady had added, as soon as its owners left for Dover to catch the ferry, it had come out of hiding and existed on handouts from herself and another neighbour ever since.

'Cats is known for being some contrary creatures,' Mrs Snell had observed, nodding her head wisely. 'Anyway my flower, me and Albert guessed you'd be back, what with the house being vacant and all. I said to him, I said Caitlin's always bin an animal lover ... she'd never knowingly let a little creature like that starve to death.'

Mrs Snell would have taken it in herself, she'd said, but her husband had an allergy to cats. They'd had cats in the past, she told Caitlin, but as soon as she was beginning to grow fond of them Albert always broke out into a rash.

Gazing vengefully at her spouse working in the adjoining garden, Esme Snell had added in hushed tones, ''Course, that sets 'im off worse than he already is ... he's a miserable sinner ever since he've bin retired.' She sighed, and rubbed her forehead wearily, adding, 'To be truthfully honest with you, Caitlin, my love, I'd ten times rather have a cat around the place than *he*.'

She'd gone on to enquire how long it would be

before Tyler came home, annoying Caitlin no end with her ridiculous, inquisitive chatter.

'You must be missing him sorely, my flower,' she'd said. 'I remember how close you was before you went away, like two little turtledoves, billing and cooing – I never did know that sort of closeness with *him*.' The old woman had inclined her head towards her husband again, who, sensing they were talking about him, looked up from his digging to nod gravely at Caitlin.

Caitlin's real reason for keeping the cat was that she'd been desperately in need of something warm and cosy to cuddle. She'd named it Pepsi, and it had certainly helped to salve her loneliness ... her sadness at living alone in a house where she and Tyler had once been so happy and full of hope for the future. The thing she hated most was having to sleep alone in the king-sized bed where they'd cuddled up so cosily together. With the kitten, though, she didn't feel anywhere near as isolated.

Her thoughts strayed back to the conversation she'd had earlier with her parents. She still hadn't told them she was expecting a baby. Some vital instinct had warned her not to and, after Tyler's call to her father, she was certain her instincts were correct. Neither of her parents could be trusted not to blurt the secret out to him when he next came on the telephone.

She had reached the tenth week of her pregnancy and had, only this morning, fixed an appointment to attend the ante-natal clinic at her neighbourhood health centre. In view of her past history, she knew it was crucial that she took special care of herself – both emotionally and physically – in the course of the next few weeks. They'd told her at the surgery she would be referred to hospital a few weeks from now, to have a scan. It would be a relief when that time arrived, she thought. Seeing the pictures of her unborn baby would help her to accept it as a real-life proposition, not just some beautiful dream.

For the present, however – as soon as she'd rustled up something to eat – Caitlin was looking forward to watching the latest instalment of *EastEnders*. It was one of the things she'd missed most in the two years she'd been away.

The Channel was as still as a millpond ... if there was such a thing as a *tidal* millpond, Calum reflected. Overhead a full moon, large as a giant melon, cast down its bright beam of silvery light like a wide pathway in front of *Green Pepperoni's* bows. They were level with Porthkerry to starboard, headed for the wider estuary off Porlock Bay and, with the tide in their favour, maintaining a speedy rate of knots. By his calculations, they would be weighing anchor at the fishing grounds a little before midnight.

There were occasions when Calum missed his sailing dinghy, and yet he had to admit the use of his brother's thirty-foot cabin cruiser had opened up a whole new dimension to his fishing ex-peditions.

There were five aboard tonight, including himself. Kev and Dexy were trailing the lines, hoping to entice a few late cod, though turbot and bream were likely to be the main catch tonight. Jacko Jackson, after sorting bait in readiness for the serious fishing to start, had taken the helm, while his young son, Darren, was in the galley, brewing them all a mug of char.

The overhead radio crackled noisily, interrupting the weather report, though Calum had heard all he wanted: visibility good, temperature twelve degrees Centigrade, and plenty of sunshine forecast for tomorrow. He could have told the weather forecasters *that* for nothing; he'd never before seen such a brilliant sunset as last evening. It had shimmered across the bleak Welsh hills, a lustrous conflagration of gold and crimson, as impressive and scary as a raging forest fire.

'Tea up, Rusty.' Fifteen-year-old Darren deposited a pottery mug at Calum's side.

'Ta, kid. I reckon you've earned yer keep. You'll be going up on deck now, I dare say. See what you can do to help yer dad.'

The boy looked at him, deadpan. 'Kevin says he'll learn me how to cast.'

'*Teach* you how to cast,' said Kevin, coming into the cabin, and flopping his large bulk down on a bunk. In his day, Kevin Buttercup had passed his eleven plus and gone to a grammar school in Bristol – it showed, too, Calum thought. He was more knowledgeable by half than the rest of them, and that included Calum himself. Kev always knew how to get the words out right, something that Calum could never quite do. He envied people who could. It was probably the reason why Suzi had been so good for him, he told himself, yet he could never bring himself to tell *her* that.

'You wanna see that moon out there,' Kevin went on. 'So bright on that water, you'd think you could walk across it ... like it was solid.'

'Spooky – sort of night what used to bring out the werewolves,' remarked Calum.

'Trust you to reduce it to that level. I was thinking more of the man from Galilee.'

'Yeah, well, there is that, I grant you.'

Not serious for long, Calum made a sudden movement, flapping his arms at Darren, who scurried back to the galley to fetch the other men's tea.

'I was thinking ... been talking to Dexy just now,' said Kevin. 'What's the position with you and Suzi, with regard to the kids? Does it mean you won't be seeing them again, now that she's got this new bloke calling on her, acting like he owns the flipping place?'

When Calum didn't reply, Kevin commented, 'It's even putting Dexy off collecting the babbies and taking them to see his old lady – their gran – anywhere near as often as he used to.'

Calum scratched his head contemplatively. He'd been trying to avoid tackling the subject all week, ever since his own mother had said she was thinking of inviting Suzi and the girls to Josh's place one Sunday for tea, now that she was all settled in.

'It's a sod,' Calum said. 'I'm going to have to do summat about it if Suzi allows the bugger to carry on like this much longer.'

'It's getting serious,' Kevin agreed.

'I know 'tis, Kevin. *Blooming* serious. I don't

know where this bloke's appeared from, do you?'

'Dexy tells me he's in insurance. Got the gift of the gab, and all that.' He paused a while, and looked at Calum thoughtfully. 'I wouldn't have thought she was the type to be impressed by all that, would you? Not Suzi Glue...'

'There's no knowing what gets into their heads when they takes a mind to it,' said Calum.

'Umm,' said Kevin, 'I suppose you're right.' He rolled off the bunk and disappeared up on deck, leaving Calum alone again, surrounded by his thoughts.

It wasn't only the problem of Suzi and the nippers that was bothering him now. Jake and Luke had begun to pester him to take them offshore fishing. Both they and he knew, though, that their mother would throw a complete wobbly if they so much as raised the subject with her. Angie would be filled with worry that something might happen to them, and she'd lose them by drowning, the way she had their dad.

Calum got to thinking about his brother's disappearance. It was on a night like this, clear and calm, that Curtis had sailed out in *Solitude* and never been seen again. Nothing would have warned him of impending disaster, any more than the balmy atmosphere out here in the Channel tonight would do. Yet it seemed that he'd completely vanished off the face of the earth. Supposing he'd been capsized deliberately by someone, Calum asked himself.

It could have been me, he thought again. He'd been thinking that ever since it happened. A secret voice inside his head went even further than that. What if it had been a case of mistaken identity – and if so … why? Calum knew himself to be no angel, but however hard he racked his brain, he just couldn't come up with a serious reason for someone wishing him dead. He bloody hoped not, anyway. He'd never touched anything that looked *too* dicey. As for Curtis, the poor bugger had never done *anything* that would warrant a case of foul play. *Or had he?* Perhaps he *had* been dabbling in something that Calum didn't know about. A very private person, Curt had always played his cards very close to his chest.

Shaking his head in disbelief, Calum left the cabin and made ready to drop anchor. The compass readings showed that they'd reached the offshore sandbanks out from Porlock Bay, where, all the indications were, they'd soon be hooking some black bream, ray, or turbot.

The following day was Saturday, and Angie was interviewing applicants for the post of live-in mother's help. The second one was due to arrive at noon; Angie hoped she'd be more affable than the first. It had been hard going all the way with Berenice Boothroyd, and not just because she was an older woman either; Angie had always *loved* the company of Daisy, even before she'd married Daisy's son. It was clear to her that the woman she'd seen earlier had very little interest in babies, even though she had a couple of children herself, both now grown up, and living abroad. Divorced and lonely, she was primarily looking for somewhere to live, Angie guessed.

Stiff, and ladylike; she wouldn't have fitted in with the family. What she'd have made of Calum, Angie couldn't even begin to imagine.

'I'll let you know,' Angie had said, but Berenice Boothroyd was having none of that. 'Either tell me now if I've got the job, or I'm afraid I'll have to turn it down.'

Angie wondered what the rush was. She was relieved, though – it made it easier for her.

'I've several other people to see,' she'd lied. She actually only had one more, the twenty-two-year-old who was due to arrive any minute now. Holly had sacrificed two hours of her Saturday overtime to be on hand to provide a second opinion. She was looking after Evie at present, while Daisy had driven down from her new home at Upalong to take care of the shop.

'Ange,' said Daisy, opening the living-room door. 'Here's the young lady who's come for the job. Helga Petersen – this is Mrs MacPherson.'

When she had ushered the girl inside, Daisy beat a quick retreat. She looked to be stifling a grin, Angie thought. One look at the applicant and she understood why – Calum's idea of a Scandinavian au pair was alive and real, here, and sitting in Angie's armchair, showing an expanse of thigh almost up to her knickers. Angie, wondering what experience she'd had, proceeded to question her in depth.

After ten minutes she gave up trying. Holly needn't have bothered to come all the way home from Bristol to be here, because the girl was definitely a no-go as far as Angie was concerned. She hardly spoke English for a start, though if

130

she'd been suitable in other ways, that might have been worth overlooking.

Angie felt a little sorry for the girl, but she'd obviously had no experience with children and, like Mrs Boothroyd, it seemed more likely she was looking for somewhere suitable to live than a job with children. Norwegian Miss Petersen was far too full of herself to look after a ten-week-old baby and provide a cooked meal for two boisterous twelve-year-old boys.

'I'd have to be behind her all the time,' Angie whispered to Daisy when she went into the shop to look for Holly. Holly was of the same opinion as herself, so Angie had wished Miss Petersen goodbye, and good luck elsewhere.

'Back to square one,' she sighed, when she sat down later with her family to eat their midday meal.

While they were enjoying the delicious ham salad that she'd prepared, Holly regaled Calum with a full description of the last candidate. He was all for chasing down the hill after her before she caught the bus back to Bristol – all expenses paid.

'I could have taken her in the car,' Holly said, 'but I wouldn't have a clue what to talk to her about.'

'Never mind *talk*,' scoffed Calum. 'I don't know what this family's coming to, turning down a little cracker like that.'

'Why don't you grow up?' said his mother. 'Sort yourself out, for heaven's sake.'

'Thanks for the borrow of your car, Gran,' Holly said. 'I won't make a habit of it, I promise.

As soon as I get my rise next month, I'll be looking out for one of my own.'

'You're welcome, my dear,' Daisy told her. 'Your mother needed you here today.'

'She's got her eye on the old storeroom. She wants to live in it herself,' Angie said.

'And what about the hired help? Where will they live?' asked Daisy.

'*What* hired help?' laughed Holly.

'Oh, dear Lord, there's got to be someone somewhere,' groaned Angie, taking her crying baby away from Daisy so that Daisy could eat her lunch.

Chapter Nine

Roxanne Meredith sat down at the kitchen table to eat her Saturday lunch of sausages, beans, egg and chips. As usual, she was in a rush; she had barely fifteen minutes in which to finish her food and be back at the betting shop by a quarter to two. Her husband, Henry, sitting opposite her across the red-checked tablecloth, was drowning his chips with tomato ketchup, the way he always did.

'Can *I* have some ketchup, Dad?' Erin asked him quietly.

'You'll be lucky to find any left, the way your father chucks it over everything,' grumbled Roxanne, refraining from blowing her top.

'That's what I was afraid of,' Erin said mildly.

Roxanne was aware she sounded a right cow every time she went for Henry in front of their daughter, but he got right on her wick with his lifetime of unchanging habits – his passion for dousing every sort of potato with tomato ketchup being one of them.

She always finished up regretting her carping criticism of Henry; she knew how much Erin hated it when Roxanne drew her into the argument. They were both so different from her, she thought, yet, for all that, she loved them to distraction. She'd be lost without them, she knew.

She speared a sausage sharply, her thoughts far away as she ate half of it. A rosy flush suddenly suffused her neck and face; she felt like an overheated boiler about to explode. Damn the bloody change, she told herself. It had come upon her early, the same as it had with her mother, and most of the other Cox women. She laid down her fork with the remnant of sausage still on it, and pushed her plate away.

Henry looked up in surprise. 'What's up, don't you like these bangers?' he said. 'I got you pork, like you said you wanted. You said not to get the beef.'

'I've lost me appetite, love,' Roxanne assured him. ''Tisn't nothing wrong with the grub – I'm feeling a bit odd, that's all.'

When Henry wasn't at work, he always cooked the Saturday lunch. Roxanne had been more than glad of his help today; Saturdays were busy at the betting shop, and she'd recently been finding the job more heavy going than she used to. The last thing she wanted was to upset Henry, when all he did was try to keep everything running smoothly for herself and their daughter. Roxanne glanced at Erin and noticed that she, too, had pushed her plate aside, with a mountain of food still on it.

'Just because I didn't want no more, young lady,' she scolded, 'that don't give *you* the all-clear to leave all that nice fried egg and beans – and you've hardly touched any of your blooming chips.'

Roxanne scraped back her chair and, rising abruptly to her feet, said 'Talk to her, Henry, for pity's sake. Tell her she ain't leaving this table until she've ate every bit of that food what's on her plate.'

Erin grimaced, but didn't reply. She knew that when her mother left, she would be able to con her father into thinking she'd eaten more than she had. On Sundays, when Roxanne cooked a roast dinner, Erin was forced to resort to drastic measures. Locking herself away in the bathroom, she would stick her fingers down her throat to make herself vomit.

I'm a lot better than I was, though, she thought, remembering how two years ago when still at school, the added pressure of exams had brought her very near the edge. There were times when she'd been seriously suicidal. Now everything was fine: as a care worker in an old folk's home, she was under no compulsion to carry out her tasks to any rigid deadlines. Happy in her work, she loved the old ladies – most of them! – and was also especially fond of the two elderly gentlemen who made up the complement of twenty-four residents.

Like her father, who also worked shifts, it was Erin's day off today. She'd volunteered always to work on Sundays, however, just to avoid being forced to eat the meat and four veg her mother served up for Sunday lunch. That was one nice thing about working at The Conifers, Erin thought. The residents were too busy concentrating on getting the food into their own mouths to worry about what anyone else was doing.

Erin glanced at the wall clock. Her mother would be leaving for work any minute now. She only needed to spin out the pretence a little while longer and then she, too, would be out of here. With her girlfriends, she planned to catch the two-thirty bus into Bristol for an afternoon's shopping in the Broadmead shopping centre.

Her spirits plummeted when she suddenly remembered that Holly and Jazz both had dates for tonight ... and the only thing *she* was foolish enough to do was fall head over heels in love with a boy who hardly knew she existed. Dominic Stone was on duty this weekend at his hospital in Gloucester; she'd overheard him telling Holly at the pub last week. As if Holly cared a tuppenny tinker's cuss what he did with his time, Erin sorrily told herself. And yet – viewing the situation from a more positive angle – her hopes rose that *if and when* Dominic did finally accept the fact that Holly was in love with someone else, it might just turn out there was a ghost of a chance for *her*.

135

Holding her long blonde hair away from her face, Erin shovelled up another forkful of the horrible mixture of egg-yolk and baked beans, and crammed the lot into her mouth. While her mother was still faffing around, plastering on her usual twenty-two layers of make-up in front of the steamed-up wall mirror, Erin did a passable imitation of enjoying the putrid concoction.

Roxanne applied the rich crimson lipstick to her full, sensual lips with a final flourish. 'There,' she announced, cheerful once more that she would soon be back where she felt most at home, trading insults rich with innuendo with all the regular punters. As an example of steadfast loyalty, none of them were a patch on Henry – she knew that only too well – but, boy, oh boy, did they ever cheer her up when she was feeling low! And, if it sometimes went a little further, well, life was too short to waste on missed chances. You only had to think of the poor old codgers along at The Conifers to realise *that*, she told herself.

'We must do this again,' Marty Riley had whispered in her ear, when they'd snatched a few stolen moments together in the back yard of the Smuggler's Retreat two Saturdays ago; a most unsuitable venue for what they would both have liked to be doing but, in the event, there was only time for a few passionate kisses before he'd been called to go back on stage.

She lived in hope that the next country and western night would prove altogether more rewarding. Marty had promised her he would do everything he could to persuade his highly suspicious wife to remain at home that evening. Henry would be working the night shift at the hospital then, and wouldn't have a clue where she was or what time she got in.

Poor soul, she thought, as Henry rose to his feet to accompany her out to the front door. He looked so decent and unsuspecting, she experienced a rare pang of conscience. Yet she couldn't survive – and, she knew, neither would their marriage – if she couldn't indulge in her extra-marital peccadilloes.

'Cheerio then, my love,' Henry said, kissing her goodbye on the doorstep. 'Try and not work too hard this afternoon, eh?'

'I won't,' Roxanne assured him breezily. Fixing him a serious look with her sharp brown eyes, she said, 'Make sure our Erin eats the rest of her food, won't you, Henry?'

A few minutes later, as she was walking along by the harbour wall on her way back to work, she pondered the possible reasons for her daughter's sparrow-like appetite. There wasn't another mother on earth who'd loved a baby daughter more, but there had been moments in those early years when Roxanne had got her hair off with Erin good and proper because she'd refused to eat the mashed-up baby food she'd so lovingly prepared for her. At times like those, she had to admit, Henry had always shown a good deal more patience than herself.

'Oh sod it – that's ancient history,' Roxanne murmured, hastily restoring a cheerful smile to her rosy countenance. She had spotted Rex Carpenter coming towards her; it wouldn't do for him to see her looking so glum. He'd recently split up from his wife, she'd heard – a sour-looking girl who had steadfastly rebuffed Roxanne's every overture of friendship.

Rex was in the process of building up his own market-gardening business on some rented land high on the slopes of Hooper's Hill. He now lived alone in a caravan overlooking the Channel at Portishead, while his wife, with their two school-aged children, remained immovable in their smart four-bedroomed house at Easton-in-Gordano. According to gossip in the betting shop, there was every sign that his business was doing well. Roxanne was pleased about that; he deserved it for all the hard work he'd put in. She thought it highly likely, though, that most of Rex's hard-earned profits would end up in his crabby young wife's hands. She gave Roxanne the impression of being a penny-pinching type.

'Hello there. What brings you down to this part of town?' she gushed, when he drew near enough to speak to.

'Hi,' Rex replied shyly, halting in his tracks and looking a bit bemused.

'Lost your way, have you?' asked Roxanne. She wouldn't have put him down as the nervous sort, yet nervous he definitely was.

'I've just taken twelve large punnets of strawberries along to the Yachting Club – they're having a do tonight,' he said.

Roxanne expressed surprise. 'You haven't never carried them all the way down from Hooper's Hill?'

'No.' An uneasy smile slid across his features, as

if he was fearful of giving too much away.

'I left the van outside MacPherson's Store,' he explained. 'It's such a lovely day, I thought it would do me good to have a little walk.'

'It is that.' Roxanne eyed him up and down, from his beige bomber jacket to the white Adidas trainers he wore on his feet. 'Oh, well, I'd best be on my way,' she said. 'Old Norman gets a bit umpety if I'm not back before two – especially on a Saturday afternoon.'

In a last attempt to lure him into her web of secret – and not-so-secret – admirers, she fingered the sleeve of his jacket, her mouth pursed seductively, like a freshly opened poppy.

Rex backed away quickly, almost toppling over, and disturbed a pair of seagulls canoodling on the harbour wall. Startled, they winged off into the pale blue yonder, shrieking raucously.

'I've never seen you in the Smuggler's of a Saturday night,' Roxanne continued, squeezing his arm in an intimate way. 'I was wondering whatever you finds to do with yourself of a night-time, now that you'm all on your own.'

'Eh?' Rex said, flustered. 'I suppose I don't get out very much – you're right.'

'You wants to do summat about it then ... come to the quiz night tonight. Life's too short to keep your light hid under a bushel ... nothing but a waste, I'd say – a good-looking young chap like yourself.'

Giving Rex's arm a final pat, Roxanne went off across the green, leaving him to digest her invitation to come to the Smuggler's Retreat that evening.

Quiz nights were the form of entertainment Roxanne enjoyed least of all. They could either be utterly boring – like when old farty-ass Stone and his even more obnoxious son, Giles, made up one of the teams – or downright annoying if they were joined by his high-falutin, horse-featured wife. Whether or not she could answer the questions correctly, Mirabel – Her Royal Highness – Stone liked to give the impression she was a cut above everyone else in the place. Roxanne often wondered about their sex life. How those two oddities had produced an attractive-looking boy like Dominic, and a beautiful black-haired daughter like Jasmine, she failed entirely to know.

Quiz night would be just the thing for young, extremely lonely looking Rex Carpenter, she thought. He seemed the intelligent sort. It occurred to her then that she might try to fix him up with her own daughter, Erin. If he was looking for a nice girlfriend, he would have to go a very long way to find one nicer than *her*.

Erin could do with getting out and about a bit more often, Roxanne told herself. At the same age, Roxanne had been having an absolute ball. She preened at her reflection in the green-painted window of the betting shop. Perhaps it was as well Erin didn't take after her. One glamorous female in the family was more than enough; she would hate it if she had to compete with her own daughter.

Waiting on the doorstep of the betting shop, and holding the door open for her, was Bob Gascoigne from the barber's shop next door.

140

'Thanks, Bob – you're a hero,' she laughed, pressing her bosom, accidentally-on-purpose, tightly against his chest as she passed.

'Caw, that was nice,' the fellow enthused. 'Can't we go back and do that again?'

'Now, Bob – you know I never did it on purpose,' protested Roxanne. 'Just as if I would!'

'Not *much*, you never,' he remarked. 'Not that I'm complaining, mind. I don't get to rub up against many like *those* in the course of a day's work.'

'I should think not; it's only blokes what comes into your shop. You should go unisex – or bisexual,' she riposted, giving him a last flirtatious grin as she let the door swing shut behind her.

'Holly wants you to come outside and talk to Mr Fletcher, Mum. She says to come quick.'

'One moment, please, Luke – you can see what I'm doing.'

Angie had taken advantage of a few quiet minutes in the lunch hour to put Evie to the breast. She was a great believer in babies getting a full ration of their mother's antibodies if at all possible.

'Sorry, little pippin,' she said, disconnecting her nipple from the baby's mouth. Evie's lips continued in a sucking movement, but she was full to the brim now. Angie settled her back in her pram, knowing that she would have to come back and burp her later, otherwise there would be trouble.

'You'll soon let me know, I don't doubt,' she

141

whispered softly before turning her attention to Luke, who was gesticulating wildly and pointing to the door leading into the shop.

'*What?*' demanded Angie, steering him round in front of her and closing the living-room door quietly.

'It's Mr Fletcher,' Luke told her. 'He says he's going to smash Rex Carpenter's windscreen, and he's been throwing our courgettes and broccoli all over the place. His wife's here, too; she's been trying to stop him. Holly and Jake are doing their best to protect the rest of the stuff. That's why she asked me to hurry up and fetch you.'

'Where's your Uncle Calum?' asked Angie as she rushed outside, where Holly was trying to prevent Adge Fletcher taking another hefty swipe at the neatly laid-out vegetables.

'Go see if you can find Calum ... quickly,' Angie instructed Luke.

'But *where*, Mum?'

'Anywhere,' Angie snapped.

'Stop it,' she heard Holly yelling. 'Bloody get off, I tell you.'

'I'll bloody get off,' Adge Fletcher snarled. 'I'll bloody get off when you MacPhersons puts a stop to selling all this-yere fancy foreign rubbish. You're fast putting me out of business, you are. I'll be lucky to sell a bloody Bramley cooking apple at this rate.'

'Now come on, Arthur. You'll do yourself a mischief,' coaxed his wife. Minnie Fletcher, less than five feet tall and as wide as she was high, was trying to stop him from doing more damage.

'Whatever's got into him, Min?' Angie

142

demanded, joining in with Holly to defend their produce.

The woman, panting and pulling at her equally rotund husband's sweaty body, rounded upon Angie angrily. '*What's got into him,*' she echoed. 'You got the cheek to stand there and say that, you precious little tart? It's *you* what've caused all *this*. We never had a ha'porth of trouble when Dais were running the place. Daisy knew better than to try and take away somebody else's livelihood.'

'*Livelihood?*' answered Angie. 'The stale old rubbish you were selling, nobody would ever buy — not unless they were absolutely desperate, that is.'

'Our customers were always asking Gran why she couldn't sell fresh fruit and vegetables,' Holly interjected.

'She didn't because she knew it was *our* livelihood,' retorted Minnie Fletcher, her face as purple as the plums on display.

'*Livelihood.* If I've got to hear that word again, I'll go totally out of control,' Angie shrieked.

The anger was getting to her now, and she wished that Calum had been here to help her handle the old man. A wave of self-pity swept over her: if only Curt hadn't been taken from her, she wouldn't be in this position at all. It just wasn't fair. The Fletcher family were doing OK. They already had a thriving coal and anthracite business down at the old railway yard. And in addition to that, next door to the scruffy shop where they sold their rotten fruit and veg they owned a small service station with petrol pumps, where on the forecourt they sold bags of coal,

143

chopped wood and confectionery.

You name it, they've got it, she thought, as the items ran through her mind like the prizes on the conveyor belt at the end of the *Generation Game* show.

'It's *not* your livelihood,' she argued. 'You've got coal ... paraffin...' She began counting off the items on her fingers.

'Bottled bloody gas ... everything except the kitchen sink,' put in Holly. 'You're nothing but a greedy pig! You want it all, that's your trouble.'

'You just mind and keep your little nose out of it, young madam,' yelled Minnie. 'Your mother's causing us enough damn trouble, without you joining in as well.'

'Where my mother's concerned, I *will* join in,' retorted Holly.

Puffing and panting, Adge Fletcher leaned hard back against Rex Carpenter's van, his pale bulging eyes glaring at Angie and Holly in turn. His off-white striped shirt was straining at the buttons across an immense stomach, jutting above a pair of shiny grey flannel trousers held up around the waist with a length of grubby string.

He had always been a repulsive sight, and his wife wasn't much better, Angie thought. Min's great bare legs and fleshy arms protruded from a floral patterned dress which had long ago seen better days. With all the money they must have, they looked like a pair of down-and-outs. Angie was tempted to tell them about the recently opened charity shop in the High Street; you could get decent clothes there for almost next to nothing.

'Yere he is then. Yere's the very bloke I wants to see,' growled Adge Fletcher suddenly as Rex Carpenter appeared over the brow of the hill. Luke, who had been walking with him, ran towards Angie, panting, and out of breath.

'I couldn't find Uncle Cal, Mum,' he explained, 'but I thought you'd want me to tell Rex what was going on.'

For a moment Rex didn't say a word. Shaking his head in disbelief, he looked around at them all, as if searching for an explanation.

Poking the air with an irate forefinger, Adge Fletcher yelled, 'You and your fancy bloody marrows – all thik bloody rubbish what nobody round yere knows how to cook – you'm driving a long-established Fuzzy Cove trader straight into liquidation – that's what you'm a'doing, young feller-me-lad.'

'Yeah. What you got to say for yerself, I'd like to know?' chimed in Minnie. She looked as though she might spit in Rex's eye any minute, Angie thought.

Rex shrugged. 'It's a free country. Everyone to their own business, I say. If you don't like the heat, then get out of the kitchen ... isn't that how the saying goes?' He paused, and looked straight at the older man. 'I don't wish to sound disrespectful, Mr Fletcher, but with all your other interests, you have what seems to me a very lucrative trade. I hardly think my supplying Angie MacPherson with a few pounds' worth of vegetables is going to bankrupt you overnight.'

'You hardly ever sold any of your rotten old stuff anyway,' Holly said. 'That's why it was

145

always stale, because not many people bought it from you in the first place.'

'You can belt it up; you young hussy. I shall have summat to say to your gran when I next sees her, that I blooming will,' Adge Fletcher roared.

'And *she's* no better than she ought to be,' added his wife. 'Living in sin in my dear dead sister's property. Josh Berry should hang his head in shame.'

'At least my gran makes him happy. That's different to what I heard about your sister,' Holly replied.

'Now, Holly, don't get into *that*,' warned Angie. 'It was long before your time.'

'What are all these marks on my van?' Rex asked suddenly, going over to examine the paintwork which was covered with a series of deep dents.

'Mr Fletcher did it with this stick,' said Jake, picking up a thick wooden stump from the gutter.

'I've a good mind to report you for malicious damage,' said Rex. 'You'd better assure me this will be the end to it. If I get to hear you've been back up here – I'm warning you – you'll leave me with no alternative.'

Outnumbered, the Fletchers recoiled, though the old man sniffed and snorted angrily to himself.

'There's no law that says Angie can't sell fresh vegetables,' Rex went on, 'so I suggest you both go home and have another think. You'd do best to concentrate on selling the things you're good at.'

Muttering insults and grumbling to each other,

the couple stalked off down the hill towards their own shop. Angie could hear the baby crying indoors and, leaving Holly to serve the few customers who'd been watching and waiting patiently, she excused herself and went back into the house to see to her.

When she re-emerged, after settling the baby down, she was pleased to see the twins had managed to set her display stands to rights, while Rex was on his knees picking up the pieces of courgette and crushed marrow that lay all over the pavement.

'You're not bothered about what Adge might do, are you, Angie?' he said, looking up at her from his crouching position on the floor.

Angie shook her head. 'I've got more pressing things to worry about than what those blessed Fletchers are up to, Rex. First and foremost, I need to find a reliable mother's help, so that I can concentrate on earning us all a living. Mum's moved out, I expect you know. She's living with Josh Berry in his bungalow at Upalong now.'

'I know,' said Rex, nodding. 'I see her almost every day. I have to pass by there on my way home.'

'Of course!' exclaimed Angie. 'Anyway, I'm a little worried about her health. She's been getting these nasty pains in her chest.'

'But she looks as fit as a fiddle – there can't be a lot wrong with her,' he replied. He shook his head. 'Oh, well, perhaps she'll be able to take things a bit easier now, with no more shop to take care of.'

'Or *baby* ... once we can find someone to take

over completely,' Angie said. She nodded thoughtfully. 'So if you hear of anyone who's looking for a live-in, or out, nursemaid's job, promise me you'll let me know, eh?'

'I'll certainly do that, Angie. I'll certainly do that,' Rex agreed.

As he turned to leave, he appeared to have had a further thought. 'I suppose it's out of the question you can get away for an evening?' he said.

'It is really,' Angie told him. 'Why, what did you have in mind?'

'Tonight ... there's a quiz night at the Smuggler's Retreat, so Roxanne Meredith tells me. I wouldn't mind having a go at it myself.'

'Tonight,' echoed Angie dubiously. 'It's rather short notice. Perhaps another time, eh Rex? My mother-in-law would never mind coming in, but I'd want to give her more notice than *that*.' She glanced at Holly who was weighing potatoes. 'And Holly's got a red-hot date, I know. She's been seeing this boy for a fortnight now. They seem really keen on each other.'

'Lucky old *them*,' said Rex wistfully, as he climbed into his delivery van, ready to drive away.

As Angie watched him go, her heart gave a little lilt. She hadn't noticed before how good-looking he was. Not strictly handsome, she thought, but definitely good-looking, with crinkly brown hair that was just beginning to recede from either side of his forehead, and an attractive mouth that seldom ever smiled, but when it did, would transform his whole face. She'd never noticed his

148

eyes before, either. They were a really warm and friendly brown, like the conkers the twins went searching for when autumn came.

'Mmm,' Angie sighed. He's rather nice, she thought. Yet she still wasn't sure what to do. Until this moment, the idea of getting to know another man had never seriously entered her mind. She would need to give it a lot more thought, and not rush into anything simply because the person concerned seemed to be just as lonely as she was.

Chapter Ten

Caitlin decided to sort through the storage boxes that she and Tyler had left in her father's garage before they departed for America. Her cat, happy to see her, was full of mischief and getting into everything. Outside, the rain poured relentlessly down. It drummed deafeningly against the concrete sides of the garage, while an irritating drip from an overhead gutter hammered repeatedly on to the corrugated roof.

Caitlin's mother had been nagging her husband for the last three days to do something about the broken gutter, ever since the weather changed for the worse. Roland wouldn't hear the last of it, Caitlin knew, until he'd hoisted up a ladder and, at almost seventy years of age, climbed to the roof to scoop out the accumulated debris from every last centimetre of guttering.

The weather was typical of the wet weekends

she remembered from when she'd lived at home previously, until she reached the magical age of eighteen and escaped to college at Exeter, where she'd taken a diploma course in holiday travel and – the thought suddenly struck her – sealed her fate by meeting Tyler Sinclair! Out of the frying-pan into the fire, she mused. The truth of that old adage had since come home to her in abundance.

Since she'd come back to Weston, she kept remembering her early childhood. Often, on rainy days like today, she and her brother Gwyn had loved to go swimming in the open-air pool which, in recent years, had been revamped and renamed the Tropicano. She recalled how they'd frolicked in the clear turquoise water with the other kids staying at Weston-super-Mare on holiday. Caitlin could still see the adult holidaymakers there, as they huddled beneath their sodden beach towels, trying vainly to protect themselves from the appalling weather.

The harder the rain had poured from above, the greater was the spirit of adventure, she remembered, though an adventure best kept hidden from their mother. Olive Hutchison would have thrown a fit if for one minute she'd suspected her precious offspring were in dire danger of giving themselves pneumonia – bronchitis or croup, at the very least!

She reminisced, too, about the long school holidays when she and her brother, well wrapped up in scarves and gabardine macs, had walked the length of Weston Bay, from Birnbeck pier at one end to the old Sanatorium at the other. She'd been dismayed to discover that the old hospital building was derelict now, with broken windows, and wire netting barriers over the entrance gates. Nothing and nobody stayed the same, she thought. An era had ended. And with her decision to leave Tyler, she realised, so had another.

Caitlin was jerked from her daydreaming by the sound of the telephone. 'Caitlin ... telephone...' she heard her mother calling from the kitchen doorway.

She sounded irritated; Caitlin could understand that. Neither she nor Caitlin's father had ever expected to have their daughter – twenty-eight years old, and separated – living at home again with them.

She went through the kitchen, where her mother was baking a cake for tea, and out to the hallway to answer the phone which was still ringing furiously. A frisson of fear gripped her stomach; she hoped with all her heart it wasn't Tyler calling from America. Why couldn't he accept the fact that she wasn't coming back? She'd made her decision to leave him several weeks ago, and it hadn't been a difficult one to make. There was no way she was going to weaken. It wasn't as though he was all alone. He'd been having an affair with a chorus girl, for heaven's sake; why else did he think she'd left him?

'Hello,' she said warily, before breathing a sigh of relief when she heard Julie Moon's slightly nasal tone.

'Hi, Caitlin. Sorry to bother you on a Saturday

afternoon, but can you explain again how the gas regulator works? Wayne wants to have a bath but every time we turn the hot water on, the radiators go off. It's miserable looking out at all this rain when you've got no heating on.'

Caitlin had gone over the heating instructions with Julie and her boyfriend the day they moved in, along with everything else she'd thought they would need to know. She'd suspected at the time they weren't taking it in. The boyfriend in particular had seemed especially thick, and Julie, she knew, was the worst scatterbrain ever. She took a deep breath, and went over the instructions again. When she'd finished and put down the phone, she returned to the kitchen where her mother was polishing her already spotless marble-effect Formica worktop. She would be making a start on the well-scrubbed table top next, Caitlin had no doubt.

'Who was that?' Olive enquired nervously. She too, was worried it might be Tyler, as Caitlin knew. Her mother hated the thought of any aggro.

'Only Julie, still trying to figure out the hot water system,' she said brightly. 'Mind if I make a cup of tea?'

Her mother glanced at the wall clock, paused for a moment as if debating the point, then nodded. 'Mmm, that might be a nice idea,' she agreed.

Caitlin picked up the kettle and carried it to the tap. Her mother was watching her – bursting a gasket, Caitlin was sure, in case she splashed water on the kettle's pristine exterior. It was also a departure by twenty minutes from her parents' usual timetable, she realised.

Olive rinsed out the blue J-cloth she'd been using, and put it away, folded neatly, into a cupboard below the sink.

'I'll just pop upstairs and ask your father if he'd like one too,' she said.

Since Roland's retirement, he and Olive did absolutely everything together. Caitlin wondered how they ever managed to go to the loo separately. She sat down at the table, and cupping her face in her hands, deep in thought, waited for the kettle to boil. With Tyler refusing to pay the mortgage on the house at Worle, letting the property out to Julie had seemed a sensible thing to do. But at *what* a price, Caitlin mused ... being forced to live back here again ... she could only hope and pray it wouldn't be for long.

The tea brewing, Caitlin covered the brown china teapot with a thick padded teacosy in the shape of a hen, and reached into the fridge for her mother's small bone china milk jug.

Milk straight out of the bottle was anathema to Olive, Caitlin knew. What a fusspot she is, she told herself, recalling how, as a teenager, she'd been desperate to get away from her parents' petty restrictions. Her dad always went along with her mother's stupid hangups, while he, too, had some fairly weird ideas of his own. Caitlin wondered how long she would be able to survive it *this* time, without going completely round the twist.

Her brother, Gwyn, two years younger than

herself, had also left home at the first available opportunity. He later married Elizabeth, a sensible, friendly girl whom he'd met when they were both at university in Birmingham. Now the proud parents of two small boys, one aged four and the other two and a half, they lived in a quiet village on the slopes of the Malvern hills where Gwyn taught maths at a local grammar school.

They would be driving down to Bristol to stay with Elizabeth's parents next weekend, when the annual Balloon Fiesta was due to be held at Ashton Court. Caitlin was looking forward to meeting them there for a picnic lunch. She'd missed seeing her brother the whole time she was living in America, and would have gone to Malvern to visit him and his family before now if she hadn't been lumbered with Pepsi the cat.

The cat, used to having a whole house to itself, had been banished to Caitlin's parents' garage and wasn't settling in at all well. Her father's dog, a Boxer called Franklyn, resented its presence, as Caitlin had suspected it would. She was banking on her stay being a temporary one – a sad little cat was a worry she could well do without: the poor anxious thing was hardly touching its food, and growing skinnier by the minute it seemed.

Caitlin heard her mother and father coming downstairs. Rising to her feet, she poured them each a cup of tea. They sat at the kitchen table to drink it, while Caitlin busied herself with a potted pink geranium on the windowsill, deadheading its wilted blooms and pulling off the dead leaves.

As she worked, she pondered her future plans.

She was looking forward to telling Gwyn and Elizabeth about the baby, and would ask them if she could use their home as a forwarding address until she'd sorted out where she would be living. She would be trying to find a job some distance away from home so that Tyler, when he came looking, wouldn't find her easily or entirely by surprise.

The cat was the nuisance now. The trouble was that Caitlin had become enormously fond of it. The little animal had become as attached to her as the limpets were to the rocks at Anchor Head where she and Gwyn used to play when they were children. Caitlin's mind went back to those long summer days when she and her brother had wandered the beach near the lifeboat slipway; searching for the hoard of pirates' gold they were certain was buried there, they spent many hours prising limpets from the rocks, believing they were oysters with precious pearls inside.

The rain continued to pummel the kitchen window with a sound like the ricochet of a thousand bullets as Caitlin's mother and father sat sipping Earl Grey tea from their Royal Doulton china teacups, chattering about the inconsequential happenings of their day. The small finger on Olive's right hand remained delicately poised, the way she'd always taught Caitlin to hold a cup.

Such awful snobbery, Caitlin thought and, letting their waffle soar clear over her head, she turned away and rested her hand on her gently emerging lump. Just like the imaginary oysters on the beach at Anchor Head, she, too, lovingly held a hidden priceless pearl. A secret smile lifted the corners of her mouth, but when she sat down at the table with her mother and father to drink her tea, she made sure her demeanour was suitably composed.

Instead of embarking on a Saturday afternoon shopping trip as they had last week, Holly, Jazz and Erin were whiling away the time at the Bluebird Café, run and owned by Dorothy Glue, mother of Dexy and Suzi.

The small café overlooking the harbour at Fuzzy Cove was a favourite meeting place for local fishermen. A framed notice hung on the main wall, with letters six inches high:

Work is for people
who don't know how to fish.

That just about says it all, Holly told herself, thinking of Calum, and recalling her mother Angie's shrewd observation about him when she'd read the notice one day.

Dottie Glue had gone home a while ago, in order to rest her feet. She'd left Dexy in sole charge, and that included washing up the enormous stack of plates and cups used during the lunch-hour trade.

'The Witches of Fuzzy Cove – doesn't sound half so interesting as the Witches of Eastwick, does it?' remarked Jazz.

'No – and neither does Dexy over there look anywhere near as attractive as Jack Nicholson,' answered Holly.

Erin smiled quietly, but said nothing. She, too, thought Jack Nicholson attractive but, not comfortable voicing her opinion, she decided to keep it to herself.

'That's what Guy said we reminded him of, anyway,' stated Holly, 'the three witches of Eastwick.'

'Good – he must think I look like Cher,' Jazz said, getting to her feet and studying herself intently in the large mirror that ran the length of the serving area, and which also reflected the back of Dexy's head, and his domestic efforts at the sink.

Dexy threw Jasmine a look of surprise. 'Cher? What the Gordon Bennett makes you say that?'

'My hair, of course. I'd *have* to be the dark-haired one, wouldn't I?'

'Perhaps you would ... yeah ... but you can't sing anywhere near as good as her.'

'You've never heard me sing,' said Jazz.

'Oh yes I have. Along at the Smuggler's of a Saturday night.'

'You thc great expert now, are you, Desmond, lad?' Jazz knew how much he hated to be called by his given name, though his mother never called him anything else.

'She might not sing *like* Cher, but she sings pretty good, all the same,' said Holly. 'And she certainly does look a lot like her, I think.'

'Mmm, I happen to think so, too,' remarked Erin shyly.

'You – little mouse ... Jack Nicholson 'ud have eaten you alive if you had bin in a film with him,' Dexy said, wringing out his washing-up cloth, and hanging it over the side of the sink to dry.

'Nice way to go, eh Erin?' laughed Holly.

'Eaten alive, and loving it,' put in Kevin Buttercup, who was drinking tea and eating a jam doughnut at the table he was sharing with a shabby little man.

'You're meeting Guy again tonight, I suppose,' Jazz said to Holly.

'Mmm, I'm taking him home, to meet my mum. I think it's about time. It's his birthday on Monday and I shall be meeting all of *his* family then – the thought gives me the ad-jabs. Admittedly, I've met one of his brothers – but not his mum and dad. He's got three gorgeous-looking sisters, too, so wish me the best of luck.'

'How d'you know they're gorgeous looking if you've never ever met them?' quizzed Jazz.

'I've seen their photos, of course.' Holly took a sip of Coke. 'So I thought I'd better introduce him to *my* mum first. Later, he's taking me out for a drive. I also want to introduce him to our countryside.'

'For a dirty stop-off in a layby, more like, so you can go at it like a pair of rabbits.'

Kevin looked up from the paperwork he'd been discussing with Snooky. 'You've got a mind like a flaming sewer rat, you,' he told Jazz.

'I'm not having you slagging Holly off in this establishment,' said Dexy. 'She and I are as good as related – or could have bin.'

'If only my uncle had got his skates on and married Suzi when he had the chance,' Holly agreed. 'What's the latest there, Dex, do you know?'

'I wish I did, love. I reckon your Rust needs his brainbox testing, letting that flaming yuppie get his legs under her table, the way he have.'

'*Rusty, Rusty,*' Holly sighed, 'that man's his own worst enemy, always.'

'He's a nincompoop of the first order,' commented Kevin, scribbling notes in the margin of an official-looking letter. 'Leonard Stockingham Snook!' he exclaimed suddenly. 'My crikey, that's a posh name you've got there, mate. Your wife, too – Esmeralda Rita – you ought to be sitting on the Council, or summat, with a smart moniker like that.'

'To get back to Rusty,' interrupted Dexy, 'he wants to get over there and sort it all out before it's too late...'

'He's acting like a complete wanker – pretends he doesn't care a toss,' replied Kevin.

'Who's a wanker?' demanded Calum, entering the café through the open door, his dog Gyp at his heels.

'You are,' Kevin told him. 'And you know exactly why.'

'So who rattled your cage, Buttercup?' Calum responded. 'Zap one of they meat pies in the microwave, Dexy, my stomach's just about stuck to my ribs.'

'He's missing Gran's cooking,' Holly said. 'I feel so sorry for him. Here Gyp – come and see me. Holly's here – there you go ... there's a good boy then.' She ruffled the soft curly fur around the dog's tan and white neck.

'Anything's better than all thik rabbit's food what you keeps giving us, day after day, my girl,'

Calum told her.

'I notice you don't refuse any of it when it's put on the table in front of you.'

'That's only 'cos there's no alternative,' he replied. 'What would I give for one of our mother's lovely hotpot stews? That Joshua Berry's a lucky bugger. I hope he realises just how lucky he is.'

'He does and, what's more, he doesn't mind cooking *her* some lovely meals, too! It goes both ways, pudding head – a little bit more give, instead of take, and you could have had just as good a thing going with Suzi as Gran and Josh have now.'

'Oh, my good God, we're back on that old track. You'm equally as bad as our mother ... there's no denying who you takes after, you meddling little cow.'

Calum got up from his seat and, whistling to his dog, flounced out of the door without waiting for his meat pie.

Holly watched through the window as he strolled away towards the slipway where his boat was moored. He raised his hand to beckon Figgis the hobbler. Holly knew it would be the last they'd see of him for the day, storm or no storm, visibility or no visibility.

She was aware that Calum was niggled with her still because he, too, had had his eye on the old storeroom, and Holly's mother had agreed to let her have it, provided she paid a token rent. Calum had argued that he could claim rent from the Social, but Kevin Buttercup had reminded him they wouldn't grant an allowance if the accommodation concerned belonged to a member of the claimant's family.

Holly was excited about moving in. The storeroom was as big as a decent size bedsit, and she'd soon have it looking like one, she knew. There was a lavatory with a small washbasin, and a separate unit containing a kitchen sink with cupboards beneath it, and two electrical points on the tiled wall above – one for the electric kettle she'd bought this morning, and the other for the microwave oven she was hoping to buy very soon. It would mean delaying the purchase of a car for another month, but well worth it if she could entertain Guy to a nice romantic evening meal every now and then. And, one day, who knows ... perhaps a double bed! Her happiness was complete. All she wanted to do from now on was to spend every moment with him.

Holly switched off her daydreams and allowed her mind to return to the here and now. The conversation had continued to flow without any contribution from her. She probably hadn't been dreaming for long, though it seemed to her that she had.

'You've got a date with Tom tonight,' Erin was saying to Jazz. 'I might as well have put in to do some overtime at the old folks' home.'

'No need for that,' answered Jazz brightly. 'What I didn't tell you is that Tom will be bringing Marcus ... and Marcus is playing rugby today with my darling brother, Dominic. We're all meeting up in the Smuggler's snug, and that includes *you*, too, my pet,' Jazz said.

A gentle blush stole over Erin's face; Holly thought her smile seemed to transform her whole personality. It suddenly struck her how pretty Erin was, with her sweet oval face, peaches and cream complexion, and eyes of speedwell blue. Holly couldn't help wondering who or what had brought this radiant reaction about. Was it Marcus, with whom Erin had danced at the nightclub? Jazz seemed to think it was.

'He really liked you, Erin, my precious,' Jazz was saying, 'and he wants to see you again. Why else would he be driving all the way out to Fuzzy Cove, when he's just come off a week of nights at Southmead Hospital?'

'They're playing rugby this afternoon, you say? *What*, in all this rain?'

'God, Erin, I don't know. It might not be raining where they are. Who knows? Who cares? Not me, I'm sure.' Jazz yawned languidly, and stretched her arms above her head.

'It don't look like Rusty's coming back,' said the weedy little man with Kevin. He shuffled over to the counter and held out his hand appealingly to Dexy. 'I know he wouldn't mind me having that pie – only he knows I'm skint: me missus've bled me dry,' he whined.

'You've only just scoffed a blooming gurt plateful of chips what he bought you,' Dexy observed.

'I know, but that 'un would see me through tomorrow as well, mate. I shan't have nothink else to eat over the weekend.'

'What d'you reckon, Holly?' asked Dexy, holding the pie aloft.

'Let him have it,' Holly said.

Dexy slipped the pie into a paper bag and handed it to Snooky. 'That's ninety-five pence you owes him then – you'll have to take it up with him.'

'He won't mind, Rusty's generous to a fault,' said Snooky.

'Yeah, so he might be usually. At the moment, though, he don't seem to be acting rationally.'

It was hardly the act of a rational person to take a boat out into the Channel today, Holly thought. It seemed very likely that Calum had, though, and if that was the case, then Dexy was spot-on in his opinion of him.

Chapter Eleven

Holly was bringing a boyfriend home for the first time. Angie had spread the table with her best lace tablecloth and laden it with an assortment of snacks. It was lucky the boys were out, or she'd have had her work cut out keeping them away from the breadsticks and the accompanying assorted dips, she thought. She hadn't been able to resist the garlic and onion one herself, and she'd also had a glass of the very nice German wine she'd been keeping for such a special occasion as this.

Angie knew that Holly had never been truly interested in any boy before, but this time she was ... and how! Everything she did and said

163

indicated she was head over heels in love, and Angie was intrigued to meet this fabulous wonder of wonders. Even after their first date, according to Holly, it seemed it might become a permanent fixture, or if not permanent then certainly long-term.

It was only a matter of time before they'd be jumping into bed together, Angie thought. She hoped they hadn't had sex already; three weeks did seem too soon to her. It was altogether different these days, though, she reminded herself, now that they had the contraceptive pill, and peer pressure, and any amount of encouragement from magazines, the media and trendy counsellors.

Angie poured a little more wine into her glass. She didn't want to be too sloshed when Holly proudly arrived with Guy, but a certain amount of Dutch courage was called for this evening. She had been hugging a secret to herself for the last hour or two, though she realised it would no longer be a secret when the twins returned from their bell-ringing practice and found her entertaining Rex Carpenter to coffee and leftover party-fare.

Earlier in the day, summoning up all the nerve she possessed, she had looked him up in the telephone book and called to ask if he would like to drop by for a bite to eat later that evening.

The bell on the shop door tinkled. She heard Holly's voice, and a masculine response. A touch apprehensive, Angie wiped her sticky palms on her skirt, and pinned on her best welcoming smile.

Well, he looks nice, was her first thought as Guy advanced towards her, his hand outstretched, a friendly grin revealing his perfectly even white teeth.

'Pleased to meet you, Mrs MacPherson,' he said, without waiting for Holly to make the formal introduction.

'Please call me Angie,' Angie told him, warming to him immediately. 'Lovely to meet you, Guy.' Turning to Holly, she said, 'You're right. He has got beautiful eyes.'

Angie and Guy began conversing and laughing together as if they'd known one another for ages. Holly wouldn't have expected Guy to be shy, but she couldn't say the same for Angie. Her mother appeared to be enjoying his company almost as much as Holly herself, though perhaps not in quite the same way, she thought.

Like Angie, Holly was pleased her brothers and uncle were out. Jake and Luke had appetites like gannets, and Calum, too, would have had no compunction about digging in as though he was starved. She wondered briefly where he was – whether he really had been daft enough to take *Green Pepperoni* out. She decided not to voice her fears to Angie; she was already paranoid on the subject. Before leaving to go to the betting shop, Calum had been boasting that he had a heavy date lined up with a woman named Marlene. Holly knew that could have been bravado, though, because Suzi was seeing someone else. Holly was well and truly fed up with Calum's prima donna ways. It was no wonder her gran was always telling him to flaming well grow up.

Well, not meeting Guy tonight is his loss, she decided. At least Guy was interested enough to want to meet her mum. Guy's twenty-first birthday was in two days' time, when Holly's turn would come to be thrown into the lions' den – for that was what she felt it was. The prospect scared her half to death. From what he'd said, there were a large number of relatives she would have to meet. She trembled at what they would think of her, not least because she didn't come from the same religious background as them.

'Happy birthday Monday,' she heard her mother say. 'Go on then, open it. Let me see what you think!'

Angie hadn't told Holly she had bought Guy a birthday present. He took a moment to unwrap the small, square parcel, and his face lit up when he discovered it was the latest CD by Nirvana – Holly knew it was one of his favourite groups.

'Fantastic...' he breathed. 'Thank you very much.'

'How did you know *that*, Mum?' Holly asked, secretly very pleased.

'Aha,' said Angie mysteriously. 'Wouldn't you like to know?'

It turned out that he'd told Jazz he wanted to buy it, and she'd mentioned it to Angie one morning when she came into the shop for cigarettes.

'Ciggies,' said Holly disapprovingly. 'I don't know where she'll get the money for ciggies, once she gets to university.'

'Well, she's still got a month to pack it in,' replied Angie. 'And if she can't, she'll jolly well have to find herself a job.'

'Her father always bails Jazz out, no matter how much money she owes,' Holly explained to Guy. 'He's even going to buy her a car to drive to Warwick in.'

'She's a lucky girl,' said Angie. 'Very lucky indeed.'

'I wouldn't say really lucky,' Holly told her, 'her mum's a right interfering old battleaxe.'

'Not like your mum, eh?' said Guy, laughing.

'Hey,' Angie said. 'I like this boy – he's welcome here any time.'

'No, not like my mum at all,' agreed Holly.

'Nor mine, thank God.' Guy crossed himself in the Catholic way. 'My mama's a very nice woman, and she's dying to meet my new girlfriend.'

'Let's hope she approves of me then,' Holly said.

Guy fixed her with one of his dark Italian stares that reduced her knees to a trembling mass of tagliatelle.

'You've no worry on that score,' he assured her, his voice as disturbingly sensual as his penetrating glance.

Sexy, very sexy, thought Holly, remembering their heavy petting sessions on the back seat of his car. She wondered how much longer they would be able to control themselves, and whether tonight was to be *the night*. She planned to visit the Brook Advisory Centre in Bristol next week; it was sensible that she got herself on the pill the very first moment she could.

Dr Chadwick at the village surgery was the

167

nicest of men, and a helpful doctor, too – Holly would have gone to see him like a shot, except for the fact she wasn't a hundred percent certain of the trustworthiness of one of his receptionists. Myrna Duffy was Roxanne Meredith's sister, though she was nowhere near as flamboyant as Roxanne. But there again, Holly reminded herself, *no one* was quite as flamboyant as *her*. None of the other staff at the surgery posed any sort of problem but, to be on the safe side, Holly intended to seek her contraceptive advice from a strictly independent source.

'Tuck in then,' said Angie, 'before the locusts get home.'

Guy and Holly made the most of the invitation, and had first choice of selecting the titbits they enjoyed best. They left enough for the others, not just as a matter of politeness, but because they were thinking of other things.

'Shall we go then?' Holly invited Guy, the moment they'd finished eating. 'I had hoped we could go for a drive along the coast road to Clevedon, but the weather's so dreadful, we wouldn't be able to see a *thing*.'

'I'm still game to go, if you are,' said Guy. 'It might be rather exciting.'

His dark gaze locked with hers again, so that not only her knees were shaking now but she could feel her intestines dissolving into jelly, deep down in the pit of her stomach. Her legs were so wobbly, she wasn't sure if she'd still be able to walk. It was exactly the same sensation as the first time she'd met Guy in the pub car park. Holly was glad that her mother had already made her farewells to them before going upstairs to check on the baby.

She wondered if Guy was feeling as strangely disturbed as herself, and when he took her into his arms and kissed her, she knew right away that he was. The way his hands were trembling was all the proof she needed – and so was the hardness of his body which she could feel pressing into her tummy, just below her waist. The physical closeness of his arousal conjured up a vision in Holly's mind of something mysterious ... exciting ... something wonderful waiting to be discovered. Discovered very soon, Holly hoped, or she would die of wanting.

They'd travelled a great distance in the three short weeks they'd been together. They'd seen each other almost every night – even if only for a few snatched minutes on her way home from work. Holly couldn't get enough of him. It was the same for both of them, and had been from the very first moment they met.

'Don't let anyone tell you there's no such thing as love at first sight,' she said, snuggling into Guy's shoulder, when they were setting off for Clevedon in his grey Volkswagen Golf.

He took his hand off the steering wheel and reached across to touch her tumbling red locks.

'I love your hair ... it's so ... *girl-like*. It really turns me on. *Everything* about you turns me on, Holly MacPherson, my love. Can you please tell me why that is?'

'I'm a witch. I can cast a spell on you,' laughed Holly happily.

'However will I control myself?' Guy said. 'I

must control myself, though – I know that very well. If anything happened to you ... you know, like...'

'I know,' said Holly, removing his hand and placing it back on the wheel. 'I'm working on doing something about it. I'm not one of your good little Italian girls. I'm a red-headed Brit, with a large dollop of wild Scottish ancestry, and I can't wait to have you make love to me properly ... like...' She hesitated.

'Like what?' he asked.

'*All the way,*' she said, after a pause.

'You mean that?' he whispered.

'Mmm ... I really do,' said Holly huskily.

She was having difficulty speaking. The desire she felt for him was churning up her insides and making her voice come out all croaky.

The storm had worsened considerably in the last hour. The Volkswagen's wipers were barely able to cope with the volume of water that cascaded down from the leaden sky. Guy parked the car on the hard verge at the side of the hilltop road which overlooked the fast-flowing waters of the Bristol Channel. The lights that usually twinkled so merrily on the Welsh hills opposite were obscured from view tonight. If there were any boats afloat down there, they were well and truly hidden from sight.

Holly wished she knew where Calum was at this moment. With any luck, he might have decided against going out at all today. He was all mixed up just now. Holly realised he was going through his own private hell, yet why he'd allowed things to deteriorate this far between

Suzi and himself was something she couldn't understand.

'What are you thinking, Holly?' Guy asked, noticing how quiet she had suddenly become.

'About my uncle,' Holly replied. 'He's very likely out there right now, in that murky old water. I only hope and pray he comes home safe and sound.'

Together, they peered down into the bleak, watery chasm. 'Gracious, goodness ... I hope so, too,' breathed Guy, his voice filled with awe.

Daisy cuddled tightly into Josh's back, pulling the duvet up high around her ears to shut out the sound of the rain beating against the window-pane. The steady downpour had continued all day, accelerated every few minutes by an extra, heavier burst, blown on to the glass by a strong east wind. Rat-a-tat-tat ... rat-a-tat-tat ... tat-tat.

How lovely it was to lie in bed, all snug and warm, with nothing special to worry about except the ongoing, ever-present matter of Curt's disappearance. But nowadays that thought was no longer so fearful – more a morbid curiosity. His memory was growing dim, even in Daisy's mind.

The thoughts that filled Daisy's head more often these days were her constant worries about Calum. She wished he hadn't split up with Suzi, who was as close as any daughter-in-law could be. And her two little girls were Daisy's own flesh and blood; you only had to look at them to be reminded of that. Lucie, especially, was a MacPherson through and through. They both

171

had the same flaming red hair, but Emma's eyes were identical to her mother's, a soft warm caramel brown. Brown eyes and red hair, Daisy thought, made an unusual and most attractive combination.

Daisy turned on to her left side, and felt Josh's bulk turn with her. It was the way they always settled down to sleep, and Daisy hadn't slept so well in years as she did these nights, in the arms of her lovely man.

She had spoken to Suzi on the telephone earlier in the evening, and was happy about what she heard. Suzi had said she was going to London for the day on Sunday, and wondered if Calum would like to take the girls to the annual Balloon Fiesta at Ashton Park. She and Josh were going there anyway, with Angie and the boys, and said they would be glad to take Emma and Lucie if Calum was unable to.

Daisy, though, was certain he would jump at the chance of having his girls for the day; Angie, too, felt sure he would, when Daisy mentioned it to her. Angie hadn't seen anything of him, however, since he'd left the house at lunchtime, taking his dog with him. Daisy had phoned Mariner's Cottage again later to find out if he'd returned. He still wasn't back, but neither it seemed was Holly. Bad weather or not, it was early yet for either of them, Angie reminded Daisy.

'Probably all cuddled up in her young man's car ... completely oblivious to time and the elements,' observed Daisy. 'This weather's getting really terrible, though. I thought just now the roof was going to blow off.'

'It is bad,' Angie agreed. 'I just hope she doesn't forget she's got a home to come to.' Angie's voice was resolutely cheerful, but Daisy knew that her daughter-in-law wouldn't be able to sleep until Holly did come in.

'What will you be like when she's living on her own in the flat?' Daisy asked.

'She's welcome to have him living with her, if it means she won't have to drive through these dark lanes alone at night any more,' Angie said.

Daisy was somewhat taken aback by Angie's reply. 'That's a bit soon. They've hardly known one another five minutes,' she exclaimed.

'I *know*,' Angie said, 'but she's convinced he's the only man for her, and they're absolutely, desperately in love.'

'It was very different in my day,' laughed Daisy, 'but who am I to be casting stones?'

'*You*,' replied Angie scornfully, 'are setting a *terrible* example to your grandchildren.'

'I know, isn't it fun?' agreed Daisy. 'You ought to try it, Angie my love. You'd have my fullest blessing, you know.'

Angie didn't answer, so Daisy explained, 'I'm not being merely flippant, Ange. On the other hand, I'm not suggesting that you should. All I want is for you to be as happy as I am right now, here with Josh at Cedar Keys.'

'I know what you're saying,' Angie replied. 'And I might just give it a bash sometime. Perhaps a little sooner than you think,' she added cryptically.

Surprised, Daisy said, 'Ooh, anyone I know?'

'Mmm ... just could be.' Angie's voice conveyed an intriguing air of mystery that fairly hummed along the telephone wires. After Daisy put the receiver down, she'd got to wondering – and was still wondering now.

Her heart gave a sudden little flutter, followed by a short – though fierce while it lasted – pounding. She explored the area beneath her left breast, and prayed for it not to happen again. Tiny, minute beads of perspiration had broken out all over her forehead, but when nothing else happened in the space of five minutes, she began to relax again. It was some time, though, before she dropped off to sleep. Her thoughts had kept running from Holly to Calum, wondering if they were home.

It was two o'clock in the morning. Calum, coming up the Channel on the incoming tide, breathed more than one sigh of relief. Earlier – at one am – above a crackle of interference, he'd heard the weather announcer warn, 'Force six winds ... threatening gale force seven, and rising.' He must have missed the earlier warnings. A full-blown gale ... the worst conditions Calum had coped with, singlehanded, in a lifetime of sailing the Bristol Channel.

At the height of the storm, he was sharply reminded of Curt's disappearance. God forbid that he, too, would end up in Davy Jones's locker, he'd thought. That would have been the cruellest thing to happen to Daisy. Her health was already giving cause for concern and another load of grief was the last thing he wanted to inflict on her.

He'd prayed then, more fervently than he ever remembered praying before, even as a nipper at the village Sunday School. He'd prayed to *Him Up Above* to have mercy upon his wickedness and deliver him safely back to port. Within a short while he had seen a miracle happen. The winds had lessened, and Calum thanked God for answering his prayers. It was a hell of a hair-raising time while it lasted. It had taken all the strength he could muster to keep the boat from capsizing, but now, at last, it was over, and his brain was starting to click back into normal gear.

In the course of the past few hours, the other hard thinking he'd done led him to the conclusion that he'd prevaricated for too long where Suzi was concerned – and now he'd probably lost her. He didn't need a lecture from the likes of Big-head Buttercup – happily married as he now was – telling him so, however. That great overweight lump of lard hadn't been exactly the world's best husband and dad the first time around. Calum wondered what gave *him* the right to think he could tell others what to do. He was like a man who'd given up smoking after a lifetime of addiction; in Calum's experience, they were always the ones with the biggest gobs on them.

He'd thought about the previous afternoon, when he'd left the Bluebird Café in a huff. Arriving at the slipway, he'd been disappointed to find that the tide wasn't high enough to lift his boat off the mud. Figgis had told him to go away and come back in an hour's time. Calum hadn't the slightest idea where to go. The thought of showing his face back at the café so soon didn't appeal to him at all, not after the way he'd walked out of there. He'd decided finally there was only one place *to* go: the place ever foremost in his mind. Settling his dog on the back seat of his car, he'd headed out for number three, Walnut Tree Crescent, in the suburb of Portmills, Bristol.

Visibility on the Avonmouth Bridge had been almost zero, the traffic crawling along bumper to bumper. The motorway was chock-a-block in both directions with holidaymakers on their way to, and returning from, the popular West Country resorts. A great many were towing caravans and boats – all the usual paraphernalia that heralded the peak of the long school holidays, Calum reminded himself. Rain, and more rain ... the weather was at its most gruesome. A typical bleak, wet Saturday in early August, with no sign of a break in the sullen sky.

When he reached the tree-lined crescent where Suzi lived he'd left his car a short distance away from her house and run for the shelter of a stand of tall beeches on the opposite side of the road. The houses had recently been repainted, each of them a different colour. Suzi's was crimson red, and parked outside the crimson front gate was a brand new black Ford Mondeo car.

For a full fifteen minutes, while the rain pelted nonstop against his face, Calum had watched and waited beneath the dripping branches of a tree. His waxed jacket had kept the top part of his body dry, but his legs, encased in sogging-wet jeans, were soaked through to the bone. Even now, almost ten hours later, his feet remained as cold as ice.

The net curtains which covered Suzi's lighted living-room window prevented him from seeing inside but, familiar as Calum was with its interior, he was able to visualise the cosy scene quite clearly. His two little girls, Emma and Lucie, were most probably playing on the living-room floor. They loved putting puzzles together and looking at picture books. He hadn't realised until now how much he missed hearing their lively chatter. The thought suddenly hit him then – if he lost all contact with his children and Suzi, he was in serious danger of cracking up.

While Calum was pondering these things, and getting wetter by the moment, the front door opened and a smartly dressed man came out. He was carrying Emma in his arms, holding a gaudily coloured golfing umbrella over their heads. Lucie, wearing a shiny new sunflower-yellow mackintosh, was right behind them.

Calum held his breath. A feeling of nausea filled his chest and the taste of bile rose in his throat, so strong he thought he might be sick. Seconds later, his dear sweet Suzi – her lovely dark hair piled high on her head, her warm brown eyes filled now, no doubt, with love for another man – came out of the house, too, and hurried down the path.

A sharp thrust of longing stirred within his loins. He wanted her. She was *his* woman ... there was no doubt at all about that. Stinging hot tears filled his eyes, blurring his vision, as he watched his family scramble into the stranger's Mondeo. A sob caught the back of his throat, while the drips from the overhead branches poured on to his head with the intensity of a cold bathroom shower. He stood as if in a trance, and saw the rear of the Mondeo disappear in the haze.

Calum didn't remember much about his journey back to Fuzzy Cove, except that he'd taken the long route along the river – into Bristol and out again – to avoid the motorway snarl-ups. When he reached the slipway, he'd hidden his car from sight, then, climbing aboard his boat, started up the engine, ready to leave. Within seconds he was chugging out into Lee Creek to where it joined the turbulent waters of the Bristol Channel.

His mind was on Suzi, tracing where it all went wrong. They'd been rubbing along fine until six months ago. Then she'd found herself a job, working three days a week as a nursery nurse. A useful job; it meant she could take the children to work with her. However, because the hours she worked were longer than the DSS's stipulated sixteen, if Calum had continued to live with her at number three, Walnut Tree Crescent, he would have lost out on his benefit entitlement. They'd both agreed it would be best if he were to move back to live in the family home at Maritime Way for the time being. And now another man had moved into her life. Calum's resentment and jealousy knew no bounds.

Anyway, he consoled himself, here he was, all in one piece – except for his heart which was broken in two – ploughing up the Channel in the early hours of the morning. Despite the grief and regrets, he was about to chug safely back into port all ready for a second crack at life …

alleluia be praised!

'And you, Gyp – you wasn't ready to die yet, was you, my old mate?' he said. The dog wagged its tail, as cheerful as if it was on dry land waiting for Calum to throw it a ball.

Calum chuckled, and ruffled its furry neck. 'We've just had a bloody close shave, old chap,' he said, ''tis a wonder we'm both alive to tell the tale.'

He *had* to think positively, he reminded himself He was in no position at the moment to do anything about getting Suzi back. Soon it might be different, though, and then it would be all stations go.

He had a few small jobs lined up for the months of August and September, and then, in early October – the *big one!* A serious proposition was put to him by Bryan Starkey when they'd met at the pub at Pilning. It involved a certain element of risk, but Calum was willing to take a chance on that. A successful outcome would guarantee him pots more money than he'd ever dreamed of before.

It shouldn't be too late to patch things up with Suzi, he thought – especially if he was able to warn her now, before she went too far, that something good was about to happen! Think what a life they'd have together, with thirty thousand lovely smackers tucked away in their bank account. In fact, it wouldn't worry him if she put the whole damn lot in her name. It would only go to show how completely and utterly he trusted her, and wanted nothing but her happiness. He'd find a job and settle down after that, he'd promise ... just like the rest of the boring old farts.

The orange semicircle of lights at Fuzzy Cove hove into view. His emotions were mixed with relief as he steered his craft through the narrow inlet and safely into port. Peering through the murky darkness, he located the small dinghy the twins had christened *Kermit* and, pulling up alongside it, leaned down to untie the painter attaching it to the buoy.

The night sky was as black as a barrel of pitch, but the storm was behind him, and Calum now felt engulfed by a strange atmosphere of calm. Water slapping gently against the stone wall was the only sound to be heard. He lifted the dog into his arms, lowered it into the green dinghy and, hopping down after it, made ready to row for shore.

Chapter Twelve

The dawn of the annual Balloon Fiesta at Ashton Court broke wondrously bright, with the sure promise of a fine day ahead. The first balloons ascended into the pale hazy sky just as the sun breasted the horizon, so that by seven thirty, when the occupants of Mariner's Cottage were rising from their beds, the medley of designs and colours of the hot-air balloons were streaming over the house at the rate of two or three a minute.

Calum sprang out of bed with a new zest for life. He would be picking his daughters up in two hours' time, to take them out for the day. His mother had left him a choice. If he felt unable to face Suzi on her own doorstep with the chance of running bang-smack into the new man in her life, then she and Josh would collect the children for him. But Calum knew it was something he had to do himself, even if he did run the risk of bumping into the bloody upstart.

'Fucking yuppie,' he cursed quietly, as he folded up the sofa-bed and packed his blankets into the cupboard below the stairs. He would need to drum up all the self-control he possessed to knock on Suzi's door. The thought of another man sleeping in the bed that he and she had shared made him almost choke with anger and grief. What he was suffering was as bad as any bereavement, he told himself. *His* Suzi giving her beautiful, sensational body to someone else was, in his mind, no less upsetting than if she'd died. He might be going a bit over the top, but the fact remained, his grief was a solid, tangible thing. Deep and real; and as for finding solace in another woman's arms ... well, he'd tried that, and it hadn't worked.

He'd stayed overnight at Marlene Trimble's home on a couple of occasions now, when she had given him not only her body, but all the other expressions of comfort she thought he needed. Calum had soon discovered, however, that she, too, was carrying the torch for someone else, and while their going to bed together had helped pass the time, and released a fair bit of built-up tension for them both, when they'd talked things through in the clear light of day they agreed that it didn't actually change a thing. They would both continue to miss the *real* loves of their lives and if in the meantime they had the chance to come together, they would keep on doing so. It was preferable to lying alone in their separate beds, pining for something they couldn't have, feeling more sorry for themselves and becoming a pair of bitter buggers, like lots of other people star-crossed in love.

By nine am the haze had cleared; the cloudless denim-coloured sky was a perfect backdrop for the kaleidoscope of balloons that drifted over the city of Bristol in a northeasterly direction. Calum went outside and, keying the ignition of his Cavalier, set off on the five-mile journey to Portmills.

At Walnut Tree Crescent, as with so many of the houses on his route from Fuzzy Cove, people were out in their gardens, some with binoculars, gazing up at the colourful spectacle. Suzi and the girls were waiting for him in the front garden of number three. Calum was relieved to find there was no sign of the black Mondeo or its owner. He wasn't at all scared of meeting the bugger, only worried he might not be able to restrain himself from punching him one in the face. He was only too aware, though, that any fracas might jeopardise his chances of seeing his daughters on a regular basis.

Suzi was first to spot him. She raised her hand and gave him a wave. It was the first time he'd seen her face to face since the God-Almighty bust-up they'd had back in June, when he'd heard through the grapevine that she was seeing someone else. Calum was determined to play it cool today, no matter what happened.

'All right?' he asked, keeping his greeting friendly, as though it was only two days ago he'd seen her, instead of practically two months.

'Fine,' Suzi answered calmly, though she was fidgeting nervously with her hair – those beautiful nut-brown curls which today, the same as when he'd seen her before, she was wearing piled up on her head.

When he and Suzi were living together she'd only worn it like that if she was breast-feeding one of the babies, he remembered, to stop them from getting their fingers entwined in it, and shoving it into their mouths. Apart from that, she had only pinned her hair up when she was taking a shower, or, perhaps, going for a swim. Calum had always liked to see her curly hair long and flowing, and Suzi knew that he did.

He had no more time for shilly-shallying now though, remembering all those little things, because here were the girls ... loves of his life, apples of his eye ... tumbling into his arms and wanting a cuddle, exactly the same as always.

'Daddy, Daddy,' Lucie called excitedly, 'Come out to the back garden, we want to show you the Rupert Bear.'

'Wupert Beah,' lisped Emma, almost three years old, and plump as a roly-poly suet pudding. 'See, Daddy ... come and see Wupert Beah.'

Calum picked her up and followed Lucie through the house and out to the back garden.

On the square patch of lawn, the lawn he had planted from seed, was a spanking new swing and climbing frame, both of which he'd never seen before. Lucie, two years older than Emma, was jumping up and down, pointing her finger skywards, to a spot somewhere amid the mass of giant air balloons.

'See, look – there it is, Daddy. And look over there – there's one like a can of Coke!'

'See, see,' urged Emma, wriggling gleefully in Calum's arms, and pointing at the sky.

'A can of lager,' corrected Calum, 'Yes, my love, I can see.' He laughed, and disentangled her little starfish hands from his hair. 'You'm pulling out all Daddy's hair, Em,' he said. 'I haven't got much as 'tis, without you yanking out what bit I *have* got.'

Her elfin eyes looked into his, light chocolate-brown, just like her mother's. Calum squeezed her knee and she began to giggle; her teeth were perfectly shaped and even; they looked like a set of miniature pearls, he thought.

'You comin' with Daddy to the fair, are you?' he said. His daughter nodded vigorously as he set her down on the neatly mown grass.

'Whose is this?' he asked Lucie, gripping a corner of the red and blue climbing frame.

'Mine and Emma's,' she told him happily. 'Want to see me climb?'

Scrambling to the top in no time at all, she called, 'I'm a tomboy. I like being one, but Emma's a baby still. John bought it for her – it's a present for her birthday, but she can't even climb to the bottom level.'

'Her legs are a good deal shorter than yours,' said Suzi, who was standing at the back door, looking on.

'I know. I'm really lucky, aren't I? I can play on it now, but Emma will have to wait for a long, long time.'

'I wouldn't think she'll be *too* long,' Suzi told her. 'By next summer, she'll be well away. Come on, my poppet,' she called to Emma. 'Let's get you ready to go out with your dad.'

When Suzi and Emma had gone indoors, Calum asked Lucie, 'Who's this John then? He bought you this contraption, did he?'

'Yes,' shouted Lucie from the top of the frame, where she was balancing, almost upside down. 'It's for Emma's birthday ... I *said*.'

'Her birthday ain't till September,' Calum said, speaking quietly to himself, so that Lucie couldn't hear. 'Come on down then and go and get ready,' he told her. 'We're going to see Auntie Angie first – she's doing all the picnic stuff.'

As he was leaving Calum asked Suzi about the climbing frame. He couldn't disguise the jealousy he felt, that some other man was buying his children toys ... the sort of toys that he or Suzi could ill afford to get.

As the children scampered away, towards his car, he heard his own voice still pursuing the subject, even though he hated what he was doing.

'Who is this bloke, Suz? I suppose you're going out with him today,' he enquired, feeling powerless to stop himself.

She didn't answer immediately, but he knew by her flustered expression that she was.

'We might be,' she said at last.

'*Might be* ... either you are, or you're not. It's more likely to be *not* – now that you've got the bloody place to yourselves.' He glared at her angrily. 'Is that what I am, eh? A bloody childminder, so's you two can get up to whatever it is you wants?'

He regretted his words as soon as they had left his lips. The prospect of looking after his two little girls for the day had filled his heart with joy, so why did he have to spoil it by letting his jealousy get the better of him?

Suzi looked anguished. Her sensitive, heart-shaped face crumpled visibly, while her smiling mouth turned down at the corners, and her eyes were clouded with an expression of sadness. Calum wished for the thousandth time that he didn't feel the need to hurt her so, grinding her spirit so low that she inevitably withdrew from him and opening up a chasm which need not have been opened.

It had always been the same, he reflected. Not *all* the time, but certainly more often than Suzi had ever deserved. If he was to be completely honest she had done nothing to warrant some of the hurtful things he'd said over the years. It was something cruel inside that made him lash out and hurt the lovely girl, and although this time there was some cause for his behaviour, it certainly didn't excuse all those times in the past when he'd hit out similarly to hurt her.

'OK. I shouldn't have said that. I don't bloody own you,' he conceded. 'What time d'you want me to bring them back? Not too early, I hope?'

186

'No,' she said quietly. She closed the gate, and turned to wave goodbye to the girls.

'Come on, you little hags. Let's get this show on the road,' Calum said, shepherding his daughters into the back of his car.

'Where's Gyp?' asked Lucie, as she scrabbled in on her hands and knees.

'He's at home, my love. Jake and Luke have taken him out for a bit of a walk,' Calum explained.

'Are we taking Gyp with us, Daddy?' Lucie asked.

'Not on your life, darling,' he told her. 'He'd be a nuisance where we'm going – jumping up in the air, trying to catch the balloons.'

'Will we be seeing Granny Daisy?' was Lucie's next question.

'We certainly will,' Calum told her. 'She's moved into a new house with Uncle Josh, and she's dying to show it to you.'

'But Auntie Angie's first, isn't it?' she said. 'I've really missed seeing Jake and Luke ... and will Holly be there?'

'See Gyp, see Gyp,' Emma butted in, taking her thumb from her mouth and waving it at Calum's head.

He glanced at them both in the rear mirror, 'What questions,' he laughed, elated that in the two months they'd been apart, his relationship with the two of them was as close and loving as ever. 'We're *all* going out for the day, and it looks like being a really good one,' he said. 'Come on now – let's have a sing-song, like we always used to do in the car.'

187

He began to sing, 'Zip-A-Dee-Doo-Dah,' and the girls joined in. 'Plenty of air-balloons heading my way,' he sang in tune with Lucie, and *'henning my way...'* yelled Emma at the top of her voice.

Before he knew it, he was parking his car alongside the pavement at the front of Mariner's Cottage again.

Angie shifted a pile of cheese-and-brown-pickle sandwiches to one side, and began on the ham-and-sliced-turkey rolls. Holly was now a strict vegetarian, and the twins were fast following her example.

'Ugh, Mum, murder and cruelty to little pigs,' said Jake, eyeing the ham warily, as if it were about to leap up and shriek in agony before them.

'And what's this – *turkey*, too? Oh Mum, how could you?' put in his brother.

'Gobble, gobble, gobble,' teased Calum who had come up behind them silently, still carrying Emma, and causing Luke to jump with surprise.

'*Uncle* – you nearly gave me a heart attack,' he said accusingly. 'Hi, Emma.' Luke welcomed his cousin with a friendly hug.

'Take them off to play,' Angie instructed her sons, after she had greeted the little girls. 'I've nearly finished in here and as soon as I've fed the baby, we'll be on our way.'

'Is Evie coming with us?' asked Lucie, holding on to Jake's hand.

'She most certainly is,' Angie assured her. 'Just as soon as I've got her ready.'

'She was only just born when I saw her with

Mummy,' Lucie said.

'And me,' added Emma, nodding seriously. 'We saw her in the hospi*kal*.'

'So you did,' said Angie. 'I'd almost forgotten that. Oh, well, you'll see a difference in her now; she'll soon be three months old.'

They wanted to inspect the baby immediately, but went off with the twins quite happily when Angie explained that she was sleeping.

'How did it go?' she asked Calum, as soon as they were alone.

'Aah, all right, I suppose.' He scratched his head dejectedly. 'As all right as it'll ever be again.'

'But the children *wanted* to come?' questioned Angie. 'They wanted to come out with you for the day, did they?'

'Aah – *they* did ... yeah ... but it don't seem right that Suzi's not with us – nor ever likely to be again.'

'Don't say that,' Angie told him. 'You don't know what might happen in the future.'

'I do. That bastard's got his foot well and truly in her door, buying stuff for the kids, and I don't know what else.'

'You still hold the trump card, though, Cal. You're the father of the girls, and if you played your hand wisely, I'm sure you could still be in with a chance.'

When he didn't reply, Angie straightened up and, fixing him a keen look, asked, 'Are you ready, though, to change your way of life to suit her?' She smoothed back a lock of dark curly hair from her forehead. 'Because that's the *only* way you'll ever get her back – if you're willing to do

189

what she sees as sensible, and you–'

Calum finished the sentence for her. 'And I,' he said, '*I* scupper all the plans I ever made.'

'All those pie-in-the-sky plans – yes, Calum. Sacrifice them all for the love of a good woman; that's if you know what's best for you. And if not ... well ... I guess you'll just have to go on being miserable. You can't have it both ways; it's up to you to decide.'

Calum shook his head sadly. He was feeling quite despondent about the situation again now. 'It's probably all too late, no matter what I try to do about it,' he said.

'Yes – and perhaps it isn't,' replied Angie. 'You've never really tried, have you?'

'I've got summat really important lined up for a couple of months' time, and then p'haps I'll be able to see my way clear,' he muttered.

'It's up to you, Cal.' Angie shrugged her shoulders as she snapped the lid shut on her large Tupperware container. 'You'd best get in quick, before she becomes just a little *too* reliant on this other man. It might be too late already, but unless you try, you'll never know for sure, will you?'

Leaving Calum to stew over her words Angie made her way upstairs, where she could hear her baby beginning to stir. Who am I to be giving advice on personal relationships, she wondered, as she mounted the stairs. On the one single occasion she'd invited a man home for coffee, they had both sat tongue-tied, stealing bashful looks at one another like a couple of inexperienced teenagers. Well, perhaps not *teenagers*

190

exactly, she corrected herself, because all the ones she'd met through her daughter Holly seemed streets ahead of her and Rex Carpenter. With the possible exception of Erin Meredith, she thought, who still seemed fairly unspoiled and sweet.

She considered the question of Rex and herself. They'd always got on like a house on fire if they were discussing mundane things like the buying and selling of his products. The fact that they'd been uncomfortable in different surroundings had come as a bit of a surprise to her. Angie hadn't given up, though, by any means. She wasn't looking for romance as such, and if she could be sure that Rex wasn't either, it was possible they might at some future stage have a really good friendship going for them.

His quiet personality reminded her of Tom Hanks in the movie *Sleepless in Seattle,* and while she was no bubbly Meg Ryan to sweep him off his feet with her sparkling wit, Angie couldn't help wishing she possessed a little of what Meg Ryan had. If only she could compel a man like Tom Hanks to fly all the way across the country from Seattle and climb to the top of the Empire State Building to profess his love for her.

In another film, the same actress had faked an orgasm in full sight and hearing of other diners in a restaurant to capture an actor whose name Angie had forgotten. Capture him she had, too ... eventually ... just before the film ended!

'*Billy Crystal,*' Angie muttered aloud, suddenly remembering the actor's name. He too was a nice, ordinary bloke, with a really friendly face;

the sort to make a woman feel comfortable.

Laying Evie on her changing mat, Angie pulled apart the sticky tabs that anchored the little one's nappy. 'Caw, Evie MacPherson ... what a pong,' she groaned, while the baby kicked her chubby legs and beamed her a happy, lopsided smile. 'Your daddy must have fancied me once upon a time, I suppose,' Angie went on, 'but I was awfully young and pretty then. Who's going to want a tired old housewife like me?'

It was a contradiction of logic, she realised. She certainly wasn't desperate to have a new man in her life; she just wished there was someone out there who could make her feel she wasn't completely over the hill.

With all these people falling in love – her mother-in-law, her daughter – and Calum wanting Suzi still, it made her long to feel some emotion, just to know she was still a desirable woman. It was worth pursuing the relationship with Rex a little further. He was such a nice, attractive-looking man. And one thing positive had come out of the experience – her memories of Curt were becoming less and less clear. She was beginning to feel she was living again, instead of partly submerged, communing with Curtis in the deep dark waters of the Bristol Channel.

Today, for instance, promised to be very pleasurable. Calum was driving her and the children to Ashton Park, where they were meeting Josh and Daisy. Holly and Guy were busy elsewhere this morning, moving into the bedsit some furniture his mother had given him, but Holly had said they would join the rest of them later on.

'Upsadaisy.' Angie lifted Evie into her arms and carried her downstairs to the hallway, where she deposited her into the folding buggy. She called out to Lucie and Emma to keep the baby entertained while she popped into the bathroom to put her make-up on.

Holding tightly to Sam's hand, Caitlin stood at the rear of a twenty-yard queue at the Mr Whippy ice cream van. As she shuffled forwards, she kept a wary eye on her other nephew, four-year-old Ryan, playing with two little girls whose father was immediately behind her in the line-up. She'd literally bumped into the red-haired, cheeky-looking fellow when they first arrived; they had both been so busy watching to see the children came to no harm.

When they reached the counter, Caitlin lifted Sam up to let him choose from the assortment of ice lollies illustrated on the price list. She was relieved to put him down the moment he'd made his choice, buying another the same for Ryan.

'My goodness, I wouldn't like to have to carry *you* far, Sam Hutchison,' she said, straightening up and rubbing her back which had started to ache quite badly. She had developed a slight backache in the last few days, but put it down to stress.

When Sam and Ryan had taken the wrappers off their lollies and dropped them into the bin, all three of them waved goodbye to the girls and set off to walk uphill to where they'd left Gwyn and

Elizabeth, with Elizabeth's parents, lingering over their lunch.

Suddenly Ryan, who was tagging a little way behind, let out a terrified cry. 'A wasp,' he called, waving his arms wildly about, and running round in circles.

Still keeping hold of Sam, Caitlin rushed to his aid, only to find that the ginger-haired man had beaten her to it.

'Got him,' he said, swatting the wasp from Ryan's bare arm with a rolled-up *Racing Post*.

'All deaded, Daddy!' his smallest daughter said, pointing to the insect, now squirming on the short turf.

Her father squashed it flat with the toe of his black Nike trainers. 'There – now we've put 'im out of his misery,' he said, and turning to Caitlin, added, 'Thik old blighter won't be stinging your little lad now. Not any more, he won't.'

She smiled. 'Thank you. He's my nephew actually, and this one here is his brother.' She paused and added, 'And these are both yours I take it. Absolutely no doubt about that, eh?'

'Yeah, both bin left out in the rain too long, like me,' he said, patting the older girl's red hair.

'I'm not rusty; you are, Daddy. That's your name, Rusty MacPherson ... everybody calls you that, 'cept Mummy and Granny, and Auntie Angie.'

'And *you*,' said Caitlin, laughing.

'Mmm ... I call him Daddy,' the little girl assured her.

'Me call 'im Daddy, too,' agreed her sister.

'Well, I'm called Caitlin,' said Caitlin, 'and

these two young men are Ryan and Sam.'

Calum nodded. 'This here is Lucie – and the little 'un's Emma.'

Now that they'd been properly introduced, the children regarded each other seriously, almost shyly, over their half-licked ice lollies. Suddenly, Sam announced with an engaging smile that wreathed his chubby face, 'My Auntie Caitlin's got a baby in her tummy. Soon, when it's big enough, it can come out and play with me. We'll have a cousin then. A little baby cousin.'

'We've got a baby cousin, too,' the older girl told him proudly – and a trifle smugly too, Caitlin thought.

'God, that's embarrassing,' she said, looking at the freckle-faced man, who was grinning from ear to ear. 'He's quite right though,' she continued, 'he must have heard me telling his mummy and dad this morning.'

'It's not a bit embarrassing – not if you wants it, like. I'm Calum,' he added, his cheeky grin putting Caitlin completely at ease. 'What was it you said your name was?'

'Caitlin,' she said, smiling back at him. He looked really friendly, she thought, and the relief of being able to talk about her pregnancy was causing her heart to sing.

'I really am pregnant,' she said exultantly. 'And yes, I want this baby more than anything else in the world.'

They had wandered uphill and almost arrived back where her brother and family were sitting. Caitlin saw that they had cleared away the picnic things.

Calum noted her wedding ring. 'What does your husband think about it?' he found himself asking, surprising himself in the process.

It wasn't something that would normally enter his head, yet this attractive girl, with her glossy, golden shoulder-length hair, and sparkling amber eyes – like the get-ready-to-go sign on a set of traffic lights – had, he thought, been looking a trifle sad when he'd first seen her in the queue. He felt she had a great weight on her mind, and recognised a fellow soul.

'That's another story,' Caitlin told him, the light that was shining in her eyes a moment ago now dimmed and sombre.

'That's a pity,' Calum said. 'He don't know what he's missing – the daft chump.'

It wasn't at all like him to stick his neck out like this, he knew, yet something told him that his intuition was right. Why couldn't it be as easy as this with Suzi, he wondered, when he was trying to fathom *her* out.

'No, he doesn't, does he?' Caitlin answered sadly. 'No one gets *everything* they want, I suppose.'

'That they bloody don't,' agreed Calum, shaking his head in commiseration. 'Oh, well, we best be off. Say goodbye to the little lads, eh, Lucie Lockett?'

The children made their farewells, and Calum and Caitlin departed with them in different directions. Calum's family had taken up a spot on the grass near the top of the hill because, all of a sudden, his mother said she had to sit down. She couldn't walk to the bottom of the park where everything was going on, because she was certain, if she did, she wouldn't be able to climb back up again. It wasn't like Daisy to make a fuss over nothing, Calum thought, yet he couldn't help feeling she was giving in to her ailment by sitting still, when a good brisk walk would probably have done her a power more good. He'd suggested that to her when she first mentioned it.

'Blow all the cobwebs away, it would,' he'd said, but his mother had been insistent. She wanted to stay within easy walking distance of Josh's car, even if it meant that she and Josh had to eat their picnic separately from the rest of the family. They didn't, of course. The others had all day in which to visit the rest of the park, to enjoy themselves at the fairground, wander around the lift-off area, and look at all the grounded balloons.

Calum had spent the last few hours enjoying his daughters' company like a hungry man who hadn't had a decent bite of food for more than two months. Angie and he planned to entertain all four children in the afternoon, when they had finished their picnic lunch, as Josh and Daisy had volunteered to look after baby Evie for a while.

It was almost three o'clock now, and Holly and her boyfriend hadn't yet put in an appearance. Calum was still a little peeved that she was taking over the tenancy of the old storeroom. It made sense from Angie's point of view, he reasoned, so didn't really hold it against her. Holly was on a decent salary and he was, as usual, skint. Though this, of course, would be rectified very shortly. *'In spades too,'* he murmured quietly to himself.

Chapter Thirteen

Humping the double bed up the narrow, twisting flight of stairs was harder than Holly had thought. A *double* bed, though – she rubbed her hands together with glee and pride. Whoever would have thought she'd have been provided with a double bed? And by Josh Berry, surprise, surprise!

When her grandmother had volunteered the fact that he had a bed stored in the garage at Cedar Keys, Holly assumed it was a single one. She wondered now why she had assumed any such thing. It was far more likely to have been the double bed from his marriage to Minnie Fletcher's sister, many moons before Holly's wicked grandmother had cast her flirty eye on him.

She didn't blame Daisy a bit for disposing of the ancient trappings of his umpteen-year-old marriage. Men never appreciated the significance of such subtleties; even the most intelligent of men could be quite stupid in matters concerning the heart. Holly was glad now she wasn't a man. She remembered clearly when she was young, and wished she was a boy so she could join the Navy as a sailor and not a WREN, her grandmother telling her it was better to be a woman. Holly had found it a little hard to accept, because at that time only a man could be a *real* sailor.

'Men miss out on an awful lot,' Daisy had said. 'I can't begin to tell you how much it is they never see. I only had boys myself, and I love them both dearly, but I'm so very glad your daddy brought me your mum. And, as for Calum, sometimes I think there's some ingredient missing. Nothing terrible, you understand, just a tiny, vital component necessary for a man to want to have a lasting relationship with someone special, so that the two of them – male and female – eventually become like one person ... knowing, and trusting each other ... certain they'll never let one another down ... *but...*'

Here she paused, and Holly remembered her exact words. 'It's the woman who is the dominant force, the one who feeds thoughts of romance into man's unimaginative soul. She's the one who makes it all come together, the keystone holding up the arch. In my experience, it's certainly the case with the great majority. Never forget that, Holly my love – because one day your time will come, and however caring the man is, you'll have to educate him in the ways of the heart.'

'Well, now it has, Gran, and now he's here,' Holly whispered quietly to herself, going out on to the landing to meet Guy who was struggling to get the mattress round the corner at the top of the stairs.

'Hey – we have a double bed,' she shouted exuberantly.

'Don't I know it?' he answered, puffing and panting from his exertions. He stopped tugging for a moment, and leaned against the wall to catch his breath.

'Oh, sorry ... let me give you a hand.' Holly rushed to help him. 'As soon as I can arrange it,' she said, 'you really must meet my grandmother.'

'I thought I was going to meet her this afternoon,' answered Guy, after they'd manoeuvred the mattress into the room and dumped it on the bed.

'Sweetheart, this is wonderful,' he breathed as, pulling Holly down with him on to the bare mattress, they cuddled tightly.

'I'll make it, shall I?' she said, pushing herself up on to her elbow and eyeing the new rose-pink sheets and double duvet she'd bought at the Index showroom in Bristol. She paused a moment, her thoughts wandering. 'They had a nice cover I liked in Lewis's,' she said. 'We won't be able to afford it this month, but I will be able to get it next...'

'Never mind that,' Guy told her. Pulling her back into his arms, he planted kisses all over her face. 'I really *love* you,' he said.

Holly kissed the sweet nape of his neck, her tongue exploring his perfectly shaped ear.

'Ooh, that tickles,' he said, shuddering with excitement.

'I'm so glad you haven't got sticky-out ears, but if you did, I promise I'd love you all the same.'

'Oh, you would, would you? I'd rate a bit lower with sticky-out ears, though, would I, you awful little perfectionist?'

'I'd bite them back into shape. I'd chew them and nibble them with love ... like this.' She proceeded to demonstrate the technique.

Their kisses became more prolonged. His

hands strayed underneath her short brown jumper, and cupped her breasts through the silky bra.

'Mmm ... let's have this off,' he murmured, in between planting kisses all around her bare midriff.

Holly helped him to pull off her jumper, and then undo the clasp of her bra.

As Guy was slipping out of his jeans, he suddenly remembered the door. 'Hey, did we lock the door behind us?' he asked.

'Nobody'll be coming up here – they've all gone to the fair,' said Holly, her voice low and throaty with desire.

'Nevertheless...' Guy padded over to the door and pushed the bolt across.

When he came back to her again, Holly saw that his desire matched her own – exactly; a man's body could express its needs a darn sight more visibly, she thought. He climbed back on to the pillowless bed and, lying beside her, swiftly divested her of her jeans, too. He kissed her passionately, his fingers caressing the soft skin at the top of her thighs, then, very slowly, creeping upwards, until they reached the delicate edging of her white lace bikini pants.

Holly's whole being shuddered to the thrill – a greater thrill than she'd ever thought possible. It wasn't the first time Guy had touched her there, and she couldn't wait to experience the same delicious sensation again. In the relatively short time that she'd known him, the whole meaning of life had become transparently clear to her.

Giuliano Paolo, she thought, whose parents

had come from Italy all those years ago, was her prime reason for living ... her reason for being *born*. Her own ancestors had hailed from Scotland. All that way – both sides – so that she and Guy would one day be united in love.

His fingers slipped inside her silk briefs, caressing and exploring the secret, hidden part of her to which, until now, Holly hadn't actually given much thought. Her body reciprocated with a powerful longing to have him continue, not to stop until she could erupt like a fiery volcano, showering sparks and burning lava all over Minnie Fletcher's sister's old bed, as she and this lovely man with the completely unpronounceable surname went into utter and total meltdown.

'Uhh,' she groaned, extracting her mouth from his for a moment. 'Let me...'

She yanked at his flannel-grey stretch briefs and pulled them down towards his ankles. He kicked them off, and she grasped the probing, throbbing part of him that was heightening her own excitement to a point beyond recall.

'I can't ... I won't be able to ... stop,' Guy gasped.

'It's OK,' she said, lifting her head and looking into his deep charcoal eyes. Blacker than soot ... blacker than a rook's wing, they were. Filled with sexual desire ... filled with love for her.

Guy's eyebrows raised into a questioning arch as he returned the stare, floundering in the dark ultramarine depths of Holly's radiant, shining gaze.

'It's all right,' she assured him, 'I'm on the pill now,' omitting to mention she was supposed to allow ten days for it to take effect. At that moment Holly had gone past caring about *anything*, except to have him fill her yearning body with his, to quench her burning desire.

Almost simultaneously, Guy was reaching into his jeans pocket, trying to pull out a condom.

'I came prepared,' he said. 'I couldn't trust myself to hold on any longer ... bed or no bed ... this place, or anywhere.'

Embracing each other tightly, they rolled over until Guy was on top of her. This was where Holly wanted him – her very first time with a man.

Gently, he slipped inside her, his easy movement lighting the smouldering volcano deep in her body and sending shockwaves out to her every extremity. No sooner had she gathered her wits than she felt Guy's climax too. For a split second, his face became blank; she saw that he was lost in a world of his own. And then he blinked open his eyes and looked at her. Those fabulous liquorice eyes, Holly thought.

They paused, silent and panting, gradually regaining a near-normal heartbeat. 'Back in the land of the living, are you?' she joked. '*Me too*. I've never felt anything like that in my life before.'

Guy shook his head and shuddered. 'Whoo ... oo, I couldn't think where I was for a moment,' he said. 'How are you, my love? Are you all right?'

'I'm fine,' she said, smiling happily, still joined to him from below the hip.

'It wasn't painful?' he asked disbelievingly.

'It certainly wasn't *that*,' Holly assured him. 'I've been using tampons for ages,' she added, as an explanation. She cast him a searching look. 'There's never been anyone else. You don't doubt that, do you, Guy?' she murmured.

'Of course not. Why ever would I doubt your word? I just didn't want to hurt you – that's all. I've always been led to believe...'

'It's probably the rumour that Italian families put around to discourage their girls from trying it,' laughed Holly.

'You and I are going to be married. It's a fact. I've known it from the first moment I saw you,' Guy said firmly.

'Aah, that's sweet. I'm sure we will be, too.' Smiling, Holly said, 'Too young ... too soon ... I can hear them saying it now. But do you know something? I really don't give a damn.'

'Nor me, neither,' Guy told her. 'All I know is, I want you with me for the rest of my life.'

'Black-eyed Italian bambinos, we'll have one day.'

'Black-eyed redheads, and blue-eyed blackheads,' he added as he withdrew his body carefully from hers.

'Not *blackheads* – ugh. Black-haired, perhaps, but certainly not blackheads in the beautiful family that you and I are going to have one day.'

'I've just remembered, we're supposed to be going to the Balloon Fiesta, aren't we?' said Guy.

'Later perhaps,' Holly said, consulting her watch. 'It's almost lunchtime. Let's go next door and have a shower. After that, I'll rustle up something to eat. I don't think anyone will *really* miss us.'

'Whatever you say, my love. I'm just as happy

staying here with you, so let's get dressed, and we can make love again this afternoon.'

'Let's have a cuddle before we go,' Holly told him, and they sat down again on the side of the bed, caressing each other, as they reflected on the wonders of love that lay before them.

Holly cast her eyes around the room, used originally by her grandparents to store dry goods for the grocery shop, which had now become an Aladdin's cave of enchantment. The assortment of polythene bags and cardboard boxes she and Guy had hauled upstairs, filled to the brim with their worldly possessions, seemed to have taken on another, more glamorous proportion. Even the most mundane of objects seemed magical: her CD/cassette player, his electric shaver, his small colour television, and Holly's hair dryer! All transformed and made precious by what they had shared and would share from now on. Tons and tons of purest, perfect love. Guy was moving in, and Holly was more content, more fulfilled, than she'd ever thought possible.

It was nearly time for the evening display to start; Caitlin calculated she could afford to stay another hour before leaving to catch her bus. It was annoying having no transport of her own, but rather than risk a recurrence of her father's anxiety state, she'd decided against asking him for the loan of his car as her brother had suggested.

'You really should know better,' she'd told Gwyn when they met this morning.

He'd given the matter more thought since then,

and was totally in agreement with her now. 'Liz suggested it,' he said, 'and...'

Caitlin smiled. '*And,* it seemed like a good idea. I know. Then you remembered who we were dealing with, and you decided it maybe *wasn't* so great after all.'

They both laughed at the idiosyncrasies of their father. They knew he was excessively touchy with regard to his possessions.

'Nearly as bad as mother, but not quite,' Caitlin reminded him.

'God, you can say that again,' her brother agreed.

Gwyn and Liz and their children had departed for Malvern, and Caitlin had turned down Liz's parents' invitation to spend the evening with them. She was perfectly happy wandering around the fairground alone, she'd said, absorbing the various sights and sounds. She needed some time to think, anyway. Now that the temporary job had finished at the travel agent's, she must do something positive about looking for work. Early next week, she would come up to Bristol and start trawling the employment agencies. Perhaps Bath, too, she decided.

The evening was warm, and all around her swirled a noisy bustle of movement. Some of the trade tents were shutting up shop; their corporate owners having clinched a satisfactory number of deals, she guessed, in the course of the last twenty-four hours. She watched the expensively dressed men and women tripping backwards and forwards from tent to tent. The tents themselves would have put a wealthy Arab sheik's to shame.

Bottles of Bollinger and Piper Heidsieck had replaced the Pils lager and Coca-Cola that had spilled like an overflowing reservoir all day.

Standing on a rise above the main complex, Caitlin surveyed the busy scene. Tents of every shape and hue abounded; hot-dog stands, still going great guns; Mr Whippy dishing out 99s and soft cornets, though there was no longer any queue.

Caitlin was feeling fairly confident about herself today. Her terracotta-coloured silk shirt flattered her shoulder-length tawny hair and eyes of treacly gold, she knew. In fact, when she'd been strolling around the funfair with her nephews earlier, she had exchanged several flirtatious glances with different fanciable men.

However, she hadn't laid eyes on anyone worth flirting with in the forty minutes since she'd been alone. It seemed to her that all the single people had paired up, and others, like the good-looking, though decidedly rough-diamond type she'd met in the ice-cream queue, were already spoken for. She remembered the older girl mentioning a mother, and saying that her auntie and granny were waiting for them to join them. Presumably they had all come to the Fiesta in a family group.

She'd been surprised to find how comfortable she'd felt with Elizabeth's parents earlier. Her brother was lucky to have married into that family, she thought. Everyone had been so pleased for her when she'd told them about the baby. Liz, in particular, had given her plenty of encouragement to go it alone as a single parent. Caitlin hadn't told them in detail her reasons for breaking up with Tyler, but Gwyn and Liz would know she hadn't taken the decision lightly. They'd invited her to stay with them any time she felt she needed a change of scenery.

Caitlin looked back down over the hill, to where a gaily striped helter-skelter towered above the rest of the fairground attractions. The merry-go-round was in full swing again now. Ryan and Sam had enticed her on to it that afternoon, she and Sam sitting astride a magnificent silver pony, and Ryan by the side of them, riding an equally exotically painted mount, all clinging to golden poles that reminded her of the sticks of barley sugar she'd bought as a child. Caitlin glanced at her watch; it was after seven o'clock. Everyone around her seemed to be eating now; it was making her feel quite hungry. There was a fast food stall at the top of the hill that she'd noticed earlier, and she made a beeline for it.

As she approached the blue and white stall, she caught sight of the red-haired man from this morning; he was sitting beneath a tree a short distance away. She searched her memory for his name, and then it came to her. *Calum*, he'd said it was. He was surrounded now by a group of people whom Caitlin supposed were his family. An older woman – most probably the granny his daughter had talked of – and another woman, nursing a baby. Even from some distance away, Caitlin could see that the baby's hair was red ... identical to *his*.

Waiting to be served with her roast chicken and chips, she began to feel quite exhausted. After walking around with the children all day, she badly wanted a rest. There was half an hour to spare before she needed to set out to catch the bus, so, spreading her cotton cardigan over the worn turf, she settled down to enjoy her takeaway meal.

The sky overhead was clear, apart from a collection of small white marshmallow clouds sailing effortlessly across its pale gentian-blue depths. For the moment, there were no balloons in sight. As she contemplated the cosy cloud formation, Caitlin was reminded of a small cluster of white doves she'd seen flying across the New Mexican desert one evening just as the sun was about to set. Tyler had been occupied with his group, who were performing at the nearby city of Albuquerque, and she'd taken the rare opportunity to drive out into the desert alone.

The primaeval beauty of the coral-red sunset was awe-inspiring. The birds became microscopic shapes of movement, silhouetted against its fiery glow. America wasn't just skyscrapers and concrete – inner cities and protective palisades – as so many people at home assumed, Caitlin reminded herself. There'd been moments when she'd found herself spellbound, lost in its breathtaking splendours.

Remembering America, she cast her mind back to a Sunday afternoon last summer when she and Tyler were strolling along the wooden pier at Santa Barbara. A flock of unwieldy pelicans had suddenly appeared, swooping in low, causing them both to duck their heads for fear of being knocked to the ground. There'd been the same sort of holiday atmosphere in the air then as now and, looking back, she recalled that she and Tyler had, for once, been in harmony. One brief day ... the rarest of days. It stood out from her other memories like a flaming beacon atop a highest hill.

After she had finished eating, and disposed of her rubbish, Caitlin checked the time again and discovered she still had twenty minutes left before she would need to set out for the bus stop by the entrance gates. Glancing at Calum, she saw he was on his own, leaning against the tree, watching the hustle and bustle that surrounded the launching of a particularly ornately patterned balloon. The older woman whom Caitlin had seen earlier was stowing a box into the boot of a car, helped by a tall grey-haired man. From a rear window of the car, a medium-sized saloon, two little redheaded moppets were peering out.

There were balloons ascending from everywhere now – the rushing, popping sounds from their gas burners came thick and fast from every direction. As soon as the rainbow-hued one that Calum was watching became airborne, he eased himself away from the tree and began to walk along the footpath, towards where Caitlin was sitting. He stopped suddenly, yards from her head, his attention taken by a balloon shaped like a giant grizzly bear. Caitlin decided it was time to make a move. God forbid he should think she was loitering with intent, she thought, finding herself amused and also a little embarrassed at this possibility.

She was halfway to her feet, and rising, when the vicious pain tore into her like an enemy missile coming directly at her from out of the blue. It forced her back to the ground and, whimpering softly, she curled herself into a tight round ball, rocking painfully to and fro.

After a few seconds the immediate agony passed, leaving in its wake a deadly dull ache similar to a bad period pain. Infinitely worse, though, because the ache was *threatening* – *menacing* ... causing her heart to leap with terror. It wasn't something which would go away the moment it had run its course, she decided. She felt a snick, and something warm leave her body ... Lord, what a spectacle she would make if she haemorrhaged all over her cream-coloured jeans! A sight to scare the horses ... a sight to scare every living soul around, of that Caitlin was certain.

Her brain had become completely numb, giving her a strong and unreal feeling of detachment from the tricks her body was playing. The full implication of what might be happening hadn't yet dawned on her. She only knew she must get away from this crowded scene, and not make an exhibition of herself. Who was there here to help, though? There was no Lisa or Marie-Carmen in this place – and her brother and Liz had left for home an hour ago. Not daring to move, she stared frantically around, willing – yet half of her not wanting it – for someone to stop and help.

'Please God, don't let it be ... let someone make it stop,' she whispered. A tear slid down her cheek, and she licked it away with her tongue. She remembered the sad salty taste so well; she,

211

who had cried so many tears before, and for exactly the same reason.

Then, to her relief, the pain lessened a trifle. As soon as she could summon up the strength, she would endeavour to lift herself up off her cardigan and tie the garment round her waist. It was a full-length one which with any luck should cover her all the way down to her knees, she reassured herself.

She was aware of what was happening now, and her common sense told her she must try to get help. If she did, then perhaps she wouldn't lose this baby, the way she had the other one. The doctors in America had been unable to save it, but this time things would be different. She was back in England now. It just wasn't possible she could lose a baby *here*.

'Uhh … hh…' A stifled groan escaped her lips as she made an effort to stand. She managed to raise her body a little way and, with fingers that felt like jelly, pull the knitted jacket loosely round her waist and tie the sleeves together. When she'd done that, she flopped back, exhausted, aware that her facial expression must give her away if anyone took the trouble to look. But everyone seemed to be intent on doing their own thing. After all, Caitlin reminded herself, they had come here to enjoy themselves.

The pain was relentless now, an ongoing torture, with no hint of a lull to deaden the awful impact. Holding her cardigan – her beige cotton, exclusive Californian fashion accessory – more tightly to her, Caitlin rolled on to her side, and slipped into a dead faint.

Later, still disorientated, she felt someone stroking her brow. A man was speaking to her soothingly, though she had no recollection of who it was.

'Stay where you are a little minute ... you just fainted off, my love. You'll be perfickly all right ... just take it steady now ... hold it ... that's right.'

All of a sudden she remembered and, with difficulty, formulated the words. 'It's Calum, isn't it?' she murmured.

'You remembered my name!' Calum said, surprised. 'You looks a bit different from when I seen you this morning, I must say.'

He was leaning over her now, his dark blue eyes only inches from her face. She closed her eyes as the dragging pain worsened, becoming so severe she wished only to faint again.

Calum patted her cheeks lightly. 'Bide there where you are,' he said, then added with a reassuring chuckle, 'not that you'm fit to do much else.'

Sensing that he was about to leave her, Caitlin tugged feebly at his arm and begged him to stay.

'Only a minute,' Calum explained, 'I'm only going to fetch my mum ... honest Gospel, I'll be back in half a tick.'

He stood up then and, fixing her a penetrating look, asked, 'Where's the people what you was with? Can't we put out a tannoy message and get them to come up yere?'

Caitlin ran her tongue over her dry lips – waves of nausea were pouring over her again. She shook her head weakly. 'They've all gone home,' she said. 'I'm here on my own.'

Calum nodded. 'OK, well, don't you worry. Our mother'll know what to do,' he said reassuringly.

It was the last normal sound Caitlin heard for some long while. Everything became a blur after that. She heard Calum telling her not to worry, that someone had summoned an ambulance and they would be taking her to hospital. He offered to ride in the ambulance with her – in case she was scared, he said. Caitlin nodded her head to that.

On arriving at the Bristol Infirmary, the duty staff transferred her to the Gynaecological Department on St Michael's Hill, where the emergency doctor did everything he could to prevent her from miscarrying a second time. It was only when they were wheeling her to the operating theatre in the early hours of the morning that Caitlin realised the battle was lost. For some strange reason – as if shutting out the unbearable truth – her thoughts switched to the kitten left behind in her parents' garage at Weston-super-Mare. It would be waiting in vain for her to come back to give it a cuddle, she knew.

'Pepsi,' she whispered, frantically licking her stiff, glue-like lips.

'Sorry, no, you can't have *that*,' the nurse who was escorting her to theatre told her. 'You'll be having an anaesthetic in a minute or two.'

'No ... *Pepsi*...' Caitlin tried her hardest to explain that this Pepsi wasn't a drink. After a while she gave up trying; too exhausted to even think.

The last thing she felt was a needle pricking her hand and, just before she fell asleep, she saw a bevy of naked cherubs hovering around her pillow, fat and cuddly. She reached out to hold one, but it slipped away from her grasp. Not *unkindly*, however, as if it didn't care. Its expression was infinitely sad. The cherubs began to croon a lullaby – the one her grandmother had sung to her when she was small and staying at her grandparents' home in Ilfracombe.

'Four corners to my bed ... four angels round my head ... one to watch, and one to pray ... two to keep...' they chanted in unison, in unbelievably dulcet tones.

Caitlin knew no more then, as the duty surgeon prepared to proceed with his fruitless but nevertheless urgent task.

Chapter Fourteen

Holly came into Angie's living room carrying two mugs of hot chocolate. Feeling just a touch guilty at not having joined her family at Ashton Park, she had left Guy back in the bedsit, watching football on television, and come next door to enquire if Angie had enjoyed her day.

'It's Options,' she said, seeing her mother hesitate. 'Only forty calories a cup. Guy's sister, Caterina, put me on to it.'

'Are they slim, his sisters?' asked Angie.

'Not too bad. They just have to watch their

weight a bit, like most people do.'

'Most people, but not you,' Angie scoffed, eyeing her daughter's perfectly proportioned figure with a sense of pride, mingled with envy. 'To think I was as skinny as you once upon a time,' she added. 'It makes me want to be sick.'

'Don't forget, you've not long had a baby, Mum,' Holly assured her. 'I think you look great for forty.'

'Thank you, my darling, for that kind remark.' Angie took a sip of the chocolate drink, 'Uhm, it isn't bad.'

The sound of the telephone ringing in the hallway interrupted their conversation. 'I'll get it,' Holly said, setting down her favourite Winnie-the-Pooh mug on Daisy's old-fashioned side-board.

Angie couldn't hear who Holly was talking to, but knew that she would have summoned her by now if the call was for her. A moment later she heard the click of the receiver, and Holly came back into the room. Standing in the doorway, she announced dramatically, 'Calum's got a new girlfriend. She's in at St Michael's Hospital having a miscarriage ... I do not jest.'

'Eh?' said Angie. 'Did I hear you right?'

'You did. That was Gran on the phone. She and Josh have just got home. They've got Emma and Lucie with them. They left his lordship getting into an ambulance with a strange woman who, it appears, was having a miscarriage. She was all covered in blood, apparently, and our knight in shining armour has accompanied her into hospital. So...' Holly rubbed her hands together

216

briskly. 'What do you make of that?'

Angie shook her head in wonder. 'It certainly sounds strange,' she said. Her mind went over the arrangements they'd made, when, because the baby was grizzly, she'd borrowed Calum's Cavalier to bring her family home. Josh was to drive Calum and his children back to Mariner's Cottage, from where Calum would take Emma and Lucie back to Portmills. Now that he'd gone off to hospital in an ambulance, only Josh and Daisy were left to make sure his girls arrived home safely.

'It's awfully late for those little girls still to be out,' she remarked thoughtfully.

Holly nodded. 'I know. Josh is just about to run them home, Gran said. They wanted to stay with her, but she's going to check it out with Suzi for another time.'

'If Calum messes Suzi about too much, she'll be stopping him having any contact with them. Dais would *die* if that happened.'

'I don't think it'll come to that, Mum.'

'You never know, love, now that she's taken up with another man.'

'As they do these days,' Holly observed quietly.

'They do seem to, yes.' Angie was silent for a moment, then, suddenly alert, she said, 'Is it *Calum's* baby this woman's having a miscarriage with?'

'God knows.' Holly dismissed her question with a shrug of disdain. 'He's like some lecherous leper, that man. He's turning into a sex maniac, if you ask me.'

'More like a regular Don Juan,' commented

217

Angie. 'Breaking up with Suzi's really going to his head.'

'To his dick, more like,' countered Holly, taking their empty mugs through to the kitchen to rinse them under the hot tap.

'You must take that mug with you when you go. It *is* yours,' said Angie.

'Dear old Winnie,' said Holly, holding the mug to her face fondly. 'Oh, well, I guess I'll be off now,' she added, coming back to give Angie a kiss. 'I shouldn't wait up for him, if I were you, Mum ... you might be up all night.'

'I won't,' Angie assured her, 'but the poor old dog's still out there waiting for his run.'

'The twins didn't take him? That was a bit mean, wasn't it?'

'They had a bath and went straight to bed; I was happy to see the back of them,' explained Angie.

'I'll see to it, don't you worry, Mum,' said Holly. 'As soon as the footie's over, I'll get Guy to come with me.'

She looked at her childhood mug again, as if in affectionate reminiscence, then continued, 'He might as well get used to it ... walking the dog, I mean. Let's face it, Calum's always gallivanting off somewhere or other these nights. He can't very well take the dog along to all these romantic sessions. Poor old Gyp would soon cramp his style, don't you think?'

She began to laugh, causing Angie to see the funny side. 'Can you imagine it?' Angie spluttered, 'Gyp jumping on to the bed with them, and licking them both all around the neck?'

218

'More likely sitting on Calum's back and enjoying the ride,' gurgled Holly, 'Ooh, I can just see it now.'

'Stop it. Go, will you?' As soon as she spoke the words, Angie realised the significance of what she was saying, but any trace of sadness she'd been feeling had disappeared for the moment. 'You'll be back to give Gyp a run presently then, will you?' she asked.

'We certainly will, but we won't come into the house, so as not to wake you up. We'll leave him out in the yard in his kennel. Then, when Calum comes in, he can do whatever he wants. Byee...' With that, Holly went off to her own pad, where she would share a bed with the boy she loved.

Angie was happy for her. She wondered what Curt would have made of the situation, though. He would have disapproved quite strongly, she thought to herself. Oh, well, it was one problem that wouldn't arise now that he'd disappeared and left her to cope all alone.

She'd never have believed it possible but she seemed, at last, to be getting used to not having him around. In the beginning she'd missed his familiar warmth in bed as much as if she'd lost a limb. Sex was a different matter – finding out she was pregnant had provided enough to think about at first, and the money worries at that time had been something else again. The first thing to go had been the car; she'd found herself completely unable to keep up the payments to the finance company.

When Christmas came, to save having to pay rent, she and the children had moved out of their council house and gone to live with Daisy at Mariner's Cottage. The seasonal festivities had passed her by in a hazy blur and, by springtime, her pregnancy was fairly well advanced. With the shop to run and preparations for the birth of the baby, she'd had no time to fret about a non-existent sex life. It was only recently that she'd given it any thought.

Angie pressed the TV handset button to change from BBC to HTV. There was a documentary reviewing the career of Dame Judi Dench due on in five minutes' time that she wanted to see. She just had time to pop upstairs to make sure that Evie was all right and see that the twins were settled for the night.

As she snuggled back comfortably on the settee waiting for the programme to commence, Angie's thoughts turned briefly to her budding relationship with Rex Carpenter. She was expecting him to be in touch soon to confirm that he'd got tickets for a concert they both wanted to see at the Bristol Hippodrome. Angie had already checked that Daisy could babysit and, failing her for any reason, well, Holly wasn't far away.

The introduction music began; Angie turned up the sound. It was little treats like this that made the living bearable, even – sometimes – quite enjoyable, she thought.

'Josh, that poor young woman! It was heart-breaking to see her so upset. She was all on her own. Her family live a good long way away, and they'd already left for home.'

'And you mean to say she was a complete stranger to your Rusty?' Josh asked, jingling his car keys in his hand and sounding extremely doubtful. He'd just arrived home again after taking Emma and Lucie back to Portmills.

'I'm certain he'd never seen her in his life before,' replied Daisy. 'He phoned a moment ago and told me a little more about it. She's recently left her husband ... he's in America, and she's living at Weston with elderly parents, who don't even know she's pregnant.'

'Perhaps it isn't her husband's kid?' suggested Josh.

'I wouldn't know about that,' Daisy said, 'but she was very lonely and scared. She was relieved when Calum said he'd go in the ambulance with her.'

'A funny old business, if you ask me,' remarked Josh, putting his keys down and going to the drinks cabinet to pour them both a drink.

'I know,' Daisy said, heaving a deep sigh.

She pulled open the sliding glass door and wandered on to the patio. Resting her hands on the stone balustrade, she looked out across the valley to the distant motorway which snaked along below the horizon like a length of blue-grey ribbon. The row of dwarf conifers that bordered Josh's garden vibrated in the gentle breeze which lifted the washing on the rotary clothes line and turned it around slowly. She was too tired to bring it in.

The sun was fast slipping from sight behind the Welsh hills, leaving wild streaks of red and orange across the western sky, as though daubed on the heavens by a master's hand. The same sort of primary colours that a child would choose, Daisy thought. A tiny child like Lucie or Emma – too young to be trendy or sophisticated.

Josh followed her on to the patio, stopping on the way to take a sip of his gin and tonic. 'I wondered where you'd got to,' he said, handing Daisy a glass of red wine.

'Thanks,' she said, turning to face him. 'Was that man there when you dropped the girls off?' she asked.

Josh shook his head, 'I only saw *her*, Dais. I've no idea if he was or not.'

He pulled out a chair and sat down at the patio table. The day had been exceptionally hot and by the look of the sky tonight it promised to be the same tomorrow. He glanced across at Daisy, and thought how tired she looked. Always her own worst enemy, he'd even had to talk her out of getting into the ambulance with Calum and the girl.

'You're looking tired, love. Come and sit down.' He beckoned Daisy over to join him.

'Haggard, did you say?' she joked, sitting down next to him beneath the green and yellow sun umbrella.

'No, not haggard – I'd say a mite exhausted, though.'

'Mmm, I must admit, I do feel fairly drained.'

Daisy had gone past feeling tired. *Devil-dragged* – a term she remembered from her childhood – was the perfect description for how she was feeling now. It was so wonderfully restful here at Upalong, though, and the reason she loved the place so much.

Resting her head on Josh's shoulder, she snuggled closer to him. 'I *love* living here,' she said, 'thank you, my darling, for making me feel so much at home.'

She kissed his cheek, and continued, 'Your wife must have been one of the luckiest women alive – not to *have* to go out to work ... her only worry, keeping this lovely home and garden tidy. A real labour of love it must have been. All those wonderful holidays you went on, and so on. Gosh, what utter bliss!'

'But no children,' Josh reminded her quietly. 'To lose the only one we had at birth was a dreadful disappointment for us both to live with.'

Daisy nodded sympathetically. 'Of course. A terrible, terrible tragedy, my love. I would have hated not to have had my boys – I realise how very lucky I am...' She paused thoughtfully. 'Or *was.*'

They lapsed into silence, each thinking their own thoughts. In the meadow beyond the trees a blackbird was trilling. Daisy thought that she'd never heard a more melodic sound and it lifted her spirits to hear it. There *must* be a God, she told herself. Only *He* could have created such perfection.

'Josh,' she said hesitantly. 'I don't know how to put this, but...' Her voice tailed off waveringly.

'Go on,' he said, waiting.

'That young woman in hospital. I'd like to bring her here. No,' she said, holding up her hand as she saw his disapproving frown. 'Not for *always*. Just until she gets over this immediate trauma. This is her *second* miscarriage, you know, and she's really and truly devastated.'

'Oh, Daisy,' Josh groaned, 'you're a glutton for punishment, aren't you? My God, and I was wondering where Calum got it from ... all this dashing to the rescue of someone he's never even met before.'

'I'm only asking you to think it over, love. Just give it some thought, would you?'

'Do I have a choice?'

'You do,' Daisy assured him.

'OK, well, I'll think it over, as you say. Come on.' He turned to go indoors. 'The best thing you can do is get yourself off to bed. We'll talk about it in the morning.'

The following morning Caitlin awoke from a drowsy doze to find Calum sitting by her bed. A most unlikely knight in shining armour ... he'd certainly come up trumps for her ... *an unexpected saviour!*

'What time is it?' she asked, straining her neck to squint at the wall clock at the far end of the ward.

Calum glanced at his wristwatch. ''Tis just about eleven o'clock,' he said.

A beam of strong sunlight cast dappling movements of light on the white bedspread by Caitlin's feet, liquid, iridescent movements, alive and constantly shifting. She stared at them quietly for a moment. The dancing motions only served to highlight the dead emptiness that lay inside the soft flabby skin of her ugly swollen stomach.

Calum put his hand over his eyes; he was still trying to get his head together. He'd spent a restless night on a couch in the hospital waiting room, twisting and turning uncomfortably. Then, just as the pink light of dawn was stealing through the east-facing window, he'd put through a call to his mucker, Jacko Jackson, asking him to come into Bristol and give him a lift home.

After a wash and brush-up, and a bite of breakfast, he had arrived back at the hospital in his own car to find that parking facilities at St Michael's were practically non-existent. He'd been circling around for the last quarter of an hour, trying to find a space.

He yawned. The lack of sleep was beginning to catch up with him now. Caitlin's eyes, too, had closed again, he noticed. She still looked extremely pale, and fragile, but she seemed like a survivor to him – not the sort to go under, or remain a victim for long. In fact she reminded him strongly of Suzi. If only he could have come up trumps for *her*, the way he had for Caitlin, he might be still in with a chance, he realised.

Caitlin was stirring again now, looking at him with those distinctive golden-tawny eyes.

'Is there anything special you wants me to do?' he asked her. 'Shall I try your brother's number again?'

There'd been no reply from the Malvern number when he'd tried it repeatedly last night.

'No rush,' she said, shaking her head, 'I'll ring him and tell him about it, as soon as I feel up to it.'

225

They were interrupted by a nurse who had come to take her temperature. Caitlin needed to go to the toilet, too, and while she was gone Calum wandered out into the corridor in search of the drinks machine. He soon located it and, slipping in the required number of coins, pressed the button marked Coca-Cola.

He leaned against a windowsill while he quenched his thirst. His thoughts returned to the previous night when he'd telephoned Caitlin's parents to tell them she'd been taken ill and rushed into hospital. Her father had appeared more annoyed than troubled, Calum thought, asking gormless questions like, 'Who's going to look after the cat?' and, 'What does she want us to do with all her things she's got stored in our garage?'

'She won't need none of that,' Calum had said firmly. 'It's an emergency operation what she's having.'

'What sort of emergency?' her father had asked.

Calum was glad Caitlin had forewarned him her parents didn't know she was pregnant or he would almost certainly have given the game away. In the event, Mr Hutchison had latched on to the idea that she'd developed an attack of appendicitis, and Calum didn't bother to enlighten him otherwise.

Caitlin had also told him in the ambulance on the way to hospital that she had lost a baby before – and for some strange reason she didn't want her husband finding out where she was, although this baby, too, was his child. From what Calum could gather, her old man was carrying out some sort of vendetta against her. It was all pretty complicated; even fishy, it seemed to him.

'America's a hell of a long way away from here, my chicken,' he'd reassured her. 'There's not a chance in hell of him hopping on a plane and arriving in England before you'm out and about again – not unless that Aladdin's Palace, where you says his band's playing, provides him with a magic carpet to fly over on.'

Before Calum had left the hospital early that morning to go home for breakfast, he'd popped into the ward to tell Caitlin what he was doing. She'd started to cry then and, although he had the deepest sympathy with her, he'd found it all quite bloody stressful.

'I really thought it was going to be all right this time,' she'd sobbed, 'I came back to England because I thought I'd be sure of saving the baby here.'

After a lengthy pause, she'd added, 'He kicked me ... *quite hard.* I thought he'd missed, but I'm sure it did some damage and that's why I've lost this one, too.'

Aha, thought Calum. It's beginning to make bloody sense.

'There'll be another time,' he assured her. 'Don't get too downhearted – tomorrow's another day, remember.' Then, squeezing her shoulder sympathetically, he'd given her a friendly kiss before going off to find Jacko Jackson who was waiting in the hospital car park.

Half an hour later, back at Mariner's Cottage, Calum had found Angie in the kitchen, having breakfast. She, of course, was curious to know

227

what had kept him out all night. Her initial response – most likely inspired by something that Holly had said, Calum guessed – implied it was probably *he* who was responsible for Caitlin's plight. He was mighty glad that Josh and Daisy had been there to witness for themselves. If they hadn't, he knew his reputation for getting women in the family way would have taken another knock.

He finished his can of Coke and deposited it in the bin before making his way back to Caitlin's ward. She was back in bed again now, but when he got nearer he saw that the tears were streaming down her face like fast-melting ice. He wondered what could have happened in the ten minutes since he'd been gone.

'Hey, hey, hey,' Calum said, drawing up a chair and sitting alongside her.

Choking back the tears, she explained, 'I bumped into a woman in the lavatory. She's expecting triplets in a few days time – all of them strong and healthy, according to the doctors, she said...'

'Not *physically* bumped into her, I hope?' Calum teased, trying to help lighten the situation. What a bugger that she'd had to run into a woman with racing hormones, he told himself.

Too weak to wipe away the tears that streamed from her sad eyes on to her waxen-white cheeks as Caitlin was, Calum had to do it for her. Everything that he found himself doing for this girl – a virtual stranger – was foreign to any previous responses he might have made. Why, he wondered, was he able to treat this girl with such tender loving care when, where Suzi was concerned, he'd charged at any emotional issue like a bloody bull at a gate?

Caitlin hoisted herself up on to her elbow and reached for a tissue from a box on the bedside locker. 'This is stupid, Calum,' she said, 'I haven't even got a tissue here to call my own. And what will I do about clothes to go home in? Mine are all spoiled and yucky.'

'Your dad's waiting for a bell to know whether he should come in and see you,' Calum told her. 'He'll bring some more, I'm sure.'

'You didn't tell him which hospital I'm in?' she asked, her voice showing signs of panic.

'I couldn't very well tell him *that*,' Calum said. 'This yere hospital's only meant to be for women's troubles. Your father thinks you'm having yer appendix out.'

She smiled fleetingly then. 'You put it so nicely, Calum,' she told him. 'I really love the way you put it.'

Calum scratched his head, a little embarrassed by the unexpected compliment. 'So what will I tell him then? Or did you want to speak to him yerself?'

'Oh, Calum, I *can't*,' she wailed. 'If Tyler finds out where I am, he'll be over like a shot to try to talk me into going back with him. He'll know I'm in a weak position – he'll be sure to take advantage of that.'

She fixed him a serious look. 'No,' she said, 'I've got to handle it *my* way. I'll find a job some distance away from Weston; I've got a week or

229

two to do it before he finishes at Las Vegas.'

Her face clouded over again. 'They'll be discharging me tomorrow, you know,' she added.

'Couldn't you go and stay with your brother for a while?' Calum suggested.

She appeared to mull over the idea for barely a moment, then said, in a monotone, 'That's the first place he'd come and look for me, I reckon. I must get right away.'

A fishy smell mixed with the disinfected atmosphere of the gynaecological ward announced that the lunchtime trolleys were on their way. The resultant aroma was not too appetising, but the thought of food began to activate Calum's tastebuds.

He stood up and buttoned his Levi jacket, ready to go. Suddenly he stared at Caitlin sharply. He'd had a brainwave ... a real fucking brainwave ... a magical inspiration, no less!

'What sort of a job will you be looking for?' he asked her.

'Anything within reason, and where Tyler won't be able to find me,' Caitlin said.

'How about looking after my sister-in-law's babby? You'd get on all right with our Ange; I know you bloody well would.'

Caitlin hesitated. 'Was she the woman I saw you with yesterday? The baby had bright red hair and looked a lot like you?'

'You needn't say it like that,' Calum told her. 'It's like as though you'm hinting I've bin up to summat I shouldn't ought to have.'

'I really didn't...' She stopped midway, and blushed.

'No – 'tis all right,' he assured her, grinning. 'The little 'un have got ginger hair, but that's because her father have too. Well, did have,' he added slowly. 'For as far as we knows, he's drowned and dead. My brother, Curt.'

'Oh, Calum, no. I'm so sorry,' Caitlin said.

'I know.' Calum shook his head sadly. 'So the little 'un'll never know her dad. There's two young boys of twelve what wants feeding and a general eye keeping on 'em too – her brothers,' he told her. 'Though Angie's only ever a minute away from the lot of 'em, working in the shop next door.'

The strained look left Caitlin's face. She smiled at Calum, and said, 'You're an angel, do you know that? I prayed for an angel last night, just as they were giving me the anaesthetic, and...'

She stopped speaking and reached for his hand, holding it in her clasp for a moment.

'Well, I'm bugg– well, I'm blowed. 'Tis the first time I've ever bin called that,' Calum remarked.

'Your sister-in-law might not think I'm right for the job,' she said hesitantly.

'Gaw – whatever are you on about? Course you'll be all right for the job.' A deeper thought struck him. 'That's if you feels able to take care of somebody else's babby, now that you ... you...'

Caitlin looked at him sadly. The sparkle that had briefly lit her tawny eyes had faded again to dull umber.

'Perhaps I'm still in shock,' she said, 'but I'll certainly give it a go. If it turns out to be too difficult a task ... you know ... then I'll discuss it with your sister-in-law, and we'll have to go on from there.'

Calum nodded. A cluster of doctors in flapping white coats had come on to the ward; they were approaching her bed, smiling, ready to greet her. They had beaten the dinner trolley to it only by minutes, he noticed. The woman pushing it was looking at them as if to kill. They'd be laid out on the floor as stiff as bloody railway sleepers, he thought, if she had her way – he'd never seen a more venomous gaze, except in the reptile house at Bristol Zoo.

Calum on the other hand was quite relieved that the doctors had arrived when they did. He had things of importance to attend to as soon as he'd had something to eat, and perhaps a quick pint if there was time. Ice cream: bloody boxes of it. Jacko had said he would drop it off sometime during the afternoon. This particular commodity had literally fallen off the back of a lorry. Calum hoped there'd be a few bob in it for him.

For the past few weeks, Jacko Jackson had been working as a delivery driver's mate for the Iceberg food company. Jacko was moonlighting – he often did it – pulling a fast one over the Department of Employment. The driver he was helping had counted Jacko in for a forty percent share of the loot if he helped him to pull off a crafty heist he'd been planning for the right moment.

At Calum's request, Daisy and Angie had cleared out some space in the shop's deep-freeze as well as their own fridge-freezers at home. They were both under the impression that the deal was strictly kosher. What they don't know won't hurt them, Calum had thought.

He made a quick dash for the hospital lift before it descended into the bowels of the building, perhaps never to be seen again until well into the millennium. By that time, he told himself, there'd be no frigging ice cream left for anybody to nick – not even a dedicated chancer like Jacko.

Chapter Fifteen

At five to one, just before Angie closed the shop for lunch, Daisy went home to finish clearing out her deep-freeze as Calum had asked her to. The baby's travel seat was strapped permanently into the front seat of the Metro, so, popping Evie inside, she hurried away to savour the delicious flan that Josh had told her he would be making.

Three months old, Evie was becoming more interesting, more observant, with each day that passed. Josh adored the baby girl, and loved having her around. Daisy was pleased; it meant that Evie would always think of him as her grandfather, and Josh had never known that particular pleasure. Judging by her squeals of glee as *Grandad* lifted her out of the car, Evie was already making deep inroads into Josh's vast storehouse of affection.

Before turning the shop sign to *closed*, Angie went into the living room to turn off the radio. The weather forecast was on, temperature ninety degrees Fahrenheit and mounting, she heard the weatherman say as she switched it off. She would catch up with the main news on television later on. It was time to be at Holly's for lunch. Holly, with so many things still to do – like hanging curtains in the large front window that overlooked Maritime Way – had decided to take the day off work to get at least that done. Angie was expecting another girl for interview for the post of nanny later in the afternoon and, as before, hoped to have the benefit of her daughter's opinion.

'Oh, no, not another one?' Holly groaned, when Angie enquired whether she'd be available.

''Fraid so,' Angie told her, 'she's due at five o'clock.'

'Sorry Mum, but you'll have to count me out. I've arranged to meet Guy in town at five. We're going to have a look at some carpets.'

'That's perfectly all right, love,' Angie assured her. 'It would have been nice to have a second opinion – that's all.'

'Will you be able to fit it all in, with the shop and everything?' asked Holly.

'The boys will still be out, with luck – they've gone off to Blue Anchor with the Scouts – and your gran will be here for the shop. I can keep the baby with me – it shouldn't be too much of a hassle,' Angie assured her.

While Holly went off to prepare lunch in her tiny kitchen, Angie lolled back on the double bed and gazed round the room. Holly and Guy had wrought a complete transformation in the place in the few days since they'd moved in.

'You and Guy have really done wonders,' she

said. 'And these curtains – they're *most* attractive. I didn't expect to find them already up.'

'I've been at it all morning,' Holly replied, 'I dashed into Bristol as soon as Debenham's opened.'

She came back into the room, carrying a tray laden with plain bagels spread thickly with cream cheese, topped with a layer of plump pink prawns. 'Josh has made a bacon and mushroom flan for Daisy's lunch,' Angie commented, making room on the bed for Holly to put the tray. 'He's even made the pastry, apparently.'

'I'm glad to hear it – it's about time Gran sat back and took things a bit easy!'

'I agree.' Angie was examining the exotic filling. 'Mmm ... this looks good, I must say.'

'*Ooh, it's Philadelphia,*' said Holly, imitating the girl in the television advert.

Leaving her meal on the tray, she went over to the window to rearrange the new curtains so that they fell into perfectly straight lines. Their pale shades of blue, green and beige blended in perfectly with the newly painted cream walls.

'We'll be looking at plain fawn Berber carpets this afternoon,' she said, 'and there's a sofa I'd very much like to have. Not that we can afford *that* yet – we'll have to wait till we've paid off some of the other stuff.'

Angie patted the uncovered duvet. 'You were very lucky to get this bed for free.'

'I know – and the telly, too!' said Holly, rubbing her hands together happily.

'You came along at the very right minute – just when Josh decided he needed one with Teletext for his racing results.'

'The main thing is, Mum, I don't have to buy a car any more, not now Guy's going to let me have his. I'd saved up quite a bit towards it, you know.'

'Are you certain he doesn't mind going back to riding a motorbike?'

'*Doesn't mind!* You've got to be kidding – of course he doesn't mind. He's in his element riding the darned thing. He and his brother, Vince, they're both motorbike mad.' Holly paused, and took a bite of her bagel. 'Sorry I won't be here to see the girl this afternoon,' she said, 'but Gran's all right at present, isn't she? Those chest pains of hers ... they've not been coming *too* often, I mean?'

'Not as far as I know. She's waiting to have an exercise test at the Bristol Infirmary. Ought to be hearing very soon.' Angie shook her head and continued, 'I wish I could spare her from having to come down here each day, but until we find someone trustworthy to take care of the baby...'

A sudden commotion in the alleyway at the rear of the shop brought their conversation to a halt. A loud clattering sound, like the opening of a lorry's doors, reached their ears. An engine was running noisily, and they could hear Gyp barking himself into a frenzy.

Holly leapt to her feet, and rushed out to the kitchen to see what was happening. She'd cleaned the inside of the window as best she could, but the outside remained coated with the accumulated dirt and grime of many years. She strained to lift the sash window but it remained stuck fast in its ancient, warped frame.

'Shit,' she swore, rubbing the glass with a dishcloth until she found a patch not completely covered with dirt.

The alleyway where the sounds were coming from was still outside her line of vision. She heard a vehicle door slam shut again, and the sound of its reversing bleeps before it accelerated away. Then, once again, there was silence.

Through the tiny clear patch on the windowpane she could see the pedigree cat that belonged to the owner of the nearby boarding cattery skulking on the wall between the two shop yards. An over-pampered pet, with a face like a flattened currant bun, it loved to tease and tantalise poor Gyp from the top of the wall, driving the dog to distraction.

'I don't know what that noise was Gyp was barking at just now, but that ugly, *frowzy* cat ... the one that cat-woman adores ... is sitting on our wall again, tormenting him like it always does. I can't imagine how anyone could possibly think that sort are at all attractive.' Holly wrinkled her nose in disgust as she came back into the living room and sat down on the bed.

'So interbred, it snuffles instead of breathing naturally. Give me a pretty-faced moggy any day – that one looks as though it's had a run-in with a steam-shovel at some stage in one of its nine useless lives.'

'The woman who runs the cattery doesn't think so,' Angie observed.

'She must have mud in her eye then,' said Holly.

'Silence ... what bliss. At least Gyp's gone quiet

again now,' Angie remarked. 'He's missed going out with Calum today. He couldn't take him with him to hospital; it's much too hot to leave a dog locked up in a car.'

'Oh, God, he's not gone *there* again, has he?' Fixing her mother an exasperated look, Holly added, 'Anyway, Mum, where were we before we were so rudely interrupted?'

'Gran's health, and you not being here to see the girl I'm to interview this afternoon. The one I saw the other day was completely unsuitable; it's the main reason I wanted your opinion with *this* one.'

'Not worse than Berenice Boothroyd and the Scandinavian bombshell? It's not possible,' said Holly.

'Certainly as bad. There wasn't one of them I'd want looking after Evie permanently – and none that I'd feel comfortable actually *living* with.'

'It'll happen,' Holly said. 'Just when you're least expecting it, the right one will come along. It's a pity Suzi's already fixed up with a job ... *a fully-trained nursery nurse* – couldn't have been better. I'm sure she's perfectly happy where she is, though.'

'Mmm, perhaps just as well. It might have proved a little awkward, the way things are with her and Calum.'

'He'd have to lump it,' replied Holly. 'Might make him think twice about where he's sticking his whatsit next time.'

'Oh, Holly, I'm sure he's not that bad.'

'I'm sure he is, otherwise what's he doing riding in an ambulance, with a woman who he says is a complete stranger, into the emergency admission department of a hospital for women's disorders and disasters?'

'We must allow him the benefit of the doubt,' laughed Angie. 'If he says she's a stranger, we must take his word for it that she is.'

'I'm buggered if I'll take his word for it, Mum. Not until he can prove to us that he's not quite as black as he's painted.'

Holly rose to her feet, and picked up their plates from the upturned orange crate that was serving as a temporary bedside table.

'Anyway,' she said, 'I'm babysitting for Suzi tomorrow night. She and this John bloke have got tickets to see a show at the Colston Hall.'

'Oh?' Angie drew in her breath sharply. 'Do you think that's wise, all things considered?'

'I certainly do. I've got no quarrel with Suzi, and if Calum doesn't like it ... *tough!* Anyway, I love Emma and Lucie, and I don't see why I should be deprived of their company just because their daddy's acting like some irresponsible dickhead.' She laughed. 'There – we've gone all the way back to where we started. My Uncle Calum letting his dick run away with his brains.'

'Only since Suzi stood him up,' Angie reminded her.

'Yeah, admitted – but why, I wonder, did she stand him up in the first place? If you ask me, she's simply got fed up of waiting for the great idiot to act responsibly. He's shown no sign of getting a job – never supported her properly – only in dribs and drabs. He's like a great big schoolkid that's never, ever grown up. Soon, little

239

Lucie will have passed him by. There's no excuse for that.'

'I know,' agreed Angie, getting to her feet and going to the door, ready to leave. 'I know,' she said again. 'He just never listens to a blessed thing that anyone says.'

The dog was legging it away down the alleyway at a fast pace, along Frobisher's Walk then right into Drake's Gardens, a crescent of neatly laid out, semi-detached prewar properties that joined up with Maritime Way. It came to a halt at the pedestrian crossing at the bottom of the hill and, after glancing in both directions, crossed the main road and took the first turning left into Raleigh Street on the south side of the village. At the back of Adge Fletcher's All-Purpose Store it lingered for a while to sniff the grass in the scruffy verge that bordered the Fletcher's broken-down brick wall.

Gyp's little black nose had picked up a particularly inviting scent and, lifting his head, his snout continuing to twitch excitedly, he set off to track it down. There, round the very next corner – on a lozenge-shaped patch of newly mown grass – an apricot-coloured toy poodle was showing off her charms to an admiring audience of three.

Calum's dog eyeballed the opposition with a certain amount of interest, and not a little trepidation. Two largish mongrels, both appreciably bigger than him – the third, a titchy Yorkshire terrier, not worth a second gander.

Gyp was encouraged no end by the poodle's

glance of recognition. They had met before in the recreation ground where they'd chased many a ball together. Her enamoured glance told him that she hadn't forgotten – *she knew him … she wanted him* – and this time not merely to chase a ball.

Something like a grin lifted the corners of the terrier's mouth. Flossie Fletcher, prettiest bitch in the whole of Fuzzy Cove, was inviting *him* to chase her, and catch her; to do it quickly, too, before their owners had a chance to step in and spoil it. Gyp made a lunge towards the larger dogs. He would see them off in no time at all. As for the pint-sized Yorkie – he was already long gone.

Angie and Daisy arrived back at the shop simultaneously at two o'clock. After Angie had unlocked the door to let Daisy in, she went over to the car to lift her sleeping baby out. Quickly and quietly, Angie carried Evie upstairs and deposited her into her roomy cot. Lying her gently down, she pulled back the Aertex blanket – it was far too hot for even the lightest of covers today.

'Phew,' Daisy greeted her at the foot of the stairs, 'Have you ever known such a scorcher, *ever?*'

'Never,' Angie agreed. 'It's too damn hot to be comfortable.'

'I hope Frank Goodyear don't keep those boys out in the sun without something on their heads,' Daisy said. 'That fair skin of theirs; they'll be looking like a couple of broiled lobsters.'

241

'Gosh no. I should hope he's got more sense than that,' Angie said.

She went on to tell Daisy about Holly's domestic setup, and how she and Guy had completely transformed the old storeroom.

'I'll call down to see her some time, tell her,' remarked Daisy. 'It's too hot to be climbing all those stairs just now. So – Calum not back yet?' she asked, after a pause.

'No,' said Angie, 'as far as I know, he's still at the hospital.'

The shop bell jangled, and they heard a woman's voice call hello. 'Here we go,' laughed Angie as she hurried away to attend to the customer.

'I'm going to tell him he can bring the girl over to our place for a few days, to give her chance to recover,' Daisy announced when Angie returned to the living room a few minutes later.

Not too surprised at Daisy's statement – nothing that Daisy or Calum did would surprise her greatly, Angie realised – she listened quietly to what her mother-in-law had to say. When Calum returned from visiting Caitlin, Daisy went on, she was going to put the idea to him. And now, in the meantime, she added, she intended to make a start on that ever-growing pile of ironing.

'I'd just as soon you didn't, Mum. I can do it tonight, when it's cooler,' Angie told her.

As she expected, her words fell on deaf ears and, while Evie slept, Daisy, stubborn as ever, set up the ironing board and, with the radio tuned in to Radio Two and Ed Stewart, ironed for the next half an hour.

At two thirty, Calum returned. 'Have Jacko called in yet with that ice cream?' he enquired, as soon as he stepped inside the shop.

Angie looked up from sorting various packets of food into their correct sell-by date order. 'No,' she said. 'Did he tell you any special time?'

'Mid-afternoon,' said Calum, with certainty. 'You've got enough space in the deep-freeze for when he do, have you?'

'I expect so. If not, your mother and I can take a few of the cartons in our own fridge-freezers.'

After pondering for a moment, Calum decided to leave the subject of Caitlin and the nannying job until later in the evening when he and Angie would have time to sit down for a proper talk.

'Great.' He nodded. 'I'm going up to have a quick wash and brush-up now.'

Angie put down the pack of vegetarian lasagne she'd been about to move, and straightened up, rubbing her back.

'Try not to wake the baby, Cal,' she said. 'The longer she stays asleep the better it will be for Daisy. I don't mind if I've got her around me all evening, just as long as your mum doesn't have to be bothered with her.'

Before going upstairs, Calum stuck his head round the living-room door to say hello to his mother. She paused and, looking up from her ironing, asked him how Caitlin was. She informed him of her plan to invite Caitlin to stay at Cedar Keys for the next few days. Just long enough to fully recover her strength, she said.

Slightly surprised, and secretly rather pleased, Calum expressed his assent before creeping quietly upstairs. Five minutes later he came down again, and went out to the kitchen to make tea. The thought crossed his mind that so far he'd seen no sign of Gyp and, even more unusually, neither had he heard him bark when he first came in.

Whistling softly, Calum set out three mugs, then reached into the refrigerator for the milk. As he turned to look for the sugar bowl, his attention was caught by a trickle of palest pink liquid seeping in under the closed back door.

'Bloody hell,' he cursed. 'Bloody hell,' he yelled again, hoping against hope it wasn't what he suddenly thought it was. He flung the door wide.

The back yard sloped downwards from the broad metal gate which, right now, was jammed open. Blocking its closure was a pile of a dozen or more cardboard boxes from the bottom of which issued a frothy stream of Iceberg Raspberry Ripple ice cream! Picking his way through the gooey mess, Calum examined the boxes more closely. *Family packs of ice cream blocks, in flimsy cardboard packaging, ready for dividing up into hundreds of individual slices,* he thought, and all of it bloody ruined – melted to buggery in the hottest-ever August afternoon that he could remember.

Daisy, having heard his angry expletives, had come to the doorway, her hand to her mouth, watching in total disbelief.

'Where's the dog got to, I wonder?' she asked quietly.

Calum cursed again – even more forcefully than before.

244

'Don't blaspheme, my son, I don't like to hear all that,' Daisy told him. 'Your dog's been waiting all day for you to give it some exercise – no wonder he's done a bunk.'

'God, bloody, hang me, Mother,' Calum groused, 'I've hardly had a minute to call me own all day. I thought the kids would have took him out. Why else 'ud I have called in the Smuggler's and had a quick pint on me way home from town? Now look what's bloody happened.'

'You can't leave *everything* to everyone else,' Daisy said, rubbing her brow wearily, 'Oh, well – he's having a nice walk now. He'll be getting all the exercise he wants!'

'If he don't get lost and never come back again,' Calum replied dolefully. 'Yeah, *nice one, Ma.* He must think he've hit the bloody jackpot this time.'

Angie, looking at the mess, remembered hearing Gyp bark at one fifteen, she said, when she and Holly were eating their lunch. Holly had looked out of her back kitchen window and noticed the cat sitting on the wall; they'd assumed it was teasing him. There *was* a lorry revving up loudly at the time, they recalled, although Holly could see no sign of it from the window.

'Over an *hour* and a *quarter* ago – no wonder the bloody stuff's melted all to hell!' exploded Calum. 'Just wait till I get my hands on that bloody Jacko. I'll marmalise the stupid sod, I will. He haven't got the pissing brains he was born with – old Kevin were right all along. He always said he were a complete moron, and now we all

245

knows he's right.'

'Is any of it salvageable?' Daisy wondered aloud.

'Do it look like it, Ma?' he growled in disgust.

'Well, we'd best try and mop it up, I suppose,' his mother said, turning to get her bucket and mop.

'We'll need a bloody snow plough on this bloody lot – not a bloody bucket and mop, Ma,' Calum groaned.

As Daisy bent down to lift the bucket, she felt the pain cut across her chest. What a damned old nuisance it is, she thought, determined to ignore it and battle on. It was no use, though – when she tried again, the pain became worse.

'Sorry, Calum,' she said, 'but I'm going to have to go and lie down.'

Before leaving, she reminded him to be sure to tell Caitlin she was welcome to stay for a while with her and Josh.

Calum gave Daisy a big hug. He was certain Caitlin would want to come, he said, and he'd be bringing her to Upalong the following morning. He was going to ask Angie to loan her some clothes to come home in.

It had crossed his mind to say that Caitlin had expressed an interest in the post of au pair. There would be plenty of time to tell her that, though, after he'd had a chat with Angie.

Calum went to get a shovel. Making a supreme effort in the soaring heat of the afternoon sun, he started to clean up the mess. 'Talk about shovelling bloody good money down the drain,' he moaned. He didn't take kindly to shifting the shapeless wodge of cardboard sodden with sticky cream which had been deposited in his back yard by the world's greatest number one nincompoop – Jacko flaming, sodding, Jackson!

'When I run into that twit again,' Calum vowed angrily, 'the prize tosser's going to wish that he'd never been born.'

Chapter Sixteen

With a look of distaste, Erin choked down the remains of her toast and stood up ready to go. It was seven thirty am and, while her mother was still in bed, she'd shared a peaceful breakfast with her father before he left for work. In no way had she succumbed to temptation – just the tiniest portion of Special K cereal, and a scrap of plain toast. She found it easy to pull the wool over her father's eyes. Henry Meredith always saw the best in everyone and never looked for their negative side, even more especially where his wife and daughter were concerned.

Despite her fulfilling job, working with the old people, Erin knew she was slipping back into her old habits again. The slightest morsel of food she swallowed had begun to assume the proportions of a three-course, slap-up meal. She hoped that her close friends – Holly, in particular – wouldn't notice and start to nag her again.

Erin knew only too well what was bothering her. It was all tied up with Holly falling head over heels in love with Guy, and the two of them setting up home together. There had been one brief period when she'd held on to the dream that the wonderful Dominic Stone, while not *fully* accepting Holly's defection, would, nevertheless, switch his amorous attentions to herself.

The dream wasn't to be, though, for a day or so ago his sister, Jazz, had casually mentioned that he would be flying out to Kampala at the end of the month to join his friend Marcus, who was already working in Uganda with ActionAid. Dominic had recently completed his six months' surgical training rotation at the Gloucestershire hospital, and was due to start the new job in September. Erin was devastated. She'd found Marcus's departure hard enough to come to terms with, even though she'd known from the first night they met that he'd soon be going to Africa. In the few weeks she'd known him, Marcus had become a really good friend ... someone she felt truly comfortable with. They had gone to several discos and parties together, and she'd missed him like stink when he went.

But as for Dominic going too – she was in despair; it seemed her whole world was falling apart. Jazz would be leaving for Warwick in October to commence her university course, while Holly, in Erin's book, was as good as gone: so wrapped up was she in Guy, she hardly had a moment to spare for any of her old schoolfriends.

Erin paused in front of the kitchen wall-mirror to run a comb through her long straight tresses. She could hear her mother moving about overhead. Roxanne would soon be down in the kitchen, she didn't doubt, demanding another cup of tea, though Henry had already taken her up enough cupfuls to fill a reservoir. Erin decided it was time to depart. Going to the foot of the stairs she bade Roxanne goodbye, before hurrying out to the back garden shed where she kept her trusty old bike.

In her powder-blue cotton blouse and calf-length flowered skirt, Erin was suitably clad for her job as care worker. She would have preferred to be wearing trousers – or shorts, maybe, on a day like today – but the matron-in-charge at The Conifers nursing home insisted on her female staff wearing skirts.

Even at this early hour, the sun was high on a promise. Its beams were strong and probing as they caressed the trickling waters of the trout stream that ran beneath the little stone bridge, near where the road forked away from the village. After the bridge, a long straight lane sliced directly through the dazzling fields aglow with summer harvest.

Dust particles danced in the rays of the sun like a million-zillion specks of summer snow and, as Erin pedalled along, a film of dust rose from the tarmac road surface painting her feet a rich copper red. In the large field on her left, a combine harvester was cruelly plundering the ripe golden corn, scarlet field poppies and saffron-centered moon daisies falling innocent victims to the indiscriminate advance of the ravenous state-of-the-art machinery.

Feeling virtually barefoot in her flimsy summer sandals, Erin pressed the pedals down, loving the feeling of freedom that cycling gave her. It was at moments like this she felt most confident; completely in charge of herself. If only *everything* in life was as simple as this, she thought. A country girl born and bred, she knew there was only one thing in the world that could possibly drag her away. If *Dominic Stone* wiggled his tiniest finger in her direction, she'd happily travel to Timbuktu, if that was where he was.

Bright, magenta-hued red campion and drifts of yellow ragwort had transformed the borders on either side of the lane into ribbons of natural beauty. In the dust-speckled grass, buttercup-bright celandines sparkled like stars beneath the hot sun's rays. Above Erin's head, for as far as she could see, the August sky stretched wide and blue as the bluest summer cornflower. She filled her lungs with the clear fresh air, breathing it out again through her nose, so that it cleared her head more thoroughly than an expensive session in the sauna room of the local health club could do.

Her thoughts drifted back to her father's conversation at the breakfast table. He'd been banging on about California again, lost in his own personal American dream. It was a pity it wasn't Africa he wanted to visit, Erin thought. She would gladly accompany him there.

In *her* private dream, she would – by some miracle – run into Dominic Stone, toiling away in the impossible heat, up to his eyes in pus and gore, tormented almost to breaking point by the buzzing mosquitoes and deadly tsetse fly. She, *Erin Meredith,* all kitted out in a khaki safari suit, like an oldtime movie star in the nostalgic movies she and Holly loved to see, would fly into his arms; he would cuddle her tightly and swear never to let her go. He'd realise at long last there was no other woman alive who would love him as much as she did.

At the crossroads at the end of the lane Erin dismounted from her bicycle to wait for a farm tractor, towing an empty trailer, to rattle past. Bobby Ayres, a boy she'd known since childhood, was in the driving seat, and she returned his friendly wave.

The dream of Dominic faded, and she reflected once more on her father's taste for the more civilised refinements of California. Whether or not to take Roxanne was what concerned him most – an imponderable problem for anyone. Erin herself wouldn't have wanted her mother with her, either, if she planned to visit the places of interest, history and culture that he did.

It would be an altogether different matter if her father's idea of a perfect holiday was a sightseeing trip to Nashville, or Dolly Parton's childhood home in the Smoky Mountains of Tennessee, she thought. Anywhere there was music playing, and glamorous people swanning around, would suit her mother to the ground. America wasn't somewhere that Erin wanted to go while the love of her life was slaving away in Africa. At Mityana, Uganda – one degree north of the equator – the heat was probably horrendous, but that was where her heart was, and where she longed to be.

The Conifers, an Edwardian mansion of some distinction, lay at the end of a winding, rhododendron-bordered driveway, which, until a few weeks previously, had been a breathtaking corridor of purples and pinks, which people came from miles around to admire. Erin preferred the more delicate shades of the creamy magnolia tree that flowered in early spring but she had to agree the rhododendrons in bloom were a truly remarkable sight. Now, in mid-August, their dense shiny leaves created a cool, shady avenue leading to the double-storeyed, grey stone house which had once been the home of the local gentry.

It was a pleasant place to work, and Erin had no qualms at all about spending the next eight hours performing some of the more mundane tasks that the job entailed. She loved her old people without exception, even the crotchety, crankier ones.

Halfway along the quarter-mile driveway, she was almost brought off her bicycle by a be-draggled, and extremely muddy-looking poodle that scuttled out from beneath the rhododendron hedge. Hot on its tail was Rusty MacPherson's wire-haired terrier, Gyp. Erin had heard her mother say that both dogs had gone missing.

'So this is where you've finished up!' she exclaimed and, jumping off her bike, grabbed them by their collars. She scooped the tiny poodle up into her arms and called to Gyp to follow her. Pushing through a gap in the hedge, she went across the wide lawn into the kitchen gardens, where she'd noticed some disused outbuildings. Shutting the dogs inside one of them, she raced back to the pathway to pick up her bike. She needed to get to a telephone, to let the MacPhersons know that Rusty's dog had turned up safely.

The phone rang at Mariner's Cottage just as Angie was settling down to breast-feed Evie. 'Sorry, my little one,' she murmured as she got to her feet to answer it.

'Hello, Erin,' she said, surprised to hear Erin's voice so early in the morning. 'Holly's not here. She's moved into her own place now. Do you want me to give her a message?'

'It isn't Holly I want,' Erin said, and went on to tell Angie her reason for calling. She advised Calum to fetch his dog from The Conifers before the Fletchers discovered that their poodle and Gyp had been running loose together.

As soon as Erin finished speaking, Angie put through a call to Upalong, where she guessed Calum would be. After relaying the message to Josh, she settled back in the easy chair to continue her baby's feed. The boys were still asleep in bed. In the blessed peace and quiet before they awoke, as she fed Evie, Angie's thoughts went back over the events of the last four days.

First, the ice cream. What a mess, she thought ... but at least Calum had satisfactorily cleared it all up! Next had come Daisy and another scare about her health; though Daisy had explained it since, attributing the pains in her chest to indigestion from the generous amount of onion that Josh had put into their lunchtime flan.

Gyp's sudden disappearance had been a further upset, if not a terribly serious one from Angie's point of view, though Calum had created a great hue and cry when the dog failed to return for its bowl of doggie-mix that evening. Since then, he'd been scouring the village and surrounding countryside looking for it.

It would be altogether hilarious, thought Angie, if Calum's dog *had* run off with Adge Fletcher's bitch. *Adge Fletcher,* his own worst enemy! From what Erin said, it seemed likely that it had. Angie could hardly wait to tell Holly the news; she'd be certain to see the funny side, too.

'Oops, darling...' Angie rested Evie over the crook of her arm to bring up the wind that was troubling her. After she'd rubbed the baby's back quite firmly for a minute, up came an almighty burp, and Angie put her to her other breast where she began to suck contentedly. Angie's peace of mind – fragile at the best of times – had been marred in the last few days by the knowledge that Calum, and up to a point Daisy, appeared to have turned against her – all because she'd offered the job of mother's help to the girl she interviewed the afternoon of the ice cream fiasco.

Serina Whitelaw, a highly suitable, neatly turned-out twenty-four-year-old, had exactly the right experience that Angie was looking for. Her excellent references and sensible attitude towards child care seemed the answer to all her prayers. Most importantly, Angie *liked* her and could imagine living with her – and that, to her mind, was the number one priority.

Serina had also agreed, though perhaps with not quite as much enthusiasm, to take responsibility for seeing that the twins were fed and watered ... *watered,* as Angie explained to her, meaning the regular use of flannel, soap and towel. Angie's pleasure at finding such a suitable girl had been dashed almost immediately when Calum informed her that he'd more or less offered the job to the young woman he'd acted as mother hen to for the previous twenty-four hours.

'How dare you, without consulting *me?*' Angie had yelled. 'It's my *baby's* welfare we're talking about, and I'm damned if I'll let just anybody take care of my kids. *No one,* unless I've thoroughly checked them out myself. Do I make myself clear?'

'Suit your bloody self then,' Calum raged back, 'but if *that's* your idea of somebody suitable, then I'll eat my bloody hat.'

He'd seen the girl leaving, he said, and neither he nor his mother had liked the look of her.

'I don't care whether you like the look of her or not,' Angie had said, secretly dismayed that he appeared to be speaking for Daisy too. Ever since then, she'd got the distinct impression that Calum was avoiding her.

As Angie had thought, Calum *was* at the bungalow. He was enjoying an early morning cup of tea with Josh when the telephone rang, and Josh went off to answer it. Through the open door of the lounge, Calum could hear his mother telling Caitlin about a miscarriage she'd had when he was just a baby. It was news to him, and he listened with interest for a while but soon his thoughts returned to the rift between Angie and

255

himself. If the atmosphere got any worse, he told himself, he would pack his bags and piss off out of there as soon as the dog turned up.

His mother had agreed with him that Caitlin would have been perfect for the job; she'd been no more impressed by the other woman than he was. Nonetheless, she had stressed quite firmly that the children were Angie's and hers alone – whoever she chose to look after them, it must be her own decision.

But Calum's disappointment on Caitlin's behalf was immeasurable. He'd seen the girl Angie was going to employ, and wasn't at all impressed. She'd looked a poncy sort of madam – the sort who'd be shocked to buggery to find herself sharing the same living quarters as *him*. He'd shock her, though, he thought ... would he ever? He'd show the jumped-up little mare just how the other half lived.

To top it all, during the course of the argument Angie had accused him of fancying Caitlin. He'd denied it, of course, yet the accusation had caused him some degree of alarm. He didn't *think* he fancied Caitlin – Suzi Glue was his one and only love – yet the way he'd been with Caitlin these last few days, so soft, and utterly unlike his usual self, it had been a complete eye-opener to him. He'd never dreamed he was capable of such softness, but now that he knew he was, he was determined he would put it to good use as soon as he patched things up with Suzi.

When he'd broken the news to Caitlin that Angie had taken on someone else, she hadn't seemed too surprised. As soon as she recovered her strength, she said, she would be making alternative arrangements. But what would she do, and where would she go, pondered Calum, miserable on her behalf.

Josh breezed back into the kitchen, smiling fit to bust. 'It seems that your dog's been having it away with my sister-in-law Min's toy poodle,' he announced cheerily.

'Never – not that bloody thing – it's no bigger than a flaming rat.' Calum was so surprised, he almost dropped his mug, spilling tea all over his newly washed jeans. Covering his eyes with his hands, he groaned, 'I'll wring the furry bugger's neck when I get hold of him ... off having his wicked way with that blasted apology for a mutt.'

'You have to laugh,' Josh chortled. 'According to Angie, they're hardly recognisable. They're caked all over with flipping mud. Erin Meredith's just rung her from The Conifers to say she's got them both shut up in an outbuilding there for the time being. She wants you to fetch Gyp quickly, before the Fletchers get wind of Flossie's whereabouts.'

Calum was aware how highly the Fletchers rated their tiny poodle. Min and her daughters often exercised it in the recreation ground where the twins took Gyp. The boys had commented on the fact that the two dogs seemed to have taken a shine to one another, and Calum had warned them not to let Gyp play too roughly with it, in case he mistook the poodle for a fluffy toy. If the Fletchers' dog sustained an injury and had to be taken to a vet's, Adge would be after him with an insurance claim, posthaste, Calum knew. There was no doubt about it, the animal was worth a bob or two.

'Bloody hell, don't anybody let on to Adge Fletcher they've bin getting it on together,' he groaned, rubbing his fist across his forehead to smooth out the worry lines he could feel forming there.

He owed young Erin Meredith a debt of gratitude, that was for sure. All hell would have broken loose if she'd telephoned the Fletchers first.

Clutching a damp J-cloth in her hand, Roxanne pushed through the swing louvre doors and went into the dingy back room of the betting shop to empty the filthy ashtrays. Tipping a heap of revolting dog-ends into the wastebin, she wiped over the surface of the table and the seats of the chairs where the dirty buggers had a habit of depositing their ash. Her thoughts a million miles away, she was suddenly startled by the sound of an almighty snore.

The snore turned into a moan, as a prone figure, garbed in an old-fashioned fawn gabardine mac, fell off the narrow leatherette-covered bench on to the tea-stained carpet by her feet. Roxanne curbed a strong impulse to stick her cyclamen-painted toenails into the shape she recognised to be Leonard Snook. She'd had just about enough of the horrible little man. The number of times she'd had to turf him out of the place recently – he was fast becoming a thorn in her flesh.

Snooky scrambled to his feet with all the finesse

of a grounded camel; his lacklustre brown eyes stared up into hers, the expression on his hapless face pleading with her not to be *too* hard on him.

'Sorry, love,' he stammered, stooping to pick up the scattered pages of his *Sun* newspaper, 'I must have nodded off a little minute.'

'Nodded off?' answered Roxanne, scornfully. 'I should bloody well think you have. What d'you think this is, a flaming dosshouse ... the Hilton Hotel, or summat?'

'Sorry, my love ... Mrs ... Mrs,' Snooky stammered nervously, eyeing Roxanne's formidable stance, arms crossed over ample bosom, legs planted firmly like tree trunks to the floor.

'*Mrs Meredith* to you – only Roxanne, or love, to my friends,' she told him. 'And you won't find me *that* easy to get round, no matter *what* you ends up calling me.'

Not the likes of you, she told herself. Different if he'd been Kevin Costner or Clint Eastwood, but there again, she mused, *she* should be so lucky!

'I'm sorry,' the little man repeated again, hanging his head low, and refusing to look her in the eye. 'I ain't got nowhere else to go, though – my missus've chucked me out.'

'I thought you was in digs, up at Missionary Row,' Roxanne replied.

The other punters had told her that Snooky had fallen upon hard times since his wife had thrown him out, due to his perpetual gambling. She had caught him dipping into their mortgage money to finance his lifelong addiction.

'The landlady've told me to find somewhere

259

else, on account of me missus taking all me money off me and I can't pay the rent this week,' he whined.

'You should've thought of that before you laid out twenty quid on that deadbeat loser at Wimbledon Dogs this morning,' Roxanne reminded him scathingly. 'All of what you've lost this week would have *more* than paid your rent.'

'Just let me wait here till me mates come,' he pleaded, 'Rusty, and Kevin, and all that crowd.'

'They ain't your mates – they'm always saying they'm fed up of you, and you needs to sort yerself out,' she told him. 'Anyway – unless you got money to bet with, I can't have you hanging about in yere. Go on over to the Bluebird, why don't you? That's most likely where they'll be.'

'I can't go in there, without the money for a cup of tea,' said Snooky. 'And it's early yet – the rest of 'em don't come in till about three.'

'Oh, I'm buggered. Yere – have a cup of tea on me.' Roxanne took some coins out of her overall pocket and flung them in his direction. 'Now take yerself off, and don't come back until you finds yerself flush again, and I don't know when *that* will be, I'm sure.'

She watched the pathetic figure scramble to pick up the ten and twenty-pence coins from the floor, and wished him gone so that she could be left alone to think in peace about the hot date she had lined up with Marty Riley at the Relax-a-Vous Motel.

Their first *all-night* date it was to be. He'd palmed his wife off with some story that he would be appearing in a one-night show at a nightclub in Cardiff when, in reality, he'd be heading out for the Bridgwater Road, where he'd booked a double room at the newly refurbished motel. With his firm promise of a cup of tea in bed the next morning, and the latest colour TV on which to watch breakfast television, Roxanne was looking forward immensely to an eventful night ahead. If wishing had anything to do with it, it would be a night filled with highly charged passion and lust.

'You don't honestly think we'll have time to sit and watch TV?' she'd told him jokingly while they were dancing together at the Smuggler's Retreat last week. 'We'll soon see what you're made of, my cocker,' she'd added huskily, digging him sharply in the ribs with her long pointed fingernails. 'You've bin telling me for the last six weeks Clint Eastwood's got nothink on *you*.'

'There's plenty of life in the old dog yet,' Marty replied, winking so suggestively that Roxanne feared his wife would spot his carryings on and knock their arrangements sky high.

The fact that Henry had been present at the time didn't worry Roxanne at all. He was perfectly capable of sitting for hours on end, not noticing anything except what he wanted to. Remembering Henry, she gave the long bench that ran all round the room an extra-hard rub with the polishing cloth. Her husband lived on a different planet from everyone else, she'd decided many years ago. It was no wonder she felt the need for a bit on the side whenever someone halfway interesting came along.

'You never knows what's round the corner, so

make hay while the sun shines,' she chirruped cheerfully to the friendly announcer whose programme she was listening to on Radio Bristol. But the chap sounded fairly young, she thought. She didn't imagine he'd reached the point in life where he needed to grab the nearest thing on offer, which was the case with her and Marty Riley right now.

With his ability to sing like Charley Pride, Marty fancied himself no end. 'Until you've seen a sample of *my* performance, ma'am, you ain't seen nuttin' yet,' he'd said to Roxanne while they were smooching together last Saturday night.

'Yee-haw,' she'd yelled out loud, causing his wife to glare at them from across the room, where she and her ancient mother, with faces like withered prunes, sat sipping their port-and-lemons at a table near the stage.

And even *then*, Henry hadn't raised his head or glanced in their direction. That just about said it all, Roxanne told herself. Sticking out her tongue through pouted lips, she threw her absent husband a loud raspberry. Twenty-four years of being married to Henry – she was long overdue for another night on the razzle, and she didn't give a tinker's cuss what anybody else might think.

'So long, babe,' Marty had murmured when the dance ended, pinching her bum slyly, so no one else could see. Then, with a wave of his hand, he'd sashayed over to join his crabby-faced wife and her equally sour-looking mother.

Roxanne remembered the last time she'd been invited to spend a dirty night away; it had never actually got off the ground – not *romantically*, that was! It was the week of the Cheltenham Gold Cup, and her boss's close friend, Sidney Digweed, had taken her there in his fast Jaguar car. After a pleasant afternoon, when Sidney had backed the big winner, they'd stopped off at an Indian restaurant on their way back to his hotel – a beautiful manor house that nestled in a gentle fold of the picturesque Cotswold Hills.

The Bombay Duck was an eating place that Sidney's best friend Norman had recommended he should try. *Some friend*, Roxanne reminded herself – they must have used gunpowder in their chicken tandoori because, later, back at the hotel, she and Sidney had done nothing but dive into the posh en-suite bathroom all night.

Sidney had got her to think up song titles, like 'Farting the Night Away', which he'd sung at the top of his voice, then, at five in the morning, he'd gone into a rendition of 'Strangers in the Night' ... for *strangers*, he'd substituted the word *farting*. A vindaloo nightmare, no less. There'd been no bonking done on that occasion, and neither, Roxanne was glad to say, had Sidney Digweed ever set foot in the betting shop since.

She hoped never to see him again. He was so far removed from Henry, who didn't even like her to use the word *fart*, that he'd disgusted even *her*. Five months after that kerfuffle, it still bothered her when she thought how shocked Henry would have been to have seen and heard the way they'd carried on in one of the smartest, most expensive hotels in the whole of Gloucestershire.

Roxanne had only one real complaint against Henry: he was too damn serious for his own good. If he'd only lighten up a little, she thought, he wouldn't be bad company at all. She wasn't really happy deceiving him by having these extramarital affairs, but she couldn't live his drab existence either – not without taking time off now and then to have a little fun.

Pursing her lips defiantly, she emptied the rubbish into a black refuse bag, and dumped the J-cloth in with it. If Henry was unable to provide her with an occasional bit of excitement, she thought, then on his own stupid head be it.

Chapter Seventeen

'This is nice,' Daisy said, sitting up in bed and taking the cup of tea that Josh had brought her.

'You're telling me. It's not many people who get tea brought to them in bed like this each morning.'

'I hope I make it up to you in other ways,' Daisy suggested.

'You do, my love – you certainly do that all right.'

Thoughts of the lovely lovemaking they'd shared earlier that morning were still fresh in his mind. They'd had to be awfully quiet, because of Caitlin sleeping along the hallway but, as always with Daisy, it had been exceedingly fulfilling and good.

Josh's only regret was that he hadn't known Daisy before she married her Scotsman, and he his wife, Rhoda, with whom he'd muddled along for more than thirty years. Not unhappily, he mused now – just a mild discontent which he'd never quite been able to put his finger on, although Rhoda's interfering relatives might well have had something to do with it.

Daisy had brought into his life a kind of happiness that he'd never really imagined existed. Warm and tender; cosy and comforting. He knew now what he'd been missing all his life.

'So Calum's gone to fetch the cat,' remarked Daisy.

'Mm ... said he'd get out before the crowds. You know what Weston's like this time of year.'

'Especially on a Saturday.'

Josh shook his head. 'A cat now! Whatever blinking next?'

'Shss,' said Daisy, holding her finger to her lips. 'She'll hear you if you're not careful.'

'A home for waifs and strays,' Josh announced loudly, grinning at Daisy's worried expression.

'*Josh* – she'll hear you,' she hissed.

'No chance of that,' Josh told her, 'she's gone for a walk up over the field, towards the coast road.'

'Oh! Why ever didn't you tell me. Thank goodness for that,' Daisy replied, reaching over to his side of the bed for another pillow to put behind her head. 'I'll be glad when I can get up there again under my own steam,' she said. 'I really miss my country walks.'

'Not to worry. They'll soon sort you out – get to

the bottom of what's wrong.'

'I hope so. I'm beginning to feel like a stranded duck that can't fly or swim. All I can do is waddle.'

'Not *all* you can do, my love. You proved that already this morning,' Josh said, smiling.

'Even *that* caused the top of my head to hurt,' Daisy said, genuinely puzzled by the strange sensation that seemed to have made her brain expand just at the crucial moment. She had experienced a rare moment of panic, hoping it wasn't the symptoms of a stroke.

Josh went back to the kitchen, and she reclined against the plumped-up pillow. Sipping her tea slowly, she wondered what the future held in store for her, healthwise. It wasn't in her nature to worry for long, though, and two minutes later, she flung back the bedclothes and went over to the window to see if she could catch a glimpse of Caitlin climbing the steep hill that led to the coast road.

The view from Josh's bedroom – hers now as well, she remembered – was of a grass-covered hillside rising high above the village, finishing at the road that led to Kilkenny Bay and, in the other direction, Clevedon. From the summit was a magnificent view of the Bristol Channel and the two road bridges that crossed over to Wales. At night the town of Newport, directly opposite, looked especially attractive with twinkling lights that stretched away along the coast for miles. As far west as Cardiff, Daisy guessed, and maybe even beyond that. Harbour lights ... street lights ... power stations ... sprawling smelting works that burned permanently with a luminous glow ... an endless, ongoing string of glittering, friendly, welcoming beacons.

Daisy stood at the window a few moments longer, thinking of the many times in the past she'd walked up there with Josh. Seeing no sign of Caitlin, she popped back into bed.

She reached into the bedside cupboard and lifted out her well-thumbed Bible. Daisy didn't consider herself a religious person as such, but since Curt's disappearance, so sudden and unexpected, she liked to start each day with renewed hope. Josh teased her about it, saying she had a direct line to *Him Upstairs*. Daisy didn't know about that; she had a strong suspicion there were plenty of churchgoers who would frown upon her for living in sin with Josh. But *He* understood, she was sure – and, in any case, it was only a matter of time before she and Josh got round to tying the knot.

'Loving someone is bound to be good,' she murmured, 'it's certainly not doing anyone else any harm.'

Turning a few more pages, she found the story she was looking for – the parable of the lost son. She couldn't explain it to anyone else, but it gave her a certain amount of comfort to read that this one had turned up safe and sound. Until someone in authority came and told her that they'd found Curt's body, Daisy knew she would never really be able to believe he was dead.

Calum was on his way to Weston, taking the old Bristol road for a change. He slipped in the

Clapton tape, then changed his mind and took it out again, substituting one of his old Eagles collection instead. The tape had started playing at 'Lay Down Sally', and he could well do without reminders of Suzi this morning or, indeed, at any other time.

As he approached the outskirts of the seaside town, a shimmer of sunlight caught his eye from the summit of a high hill to his right. Bouncing off windows, reflecting from metals, it illuminated a castle he'd never noticed before, fairytale and white, which reminded Calum of the castle in *Cinderella,* Lucie's very favourite video, which she always used to ask him to watch with her.

'Emma and Lucie...' He breathed their names and sighed deeply. How he missed those two little girls. If he and Suzi had still been together, he would more than likely have brought them with him this morning, just for the pleasure of their company. He wasn't able to do anything about that particular situation at present but, by the end of the month, when he'd completed the first of the *big ones,* he might be in a better position to persuade Suzi to take him back.

He turned his mind again to the reason for his journey. Caitlin had said her cat wasn't exactly being mistreated, but it was certainly being given the cold shoulder – unwanted by her parents, and even more particularly by her father's dog. Daisy and Josh had agreed she could keep it at the bungalow for the time being because she'd seemed so unhappy about it.

If only she had come with him now, he would have felt a lot more comfortable. They were her damned parents, after all, he told himself. Caitlin had changed her mind about coming at the very last minute, though ... said she wasn't ready to meet them yet, not until she knew what she'd be doing in the immediate future. To avoid the awkward questions he knew they'd ask, Calum decided to stick to his story that Caitlin had had appendicitis.

Calum turned into the straight tree-lined avenue where the Hutchisons lived, looking out for the number that Caitlin had given him. He didn't intend to be hanging about here for long. He'd only come to collect her cat, after all.

He parked his car outside the Hutchisons' gate and, walking up the short concrete driveway, entered the neat red-brick porch and pressed the doorbell. Caitlin's mother, when she came to the door, was a dead ringer for Mrs Bucket in the popular television comedy, he thought: her voice, her manner, almost every bloody thing about her. He wouldn't have been surprised if, like the real Mrs *Bouquet* when faced with a visitor she didn't approve of, she'd reached out and yanked him inside. Olive Hutchison spoke to him politely, though. The posh old dink didn't actually ask him to remove his shoes, but he had the strongest feeling that she would have liked him to.

Both Caitlin's mother and father seemed fairly put out that their daughter hadn't come in person and, as Calum expected, they proceeded to give him an in-depth interrogation as to the exact nature of her illness. They had been making plans to visit her in hospital and were disappointed to hear that, although she'd been discharged, she wasn't feeling well enough to see them yet.

They were a strange couple, Calum thought. Olive acted and sounded like Lady Muck, while her husband had the same lugubrious expression and thin appearance as Christopher Lee, playing the part of a ghoul. His voice was noticeably mournful and whiny; Calum could well understand Caitlin not wanting to cop an earful of *that* when she was still a bit off-colour herself.

Holding tightly to the collar of his slavering hound – an excitable, tan-coloured Boxer called Franklyn – Roland Hutchison led Calum out of the back door and into the adjoining garage. The little black cat was huddled up in a corner as far away from the Baskerville menace as it could get, and with good cause, thought Calum. Approaching it slowly, he cradled the frightened bundle of fur in his arms for a minute or two before lifting it gently into the plastic travelling container which he found, as Caitlin had told him, on a shelf above her father's workbench. Bidding her parents farewell, he put the pet carrier on the front passenger seat of the car and a suitcase of Caitlin's clothes into the boot, then set off for home. The cat meowed the whole way, so he was more than pleased to dump it off at Upalong, where Caitlin was waiting expectantly for it.

By the time he arrived back at Maritime Way Calum was feeling more down in the dumps than ever. Starkey's failure to contact him with the coded message he'd expected to have received by now regarding the next job was really getting to him, and the fall-out he'd had with Angie didn't help things a bit. It was the first time he and Angie had ever seriously argued, and Calum was wary of saying or doing anything to cause the rift to grow even wider. He still needed to sleep on the living-room couch, and keep his clothes here, too.

'Sod it,' he muttered, as he hurried past Angie who was serving in the shop, on his way out to the back porch where he kept his old trainers. He was glad the boys had gone away; they'd begun to twig that he and their mother had fallen out, and were curious to know why. They'd left for Swansea at seven this morning with Frank Goodyear and the rest of the Scout troop, aboard Jeff Starling's lavender-painted minibus.

'Oh, well, worse things happen at sea,' Calum muttered, whistling tunelessly to himself He finished tying the laces of his shabby black trainers and went out to the yard to collect his dog. He would get something to eat at the Blue-bird, he decided. He couldn't risk taking Gyp to Upalong – Caitlin's cat might not take too kindly to that.

Sharp at eight o'clock that evening, the taxi picked up Roxanne outside her house at the bottom of Fuzzy Cove High Street and deposited her twenty-five minutes later at the front entrance of the Relax-a-Vous Motel on the Bristol to Bridgwater road. She slipped the driver a nice-sized tip – she was feeling particularly generous tonight – and paused for a moment to adjust the skirt of her new, above-knee-length,

271

leopard-patterned chiffon dress, trying to get it to fall into place as elegantly as on the model at the shop at Portishead where she'd bought it. The dress had cost her an arm and a leg, but Roxanne didn't regret a single penny. Sixty pounds was more than she would normally pay, but this was a special occasion – one well worth dressing up for, she told herself

She'd also lashed out on some new black satin panties and a lacy black brassiere to match. She had purchased the flimsy apparel at an underwear party held by the woman who worked at the Clevedon betting shop. Roxanne was sure her glamorous new underwear wouldn't be wasted on Marty Riley, the way equally sexy garments she'd worn in the past were completely wasted on Henry. Her husband, she knew, wouldn't bat an eyelid if she was to parade around the house in her birthday suit if he'd got his head stuck into a book.

Pausing a moment to adjust the straps on her high-heeled evening shoes, Roxanne reflected on the present state of her marriage. She knew Henry fancied her in his own quiet way, but everything he did she found so terribly boring. He totally lacked surprises, and so did *she* when she was in bed with him. To get him to change would require her to do something so completely unusual, that Roxanne couldn't for the life of her imagine *what*. And when they were out together, he never seemed bothered when other men gave her the glad eye, as so many of them did. She was a fine figure of a woman, he always said, and he wasn't surprised they all wanted to chat her up.

'Oh, well...'

Roxanne stifled the remaining pangs of guilt she'd been feeling with regards to two-timing Henry and, stepping inside the automatic doors of the Relax-a-Vous Motel, she made her way to the bar where Marty had said he'd be waiting.

He spotted her immediately and signalled to her to join him. She was disappointed to see he was wearing a navy-blue pinstriped suit. It was the first time she'd seen him in anything but his stage costume of red plaid shirt and ten-gallon hat and she was dismayed to discover he looked not much different from anyone else. As they met, he grabbed hold of her arm and propelled her towards a table in the far corner of the room.

'Let's sit over here, out of the way,' he said. 'We don't want nobody we know seeing us, or there'll be all hell to pay.'

Speak for yourself, Roxanne thought. It wasn't only Marty's appearance she found strangely unappealing; it was his nervous manner, too, that made her wonder if he was, after all, the man of the world she'd thought him to be.

'What are you drinking?' he asked. 'I thought we'd have a quiet drink *first*,' he added, smiling suggestively.

This creeping about, and putting off the important things, wasn't at all what Roxanne had had in mind – not after their eager, passionate fumbles in the back yard of the Smuggler's Retreat on country and western nights.

'I thought you said you was getting champagne ... champagne in the room, you said,' she reminded him.

Marty pushed back his almost non-existent hairline. 'So I did ... ah, so I did,' he confessed.

'You told me Clint Eastwood had nothink on you,' Roxanne added. 'That's what we come yere for, I thought, so's we can spend the night together, making wild passionate love. Just like Clint, you said.'

'Yeah, yeah, you're right. 'Course, you're right, my love. It's only that–'

Marty glanced towards the doorway, as if he expected his wife and mother-in-law to walk in at any minute.

God, he's chickening out – he's as nervous as my Henry, Roxanne thought, and then she changed her mind about that. In many ways Henry might seem the nervous type, but he was resolutely steadfast in his love for her. She had the feeling that Henry would protect her to the death, no matter who came along to challenge him. Where she and their daughter were concerned, he could always be relied upon to put them first.

'I did ... I ordered champagne when I booked the room – I just forgot for a minute,' Marty apologised. Rising to his feet, he swilled down the remainder of his beer.

'Are you ready then, love? Let's go,' he said, leading the way out to the foyer where the lifts were.

He pressed the up button, and they alighted at the first floor. Roxanne followed her cowboy lover along the plain straight corridor until he came to a halt outside the door of room number thirty-nine.

Roxanne's spirits lifted. This was what she'd been waiting for. 'Got the key?' she asked, hitching her black velvet pouch bag higher on to her shoulder, and subtly lowering the neckline of her leopard-fabric dress to reveal her new black lace, F cup, cross-your-heart bra.

'No key, see?' said Marty, inserting what looked to her like a credit card into the round metal door handle. He shook his head and looked at her, as if bemused by the wonders of modern science.

'They'll be using them bleepers what you flips at the car door next,' he said.

After a quick glance back along the empty corridor, he appeared to relax and, taking hold of Roxanne's arm, pulled her close to him.

'There! What d'you think, eh?'

His arm round her waist, Roxanne stood in the open doorway, admiring the smart modern decor. There was a king-size bed, covered with a bedspread in an attractive turquoise and gold mock-tapestry design. The two large pictures on the biscuit-coloured wallpaper were of exotic birds, one a peacock, its tail feathers displayed in magnificent splendour, the second a flamingo, peachy-pink, long-legged and graceful. It was all very classily tasteful, Roxanne decided. Quite the nicest motel room she'd ever been in.

'Haven't they ever done it out love*lay*?' she exclaimed, 'And you was right – they *have* left us a bottle of champagne.'

'They better had – I've already paid for it with me credit card. I had to pay up front for the room, too. They never used to want *that* in advance.'

'That's to stop people from pushing off without paying,' Roxanne said, glad to know that an early morning flit was not on the list of probabilities for tomorrow. The last thing she wanted was to make her exit by the fire escape before dawn, as she had done on a couple of occasions in the past. She was too long in the tooth now for those wild, mad adventures, she reminded herself.

'Let's break open that bottle of bubbly, shall we? We've got a long, long night ahead of us, gal,' Marty announced. He went behind her and, placing both arms tightly round her body, pressed up against her sexily.

Roxanne giggled happily, 'Sharon Stone, here we come.' Flinging out her arms, she postured flamboyantly. 'If you're a good boy, Marty, I might do a pose for you with no knickers on,' she said. 'There's a chair over there just like the one she was sat on in *Basic Instinct*.'

'Yippee-yi-yo-ki-ay. Bloody hell, let's get partying then.' Marty leaned back to close the door which met with a sudden, though firm, resistance.

'I'll give thee yippee-yi-yo-ki-ay,' screamed a voice familiar to him, as his wife burst into the room with the force of a rhinoceros on the charge.

'Well, well, well ... it looks as if I've got here just in the nick of time.' The woman's eyes flitted from the double bed to the magnum of brut on the low circular table.

'I knew you were up to something you shouldn't be when I heard you ordering that champagne,' she said. 'I pressed the memory button the moment you'd gone, and it rang *here*. I soon put two and two together when I discovered you wasn't booked where you was meant to be booked – over the bridge, in Cardiff, you liar!'

Marty and Roxanne stood speechless as she pushed her way past them into the room. 'I had a funny feeling this, this ... creature ... was at the bottom of it,' she went on. 'I've seen the way she's been clinging to you, the last few times we've been out at Fuzzy Cove.'

She stared defiantly at them both. 'Well, that's the last time you'll ever appear out *there*, so you can say goodbye to him now, you common cow. You won't be seeing *him* again in a hurry.'

Roxanne had listened to enough. 'If you think I want your bloody old man, you've got another think coming,' she stormed.

'*Think?*' Marty Riley's wife yelled. 'I don't think, I *know*. You're the sort of woman that would make a play for anything in trousers. Well, you can keep your grubby paws off *my* husband from now on, you ... you flighty trollop, you.'

'Let's see what *he's* got to say about it, shall we? What's up with you, Marty? Frightened she might kick you out, or summat?' Roxanne goaded. But her erstwhile lover remained silent; he hadn't yet uttered a word.

'Just because your own husband's as wet as a dripping tap, you needn't think you–' the woman continued.

'My husband wet?' raged Roxanne. 'I'll have you know, my husband's worth fifty of the likes of him. Gormless great bloody show-off – he's

277

nothing but a waste of space, and so are you – so push off, the pair of you, why don't you? Go on, get out.'

Pushing them both out through the door, she slammed it hard behind them and sat down heavily on the turquoise tapestry armchair. She was shaking with anger, drained of strength, and positively gagging for a drink. Something strong, she thought; she hadn't had a sniff of one yet tonight. For a moment she toyed with the idea of phoning room service and asking them to send a waiter to open the bottle of brut, but then she decided against it.

'Sod Marty Riley,' she muttered. 'Sod his wife, and sod his mother-in-law – sod the bloody lot of them.'

Picking up the champagne he'd paid for, she popped the plastic door card into her handbag and made her way down to the foyer. A tot of straight brandy was the tonic she needed to help get over the shock, she decided.

Having organised her night away from home with such careful planning and expectation, she was disappointed not to be sleeping here in that lovely room. Henry was working the night shift, and she had told Erin she'd be staying with her sister, Myrna, at Clapton-in-Gordano while Myrna's husband was away. It seemed a pity not to spend the night in luxury, tell herself she was waiting for a Chippendale to come along, preferably one with no wife in tow. It crossed her mind that handsome Rex Carpenter would have fitted the bill quite nicely, but she suspected he would find her too much of a woman for him. If the poor man's only experience of sex was with that awful ex-wife of his, then it was a pretty safe bet he wouldn't be up to going the full Monty with someone as versatile as *her*.

'Oh, well.' Roxanne pushed aside any further thought of spending the night in that super-luxurious bed. 'I'd better get on home,' she murmured, 'just as soon as I've had me drink.'

Perching her bottom on a bar stool, she placed the bottle of champagne on the stool beside her while she ordered a double brandy. Emptying the goblet in one fell swoop, she called for another the same. She didn't drive ... *couldn't* drive, so at least she had no fear of a breathalyser test.

How to get home, though, was her main consideration. Should she order a taxi, or call a friend? Supposing she were to dial the Smuggler's Retreat, speak to Barry Buckley, and ask if Rusty MacPherson was drinking there tonight? Rusty would be certain to come and fetch her if he knew she was stranded here all alone. And the good thing was, she wouldn't need to go into any details with him – she and Rusty went back a long way: all the way back to the village nursery school, in fact.

They shared a secret that no one else knew – and though others might *suspect*, they would never know for sure. At the age of fourteen, Rusty and Roxanne had taken the biology master's lessons seriously ... very, very seriously ... and put into practice what everyone else in the class was merely writing about. Sex in the sixties wasn't rife among schoolkids the way it was now, Roxanne reflected. It was viewed by responsible adults as a taboo subject, and remained a closed book to most kids of their age. It wasn't something they ever mentioned now but, all the same, the knowledge smouldered beneath the surface, binding them together in some strange way, like a strong, invisible rope.

Roxanne ran her fingers lovingly over the magnum of brut. If she'd been thinking rationally when she came downstairs, she would have left it in the ice bucket to keep cool. Her brain carried out a quick assessment. If Rusty did come to fetch her, it oughtn't to be too difficult to persuade him to accompany her to the bedroom, just to pop the cork.

Smiling a tiny smile, Roxanne picked her way across the luxuriously carpeted foyer to the row of public phone booths inside the main entrance doors. Before she took the champagne back to room thirty-nine, where the silver ice-bucket awaited, she had better find out for certain if Rusty was willing to do an old friend a favour.

Chapter Eighteen

For the first time in months Angie felt like a real woman. Dressed up to the nines for once, tonight she was not just a stay-at-home mum. Admittedly when she sniffed the front of her blouse she thought she detected a slight whiff of milk, but it wasn't that noticeable – not enough, she hoped, to put Rex off.

He'd got the tickets for the one-man tribute to Roy Orbison they both wanted to see. They had good seats, two rows away from the front of the stalls. It was the interval now, and as she sipped her glass of medium white wine Angie looked around the bar, soaking up the sights, hardly able to believe she was here. The night was all hers. Daisy and Josh had taken the baby home to Upalong, with a good supply of nappies and bottles and a packet of powdered baby milk from the village chemist's.

With a movement of his head, Rex indicated to her to follow him, and they elbowed their way through the crush to a place that was less crowded. Out in the cool passageway, they leaned against the crimson wall, able to enjoy their drinks without fear of being jostled. As before, she felt strangely tongue-tied in Rex's company now they were in a social situation.

For a moment neither spoke, and then they did simultaneously. 'He's really...' Angie began.

Rex continued the sentence for her, adding, 'This guy's excellent, isn't he? Sounds exactly like the Big O.'

'Wonderful.' Angie nodded in agreement. 'What talent that man had! I didn't dream he'd written all those other songs – not only the ones he recorded himself.'

'I know.' Rex tipped his glass and finished the remains of his lager. His nut-brown eyes regarded her seriously. 'Incredible,' he added quietly, as he turned away and began studying the programme.

Angie sipped the rest of her wine, and they

lapsed into silence again for a minute or two. The words of the song she'd been listening to earlier, 'Too Soon to Know', were dancing a tantalising pirouette through her head.

'Time to go, I think,' Rex said after a while, taking her glass and resting it on a windowsill.

People were starting to move, although the bell hadn't gone. They went back to their places in the stalls and, the moment the curtain went up, Rex reached across and took hold of her hand.

'Pretty woman,' he murmured appreciatively.

A tingle of pleasurable anticipation surged through her heralding the possibility of future sweetnesses to come. It was ages since she'd experienced a similar sensation. Twenty-five years ago, she thought – the day she'd run into Curtis MacPherson at the annual Pill Regatta.

It was boosting her confidence no end to be out on the town again. A few more trips like this and she'd be good and ready to face the world once more, to pick up the lost threads of the life which had ended for her the night Curt went fishing in his brother's boat, but failed to return with the morning tide.

Erin emerged from the pub toilets, her throat raw and sore from having vomited up the veggieburger that Jazz had insisted on making her eat some fifteen minutes ago, with two half pints of Strongbow cider to swill it down. Jazz was watching Erin's food consumption like a hawk, and when Jazz was determined, Erin knew there was no escape.

Catering for vegetarian tastes at the Smuggler's

Retreat was an innovation which Barry Buckley had introduced only recently. Jazz was a veggie, and her influence over Barry, a strapping great ex-rugby football player, was obvious to anyone who saw and heard them conversing together. When Jazz was sixteen and still at school, they'd had a secret love affair; Erin and Holly were the only people she'd confided in and, at just fifteen themselves, they'd viewed the romance between their friend and the thirty-year-old barman with curious, and almost horrified, fascination.

Holly and Guy were in Bristol tonight, attending the twenty-first birthday party of one of Guy's numerous cousins. His elderly grandparents and some other relatives had come all the way from Sorrento in southern Italy to be there, Holly had said. Erin missed Holly badly. Jazz was a good friend in many ways, but it had been much nicer when the three of them were a trio. *The three witches of Fuzzy Cove,* as they'd liked to be called, hadn't had a night out together for quite some while. In fact, Erin told herself, the name hardly applied to them any more.

However Erin didn't for one moment begrudge Holly the love and happiness she'd found with Guy. If the miracle she prayed for ever occurred, and Dominic Stone asked Erin to be his girl, she knew she would positively leap at the chance – there was absolutely no question about that.

'And pigs might fly, and my mother become the Archbishop of Canterbury's wife,' she muttered disconsolately.

Suddenly she smiled; her blue eyes lit up with merriment as a vision of the extrovert Roxanne, prancing around the portalled halls of Lambeth Palace, slid into her mind. Roxanne with her low-cut dresses, revealing acres of cleavage at the top, and her wiggling bottom below, would liven up even *that* place, Erin was sure. Those hallowed halls would never be the same again. You had to laugh ... *really!* If you didn't, you would cry.

A smile still flickering across her face, Erin sat down next to Jasmine who was chatting away ninety to the dozen with Rusty MacPherson and a group of his mates.

'She's putting on a brave face, aren't you, my precious?' remarked Jazz. 'She's missing her bloke like billy-oh. He's swanned off to Africa, you know.'

Erin said nothing. If Jasmine knew who it was she was *really* pining for she would be just a little surprised, she mused.

Calum went off to get more drinks and Jazz followed him to the bar, leaving Erin sitting with the men.

Kevin Buttercup glanced up at the clock suddenly. 'Hell's flaming bells,' he exclaimed. 'It's nine o'clock. I told her faithfully I'd get home by nine, in time to watch that telly pro-gramme we've been following.'

Suddenly the idea of being home – alone – reading or watching television, seemed im-mensely inviting to Erin.

She nodded. 'I think I'll be making a move, too,' she told him.

'I'll give you a lift if you're going right now,' Kevin said. 'I'll have to get going right away, else the love of my life will have my guts for garters.'

The big, jovial council worker had married for the second time only a few months ago, Erin knew; she was impressed to see how mindful he was of his new responsibilities.

She swallowed the last of her drink and, picking up her pale canvas sling-bag, rose to her feet, all ready to go. Jazz, she saw, was deep in conversation with Barry at the bar. The thought of crossing the room in full view of everyone to say goodbye to her seemed strangely intimidating. While she was still hesitating, Calum returned with three flagons of ale which he plonked down on the table.

'Talk about bloody henpecked – I've seen the lot now,' he remarked, taking a slow, deliberate swig of beer, and looking pointedly at Kevin.

'I don't know about that,' said Jacko, leering at Erin, suggestively. 'He's just offered to give this lovely young lady a ride home in his new car.'

Calum swivelled round to face him. 'What the hell are you insinuating, you low-life creep? That our Erin here's not the respectable young lady she always gives the impression of being?'

Jacko slumped back in his chair, conscious that he'd upset Calum again. 'Well, she's her mother's daughter, ain't she?' he muttered quietly, a slight smirk on his face.

He was trying his best not to upset Calum at the present time. It would be a while before he forgot about the ice cream delivery that had gone so disastrously wrong, Jacko knew.

Calum cast him a withering glance then, patting Erin's arm companionably, said, 'Thanks a billion for what you done. You just about saved my bacon, I reckon.'

Jacko's ears pricked up again. He wondered what the big blowsy tart's daughter had done to warrant such gratitude from Rusty MacPherson.

'That's OK. I'm glad it all turned out all right,' Erin replied, throwing Calum a grateful smile.

As she passed by, she glowered at Jacko Jackson. She'd heard what he'd said about her mother, and it had made her so angry she felt like slapping his face.

'Erin – my sweet one – you're surely not going, are you?' Jazz called to her from the far side of the room.

Erin nodded. 'Mmm, I've got a really bad headache, I'm afraid.'

Jazz rushed across to hug her. 'What foul luck, sweetie, a headache on a Saturday night,' she exclaimed. 'We'll meet up tomorrow then, eh? I'll give you a bell to let you know just where and when.'

Jazz sat down beside Calum again. The only person she fancied in the whole wide world was Barry Buckley, for whom she was still carrying a torch. He'd yonks ago made it plain that he intended to remain only a blast from the past, however, and there was no sign of him having changed his mind. Why did she keep hanging on, she wondered. He wasn't the only pebble on the beach. The thought of going away to college was raising a fair number of bittersweet emotions in her mind.

After an uncertain start, the evening had turned out to be quite enjoyable, Calum thought. The drinks were flowing freely, and the conversation had begun to warm up nicely. Jet-haired Jazz was always happy to see him and, he had to admit, he always enjoyed her company. The moment she and Erin had come into the pub this evening they'd headed straight over to where Calum was sitting, to ask him how Gyp was, and whether the dog had suffered any ill effects from his recent gadabout.

Overhearing their conversation, Calum's mates had chipped in with a few ribald remarks.

'Apart from walking on all four knees, he's recovered quite well,' Dexy Glue had assured the girls.

'Just a little frayed around the edges and showing a few signs of wear and tear,' quipped Kevin Buttercup.

Jacko Jackson had, of course, had to put in *his* five cents' worth. 'Shagged out – just like his bloody owner – if I knows anything about old Rusty here,' he'd chortled.

'You don't know the first bloody thing about me, mate, so don't go acting as if you do,' Calum had flared back angrily.

That Jacko got right up his nose. He wished to high heaven he didn't have to clap eyes on the bugger ever again but, unfortunately, Starkey had already roped him in on the proposed trip to St Malo, and the notion had gone to his head. He was even more obnoxious than he usually was, and that was saying something.

Jazz, sitting next to Calum, nudged his elbow now, and said cheekily, 'So – who *was* the lucky female then? Does anyone know *that* yet?'

'Whose – his, or his dog's?' laughed Dexy. 'I

think we'd *all* like to know that, Jazz, my love.'

Calum tapped the side of his nose. 'That's for me and little blondie to know, and the rest of you to guess,' he said firmly.

'He likes keeping secrets. I hear he's got a mystery woman hidden away at Upalong,' Barry Buckley whispered loudly into Jazz's ear as he picked up a cluster of empty beer glasses and swiped a damp rag over the top of the polished wood table. 'Hey up, the phone's ringing.' He beat a hasty retreat back to the bar. 'A call for Calum,' he called out, waving the receiver aloft. Calum put down his drink and went to answer it.

'It's Roxanne – asking for *you*,' Barry told him quietly, keeping his voice low so that no one else could hear. There were some nosy buggers around and Barry was aware when to keep his trap shut and when to open it.

Roxanne explained to Calum that she was stranded at the motel Relax-a-Vous, on the Bridgwater road, a few miles out from Bristol. Henry was working nights, she said, so couldn't come and get her, and Calum was aware that his old schoolfriend didn't drive.

'I'll come over straight away,' he assured her, only too happy to do an old friend a favour.

'I shan't be long,' he told his companions. 'Keep my seat warm till I gets back.'

'And where might you be off to now?' enquired Jazz. Her ebony eyes – twinkling cheekily – put Calum in mind of the shining dark currants in a glazed hot-cross bun.

'Going to do my good deed for the day,' he replied. 'I should ought to be back fairly soon, but there again, you never knows what might come up.'

'With *you*, we do,' Dexy said suggestively. There wasn't a peep out of Jacko this time, Calum noted.

Barry nabbed Calum on the way out. 'Sounds to me like Roxy's been stood up,' he said in his lilting Welsh accent. 'Asked for you by name, she did, but I know for a fact she was meant to be meeting another bloke tonight.'

'Oh?' said Calum. 'Who were that then, me son?'

'I'd rather not say, but he was in here boasting about it the other night. I very much fear he'll live to regret his big mouth – there were plenty of others who must have overheard.'

'And you're not going to tell me who it was,' said Calum, his curiosity aroused.

'Least said, soonest mended,' Barry replied philosophically, drifting away to attend to another customer.

Twenty-five minutes later, Calum arrived at the Relax-a-Vous motel's car park. He could see Roxanne waiting inside the entrance foyer and, by the look on her face, she seemed pleased as well as relieved to see him.

She greeted him with a warm hug. 'You don't have to rush away, do you, Rust?' she said. 'Come and let me buy you a drink. I owes you summat special for coming out all this way.'

'All right,' Calum agreed, 'I don't suppose one quick *one*'ll hurt.'

'My shout,' Roxanne told him, 'I was having a brandy myself – d'you fancy joining me?'

'Nothing so strong as that. I'm driving,' Calum reminded her.

'You don't have to, Rust ... drive home, I mean,' she suggested invitingly. 'I've got a lovely room upstairs doing nothing.' She cast him a flirtatious glance with her foxy brown eyes, and added, 'There's a magnum of champagne waiting up there, too. I'd be really grateful if you could come up and open it.'

'I'll certainly do *that*,' Calum said, 'but I can't hang around for long. The fellows are lining up the drinks for me, back at the Smuggler's.'

'Oh, well, we won't bother with having a drink down here then. Let's go upstairs and open that gurt big bottle of brut. There's glasses up there, and everything,' she explained.

They took the lift to the first floor, and Roxanne led the way along the corridor to room thirty-nine, unlocking the door with a card she took from her purse.

'Gurt posh, eh?' she said.

'Aah, 'tis *that*, all right,' Calum replied. Taking the bottle from the ice bucket, he popped the cork so that it hit the ceiling with a loud bang.

'Yippee,' laughed Roxanne. 'Come on and fill the glasses up.'

Her enthusiasm was contagious and, although Calum hadn't intended to stay, he filled the two glasses that she handed him. The champagne, too, proved to be contagious and, before he knew it, he was drinking a second and third.

'You're right ... this is a bloody great bottle,' he remarked as he poured them both another.

'It's a magnum – I told you,' Roxanne giggled.

'Oops, I'm bloody sloshed,' she added, falling into a heap on the bed. Patting the pillow beside her, she invited Calum to join her.

'Come on, Rusty-bucket ... don't be nervous. We had it real good once upon a time; let's get it together again now, just for old times' sake.'

Scrambling over to the side of the bed, she slipped out of her dress and kicked her high-heeled shoes to the floor.

She pulled Calum down by her. 'Come on, get this off,' she chuckled, helping him remove his polo shirt, and unzipping the front of his jeans.

Soon he was completely naked apart from his underpants. All wrapped up in Roxanne's arms, he buried his face in her cleavage, luxuriating in the sensuous warmth of her breasts.

She sat up suddenly. 'There,' she said invitingly, 'I got this brand-new brassiere specially for you, but I think you've had your eyeful now; it's time to take it off.'

As she spoke, she undid the back fastener of her black lace bra and let it all hang out.

'You got it for *me*?' Calum said, puzzled. He didn't see how that could be, unless she had planned this all along.

Roxanne eyeballed him closely, enjoying his stunned reaction. 'Of course I did – who else?' she protested earnestly, laughing as he shook his head in a bewildered way. 'So, how do you like my titties? A bit bigger than when you seen them last, eh?'

'Caw, I'll say.' Calum was speechless, mesmerised by the sight. Like two huge Christmas puddings, he thought, but white, instead of all black and speckled. In the place of sprigs of holly, two hard brown nipples stared him in the face.

'It's time we had these off, too,' Roxanne said, pulling at Calum's underpants.

He rolled over on his back and slipped them off, then snuggled back into the circle of her outstretched arms. Her breasts, pushing softly against his chest, were soft and warm. Everything about her seemed suffocatingly vast. He tried not to think of Suzi ... petite, perfectly proportioned and, what was more, a cracker to look at in the nude.

A sudden thought occurred to him. 'Who the hell's paid for all of this?' he asked.

'Never you mind about that. Let's say somebody did me a favour. They owed me one, and I asked them for *this* ... and then,' Roxanne hesitated, 'and then I invited you.'

'Yeah, *but...*' Calum was having doubts about the authenticity of her statement. A serious expression darkened his eyes.

'Come on, Rust,' she coaxed, 'it's no good worrying about your young lady. She's having it away with a travelling salesman everybody knows that.'

When Calum didn't answer, she flung back the bedclothes and slid her body inside the impeccably ironed sheets. Calum caught a glimpse of her as she went; she looked like a great white whale.

'I want you to make love to me, and I know you want me – so what the devil are we waiting for? Have a drop more shampoo if it makes you feel more relaxed. I'm quite happy to wait till you're good and randy,' she laughed.

Questioning what, if anything, he had to lose, Calum slipped into bed beside her. He ran his hands along the inside of her thighs, feeling her ample body quiver with lust. Lust was *all* that it was ... all that it could ever be, Calum reminded himself.

When they were both fourteen, touching each other up behind the cricket pavilion, it was curiosity, pure and simple and then, in the space of a few months, their curious fumblings had flamed into high passion – the passion of newly discovered delights; hitherto unimagined delights. *Animal* delights, thought Calum now, though he'd always doubted whether animals felt anything like the delicious sexual release that human beings did.

Her warm hands were stroking his flaccid penis, coaxing it back into life, but Calum experienced none of the eager reciprocation he'd felt in situations like this before. No stupendous electrical current coursed through his body this time. His little willy hadn't throbbed a beat; it remained as still and limp as a lifeless fish on a fishmonger's slab.

'We'll have to do much better than this,' Roxanne whispered, cupping his balls in her hot, squeezing palms.

But nothing happened ... *zilch!* Never before, in the whole history of Calum's adult lovemaking, had such a calamity occurred. It seemed that the more attention he paid to it, the tinier his organ seemed to shrink.

'Get yer pecker up,' Roxanne demanded, still

fondling his balls and nibbling the lobe of his ear in a breathless, seductive way. 'Come on, Rusty ... Calum ... love – I'm desperate to have you come inside me. You were the first, remember? And I was the first for you.' She paused, her small brown eyes burning into his like hot roasted peanuts. Then she laughed, and gave his testicles an extra squeeze. 'Well, you *said* I was. I don't s'ppose you was lying to me, Rusty MacPherson, you bugger?'

'You're kidding, ain't you?' Calum told her. 'I'd only bin out of short trousers a few minutes.'

'Naughty little boy then, wa'n't you?' Roxanne teased. 'You knew what you had it for, though, even then.'

'Which is more than I do now. Go on ... say it.' Calum smiled ruefully, wishing that he'd never agreed to come upstairs to her room.

He was unable to raise a flicker of response – not for the life of him. It wasn't that he found making love with Roxanne at all distasteful – after all, Marlene, the woman he'd been seeing recently, was equally plump. It was the sudden thought of Suzi that had caused his willy to shrink so small. It would need a splint applied to it if it was to do Roxanne any good tonight, he thought.

'It must be all that drink I had,' he excused himself, 'I ain't used to supping all that good-quality booze.'

Roxanne lay quietly beside him. He could sense disappointment exuding from her every pore.

'Never mind – it can't be helped,' she said, 'Perhaps we'll get it right the next time.'

But there'd never be a next time for him, Calum thought; not with Roxanne Meredith. He would never again put himself in the position of having *this* happen to him.

'Let me love you anyway,' he said. 'I'll make it good for you, even if we can't do it the proper way.' He rubbed his forehead puzzledly. 'It must be all the drink,' he murmured in disbelief.

'If you ain't used to it, it must be that,' Roxanne told him and, because they'd dabbled in sex before, and weren't exactly strangers in that respect, she soon responded to the touch of his hand. Within minutes, she had entered her own private world of sensual enjoyment.

Yet, even at the point of her greatest arousal, when she heaved and groaned, and let out wild exclamations of pleasure ... even then, Calum was unable to get an erection. It was the greatest calamity that he'd ever experienced. He wondered if he would ever know what it was like to feel sexually turned on again.

In Rex's delivery van, on the way home from the concert, Angie deliberated whether to ask Rex in for coffee as before. Last time, the twins had been around – a safety valve which had stopped her from having to worry about things proceeding too far. The boys weren't here now, though, so she didn't have that excuse. Was Rex expecting her to invite him into her bed, she wondered, or would she come over like a floozy to him if she did? Women like Roxanne did it all the time. It was village gossip, Angie knew but, nonetheless, Curt had assured her that a large portion of the gossip was true.

Daisy's feather bed was where Angie was sleeping now, and the idea was altogether tempting. She was badly in need of a masculine frame to cuddle. She stole a look at Rex's handsome profile, his vision concentrated on the road ahead. Did he have hairs on his chest, she thought. If so, they'd be dark, not ginger like Curt's ... the only man she'd ever shared a bed with before.

And there again, how would she be able to look Curt in the eye, knowing that she'd made love with someone else? But Curt might never come back, she mused, so why deprive herself of some simple human affection with a nice man like Rex? Because that was what Rex was: really and truly *nice*. So what, if he didn't *turn* her *on*, as Holly was fond of saying? He was excellent company, and they'd had a wonderful time tonight; did it matter that he didn't set her pulses racing? Upon reflection, it was a long while now since even Curt had done that – so what was the reason for all these self-doubts?

Reaching her door, she made an instant decision to invite Rex inside. He – like her – seemed shy and ill at ease, but he came in without any hesitation.

Sitting closely together on the settee, after they had finished their coffee, Rex pulled Angie gently towards him and kissed her on the lips. It was almost as if he thought that he should, Angie found herself thinking, as if it was the right thing to do in the circumstances. Although a little wary at first, she soon felt herself responding to his kiss. Warming to the caressing touch of his hands, she felt a physical desire to have him proceed still further.

But was it enough, Angie wondered – her earlier doubts resurfacing once more. Her slight, hesitant withdrawal caused Rex to take pause. He leaned away, and released his hold on her arm while the hand caressing her knee halted its exploratory movements. They pulled apart, and Angie gathered her composure; not a moment too soon as it turned out, because, entering the shop through the front door, she heard Calum. She hadn't expected him for at least another hour.

'Drat,' Angie muttered, yet secretly she felt somewhat relieved. The decision, she realised, had been taken from her now.

To her relief Calum went straight out to the back yard to give the dog a run. Rex shot to his feet and, helping Angie up as well, whispered, 'Best if I slip out now, I think. So very, very sorry ... some other time perhaps,' he added, as they parted at the door. He gave her a warm kiss on the cheek before he slipped silently away.

Angie didn't wait for Calum to come back and, within less than a minute, found herself sliding into the warm feathery depths of the old MacPherson bed, going over again in her mind her feelings for Rex. Would she or wouldn't she have let him into her bed had Calum not come when he did? And if she had, would they have woken up tomorrow morning knowing that they'd ruined a good friendship?

She knew instinctively that however decent Rex

Carpenter might be – however friendly they might be in the course of their day to day relationship – unless he was able to conjure up from deep within her the longings and feelings she knew were there, then he wasn't the right one for her.

Perhaps, somewhere out there, there was such a man, she thought, her optimism unexpectedly and pleasantly restored by Rex's not altogether disinterested advances towards her.

Chapter Nineteen

Daisy's feelings were mixed as she followed the signs along the corridors to the hospital cardiac department. Relief, because someone was, at last, looking into the cause of her troublesome chest pain, and then a scary sort of feeling that the test she was about to take was a hundred times more important than any other medical examination she'd ever had before.

She wasn't kept waiting long. Only four exercise tests were scheduled for this afternoon and hers was the second. A nurse who looked no more than fourteen, Daisy thought, handed her a flimsy hospital gown and told her to strip off all her upper clothes.

In the privacy of the small cubicle, Daisy felt fine but, before she could don the gown, there were monitors to be applied to her back and chest. 'Oops,' she said, half-embarrassed, as the nurse pushed Daisy's breasts hither and thither.

'Not a pretty sight, I fear,' Daisy murmured almost apologetically.

'I've seen a lot worse,' the girl assured her, as she carried on applying all the bits and pieces of wired equipment to Daisy's wobbly parts.

The test, due to last fourteen minutes, lasted only four. No sooner had the rhythm increased a little than Daisy felt the humongous pain. She glanced at the monitor screen to which she was attached – the pattern now resembled the stalagmites and stalactites she'd seen in the underground caves at Cheddar Gorge.

'Step down for a minute, Mrs MacPherson,' a young physician in a white coat said and, as Daisy rested her rear end nervously on a chair, he added, 'you'll need to see your cardiac specialist, I'm afraid, Mrs MacPherson.'

'My *what?*' said Daisy, too mystified to be scared.

'You mean to say you've never been referred?' the doctor asked. 'In that case, I'd better book you in right now ... excuse me a moment, won't you?' and he dashed out of the door.

'But nothing showed up when I had the tests lying down,' Daisy told the nurse, who was unclipping all the leads and yanking off the sticky tape which attached the monitors to Daisy's fragile skin.

The girl's face remained totally non-committal. 'There, does that feel comfortable?' she asked as she pulled the last one off.

Ten minutes later, with shaky steps, and an appointment to see the specialist in a week's time tucked into her bag, Daisy retraced her route to the car park. She had declined Josh's offer to come to hospital with her, but she'd have given anything to have him here now, she thought, as she opened the Metro's door and flopped shakily into the driving seat.

'Are you certain you'll be well enough to take care of the baby for Angie in the morning?' Josh asked as they lay in bed that night.

'Perfectly,' Daisy assured him. 'Unless I go uphill or run anywhere, I never feel a thing.'

'You'd better not let me catch you running anywhere,' Josh teased, 'and it's a darned good job Angie's got this girl starting soon.'

'She'll be moving her stuff in on Sunday, ready to start on the Monday,' Daisy said.

'And what about Caitlin? Is she very disappointed?' Josh lowered his voice to a whisper, aware that Caitlin was nearby, and the walls weren't terribly thick.

'I don't know, I'm sure,' replied Daisy. 'But she's determined to find herself a suitable position before that horrible husband of hers comes over from America. She won't be stopping here long.'

'If it's a living-in job she wants, it's unlikely they'll let her keep a cat,' Josh observed.

'Mmm,' Daisy said thoughtfully. 'Mmm, I was thinking about that.'

'Oh *no*,' he groaned. 'Daisy, we don't want a bloody cat.'

'Not for always, no, we don't, but I thought, just until...?'

'Pets are a nuisance. What if we want to go on holiday?'

'We won't be going anywhere just yet, my darling. I've got to see the specialist next week, remember?'

'Well, let's hope the girl sorts herself out before too long,' grumbled Josh. 'The last thing I want is to be saddled with a *cat*.'

'Poor little Pepsi's a sweet little thing – how can you say things like that?'

'So it might be a sweet little thing, but I don't want it living here permanently.'

'Well, it won't be; she's already told you that.'

'Good – the quicker, the better, as far as I'm concerned. Come here and give me a cuddle.'

Curled up in each other's arms, they finally fell asleep. Long before the light of dawn, though, Daisy's thoughts were whirling round, partly thinking about the letter she'd received the day before from her sister-in-law, Vinnie, in Scotland. Vinnie's son Stuart was visiting the West Country at present, in the course of his job, she said. He worked on the steamers, ferrying passengers to and from the Western Isles, and his firm had connections in Penzance. He was due to travel down again in a few weeks' time, and had promised to bring Vinnie with him then so that she could spend a little time with Daisy before winter set in.

Josh, after he'd read the contents, had handed the letter back to Daisy with a devilish wink.

'Tell her she's welcome to come any time,' he'd said, adding, 'as soon as we've got rid of the cat, of course. We haven't got room for them both.'

Daisy had phoned Vinnie straight away, telling her Stuart should bring her soon, while it was still warm enough for her to sit out in Josh's amazingly beautiful garden and enjoy the fabulous view. It occurred to Daisy that she'd entirely forgotten to enquire how Stuart was coping since his wife died: it was strange that Vinnie never brought up the subject at all. At least it was a relief that his daughters were both grown up, Daisy thought. The youngest attended one of the universities in Scotland, the older one worked for a top hair stylist and lived with her boyfriend in London.

It was quiz night at the Smuggler's Retreat, a week since Angie had been tempted to invite Rex into her bed, and here they were again, out on another date, their earlier easy friendship restored to its usual firm footing.

From her seat on the covered windowsill she watched Rex and his team, whose turn it was, competing against the Stone family. The other members of Rex's team were Kevin Buttercup, Bobby Ayres, son of a local farmer, and Carly, his girlfriend, a chubby, rosy-cheeked lass from Weston-in-Gordano. The opposing team – reigning champions – were Mr and Mrs Stone and their two sons; Giles, the eldest, who looked and sounded every bit as supercilious as his parents, and Dominic, the good-looking young doctor who, Angie knew, had always had a fancy for Holly.

Dominic looked up and gave her a friendly wave. With his mass of thick brown curls, he was truly a fellow with film-star looks, Angie thought; tall, whereas his brother and father were short, and with aquamarine eyes that most girls would swoon to see close up. Just like his sister Jazz, however, he seemed totally unaware of the effect he had on the opposite sex.

'Hi, Mrs Mac. I wondered who my bruv was waving to.' Jasmine Stone, a handsome, dark-haired boy in tow, sat down next to Angie. 'Holly not here – *of course?* We hardly catch a glimpse of her these days,' she said.

'You and me both,' Angie sympathised, 'And I'm missing having you and Erin popping in to see me, too. Where *is* Erin tonight?'

'Would you believe? Gone to the pictures with her dad. It was a film he specially wanted to see and Mrs Meredith, apparently, didn't want to go. The Shakespearean one, with Kenneth Branagh. Sounds really good. I can't wait to see it myself.'

Turning to the young man, she said, 'Hey, Tom – fancy coming to the flicks with me one night? I'm sure *you* would appreciate a dose of uplifting culture.'

'Perfectly happy to oblige, sweetie ... just waiting for you to give me the nod.'

He looked a bit effeminate to Angie's way of thinking, and spoke with exactly the same upper-class accent as Jazz's parents. It was a miracle to her that Jazz was as ordinary and down to earth as she was. Angie's mind went back to the many times that Jazz had breezed into their house when she was at school with Holly. They'd been living on a council estate then, yet Jazz had never let *that* put her off. She'd entered into everything

303

they were doing with the greatest enthusiasm.

'Yeah! What a fantastic score!' Jazz yelled, cheering on the village team, even though they were in opposition to her own family.

Tom put a restraining hand on her arm as she bounced up and down in her seat. 'I say, old bean,' he muttered quietly.

'*Yeah* ... *Kevin* ... sock it to 'em, mate,' Jazz screeched even louder.

Angie clapped too as Kevin Buttercup scored another five points in a popular win greeted with deafening applause.

'Good to see you out and about again, Angie MacPherson,' she heard a voice say. A suffocating scent of musky perfume wafted towards her, and Angie looked up to see Roxanne Meredith standing there.

'Shove up,' Roxanne ordered Jazz. Hitching up her short red skirt and smoothing her silver Lurex top down around her bulging waistline, she squeezed into the remaining space.

Jazz elbowed the boy along the seat. 'Wotcher, Mrs M,' she said. 'So you didn't much fancy an hour or two of highly cultural entertainment at the cinema tonight, I hear?'

Roxanne shook her head adamantly. 'Not my cup of tea, dear, that. I'd rather have a spot of *Dirty Dancing,* any day. So – how's you?' Roxanne asked Angie, who was wedged so tightly in her seat she had difficulty raising her glass.

'Fine...' Angie grinned. She might be squashed, but she didn't care. She was glad now that she'd accepted Daisy's offer to take the baby home to Upalong again for the night. Daisy had assured her that she and Josh loved having her there.

When Daisy had heard that the boys wouldn't be arriving from Swansea until late she had informed Rex of the fact, adding that Angie would be on her own again this evening. He'd invited Angie to join him at the pub quiz, making no mention of the previous Saturday night's events. That suited Angie fine. She had been afraid it would raise a barrier of embarrassment between them. The twins had phoned her from Wales that morning and she'd told them she would leave the key in the dog's kennel, where she always did, and that she'd be at the Smuggler's Retreat if they needed her for anything.

As Roxanne rose to her feet again another strong burst of the cheap, musky perfume wafted into Angie's face. 'Can't see your Rusty here tonight,' she said, staring all round the room.

'No – I haven't a clue where he's got to,' replied Angie.

Roxanne shook her head disappointedly, her honey-coloured bouffant hair-do remaining as stiff and rigid as a guardsman's busby.

'No, 'e don't appear to be anywhere around,' she sighed, sitting down again. ''Tis a good job 'e were in yere this time last week, when I needed him to do summat for me.'

'And I guess he did do,' remarked Jazz. 'I was with him when he got your call; he didn't appear again, though all his drinks were waiting.'

'No, that was 'cos I had summat special on, and I couldn't do it without his help – bless his little cotton socks.'

'Oh, well, what are friends for, I always say? You

can't have enough of them, Mrs M.'

Jazz put down her glass and stood up, too. Nudging Tom's arm, she said, 'We'd best go and mingle now, old love. I'll never live it down with my lot if I don't. Let's give a cheer for Dominic – make him look brighter than he is.'

'Come off it, Jazz, Dom *is* bright. Don't make him sound as though he's dim.'

'None of my family are dim, I know – that's the bloody trouble. It's a real pain to have to live up to, but that's the story of my life...'

She paused, and gazed over towards the bar. 'One can't have *everything* one wants in this life, I've come to realise,' she added wistfully.

When they had gone, Roxanne whispered confidentially into Angie's ear, 'Yere, when you sees your Rusty next, tell him I got summat for him, will you? It's summat I got in the health food store; I think he'll find it useful.'

While Angie was still digesting this piece of information, Roxanne shot bolt upright in her seat. She was looking at the small raised stage, Angie realised.

'Is that Rex Carpenter I can see up there?' she enquired.

'Mmm, he's with me ... I mean...' Beneath Roxanne's inquisitive gaze, she found herself explaining, 'The boys are at camp. Well, they're on the way home now, and mother-in-law offered to take care of the baby for the night ... so...'

'I'm glad to see he's coming out of his shell at last. I was beginning to wonder.'

'He's really very nice,' murmured Angie.

Roxanne fixed her an admiring stare. 'Good for

you, my blossom. I'm glad to see you're not still sitting at home, moping. You're a long time dead, I say.' She squeezed Angie's hand tightly. 'What I mean is, love, life's too damn short to care what all them nosy buggers might think.'

Angie shook her head, unsure of Roxanne's meaning. Was she hinting that people were curious about herself? Angie very much hoped not. She hadn't yet done anything amiss. There were times, though, when a person couldn't do right for doing wrong, as her old Aunt Bridget in Cornwall always used to say.

It was Sunday morning again and Holly adored her Sunday lie-ins with Guy. She hoisted herself on to the pillow and peered at the clock. It was almost nine thirty.

'I hope you don't mind, but I've asked Erin round for coffee later on,' she said. 'There's a chance we'll be going to the market at the Bristol City football ground.'

'Your friend won't arrive *too* early I hope?'

'No, no.' Holly stroked his tanned face, her fingers moving down to his shoulders to caress and smooth the soft flesh at the top of his arms.

'Ooh – that's naughty ... I like it, though. *Ooh, do I like it?* Hey...'

Guy wriggled his body closer to her, and Holly felt his erection pressing on her leg. 'Come on; lie down,' he instructed, pulling her down beside him.

'*Again?*' she asked, but already her body was responding. She loved him more than she could ever have imagined loving anyone or anything.

His smouldering black gaze was hypnotic. A rabbit frozen in its tracks by a stoat could be no more powerless than her, Holly thought. Not that she was unwilling – far from it. Her response to this dark-eyed predator was eager, hungry, slavish, desperate to have him come inside her – to *conquer* her with his urgent, primitive desire. Not in any way was she a victim. Inside her body burned a cauldron of molten, fiery heat, crying out to be filled with that part of him which was primed like a piston, all ready to enter her.

'I never knew it was possible to love anyone so much,' she whispered, her voice choking in her throat, so suffocated was she with passion.

'I know ... it's almost frightening,' answered Guy, his fingers exploring her honey-filled vagina, precipitating her into outer space far beyond the point of no return.

'Keep, keep...' Holly gasped, and then the sublime orgasm overwhelmed her, like a flooded river bursting its banks, a tidal wave engulfing the waiting shore.

A moment later she felt Guy's final thrust – warm and unimaginably fulfilling. This was the ultimate bonding Holly had dreamed of since the first moment she clapped eyes on him, her wonderful, fabulous man.

They lay together, locked in love, for almost five minutes more, and then Holly remembered that Erin was coming at eleven and she would need to have a bath or shower before then. This would entail a visit to her mother's house. She only hoped her brothers hadn't taken all the hot water.

Angie was preparing the Sunday lunch. She wasn't expecting Calum to join them. She'd heard his car start up early this morning and, when she came downstairs, noticed that his fishing tackle was gone from the back porch. There was no sign of the dog, either.

With a nice joint of pork roasting in the oven, she was debating whether to invite Holly and Guy to lunch ... that was if they were interested in eating, she thought. It was a more likely bet they were still happiest living on love. Angie paused from peeling a potato to wonder if *she* would ever feel that way about a man again. She shook her head doubtfully. Even with Rex – nice as he was – she didn't really think there was any serious possibility of that.

She carefully pared the last piece of peel from a potato, and turned her thoughts away from the subject of romance. The house seemed awfully quiet without Evie. She realised how much she was looking forward to having her back. She was pleased to have had some time to spend with the boys, though. They'd been regaling her all morning with tales of their adventures on the Gower coast and, from their description, it sounded very similar to Cornwall.

'Do you realise, I grew up in a place like that?' she said, listening to Jake rattling on about the steep cliffs he'd climbed, the lichen-covered boulders, the rock pools, crabs, limpets, and long sandy beaches. It was *years* since she'd been to the *real* seaside, she reminded herself. The dull gunmetal waters of the Bristol Channel were no substitute for the wild Atlantic rollers that crashed incessantly and majestically on to the rugged rocks and shores of her birthplace. 'We *must* go there again, kids,' she announced suddenly.

Her sons looked at her eagerly, freckled faces burned slightly pink by the sun, each with his father's dark marine eyes – Luke's just a little shade lighter than Jake's, Angie noticed, the same as she always did.

'To Polzeath... I'll take you there, the moment we can afford to shut the shop and take a holiday,' she said, her voice dreamy and wistful.

Their faces fell. They had heard her say it so often before. 'Aw, Mum,' Jake complained. 'That'll be *never*, I know.'

'Not never, Jakie,' Angie assured him. 'Look how well we're getting back on our feet.'

'You always say that,' Jake said.

Luke, more thoughtful of her feelings, added, 'Maybe next year, eh, Mum?' He frowned at his brother. 'We've just had the greatest time in Wales, Jake, don't keep going on...'

'*And* I managed to pay for *that* all on my own,' Angie reminded them.

'I know you did, and we're really and truly grateful,' Luke told her.

Jake said, 'Yeah, don't think we're *not*, Mum – we've had a real great time with all our mates ... and maybe next year...'

'That's right. Just think, Evie will be toddling by then and, if you put aside some money from your paper rounds, you'll both have a nice bit to spend.'

She held out her arms. 'Hey! Come here, my handsome big sons,' she said. 'It's so good to have you back. The place just hasn't been the same, not with you *and* Holly gone.' She pressed her face into their necks, loving the boyish, earthy smell of them. They would never know how relieved she was to have them safely back home, she thought.

'Only the noisy, troublesome one left,' said Luke solemnly. 'I hope she didn't cry too much and keep you awake at night.'

'No, she wasn't bad at all,' replied Angie, 'and she'll be easier still once she starts to sit up and do things.'

'Mmm, it must be boring just lying down – I wouldn't like it at all,' agreed Luke.

'I can't wait to see her again,' Jake laughed, 'that funny little face, I've forgotten what she looks like.'

'Like a pudding,' Luke said, 'but I'm dying to see her again, too.'

The back door opened and Holly came in like a whirlwind, disrupting their peaceful conversation.

'Oh, my God, they're home again! It doesn't seem five minutes since they went.'

She ruffled Luke's cropped auburn hair, 'Hi, copper-knob,' she said. 'Look at you...' She stood back to inspect them. 'You look like two prize turkey-cocks.'

'Roosters, I think you mean,' said Angie, 'I don't think turkeys have got red topknots.'

'I'm sure they have,' answered Holly. 'Anyway, chaps, did you have a good time?'

'Fab,' Luke said. 'It was really fab. We followed the source of a group of rivers, and learned a lot of stuff.'

'I'll bet this one didn't,' said Holly, poking her tongue out at Jake, with whom she often clashed.

'Don't start any of *that*,' Angie warned, silencing Jake before he had a chance to get his own back.

'So, what time did you get home?' Holly asked her brothers.

'Late, and even then Mum wasn't in when we got here,' said Jake.

'I knew you'd be late,' Angie told him, *'and* I left you a note to say where I was.' Turning to Holly, she went on, 'They didn't want to wait at Gran's, and nor did they...'

'Want to wait with me, eh? Cheeky monkeys,' replied Holly, sounding a little miffed.

'*Uhh, no* – just as *if*...' Jake pulled a gruesome face.

'Just as well then, 'cos I was out myself,' she retorted.

Angie, secretly amused, knew the boys disapproved of Holly's sudden transformation from the good older sister who always came home at night, to the crimson Jezebel she'd lately become – living with, and *having sex with,* a *man.* As much as they liked and were friendly towards Guy, they weren't ready for Holly's sudden metamorphosis from teasing sibling into the worldly-wise, twenty-year-old woman she was now.

Jake had refused pointblank to even visit her new home, though Luke had once gone there with Daisy. Daisy had described to Angie how he'd poked his nose round the door, then, seeing the bed – so obviously made for two – he'd practically fallen down the stairs in his haste to get away.

'Yuck – me neither,' Luke said now, echoing his brother's disapproval. Avoiding looking at Holly, they went upstairs to their room.

'They're horrible,' Holly exclaimed, 'Makes me feel like a prostitute, or something, and it's not at all like that.'

'I know it's not,' chuckled Angie. 'You have to remember, though, they're still only kids. It's an awful stage to be at – not grown up, yet not a little child.'

'I guess so, but they'll be thirteen soon – *teenagers* – it's time they knew about the facts of life.'

'They've known the facts of life a while, love. It's the emotional factor that's missing still. They won't know about that until it hits them personally.'

Holly said quietly, 'D'you think they're missing Dad more than we realised, Mum?'

Angie thought for a minute. 'Not in *this* respect, I wouldn't think. They know all there is to know about sex. How could they not, living out here in the countryside?'

'Mmm,' Holly agreed. 'I'll be glad when they accept Guy and me together, without looking at us as if we're two sex maniacs, though.'

'They will – sooner than you think. I was wondering if you and Guy would like to have lunch with us presently. I've more than enough for five.' Angie paused, and smiled, 'It would be smashing if he could carve the meat, being as Calum's not likely to be eating with us today.'

'Dip-stick ... loopy bugger...' Holly waved her hand dismissively. 'He's not worth you worrying your head about, Mum.'

'All to do with me taking on someone to look after Evie! How did I know he'd more or less told this other woman the job was hers?' Anger welled up inside Angie again. 'How *dare* he?' she said, stamping her foot hard on the tiled kitchen floor.

'He could, and he did, because he's Rusty MacPherson – the biggest, daftest nutcase ever born.'

'I know,' sighed Angie, 'but it's got out of hand. I hate this awful atmosphere.'

'Where is this girl, anyway? What time's she meant to be dumping her stuff off, Mum?'

'I've been expecting her all morning,' Angie said worriedly.

'D'you have a telephone number?'

'Mmm, but it's where she was working at the time, and she said she'd rather I didn't ring her there.'

'Oh, God, Ma. She's supposed to be starting *tomorrow*. The other people are bound to know by now; that's if she gave in her notice when she said she would.'

Angie nodded. 'Two weeks' notice, she said, but I haven't heard a dicky-bird from her since.'

'Let me have that number, Mum – we need to know what's happening.'

Angie produced a scrap of paper with a number, which Holly promptly dialled. There was no reply, however, only an answerphone.

Holly left a message, then, sitting down on a kitchen chair, grinned cheekily at her mother.

'Well?' she asked. 'Come on, you dark horse. I can't keep it in any longer. How did you and Rex get on on your second big date? That's what I want to know.'

Angie looked confused. 'I wish you hadn't asked me that. The same as before, I suppose ... not bad, but...'

'He doesn't turn you on?'

'He *does*,' Angie exclaimed. She hesitated. 'Well, he does in a way. Physically, I find him very attractive, and yet somehow...'

'He doesn't turn you on,' Holly said emphatically. 'Has he kissed you yet?'

'Of course, he has. Gosh, Holly – what else do you want to know?'

'Nothing in *detail*, Mother dear. I just happen to have your best interests at heart, and *I'm* so happy with Guy – in bed – you know – and I want you to be happy too.'

'And then what? What if your dad should come back?'

Holly hesitated. 'Oh, well, then you'd have to do what you think best. He can't expect you to not have changed in all these months.'

A puzzled frown wrinkled Angie's brow. 'It's strange with Rex, bearing in mind how well we get on on a day-to-day basis.' She paused. 'I think I'm not ready for a proper relationship yet – not a physical one, anyway.'

'I think in that case Rex isn't the right one for you,' commented Holly. 'Yet, as you say, you and he laugh and joke around together like nobody's business when he's delivering the fruit and veg.'

'I know. It's a mystery, love. I do enjoy his company – and he's a gorgeous-looking man. That crinkly brown hair makes you want to run your fingers all the way through it, and yet...'

'There's ·something missing, Angeline Mac-Pherson – that wonderful, secret something you talked about just now when we were speaking about Jake and Luke – the *emotional factor*. It might be that you're subconsciously still hankering after my good old dad, in which case you're certainly not ready for anyone else at the present time.'

Holly stood up, and wrapped her arms round Angie's waist. 'Food for thought, eh, Mummy dearest – and while we're at it, talking about food, yes, Guy and I would very much like to come for Sunday lunch with you and my lickle bruvs.' She glanced at her watch. 'Oh, hecky-thump, is that the time? Only I need a quick shower if that's all right with you. I trust the boys have already had their baths?'

'Only showers, so there's plenty of hot water left. They were both surprisingly clean. Said they liked mucking around in the showers at camp.'

'Them *clean* ... well, there's a surprise! Oh well, there's a first time for everything, I suppose,' Holly said.

'In my experience, life's one long continual source of surprises,' commented Angie. 'I spend half my time wondering what the next one's going to be.'

Chapter Twenty

Caitlin had put butter on Pepsi's paws – an old wives' tale maybe, but she hoped it would prevent the cat from straying. She didn't anticipate remaining at Upalong much longer, and thought it best if Pepsi didn't get a taste for wandering too far. Caitlin, sunglasses on, was sitting on the patio at Daisy and Josh's, soaking up the sun. As well as keeping a wary eye on the cat, she was watching baby Evie who was sleeping quietly nearby in her buggy, in the shade.

She'd helped Daisy take care of Evie the previous evening, though the baby had spent the night in her travel cot in Daisy and Josh's bedroom. She recalled now how she'd wondered whether it would upset her too much to hold a small baby in her arms; remind her too vividly of all that she'd lost. Instead, however, she'd found it strangely comforting. Evie wasn't *her* baby, she'd had to tell herself – she was Angie's, and Caitlin just loved looking after her.

'You'll be going back to Mummy soon,' she whispered quietly, so as not to awaken the baby. Evie's rosy pink cheeks reminded Caitlin of a china doll she'd had as a child, though the doll, she remembered, had been blonde, and the cute little wisps of hair on Evie's head were bright carroty red.

Relaxed though she was, Caitlin was also aware

of time whizzing by far too swiftly. She'd have to do something soon about getting a job. She had no doubt that when Tyler's contract was finished, he would come looking for her. At least there was no danger of her parents telling him where she was; she'd made sure they didn't know. Tyler, when he wanted, could be so utterly charming he'd pull the wool over Olive and Roland's eyes without any trouble just as he did his own parents who lived not far from them at Burnham-on-Sea. It was best, she thought, to continue playing the role of fugitive. The only members of her immediate family who knew where she was were her brother Gwyn and his wife Liz. Caitlin knew she could trust *them* not to give her away.

A few yards from where she was sitting, on the other side of the terrace wall, grasshoppers were chirruping loudly in the long grass. The scent of honeysuckle was overpoweringly sweet, and a speckled thrush on the fence near the fir trees was warbling an aria from grand opera, its spotted breast all puffed up like that of Luciano or Placido. Caitlin breathed in the clean clear air, feeling more in charge of her life than in a long time. Tyler and the trouble he was capable of causing seemed a million miles away on this sunny Sunday morning.

In the distance, but out of sight, the Bristol Channel flowed its steady course to the sea. Caitlin thought of Calum, who was headed for Porlock to fish for ray or bass, perhaps some conger-eel, he'd said. He'd asked her if she'd like to go with him one day soon, and she was looking forward to the experience. The black cat was playing footie with a giant beetle, knocking it over with its paw each time it managed to right itself. Caitlin was tempted to rescue the poor thing, but to do that would take energy, and energy was what she lacked. A giant bumblebee buzzed past her ear, and she watched its progress with caution as it wavered around the baby's pram until it finally settled on a lilac-hued buddleia some little way away. Inside the bungalow, she could hear Daisy flitting from room to room, gathering up Evie's million-and-one belongings in readiness to take her back to Angie.

'Can you see her bottle in the kitchen?' Daisy called out from the bedroom.

'Yes, it's here,' Josh answered.

'Ooh, Josh...'

Caitlin thought she detected an element of distress in Daisy's voice, and a prickle of fear crept the length of her spine.

'Josh, *please* ... stop what you're doing and come,' Daisy cried out. Then everything was silent.

Caitlin jumped to her feet and hurried over to the open window. She could see Daisy lying in the bedroom doorway that opened into the hall. Rushing past the baby, who was beginning to stir, Caitlin ran to where Daisy lay. The older woman's face was completely drained of colour; as white as death.

Josh was speaking into the telephone, his face almost as pale as Daisy's.

Caitlin drew in a deep breath. 'Is she...?'

'She'll be all right. I know she will,' Josh said, as if he was trying to convince himself as well.

The baby began crying in earnest outside, her wails of distress gathering momentum by the second. But she was safely strapped in her buggy, Caitlin quickly reminded herself. She might be crying loudly, but she couldn't come to any harm. Right now the most important thing was to make certain that Daisy received urgent help.

Ten minutes later, as the ambulance taking Daisy and Josh to hospital disappeared down the hill, Caitlin reflected how only a fortnight earlier she, too, had been carted away just the same. Yet here she was, back on her own two feet, and feeling stronger every day. She prayed that it wouldn't be long before Daisy was home and fully recovered too.

The baby was crying up a storm now. It suddenly occurred to Caitlin that in all the commotion she'd forgotten to ask Josh for Angie's telephone number. She hoped it would be in the address book on the hall table near the front door.

Rex Carpenter, returning to his mobile home on the seaward side of the coast road, pulled over on to the grass verge to make way for the ambulance coming at high speed down the hill. Earlier that morning he'd driven to Easton-in-Gordano on what proved to be a fruitless errand, and now he was on his way home to prepare a lonely snack lunch. It was more than a week since he'd telephoned his estranged wife, Delphine, to say he would take his son and daughter to the seaside for the day. Although he'd given her ample warning, when he reached the house at eight this morning, he'd found the place deserted. It wasn't the first time she'd done it to him, and Rex was fed up to the back teeth with her spiteful behaviour.

On the way back to Fuzzy Cove he'd stopped off at his brother's house at Pill for a cup of tea and a chat. *Tea and sympathy*, his sister-in-law had called it, giving him a consoling hug. A keen gardener, she had presented him with cuttings that she'd taken from her flowering shrubs. There were far too many for Rex's tiny garden and, with his sister-in-law's blessing, he intended to offload a few on to Josh and Daisy.

He halted the van near their gate and walked up to the front door, which was slightly ajar. He was just about to ring the bell when an attractive young woman appeared like magic in the doorway. Her eyes were pools of purest amber – so unbelievably beautiful, he was unable to stop himself from staring. Never before in his life had he seen eyes as wondrously expressive. Her hair, falling loose around her shoulders, was an unusual shade of tawny gold – wild, like a lion's mane. It was a moment or two before he felt able to speak.

'I'm sorry,' he muttered, feeling a right idiot.

Whatever must she think of him, he wondered, and who on earth was she? What was her connection with Daisy and Josh?

'I'm a neighbour – a friend of the Mac-Phersons,' he explained, concentrating his gaze on her sandalled feet, the coral-coloured varnish on her toenails. 'I ... I've brought a few plant cuttings I thought they might like.'

The woman nodded, but didn't reply. It was as if he and she were statues, frozen in a moment of time.

Rex swallowed deeply and, having to force himself to look her in the eye again, said, 'I've just passed an ambulance in the lane. Is it ... I mean...?'

The young woman nodded gravely, a worried expression clouding the lustrous glow of her eyes. She opened the door a little wider and beckoned to him to enter. 'Come inside a minute,' she said, her voice as melodiously perfect as everything else about her.

Rex inclined his head in the direction the ambulance had taken. 'The ambulance...' he said again.

'It was for Daisy. I think she's had a heart attack. It all happened completely out of the blue.'

'*Oh, no*. How did she seem when they took her away?'

'If you mean do I think she'll live – I can't answer that one, I'm afraid.'

She paused in the kitchen doorway. 'Look, if you'd like to put the kettle on, I could sure do with a real strong cup of coffee. I have to go and get the baby but I'll be right back.'

Evie, when Caitlin reached her, had stopped her frantic screaming and was hiccupping quietly with pathetic little sounds as if she'd been abandoned for hours.

'Poor little baby, come to Caitlin then. *We'll*

take care of you, my sweetie-pie,' Caitlin said, scooping Evie into her arms and rocking her soothingly.

'You must be the girl that Angie's been telling me about,' Rex said, when Caitlin returned to the kitchen. 'You'll be looking after the children, she tells me.'

Those strange golden eyes darkened momentarily. 'No, I'm just a friend of Calum's,' she said quietly.

'Does Angie know about Daisy yet?' Rex wondered, switching off the kettle.

'No, I'm afraid she doesn't. I was just looking up her phone number when you appeared.'

'I'll ring her for you if you like,' Rex offered.

She smiled at him weakly. 'I'd be really grateful if you would. I think she might take it better from somebody other than me,' she added quietly.

'Why d'you say that?' Rex asked, dialling Angie's number.

'Because ... well, Calum and her, I guess they've fallen out over me.'

'I wouldn't think–'

Rex stopped in mid-sentence, and began to explain the situation briefly to Angie.

'The baby's fine, Angie, just fine. This young lady here's been looking after her a treat. I shouldn't think you need wait till Holly gets home – no! Hang on a minute and I'll ask her.'

Turning to Caitlin, he hesitated. 'I apologise – I haven't even asked you your name.'

'Caitlin.'

'*Caitlin*. Do you know which hospital they were taking Mrs MacPherson to?'

'The BRI, they said.'

Rex tried not to stare too deeply into those strangely iridescent eyes. Until this moment, he'd always prided himself on being completely in control of his deeper emotions. He only hoped that he looked a dam sight calmer than he felt.

'Would you mind looking after the baby a little while longer?' he said. 'If it's all right with you, I'd like to take Angie in to see her mother-in-law.'

'Of course I will,' Caitlin said, cradling Evie more tightly in her arms. 'She'll be absolutely fine here with me.'

Rex, speaking again into the telephone, said, 'Angie ... that's all right. Caitlin's perfectly happy to keep her here until we get back.'

Replacing the receiver, he said, 'Sorry I've rather dumped you in it, but Angie's desperate to know what's happening with Daisy. Her daughter – Evie's big sister – has gone into Bristol, to the Sunday market, so there is no one else.'

Caitlin nodded. 'There's baby food here, and a nearly-full packet of diapers – nappies,' she corrected herself. 'Tell Angie not to hurry back. I'll love looking after her baby.'

'Bless you,' said Rex as he rushed out of the door. He reversed the van into the lane and sped away down the hill at a high rate of knots.

With the winnings from a horse he'd backed earlier in the week, Calum had treated himself to some decent rig at last and, using squid for bait, had, in the last hour, caught no fewer than *three* large bass. Well content with this hat trick of beauties, he decided to pack his fishing tackle away and call it a day. He had a firm order for his fish from the head chef at a smart Bristol hotel, provided he delivered it there while it was a hundred percent fresh.

Calum, with Jacko and his son Darren, had spent the last few hours fishing the offshore sandbanks out from Porlock Bay, though the Jacksons had only caught a couple of very small dogfish. Jacko, who was still hoping to hook a spotted ray, or bass, turned to look at Calum who recognised a surly look of envy in the man's dark hooded eyes. But Jacko was a sly one, Calum knew; he was desperate to stay included on Starkey's next heist and, in his eagerness to get his snout in the trough, it was highly unlikely he would expose his true feelings towards Calum at this time.

'Yere – where d'you want this fucking tea?' Darren Jackson groused irritably, thumping a mug of tea down on the deck near his father. It was as well that Angie *had* got a hangup about the twins coming fishing, Calum thought. They would certainly have picked up some colourful swearwords from the fifteen-year-old in the last few hours. 'Bloody hell – don't piss me about,' the boy went on, treating Jacko to another long string of expletives. He returned to the fo'c'sle and, a moment later, Calum's dog let out a shrill, sharp yelp from below deck.

The hackles rose on the back of Calum's neck like bristles on a brush; he flew down the gangway stairs with the speed of greased lightning. His anger rose even higher when he saw Gyp cowering beneath a bunk. He knew if he raised his voice it would cause the dog to shiver and tremble more but, for once, the daft mutt would have to put up with it, he decided – the great gangling, spotty-faced youth needed putting right in a big way.

'You've bloody kicked him,' he yelled accusingly.

'No, I bloody have not,' the boy protested.

'And I'm saying you bloody have. Old Gyp'ud never have screamed like that, not unless you'd done summat to him.'

The kid didn't reply, and Calum put his face closer to the lad's.

'If you hurt my dog again, it'll be the last thing you ever do. Got that, you stupid, bald-headed punk?'

Darren blinked for a moment before hurling a mouthful of abuse back at Calum.

The boy had altered out of all knowledge in the last couple of months. It was common gossip in the village that the kids he ran around with were into taking drugs. Calum had a fairly strong suspicion that Darren was dabbling too.

'Here Gyp,' he called, and the dog followed Calum on to the deck and settled down on a tangle of rope by his feet, its soulful great eyes were oval brown loops, staring trustingly up at him.

The late afternoon sun cast a shimmery lemon glow over the calm waters off Porlock Bay, and a moving shadow from a swooping gull darted over the dog's nose as swift and silent as a passing meteorite.

'You're all right now,' Calum said, patting the

terrier's head. 'You got more rights to be on this boat than either of those two buggers.'

Old Gyp had been coming fishing ever since a pup, Calum, reflected, musing on the trips they'd taken on *Solitude* when, indeed, the dog was his only companion – the only one he'd needed.

Solitude, he thought. It set him off wondering again whether someone had had it in for him, had meant to finish him off but got his brother instead. Curtis, with the same red bonce as himself, and not a single enemy in the world. There were plenty of things that Calum had done in the past which he truly regretted now – all manner of scams he'd been involved with where someone might have wished him a goner – but none of it applied to Curt. He shook his head and sighed forlornly. You could wonder about it until the cows came home, but every avenue you went up had a way of turning into the same flipping dead end.

The telephone rang in Mariner's Cottage just as Luke and Jake were seeing Angie off in Rex Carpenter's van. When Jake answered it, a strange woman asked if she could speak to his mother. When he explained she wasn't in, the caller told him to ask her to ring back the moment she returned.

'My name,' she continued, 'is Mrs Adams-Farqueson, and here is my number – do you have a pen?'

'No, I've got a pencil, though,' Jake said, picking up a stubby piece of pencil that needed sharpening, and writing down the number. He left the message on the wooden chest at the bottom of the stairs where the family always left messages.

'A gurt posh voice, she had, like she had a plum stuck in her gob,' he told Luke, who had come inside to listen. He knew it wasn't an expression his mother would have approved of, but he'd often heard their Uncle Calum use it.

It was late afternoon when Rex and Angie arrived back at Mariner's Cottage, where Holly, Guy, and the twins were waiting anxiously for news. Angie explained that Daisy had been given a bed on the emergency admissions ward and was taped up to machines and wearing an oxygen mask. However the doctor who admitted her had said no diagnosis could be made until the specialist examined her the following morning.

'Why oh why did I ever think she was fit enough to take care of Evie two Saturday nights in a row?' moaned Angie, her eyes bottomless pits of despair.

'But it was your mother-in-law who insisted,' Rex reminded her. 'She always said how much she and Josh loved having her there.'

'I know she *said* that. But the fact remains, I was home early for the boys; I could easily have gone up and fetched Evie, too.'

'And you have no car, and *I* wasn't in – and Calum's never around,' Holly reminded her. 'Come on, Mum, it's nobody's fault that Gran was taken ill.'

'I'll bet Rex would have popped me up there to fetch her if I'd asked him to – wouldn't you, Rex?' Angie said worriedly.

'Oh, for pity's sake, Mum, don't keep blaming yourself. We'll go and collect her now. I didn't bother before because I spoke to Calum's lady friend and, I must admit, she sounded very pleasant. *And* she seemed to have everything under control.' Holly squeezed her mother's arm and added, 'So I thought let's do what Mum's always saying we should – let sleeping dogs and babies lie.' She wrinkled her forehead, 'Or was it sleeping *logs?* Anyway, we'll go and get her now.'

'Has there been any message from the au pair, boys?' Angie gave the twins a questioning look.

'Serina ... Semolina. What did you say her name was?' Jake said.

'Serina Whitelaw, and she's due to be starting tomorrow. She said she'd be dropping her baggage off some time this morning.'

Jake rubbed his nose, 'Oh no, well, that wasn't her then. This woman who phoned was all lah-di-dah, and her name sounded like Adam Farker – *Farter* – something like that, I think.'

'Adam Farter,' repeated Luke, and they both dissolved into great peals of laughter.

'If it was that important, she'll ring again, I suppose,' Angie said.

She turned to Rex. 'Thanks for taking me to see Daisy. I'm really grateful, Rex.'

'Only too pleased,' he assured her.

Rex was aware that he liked Angie a lot; she was a smashing person and a very good mother, so different from his quarrelsome wife, from whom he'd been separated for almost a year. But – and he wished he could dispel the intrusive thought from his mind – who was Caitlin, and where had

329

she come from? He didn't want to believe she was *that* close a friend of Calum's. Yet it takes all sorts, he reminded himself. One man's meat was another man's poison, and if this gorgeous woman turned out to be Calum's latest lady friend, then that old saying was indeed true.

The sun was sinking over the Welsh hills as Calum steered his boat back into port. A brilliant red sky boded well for another fine day to-morrow. Though content with his catch, he was tired and thirsty and longing to rest his weary limbs. He'd been standing at the tiller for several hours, not wanting to hand the steering over to Jacko, and especially not to Darren who had been sulking like a big girl's blouse ever since Calum had ticked him off for frightening the living daylights out of the poor old dog.

Calum's high spirits were suddenly lowered when he noticed Snooky waving to him from the quayside. 'Oh, bloody hell's bells,' Calum muttered, throwing out a rope and signalling to the little man to attach it to an adjacent capstan.

Snooky was bubbling over with important news. The great Bryan Starkey had been down to Fuzzy Cove, he said, looking for Calum and Jacko. He had slipped Snooky a pound coin to be sure to tell them that the planned trip to France would take place in two days' time.

'Good. I'll give him a bell from the pub,' Calum said, hauling up a large bucket containing the trio of gaping-mouthed, surprised-looking bass.

Jacko was hopping around like a cat on hot bricks, wanting to know what was going on.

Calum had had it up to the eyeballs with the stupid git today. He passed Snooky's message on to him as quickly as possible, impatient to see the back of him and his pesky son. When the Jackson Two finally drove away in their old Austin Princess, he breathed a hearty sigh of relief.

Calum's relief was momentary, though. The Jacksons had no sooner left than Snooky began to fire a whole lot of idiotic questions at him. He wanted to know if Calum intended going fishing the following day and, if so, whether he'd be taking out his own boat. Calum couldn't help wondering what lay behind his questioning. The shabby little scrounger had never been known to show a jot of interest in *anyone's* vessel before.

'Certainly not tomorrow – I got other things on,' he replied tetchily. *'Tuesday* ... well, you heard what Starkey said about Tuesday, you daft sod.'

Snooky made no answer, and Calum switched his mind to more important things. He hoped he'd be in time to deliver the bass to the hotel before the chef locked his refrigerators for the night.

To Calum's intense annoyance, Snooky didn't stay silent for long. The horrible little man began bombarding him with questions about divorce.

'I don't know why you keeps on bloody asking *me*,' Calum snapped, crossly, 'I've never even bin married meself.'

''Cos I ain't got nowhere to live, and I wants half the house what's my due and legal rights,' Snooky whined.

Calum, his patience already worn to a frazzle

331

by the two berks he'd been forced to spend the day with, had come to the end of his tether. He turned his back on Snooky and, calling to Gyp to follow him, strolled off across the green. He could kill two birds with one stone, he thought, if he made his telephone calls from the Smuggler's Retreat while supping a pint of bitter at the same time.

Snooky waited until Calum had disappeared inside the pub, then, retrieving his plastic carrier bag from behind a tree where he'd hidden it earlier, he ambled back to the quayside. Casting a furtive glance around to make sure that no one was watching, he descended the rusty ladder and scrambled on to *Green Pepperoni's* deck.

He knew where Calum hid the key to the cabin door, he'd heard him telling Dexy Glue one afternoon at the Bluebird Café while drinking a cup of tea that Calum had treated him to. Snooky, ever alert to methods of self-preservation, had stored this snippet of information away in his head, suspecting that he might one day be in need of somewhere warm and dry to come to. That time was upon him now. He'd been sleeping rough for the last six days, ever since his landlady had chucked him out for non-payment of rent.

He'd been thankful to hear that Calum had no plans to take his boat out again tomorrow. It would give him the opportunity to linger a little longer, perhaps cook himself something to eat. A bit of fried bread, maybe; provided there was a stove.

Still clutching the Tesco carrier bag that

contained all his worldly possessions, Snooky retrieved the small Yale key from its hiding place beneath a broken lobster pot, and slipped it into the lock on the cabin door. Checking again that the coast was clear, he slid stealthily inside.

Chapter Twenty-one

Angie was all alone, lying on the living-room sofa, when Calum arrived home. To his great surprise, she called out 'Hi' as he passed the door. Gyp ran over to greet her, his tail wagging furiously, and Angie nuzzled her face in the dog's neck.

'Oh, Gyp,' she said, 'am I ever glad to see *you*.'

To Calum's dismay, he saw that she'd been crying. Gyp was leaping all over her now, whining, and licking away her tears.

'I'm so relieved to see you,' Angie murmured, running her fingers through Gyp's wiry coat.

But it was *him* she was speaking to, Calum realised. Angie was speaking to him again, at last.

'What's happened?' he asked as all sorts of wild ideas crowded into his mind.

Angie looked at him tearfully. Wiping her eyes with a tissue, she said, 'Oh, Calum, it's been an awful day. One disaster after another.'

She told him about the scare Daisy had given them, and how Rex had given her a lift to the hospital to see her. She also said how much she appreciated Caitlin's help in looking after the baby.

Calum was dumbfounded. So Angie had had to rely on Caitlin, after all, he thought.

'When's the new girl due to start?' he asked. He needed to clear his head; he'd never dreamed that the situation might have changed, let alone so completely.

'She isn't – that's just it,' replied Angie. 'The woman she's working for has upped her salary, and she's staying where she is. They're taking her with them to the Caribbean next week. There's no way I can compete with that.'

'I should bloody well think not,' Calum said. 'Well, not until the old lotto comes up, anyway.'

'I've given up buying lottery tickets ... can't even afford them any more,' Angie sighed.

'Oh, blimey, Ange, you are in a bad way.' Calum sat down beside her and squeezed her wrist. 'Where's the little 'un now?' he asked.

'Fast asleep in bed. The boys, too.'

Angie put her arms round him. 'Oh, Cal, I'm so sorry. You were right all along ... she wouldn't have fitted in. Do you know what that old bossy boots said to me on the phone?' Angie put on a swanky voice. '"Serina's a qualified nursery nurse, and it wouldn't be right to expect her to take charge of two grown boys as well as attending to a baby." I was only asking her to keep her eye on Jake and Luke – make sure they washed their necks when told to.'

'Bloody bitch. You're better off without the likes of that sort,' Calum replied. He stood up, pulling Angie to her feet too. 'I thought she seemed a bit of a madam, and so did our–'

'I know, Cal, and I was wrong about Caitlin

too. She's really turned up trumps today. To think, I didn't even want to meet her.'

'Never mind about all that – the scare you've had with Mother today is quite enough for you to be going on with.'

'I know ... I thought...' Angie slumped back on to the sofa. 'Phew – I feel utterly exhausted.'

'I feel pretty knackered, too,' Calum said, 'but not half as bad as you.' He paused. 'I've got to go out again in a minute to do a bit of business, but I should ought to be back home by eleven at the latest. If you like, I'll sleep in 'long with the babby, and you can go in Holly's room and get a decent night's shuteye.'

'What if she wants feeding?'

'Make her up a bottle, then I can give it to her. I used to do that with our Emma when Suzi were working nights at thik old nursing home.'

Angie brightened. 'Of course you did. Bless you, Cal – I'll take you up on that offer.'

'And I'll give Caitlin a ring in a minute to see if she'll mind coming in and helping out to-morrow.'

'Calum – you can be such an angel at times. Why is it you're always so terribly misjudged?'

'That's the second time in as many weeks that somebody has called me *that*. I shall have to try and make sure I keeps my halo in place.'

'You will if you put your mind to it. You're a real sweetie when you want.'

The rare compliment had made Calum feel good. Once he'd completed the next bit of business with Starkey, he really would try to make an effort to change his ways, he reflected quietly. In the meantime, the chef at the Bristol hotel wanted the bass. They'd settled on a figure of over a hundred quid, as long as Calum got it to him tonight; the exact amount only when the chef had seen the fish.

On his journey into the city, along the Portway, after Avonmouth, Calum dreamed dreams all the way, thinking of the things he'd be able to buy with a few spare pounds in his pocket. As well as jeans and a couple of shirts, he'd be able to get the new waders that he'd need to take on his expedition to France. The ones he was making do with at present were covered all over with bicycle patches; there were more bloody patches than boots!

Apart from the worry about his mother, things were beginning to look up nicely again. New boots, a new venture, and – he hoped – a new way of life in the near future.

The mixed ward was noisy and Daisy hardly got a wink of sleep all night. So relieved was she to be there, though, she didn't much care how long she remained awake. At least this way she knew she was *alive*. The previous morning, when she was feeling so groggy, she'd been sure that her number was up.

The bed adjacent to hers was occupied by a man young enough to be Daisy's son. They were separated from each other by a few feet of floor space. Daisy, lying awake, had heard every word spoken to him by the male nurse keeping vigil at his bedside all night.

The nurse had roused the boy hourly to have

his blood pressure taken and also, at regular intervals, fed him with large doses of some foul-looking white fluid. It wasn't until the first light of dawn came creeping through the grubby hospital windows that Daisy saw the policeman sitting in a chair at the foot of the boy's bed.

The male nurse was coaxing his patient to drink more of the white medication. 'Swallow it down,' he urged, holding a glass tumbler to the boy's lips. 'It'll help to pass it through your intestines. If *that* stuff breaks open in your stomach – *then you're a dead man, pal.*'

Daisy watched the boy gulp the concoction down and, when the nurse moved away, he lay back exhausted, resting his head on the pillow. He turned to look at Daisy who was staring at him with compassion. There but for the grace of God, she'd been thinking, her sons and grand-sons very much at the forefront of her mind.

'You wouldn't happen to have a cigarette on you, would you?' he asked her.

She shook her head. 'Sorry. I don't smoke.'

The situation was surreal, she thought, or rather, completely *unrealistic*. But how could anyone begrudge him a cigarette when, within the space of the next few minutes, he could very well be dead?

Later, when Calum and Angie came to visit, they found that Daisy had been transferred to another ward. Everyone in here, Daisy informed them, was awaiting, or recovering from, some form of heart surgery.

'I'm booked to have an angiogram on Wednes-day,' she announced. 'Then they'll know exactly what's going on.'

'*Wednesday,*' repeated Calum, 'That's a bugger, 'cos I won't be around on Wednesday – not until the evening, that is.'

'Why, where are you going?' Daisy asked.

'France,' said Calum. 'We're leaving tomorrow morning; staying there overnight.'

'Who's *we?*' queried Daisy warily. After her night-long experience in the emergency admissions ward she was rather more suspicious of Calum's trip to France than she would otherwise have been.

'Not nobody you'd know, Dais,' Calum assured her, adding after a moment, 'oh, well, yes – you would know Jacko Jackson, I suppose, but he's only coming along for the ride.'

'Are you going over in *Green Pepperoni?*' Angie asked.

Calum shook his head. 'No, the bloke what's organising the trip, we'll be going on his boat.'

He didn't think it necessary to mention that he had arranged with Bryan to anchor *Pepperoni* in a little bay not far from Lynmouth, on the coast of North Devon, ready to transfer his share of the loot aboard when they arrived back on Wednesday afternoon.

'You worry me, my son,' said Daisy, her clear grey gaze fixed on Calum's face.

'There's nothink at all to worry about,' he assured her, 'Would I do that to you now that you'm ill?'

'I think perhaps the die might already be cast,' answered Daisy.

Calum frowned at her indignantly. 'What

exactly d'you mean by that?'

'That you'll do whatever it is you've got planned, regardless of what anyone else might think.'

Daisy told Calum and Angie about the boy in the next bed, and the policeman who'd been keeping a close watch nearby.

'Sitting on guard all night, ready to cart him off to the cells the moment he's passed the stuff through him,' she elaborated.

'Let's hope he has done, and the bag's not burst,' remarked Angie. 'Otherwise he'll very likely be a goner by now.'

'Condom, I expect 't'was,' said Calum.

'Is that what...?' Daisy paused; giving him a concerned look, she said, 'You seem very well up on these things. Are you absolutely, completely sure?'

'Oh, God blimey,' Calum cursed, 'now she's got me down as a drug-smuggler, Ange.'

'I'm sure he's got more sense than that, Mum,' Angie said.

'Where sense and Calum are concerned, Angie love, I wouldn't like to place my last best bet on it.' Daisy glared at Calum again. 'That *Jackson* fellow – remind me. Isn't he the one who robbed his employers of more than a dozen boxes of ice cream the other week?'

'I wasn't to know it was knocked-off property,' protested Calum.

'Come off it, my son,' said his mother. 'I wasn't born yesterday, and neither was Angie here. We knew as soon as we saw the way he dumped it there that someone was attempting to pull a fast one over us.'

'Oh, well, no one exactly profited from *that* little shindig,' said Angie laughingly.

'You'd better not be bringing in drugs.'

Daisy frowned at Calum, whose face remained wreathed in innocence. Angie too hoped and prayed with all her heart he wasn't involved in so heinous an activity.

'On my babby's life, I shan't be touching no drugs,' he declared adamantly.

'In that case, I'll accept your word for it, Cal. I'm sorry to have gone on, but that young man really upset me so. I couldn't help thinking, he's got a mum somewhere – probably without a clue as to the trouble her son's got himself in.' Daisy shook her head sadly. 'I should hate to think it was you, Cal. That's all I'll say on the subject for now.'

'If it isn't drugs then what is it?' Angie asked Calum when they had returned to his car, and were on their way home to Fuzzy Cove.

'Oh, blimey, Angie – don't *you* start,' he replied, changing down to low gear to avoid running into the back of a tractor towing a trailer loaded with hay.

'Well, it doesn't sound to me as if you're going fishing,' Angie said.

'Nobody said we was, and neither has anybody said that it's anythink else, neither.'

'Oh, well, if you don't want to tell me, I can't force you to, but please don't bring whatever it is back home with you this time. I'm very glad the boys were out when all that ice cream came, or we would have had some very awkward questions from the pair of them.'

'It's nothing like that. This is proper, official business, Angie-baby.'

'I'll bet it is, Calum-honeybunch, only please make sure you keep it to yourself.'

'Changing the subject, Ange, I got over a hundred smackers for that bass I sold last night.'

'Good, so when you've made all this other money you're definitely going to make, you'll be able to do your bit towards helping Suzi with the girls.'

'That's what I'm doing it for – so's I can give her a bit of extra for a holiday, or summat.'

'If that's what she needs...'

'She do. I spoke to her on the phone last night, and that's just what Lucie had been going on to her about. A holiday, somewhere nice.'

Calum remained silent for a moment, before adding, 'Lucie were running a bit of a temperature. I should ought to go over and see her later, but I don't want to chance running into that bloody bloke.'

'As long as Suzi's happy for you to keep seeing the children, you've got a perfect right to be doing so,' Angie told him.

'Yeah, well ... perhaps it would be best to leave it until after I gets back.'

'Yeah, and what if Lucie's temperature has soared even higher by then? You'd do better to see her today, Calum, I'm sure.'

'I'll think about it, Ange. With all what I got to do, I might be a little bit pushed.'

'Oh, Calum – excuses, excuses. Look what's happened to Daisy now! There's no time like the

341

present, so do what you have to do.'

The following morning, after Calum had left for France, Suzi phoned Mariner's Cottage to speak to him. Caitlin took the call and fetched Angie from the shop. Lucie wasn't at all well, Suzi told her, and all she kept saying was, 'I want my dad.'

Angie explained to Suzi where he was; she even apologised for him. In view of her recently repaired relationship with Calum, though, she decided not to let him down by telling Suzi that he'd known about Lucie's illness for several days. But, boy oh boy, she told herself, was she ready to tear him off a strip the moment she set eyes on him again! There was Daisy, too, all ready to have an angiogram to discover if she needed angioplasty – even an arterial by-pass – and her son nowhere to be seen.

'That Calum,' she told Caitlin, 'would try the patience of a saint.'

Without wanting to paint too black a picture of her brother-in-law, who after all had stood by Caitlin in her hour of need, Angie went on to tell her a little about his failings as a father and provider to his two small daughters.

'He's a case – a one-off, Calum is. Always certain he can pull rabbits out of hats and, sometimes – just *sometimes* – he's actually able to do just that,' she concluded.

On Wednesday morning, Daisy was wheeled down to theatre early – so early, she didn't have time to feel nervous. An hour or so before the porters were due to collect her, a nurse handed her a safety razor, though no soap, and directed her to the toilets to shave the hair from her right groin.

There, in the hospital loo, with a male patient waiting outside the door and, even more importantly, the knowledge of what the shaving was for, Daisy's hand had shaken like an alcoholic's in desperate need of a drink. The man waiting also had a safety razor in his hand, she noticed when she finally emerged. No sexual discrimination here, Daisy thought, and supposed that her task had been easier than his, unencumbered as she was by what Calum would call a full set of wedding tackle.

Later, fully conscious, and without fear, she watched her heart beating on a screen against the wall above her head. It looked too much like a cabbage or a lettuce to resemble anything that Daisy could recognise as being a part of *her*. It was only now and then, when the radiologist called, 'Right, Mrs MacPherson, I want you to take a deep breath now,' then, 'hold it until I say,' as the cardiologist passed a fine catheter all the way through her body, from a little excision he'd made at the top of her thigh, that she was able to grasp the full significance of what they were doing. She was very lucky as it turned out. The surgeon was able to insert a tiny coil of stainless steel mesh – scaffolding, he called it; it was easier to remember than its medical name *Stent* – into the blocked artery. It would prevent it from furring up again, he explained.

By Wednesday evening the spell of dry weather

had broken and a heavy grey drizzle had set in all across the Severn estuary. Calum, steering *Green Pepperoni* past Kilkenny Bay and into Lee Creek, could just make out the lights of Fuzzy Cove ahead. In fifteen minutes from now, he'd be safely home and dry, his own portion of the loot hidden away in the space below the cabin bunks. After he'd secured the outer door with the two new double padlocks that he'd bought at Fletcher's hardware store, the place would be as safe as Fort Knox.

All that remained was to get Jacko's share of the loot on shore. The first thing he and Jacko had to do when they touched base was get it on to the jetty, and then into the boot of Jacko's car. Calum almost burst a fuse a few minutes later when he discovered the stupid damn idiot had parked his old banger smack-bang behind the Customs and Excise shed, without a valid tax disc on show.

His stomach churning nervously, he waited for Jacko to bring the car round. *Ten boxfuls of good English rolling tobacco,* he told himself ... brought all the way from St Malo, and so far un-challenged! It would be the stuff that nightmares were made of if they were apprehended on their own home patch. The stress he was suffering was enough to bring on a seizure, and he wished Jacko Jackson would get a move on. Still, whatever the daft sod did from now on would no longer be any concern of his, he consoled himself. Enough was enough and, as from tonight, he would be finished playing nursemaid to the dopey bugger for ever.

The transfer into Jacko's old jalopy completed

successfully, with no untoward incident, Calum congratulated himself again on the success of the mission. His share of the haul would amount to a thousand pounds clear profit, even when sold at a knockdown price. He rubbed his hands together in joyous anticipation.

With Jacko safely gone, Calum was himself getting ready to leave when he ran into a snag. The two new padlocks he'd bought for the outer door were still in the galley where he'd left them but both the keys were missing. It was a complete mystery. Where could they be, he wondered. The cabin door was securely locked, he remembered, when he and Jacko came aboard at Lynmouth, and the key had been where he always left it, beneath an old lobster pot chained to the railing at the vessel's stem.

Calum frowned, puzzled, his eyes scanning every nook and corner of the fo'c'sle. He'd looked just about everywhere there was to look, and now it was midnight; he was longing for his bed. There was nothing else for it but to lock the cabin door the same way he always did, making a mental note to buy new padlocks early the next day. Ten minutes later, sitting in his car, and still preoccupied with the mystery, he failed to see a dark figure emerge from behind the wheelie bins at the rear of the Bluebird Café.

Across the green, on the far side beyond the duck pond and the children's play area, Snooky, hiding in the shadows, watched the Cavalier's tail-lights vanish from sight into the watery blackness of Harbour Walk, leading to Maritime Way.

He waited five minutes – just in case Rusty discovered that he'd forgotten something – and then, clutching his Tesco carrier bag, he beetled across the green to the harbour. Well practised now at surmounting the iron ladder, he shinnied down it, and on to the deck of *Green Pepperoni*. He had no need to grope beneath a stinking old lobster pot for the key; since his sojourn on Sunday, he'd had a spare one cut.

He wondered what Calum's reaction had been when he discovered the padlock keys were missing. Though Snooky hadn't got a clue what the locks were for, he didn't want to chance being locked out of the boat because Calum had put them to use. Just to be on the safe side, he'd slung the keys overboard and watched them sink into the oozing grey mud of the harbour.

He set the old-fashioned alarm clock that he carried with him to go off at five thirty am, standing it on top of the fixed gas heater by the bunk where he'd slept previously. The temperature had dropped considerably since Sunday, though, and he found it difficult to get off to sleep. He eyed the propane heater with interest, wondering if it was in working order. It might be the end of August, he thought – still officially summer – but Snooky was shrammed through to the marrow with cold and wanted a bit of heat.

He climbed out of the bunk and, moving his clock on to a shelf, groped in his jacket pocket for his matches. He turned on the gas jet, and gingerly applied the lighted match to it. The fire hissed for a moment, then started to redden nicely. As an afterthought, Snooky placed his wet jacket on top of the heater to dry.

He eased himself back into Calum's green plaid sleeping bag, pulling the top up over his shoulders and around his neck. 'This is better,' he told himself. Now he'd be able to sleep all nice and warm; at least until the dratted alarm clock went off and shattered his peace for another day.

Chapter Twenty-two

Josh brought the radio into the bedroom for Daisy to listen to *Wake Up With Wogan*. It was a little over two weeks since her heart surgery but she was still supposed to be taking it easy. All of her parts were ticking along nicely now. She remained very pale, but pale was interesting, as Holly kept reminding her.

In Josh's opinion she was looking better with every day that passed.

'Marry me, Daisy,' he said again now, purely out of habit.

Each time he'd asked her before, Daisy had always said, 'Not now, Josh – let's wait and see,' but this time she surprised him with her answer.

'OK. Now that I think there's a chance I'll not be a burden to you, I will, Joshua, darling ... I will,' she said.

'Eh?' Josh stopped in his tracks, unable to believe what he'd heard.

Laughing at his incredulous expression, Daisy

added, 'Yes, I'll marry you, and very soon –
though *not* a fancy wedding.'

'I don't believe it,' Josh gasped.

'October would be a nice time, as Vinnie will be
down from Scotland then. We'll invite Stuart and
his two daughters, too.'

With Wogan chattering away in the background, Josh sat down on the bed and gave Daisy
a hug. 'Good,' he said, 'so that's settled then.
We'd better get on and fix it up.'

'October is next month. Not long to get things
moving. It might mean shutting the shop if
Angie's to get a day off,' Daisy reminded him.

'Well, *that's* not the end of the world,' answered
Josh.

There came a light tap on the bedroom door,
and Caitlin stuck her head round it.

'Just off to work,' she announced. 'Rex will be
here any minute. Five minutes to eight, he said.'

'How's the cat settling?' Josh asked, rising to his
feet.

'Fine, Rex says. Pepsi's latched on to him good
and proper – the giver of all food, and other
bodily comforts.'

'Cats aren't daft,' remarked Daisy.

Caitlin smiled. 'It's good to see you looking so
much better,' she said. 'There's Rex's van now.
I'd better not keep him waiting.'

After Caitlin had gone, Daisy and Josh
exchanged glances. 'D'you reckon there's something cooking there?' Josh said.

'I was wondering that myself. She dashes out
every morning with that radiant look on her face.
Let's hope nothing or no one turns up to cloud

those lovely topaz eyes.'

'Sooner or later, I suppose her husband's bound to come looking for her,' observed Josh.

'Could be *soon* rather than later, but that's the reason she's still sleeping here, and hasn't moved in with Angie. It's also why Rex drops her off at the rear of the shop, and never the front entrance, of course.'

Frowning slightly, Josh nodded. 'Caitlin said his contract was due to finish at the end of August and we're well into September now.'

A golden September morning ... Angie was reminded of the Neil Diamond hit of the same name. On a glorious day like this Calum really ought to be out fishing, she thought. Two weeks had elapsed since his boat had been inexplicably burned to a cinder, and Calum with no boat was a lost and haunted soul.

He'd taken over Holly's old room permanently now and, with nothing special for him to get up early for, Angie was in no hurry to call him down. She'd taken up a cup of tea at breakfast-time but wasn't expecting him to have drunk it. The only thing was, she'd have to make sure that he was up in time to meet the insurance man, due at eleven.

The insurance implications of the two lost boats were proving most frustrating. *Green Pepperoni* had been registered in Curtis's name, and still was; the thirty-foot cabin cruiser was part of his estate, and the compensation would come to Angie if Curt was found to be dead. On the other hand, the sailing dinghy, *Solitude* – missing with Curtis on board – had actually

349

belonged to Calum. He'd still not received any compensation as *Solitude* had never officially been declared lost.

'And goodness only knows what Calum had got stashed away after his trip to St Malo,' Angie commented to Caitlin, who had come into the house from the back lane after waving the twins off to school. 'I'm trying to make some sense of it,' Angie continued, rustling through a thickish pile of papers. 'The claims officer is coming to see us this morning, but it's all such a hopeless mess.'

'Poor Calum,' Caitlin said. 'Will he ever get over it, I wonder?'

'He will – just as soon as he gets another boat, and goes out sailing again.'

'Do you really think he had something illegal on board?' asked Caitlin.

Angie nodded. 'Mmm ... judging by Calum's reaction, it was something pretty important to him. He was in a dreadful state the night it caught fire, jumping around, like a cat on hot bricks!'

'And there was absolutely nothing left for the police to identify,' Caitlin observed. 'I know it's very wrong of me, but I couldn't help feeling glad about that.'

Angie grimaced. 'He's a one-off, that brother-in-law of mine. I'm very glad he is.' She glanced at her watch. 'Time to open up,' she said. 'I'd better go on through.'

'Rex told me to tell you he'll be calling in between nine thirty and ten with some more fruit and tomatoes.'

'OK, thanks.' Angie flipped the words out as casually as she could while, deep inside, her tummy was looping a dozen loops. She couldn't explain the jolt of jealousy she was feeling, not even to herself. It wasn't that she wanted Rex for herself, so why – now that he'd become friendly with Caitlin, and given a home to her cat – did she give a damn about it, one way or the other?

The truth was she *did* care. She was just plain envious of all the attention Rex was paying to Caitlin when, if Caitlin hadn't come along just now, he might well have been paying it to *her* instead.

'You stupid cow,' Angie muttered quietly to herself as she unlocked the shop door. If Rex had been as smitten with her as he seemed to be with Caitlin, she'd have been the first to urge him to back off, not to hem her in because she wasn't ready for it yet. Her common sense told her that Caitlin had no transport; it was only sensible for Rex to bring her to work in the morning and then give her a lift home at night.

Angie could hear her baby gurgling with laughter as Caitlin rolled her around on the living-room floor. Ever since Caitlin had stepped in to help, all the worry of seeing to the baby – not to mention the boys – had been taken away from her.

She paused in the doorway. Caitlin was kneeling down, removing Evie's nappy on the changing mat on the floor. 'Ooh, tickle, tickle,' she was saying, as she lovingly caressed the baby's chubby tummy and back.

What a nice girl she is, and what a miserable cat

I am, Angie rebuked herself silently.

'I'll just give Calum a call,' she told Caitlin as she turned to go upstairs. 'Give me a shout if you hear the shop bell.'

Calum MacPherson, all rolled into a sad little ball, shrugged away from Angie's initial touch.

'Time to get up, Cal,' she told him, 'The man from the insurance company is coming at eleven.'

'It *were* Snooky ... the sneaky git ... I'll lay my bottom dollar on that,' Calum said, sitting up and staring her in the eye.

'You can't be sure, love – it hasn't been proved that it was,' Angie said sympathetically.

'It *were*. I know it were. Figgis were almost certain he caught sight of the bugger, jumping over the side.'

'Just as well the tide was in then, or he'd have been lost forever underneath all that mud.'

'I wish he were – the little creep. That would teach him not to hang around my boat ... we know very well he was doing that.'

'The police had him in for questioning, Cal, but they had to let him go.'

'That was some days later, don't forget. He buggered off to his sister's in Bristol first thing after the fire. She probably cleaned him up and kitted him out in new clobber, chucked all his old stuff away.'

'Perhaps, Cal. But you haven't any actual proof it was him.' Angie gave him a measured stare. 'Are you going to see Lucie today, or is she well, and back at school?'

'She's back at school, but I'll try and get over there for when she gets home. It's riling that John 'no end – me calling in there regular, like.'

'I'm glad you're seeing the girls more often, but what does Suzi have to say about it?'

'Not a lot when he's around, but there isn't much she can do. 'Tis the little 'uns that wants me there.'

'Piggy-in-the-middle – poor old Suzi,' observed Angie, as she went out on to the landing. 'There's Caitlin calling now. Must be someone in the shop. *Calum*, don't go back to sleep. You're needed for eleven o'clock, remember?'

'Oh, ah,' answered Calum, his eyes scanning the bedroom floor for his socks.

He was certain in his own mind that what Figgis had said was true, that he'd seen Snooky jumping off the boat just before the fire took a firm hold. It was a real shitbag whichever way you looked at it, Calum reckoned; the greatest disaster ever, to have all that good merchandise go up in smoke, before it ever got to the bloody customer! Fifty-gram packs of best rolling tobacco, costing two pounds sterling each, bought in Belgium then hiked all the way over to St Malo, France, without an incident of any sort ... and all for bloody nothing ... *zilch!*

Calum knew that he could have resold the packs for at least a fiver apiece. What sickened him most, though, was to see Jacko, who'd only had a quarter of the cut that *he'd* received, swanking around the neighbourhood like a sodding lord.

Calum's only solace at this time was the love and cuddles he was receiving again from Lucie and little Emma. He wasn't able to give his daughters his full attention yet but, after October, when Starkey was preparing to bring off the super-duper *Big One,* he'd be well and truly able to make up for lost time. Starkey had sorted out a boat for Calum's use, he said, and, after the job was safely completed, Calum intended to finish with smuggling for good. He'd patch things up with Suzi then; tell her fancy man to get lost because Calum MacPherson, father of her children, was taking up residence again. This time the rewards from the heist would be stupendously great, not the piddling little thousand smackers that would have been his had all those lovely-jubbly packets of rolling tobacco not gone up in sodding smoke.

Myrna Duffy resembled her younger sister, Roxanne, physically, though that was where the resemblance ended. As amply proportioned as her sexy sibling, her body-weight was very differently distributed to give her a matronly air, as opposed to that of a wild western hoochie-girl. She was sorry to say it, but her sister was a hustler; she hustled men just like those busty women did in the old Western movies they'd seen as children at the cinema matinees on Saturday mornings.

'Any messages for me, Myrna?' asked Dr Chadwick, her boss, in a rush, as usual, to start his morning visits.

'There was an enquiry earlier from someone at a Weston health centre, Doctor,' Myrna told him, 'but they said if they didn't hear back from us by eleven, they'd get the information they needed from the Committee of Family Practitioners.'

'Good stuff. Fair enough.' The doctor nodded and departed towards the car park. As he was driving out on to the main road, a car, driven by a man, passed him on the way in. The occupant got out and went into the surgery, meandering casually up to Myrna who was sitting behind the glass-fronted appointment desk.

'Can you tell me please if you have a patient registered with you by the name of Caitlin Sinclair?' he enquired.

Myrna thought she detected just the slightest trace of a Yankee accent. His clothes looked American, too. He wore an expensive-looking flannel-grey sweatshirt, emblazoned with the emblem *Proud to be an LA Dodger.*

'Who wants to know?' she queried, fingering the name badge pinned on the front of her best floral Alexon blouse.

'Her husband,' replied the man – as if *that* gave him the right to be privy to Dr Chadwick's confidential files, Myrna told herself.

'Ooh, dear, well if you're her husband, dear, wouldn't you already know whether she was registered with us?' she asked.

A flicker of impatience crossed his sharp dark eyes, causing Myrna to change her mind about comparing him favourably with Al Pacino, or some other equally attractive dark-eyed visitor from the other side of the pond.

'I see she is,' the man replied. 'Well, Okey-dokey – that's all I wanted to know.'

He walked away, leaving Myrna Duffy feeling a little perplexed. She recalled the patient to whom

355

he referred, a young woman who bore a passing resemblance to Rula Lenska, she thought. She'd been introduced to Dr Chadwick's practice by Rusty MacPherson, following her discharge from St Michael's Hospital, having suffered a sudden miscarriage ... her second one, if Myrna's memory served her right.

Myrna wondered vaguely how long the young woman had been knocking around with the red-haired boy wonder of Fuzzy Cove: her sister Roxanne's favoured friend. *That* just about said it all, as far as Myrna was concerned. It didn't however stop Myrna from wanting to know more about it. She hadn't liked the husband's swift change from affable to mean, and any information she could glean from Roxanne could prove extremely intriguing. She decided to pay her sister a visit very shortly to see what she could discover.

The following evening, Jazz and Erin were sitting in the Smuggler's Retreat, enjoying a quiet drink ... as far as Jazz ever *could* be quiet, Erin thought ... when a man, late thirties, dark-haired, and rather attractive, sat down at the table next to them. He was drinking shorts; whisky or brandy it looked like to Erin, and when, several minutes later, he returned from the bar with a third, he struck up a conversation with the girls. Well, mostly with *Jazz*, Erin noticed. Erin wasn't interested in listening to some stranger's chatter. She was quite happy to leave that sort of thing to Jazz.

Before the man joined them, Jazz had been telling her about Dominic's experiences in

Uganda and as a consequence, Erin was feeling dejected. The realisation hit her how very little she figured in that dishy doctor's life. She knew now that she'd *never* meant anything to him. He wouldn't have known she existed if she hadn't been Holly's old schoolfriend.

'So what was he like?' asked Holly, the next time Erin saw her and told her about the man that she and Jazz had been talking to in the pub.

'Well, I thought he was nice, but Jazz wasn't so sure,' Erin told her.

'Jazz ought to be here soon,' said Holly. 'In the meantime...'

'In the meantime,' Guy put in, 'let me get you a drink.'

'While you're there, I'll have another spritzer, please love.' Holly held out her empty glass.

Guy took it from her, raising his eyebrows enquiringly at Erin.

'Mmm, me too, the same,' she agreed.

Guy smiled, showing his even white teeth. 'Aah, here's Jazz now,' he said. 'I'll just see what she's having.'

'You do that, my little chickabidee,' purred Holly, 'then make your way slowly over to the bar to let me have an eyeful of that lovely sexy bum.'

'You're embarrassing him,' said Erin, as Guy walked away.

'Gorgeous Italian bum,' Holly mused aloud. 'I don't think it's safe for me to go to Italy, do you?'

'Who's going to Italy?' Jazz greeted them. 'Am I missing something then?'

'Me and Guy are planning to go – probably in

357

a couple of months' time. His grandparents have invited us; the sad thing is, we won't be allowed to sleep together in their house, he says.'

'Go on – shock 'em all,' scoffed Jazz. 'I bloody well would, I tell you.'

Erin said nothing. No one had asked her opinion but, if they had, she would be forced to agree with Guy. After all, it was only for a week or two. Well worth the sacrifice if Holly was to marry into his family and become thoroughly accepted.

'Look at you ... old po-faced Annie,' Jazz remarked, sitting down and giving Erin a sharp dig in the ribs.

'It's only a few days out of the rest of your life, Holl. Surely that's not too much to ask?' said Erin, irritated by Jazz's manner.

'The Virgin Erin has spoken,' commented Jazz, and Erin blushed profusely, but said nothing more.

The dark-haired man they'd seen the other night had come into the pub without them noticing, Erin suddenly discovered. He was sitting only a few feet away. He must surely have heard what Jazz had said. She felt so utterly humiliated that she wanted to curl up and die.

'You can sometimes be a real cow,' Holly told Jazz, crossly. 'What's Erin done to ever deserve *that?*'

'Oh, good God – can't any of you take a joke?' groused Jazz, springing to her feet again and flouncing over to the bar.

The man at the next table slid along the padded seat until he was sitting next to Erin. 'Mind if I

358

join you?' he said.

'Sure.' Erin nodded shyly, without looking up.

'It strikes me your brunette friend over there has got a lot to say for herself,' he said, quietly.

'Mmm,' Erin murmured, and Holly chipped in, 'That Jasmine's got a mouth on her as big as Avonmouth Docks.'

'Good way of putting it,' Tyler agreed.

Erin thought so, too. You could hear Jazz's upper-class cackle and strident voice above everyone else in the pub.

'I'll go and speed our drinks up,' said Holly, going over to join Guy, who was waiting patiently to be served.

The newcomer held out his hand to Erin. 'Perhaps now we can get acquainted properly,' he said. 'Tyler Sinclair. My friends call me Ty. And your name, I couldn't help overhearing, is Erin.'

He paused, and fixed Erin an interested look. 'A sweet *Oirish* name for a sweet old-fashioned girl. Though not the least bit old-fashioned in appearance, if you understand my meaning.'

The suggestion of a smile flitted across Erin's delicately boned face, lighting up her forget-me-not eyes. She could feel herself warming to this man's compliments. He was very good-looking, she thought – she was sure that even Jazz would have been flattered if he'd made a pass at her. He'd made it very clear, though, that he had no interest in Erin's brunette friend at all. Erin nurtured this lovely fact. At last someone – and an extra-presentable someone, at that – a guitarist in a rock band, he'd told them he was the other night – actually preferred her company to that of the more outgoing, often quite *outrageous*, Jasmine Stone.

Suddenly she realised he was talking to her again; could it be that he was actually inviting her out?

'I'd like to see more of your village, Erin. Take me for a walk, why don't you?' Tyler said. 'I have a strong feeling that you and I are going to become very well acquainted before it's time for me to leave for the States again.'

'Your Auntie Myrna came round to see me earlier tonight.' Roxanne handed Erin a mug of Ovaltine and sat down next to her on a kitchen chair.

'She did? That was nice,' replied Erin, 'and so what did she have to say?'

'Said you needed feeding up, for a start. Said you looks like a blooming matchstick with the wood scraped off.'

'Oh, please – not that again.'

'She said you looks like you'm wasting away to nothink, and it's time you ate summat substantial.'

'I'll have you know, I've just finished eating a good-sized portion of fish and chips,' Erin retorted impatiently.

'That's summat then,' her mother said. 'You should do it more often, my girl.'

'I may well, who knows?' replied Erin, thinking how much she'd enjoyed herself tonight, listening to Tyler's tales of life on the road in America with a rock band. How her dad would have liked to hear about *that*, she thought.

'Our Myrna was asking about the woman what's stopping up at Josh Berry's place,' Roxanne continued. 'She wondered if *you* knew anything about her.'

'No,' lied Erin. 'Never met her in all my life.' The last part was the honest truth, she thought, though Holly had told her a fair bit about Caitlin Sinclair.

'Well, her husband's over from America looking for her. At least, your auntie was pretty certain that's who it was.'

'I know. I was talking to him earlier,' Erin said. 'He only wants to check she's all right.'

'You little dark horse, you – fancy that!' Roxanne exclaimed. 'So what's he like? Aren't you going to tell me? Our Myrna didn't seem too taken with him.'

'He's really nice ... an interesting man. He plays lead guitar in a well-known rock band. Well known in America, that is.'

'You don't say?' Roxanne was impressed. 'Is he going to be over yere long?'

'I haven't a clue,' said Erin, 'but he walked me home from the Smuggler's and I shall be seeing him again tomorrow night.'

'He's a married man, don't forget,' her mother warned. As if she had any room to talk, Erin thought.

'He won't be for much longer. He wants a divorce; that's what he told me just now.'

Roxanne raised her eyebrow teasingly. 'While you was eating your fish and chips?'

'Yes, Mum. While we were eating our fish and chips.'

The next day Erin made enquiries of Holly, who told her that Caitlin, while still working for Holly's mother, was anxious to avoid meeting her estranged husband. When Erin explained that he was going to put in for a divorce, Holly said she'd tell that to Caitlin, but warned Erin not to get involved.

'I won't,' Erin promised her, 'but he seems very genuine, I thought.'

'It's probably *her*,' remarked Holly. 'She does come over as rather paranoid where her ex is concerned. But Rex Carpenter's taking her in hand. He's sensible; he'll put her straight if anyone can.'

'Well, tell her Tyler just wants to talk to her. That's what he told me, anyway.'

'You like him, I think,' chuckled Holly.

'I do,' was Erin's uncharacteristically positive reply. It had made all the difference having someone think she was a nice, attractive person.

'Dad – when I wasn't very well you said you'd get me a puppy.'

Lucie, strapped in by her seat belt in the back of Calum's car, held Gyp tightly in her arms. The dog lay there, lapping up her warm affection.

'I know I did,' said Calum, 'but I don't reckon yer mother 'ud take too kindly to all the mess that puppies make and all the things they gets up to before they're properly trained.'

'Aah, Dad ... you promised me.'

'You've got Gyp.'

'No, I haven't. He doesn't live with us any more. Why can't I have a puppy, Dad?'

362

'I just told you, my lover, 'cos he'd need properly training.'

'You could train him.'

'No, I couldn't, 'cos I'm not there, permanent.'

'Perhaps John...' Lucie's dark blue eyes, so like his, stared at Calum forlornly. 'No, he wouldn't want a puppy,' she said firmly. She kicked her legs in frustration. 'It's not fair,' she cried.

'No, nothink's fair, Luce,' Calum agreed, shaking his head sadly.

Jake was kicking a ball around in the small, scrubby recreation ground that local people had for generations called the rec. Luke was a little way away, picking blackberries with their friend, Pete Goodyear. He'd promised to take some home for Angie to bake a blackberry and apple pie but the temptation to eat the ripe fruit was proving difficult to control.

Posy Fletcher, an unmarried woman in her late thirties, still living at home with her parents and sister, was walking the family's pet poodle, Floss. Since the little poodle's escapade five weeks earlier, when she'd gone missing for several days, Posy's mother, Minnie, had called in at the vet's shop in Nailsea High Street and purchased a special harness and a long releasing lead, which gave Flossie a certain amount of freedom to run about, but no chance of repeating her recent bid for escape. She could quite well have been abducted, a valuable dog like her, the Fletchers reasoned.

Flossie's ears pricked up when she saw Gyp come running towards her; she wagged her stumpy tail with great enthusiasm. Gyp, too, couldn't hide his pleasure at meeting up with his long-lost amour, the subject of all his doggy desires.

'Come *yere...*' Posy reined the little dog in, aiming a well-placed kick on the terrier's white and tan flanks with the toe of her purple-trimmed trainer. 'Get that pesky animal away from my dog,' she called to Jake.

'Call that a dog?' he mocked. 'It's more like a mouse on the end of a piece of string.'

'I'll have you know this dog's got a pedigree as long as your arm,' Posy flared back indignantly.

'So it might,' said Jake, 'but it still looks like a mouse. And not half as pretty as my gerbil, Sylvester, or the rat we've got in a cage at school.'

'Gerroff!' Posy yelled, as Gyp began licking Flossie's diminutive rear end in an extremely possessive and intimate way. 'I'm not telling you again,' she continued and, bending down, all fifteen stone of her, she hoisted the toy poodle into her arms.

Flossie struggled to get down, but Jake had hold of Gyp's collar now, pulling him well away.

When Posy reached the exit gate she lowered her pet to the ground. Flossie turned to look at Gyp with eyes filled with longing. Then, resignedly, she trotted obediently to heel behind Posy's size eight Reeboks. Still tiny as a kitten, the bitch's little abdomen showed signs of a slight swelling, though so far, neither Minnie nor the other Fletchers were aware of anything amiss.

Chapter Twenty-three

Tyler's first sighting of Caitlin in Fuzzy Cove caught him completely unawares. He was cruising down Maritime Way at a snail's pace in his hired Renault Megane, hoping to kill a few minutes before the pub opened. He was to meet Erin there and treat her to a ploughman's lunch. Afterwards, they would be going to visit the wild bird sanctuary at Slimbridge. Erin loved wildlife of every kind, and he'd been surprised to hear that she'd never been there.

As he was passing the small general store near the top of the hill a man came out and got into a white delivery van parked outside the front. Tyler was just about to look away when he saw his wife emerge from the shop; she was waving her arms to attract the van driver's attention. Tyler pulled to a halt a little further down the hill and, in his wing mirror, watched his wife in conversation with the man. Soon afterwards, he saw Holly come out of a nearby door and go over to join them. They all stood talking for a minute or two until the van moved off, when the girls went back inside the shop.

Tyler keyed the ignition and drove slowly away. His feelings towards Caitlin had changed in the last couple of weeks. He wasn't so much jealous of what she did any more; merely angry because she'd caused him so much hassle. He remembered how free he'd been in Vegas without her, freer than he'd felt in a long time. He intended to keep Caitlin on tenterhooks a while longer, though, to let her sweat a little, wondering what his next move would be.

His reason for coming to England had originally been to locate his wife and persuade her to return with him to California. Already the golden coast was starting to beckon him back. He missed the sunshine, and was looking forward to being there, *to start living again*. The trendy resorts along the Pacific coast were filled with good-looking broads, he reminded himself, and Tyler Sinclair had never had any problem pulling the birds!

A perfect example of his power of attraction was the friendship he was gently nurturing with Erin Meredith. She was a virgin, her so-called friend had said, and there weren't too many of those about these days. He'd only met her recently but he knew his technique would result, sooner or later, in yet another conquest for him.

Erin was a child of nature who loved wildlife of any kind, he'd discovered. Her baby-blue eyes would pop out on stalks, he was sure, if he were to invite her to San Diego to see the dolphins perform their tricks at the Seaworld centre. After that, they could mosey on up to Santa Barbara – take a stroll along the pier and see the unwieldy pelicans, looking like those prehistoric creatures in kids' picture books, flying low over people's heads, sending them scurrying for cover. A few piddling little wild ducks in a sanctuary in Gloucestershire were nothing compared to the majestic sight of an eagle soaring high across a clear cobalt sky above the Grand Canyon. He'd shared all these good things with Caitlin; the fact that she'd chosen to return to dull old England only proved to him how little she had appreciated the life they'd had together.

He and Erin had just finished eating when Holly came into the pub. Tyler beckoned her over to join them and, after fetching her a drink, began quizzing her about where Caitlin was living. He mentioned he'd seen them talking earlier, so Holly couldn't deny that she knew her. After some initial hedging, she told him that Caitlin was staying, temporarily, at a bungalow called Cedar Keys on the outskirts of the village.

Tyler left Holly and Erin to finish their drinks and went out to draw some money from the cash dispenser situated at the far end of the harbour. Soon after he'd gone, Jazz breezed into the pub. She rushed up to Erin and, greeting her warmly, apologised for the uncalled-for remark she'd made when they last met.

'You can't help being a dozy prat,' Holly told her. 'We were just discussing Tyler and his wife … or ex-wife. We think Caitlin must be still suffering from the effects of that miscarriage.'

'She's got to be a bit unbalanced – why else would she be afraid of a lovely man like Tyler?' said Erin. 'He didn't even know she was pregnant when she came away. He says she's changed completely from how she used to be.'

Jazz was at the bar getting in drinks when Tyler reappeared.

'So you didn't know your wife was expecting

another baby when she pushed off?' said Holly.

'No, I didn't have a clue,' he said. 'I must confess, though,' he added, smirking sarcastically, 'I did leave her resting for a whole six weeks at our beautiful beach home near San Francisco while I was performing in Vegas with the group. Poor badly treated woman, eh?'

'My dad would go crazy, hearing about all these places,' commented Erin. 'He's wanted to visit them for as long as I can remember.'

'And what about *you*, Erin?' said Tyler. 'I'm due to go back there next week; how would *you* like to come over for a short vacation? I'll fix things with Caitlin – tell her I've had enough of her neurotic, hysterical behaviour, and I'm putting in for a divorce.'

His voice was low and beguiling as he appealed to her. 'You need only come for a couple of weeks. I'll show you sights like you've never seen before in your life.' He touched her cheek gently. 'Just think about it, sweetie, and let me know, eh?'

Erin coughed and spluttered, almost spilling her lemonade. 'Gosh, I don't know about that,' she murmured.

'Hey up, what's the peony-like fizzog in aid of?' enquired Jazz, returning to their table with a fresh round of drinks, and noticing the bright red blush that had crept all over Erin's face and neck. Jazz stared at them all in turn until Holly felt compelled to tell her about Tyler's invitation to Erin.

'Oh, good golly Moses, man,' Jazz exclaimed. 'Give the poor bloody girl a chance. She'll need a year at least before she agrees to do anything as daring as that.' She placed the drinks on the table in front of them. 'That's what I told my brother a couple of months ago,' she went on. 'He was thinking of inviting her to spend a weekend with him in Gloucester, so he could take her to a farewell party at the hospital before he left for Africa.'

Holly could see by the startled expression on Erin's face that this was a complete surprise to her: she'd almost jumped out of her skin. She suddenly realised it was Dominic that Erin had been fancying all along and not Marcus at all. If only I'd had the slightest notion, Holly thought, I'd certainly have put Dominic in the picture.

At her mother's house the following day, Holly broke the news to Caitlin that Tyler had managed to worm out from her where she was staying. He'd given her no cause to think he might be out to cause trouble, she explained helpfully, but Caitlin obviously thought differently.

'Holly – how could you do that?' she screeched, looking as though she would have liked to throw some heavy instrument at her. She'd shouted so loudly that Angie had stuck her head round the shop door to find out what all the commotion was.

'For a quiet one, she's got one hell of a temper,' Holly told Guy later at their flat. Guy was engrossed in the motor racing on television, though, and merely nodded.

'*Ooh...*' Holly exclaimed, feeling like throwing a heavy object at *him*. She eased her frustration by hurling a soft cushion instead.

Caitlin hardly slept a wink that night. Lying quite still, she mulled over the problem in her mind. Every time a branch creaked outside in the garden, she was convinced it was Tyler coming to seek her out.

The next morning on the way to work she told Rex about it and he suggested that she move in with him. It made sense, he said. She already spent a great deal of time at his place, visiting her cat.

Rex's well-maintained, two-bedroomed mobile home, almost hidden behind a copse of trees, was situated at the top of a hill overlooking the Bristol Channel, and reached by a narrow, twisting pathway, its entrance virtually hidden from the lane. Unless someone actually showed Tyler where it was, Rex was sure he'd never find it by himself.

Tyler's vacation would soon be coming to an end, Caitlin told him. Persimmon Sorbet was booked to appear at Lake Tahoe throughout the month of October, and it was almost the end of September now. As she explained that, relief settled over her like a warm, comforting blanket.

Rex, as ever a quivering mass of excitement when Caitlin was near, managed to murmur, 'Good.'

God, she's so lovely, he thought, his knees having turned to jelly as they always did when in her mesmerising presence. Her perfume was intoxicating – her hair a cloud of pure spun gold! How on earth he'd managed to keep his hands to himself during all the journeys they'd made to

and from Upalong, he'd never be able to understand. But keep them to himself, he had.

Late in the evening of the twins' birthday, with
the baby tucked up in bed and Jake and Luke
gone with Josh to visit their grandmother, Angie
and Holly were clearing up the remains of the tea
party. Caitlin had stayed on an extra hour to help
Angie serve the boys and their friends with oven-
baked chips and pizza, followed by hot dogs and
burgers well-laced with bright yellow mustard. It
was a far cry from the blancmange and jelly that
Holly's guests had consumed at the birthday
parties Angie had catered for not so long ago.
Then she'd prepared platefuls of small, triangular
fish-paste sandwiches and homemade jam-and-
cream sponge which the kids had taken away
with them in paper serviettes.

By contrast, today's cake had been a pro-
fessionally iced Wallace and Gromit affair. Holly
had got it from Sainsburys with Reward vouchers
she'd been saving for some while. Twenty-six
candles had adorned the top: thirteen white on
one side for one twin, and thirteen blue on the
opposite side for the other.

'Mum.' Holly's voice broke into Angie's train of
thought. Against any logic or reason, Angie was
feeling quite upset at the thought of Caitlin
moving in to live with Rex. Somehow it seemed
the ultimate rejection of herself. 'Something I've
been meaning to ask you,' Holly went on. 'I
couldn't say anything when Caitlin was here.'

'Yes?' questioned Angie, reaching up to put a
stack of dinner plates into the cupboard above

the worktop. Best to act nonchalantly; she didn't want Holly to guess that she was in any way bothered by the situation.

'What's your opinion about Caitlin and her husband? Wouldn't you say she's acting a bit over the top?'

'How would I know, love? I don't know anything about the man,' Angie said, piling knives and forks into the cutlery drawer, and placing the remains of the cake in her large Tupperware container.

'Well, I do, and so do Erin, and Jazz. We've all reached the same conclusion that she's still suffering from the effects of the miscarriage ... postnatal depression, or something like that.'

'You might be right but, like I said, I've never even met this husband of hers,' said Angie, frowning thoughtfully.

'Well, I – me and the girls, that is – think he's rather nice. He's a great guitarist, according to Barry Buckley, and the next time he comes to England he's planning to bring his guitar and play for us at the Smuggler's. That's what Erin's told us, anyway.'

'Erin?' queried Angie. 'Why would Erin know?'

'Because she and Tyler seem to have struck up a very good friendship, that's why,' explained Holly.

'So does that mean that he'll have stopped pursuing Caitlin now?' Without catching Holly's glance, Angie finished wiping down the top of the counter, and rinsed the cloth under the tap. 'I'm sure she's under the impression he wants her to go back with him,' she added.

'He's not *pursuing* her at all. He just wants to see her; make sure she's all right, and then he'll be on his way,' Holly said.

'Mmm ... well ... I'm pretty certain that isn't what Caitlin thinks. I know from the way she's been avoiding bumping into him. She only steps outside this door to jump straight into Rex's van. She's scared stiff of him, if you ask me.'

But Holly had given Angie food for thought. Supposing what she said was right, and it was all a ploy on Caitlin's part to make Rex Carpenter feel sorry for her, protective of her, even to the point of taking her into his home to live. She wondered if they were sleeping together. The old flame of jealousy had reared its ugly head again, and it wasn't a nice sensation.

'I've come to the conclusion that it's all in Caitlin's mind,' Holly continued. 'She's a nice girl and all that. Fantastically attractive to look at; no wonder Rex is hooked. It's my opinion, though, Mum, she's taking this fear business a trifle too far.'

'You might be right,' agreed Angie cautiously. She was spared from having to say any more on the subject, however, by the sound of Gyp barking and the back gate rattling open. Suzi, accompanied by her two small daughters, came into the yard, the girls carrying parcels wrapped in gift paper.

'We've come to see the birthday boys,' announced Suzi cheerfully.

'Oh gosh – sorry, Suze, they're up at Upalong. Josh fetched them a short while ago,' Angie said, giving Lucie a kiss.

Holly swung Emma up into her arms and cuddled her tightly. 'Hi, Em,' she greeted her cousin warmly. 'And hi there, Lucie, how's *you?*' She looked down at Lucie, who was fussing with Gyp, hugging him round the neck and squeezing him tightly.

'That's all she cares about, that dratted dog,' smiled Suzi. 'A dog's all she wants in all the world, she keeps on telling me.'

'It is,' vowed Lucie firmly, her fathomless marine blue eyes fixing them all with a firm, direct stare. 'If I can't have Gyp, then I want a dog of my very own, so there.'

Holly mimicked her. '*So there*, and I don't care what anybody else thinks, eh Luce? Come on – let's go and say hello to Guy.'

'How did you get here?' asked Angie after they'd gone. She knew Suzi had no transport of her own.

'Dexy brought me over. I was hoping John would, but he didn't want to know.'

Suzi sounded irritated by this, Angie thought. 'Do I detect a note of disenchantment?' she asked.

'You could say that,' replied Suzi. 'He's pretty damn selfish but then, all men are, in my experience.'

'Mmm ... lots of them are. They mostly do what *they* want.'

Angie hoped that Suzi *was* experiencing some disillusionment in her relationship with the new man. It might give Calum a better chance of getting back with her one day.

'I'm sorry, I didn't mean all of them,' Suzi said

apologetically. 'I realise how bloody awful it must be for you.'

'Sometimes I feel it's only a dream, and he'll come walking through that door,' answered Angie. 'Then there are other times when I can barely remember his voice, or what he *feels* like ... what he looks like, even.' She sighed deeply. 'Well, perhaps not what he looks like. After all, I've only got to look at Cal to remember that.'

'These MacPhersons – they get a hold on you in some strange, mysterious way, don't they?'

'You might say that, Suze. Yet I'm just beginning to come out from under Curt's spell, I think.'

'If it makes you feel stronger, I'm glad to hear it,' Suzi told her. Taking hold of a loose strand of her glossy nutbrown hair, she pinned it into the round bun at the back of her head.

'You always wear your hair up these days,' commented Angie. 'I much prefer it loose, falling all around your shoulders.'

'John likes me with it this way. Says it makes me look more sophisticated.'

'Whatever's best for you. It's none of my business, love.'

Angie was unable to avoid the slight feeling of dismay she experienced when hearing about and discussing other people's relationships. She didn't envy Suzi with her John, didn't want Rex – not as a serious proposition, anyway – and yet she still resented his falling in love with Caitlin. She was beginning to wonder just what it was she did want, other than to turn the clock back a year and prevent Curt from going fishing that night.

At the country and western special at the Smuggler's Retreat the following Saturday evening, Roxanne was introduced to Tyler Sinclair, the man who was keeping her daughter company. After the poor recommendation given to her by her sister Myrna, she was pleasantly surprised by both his manner and appearance. It was plain to her that her husband didn't share her enthusiasm – but sod what Henry thought, she concluded. He was treating their daughter like a princess, and surely that was what Henry had always wanted for her, too.

Though she was careful not to let it show, Roxanne's pride was still smarting from the debacle with Marty Riley at the Relax-a-Vous Motel some weeks earlier. She hadn't been to a country and western night since, and she was relieved to find that his wife had meant what she said, and stopped him coming out to the Smuggler's Retreat. The old bat might not know it, but she had done Roxanne the biggest favour ever.

Tonight's singer bore no resemblance at all to Charley Pride; the songs he was singing were new ones, nice in their own way, but Roxanne was unable to sing along as she usually did because she didn't know the words. A good loud burst of 'Stand By Your Man', or 'When the New Wears off of your Crystal Chandeliers', was the finest thing imaginable for blowing the cobwebs away from your mind.

Relieved as she was not to have to face Marty Riley again, there still remained the odd, unavoidable encounter with Calum. She hadn't forgiven him for doing a bunk from the motel room that night, leaving her to make her own way home the following morning by taxi after all. There was no sign of him tonight, she was glad to see. A man's inability to get it up – especially when encouraged to by *her* – was completely unforgivable ... with the possible exception, she thought, of poor Sidney Digweed who'd had a stomach bug and could therefore be excused for his lack of performance.

She was tempted to question Henry about the cure for impotence, Viagra, but he'd be sure to wonder why she was asking, and that could lead to some *very* awkward questions. The same applied to her sister Myrna. She decided to ask Hubert Herring if he could tell her anything about it. He ought to be able to; he worked for the Health Service, too.

The music changed to a slow tempo, and Jasmine Stone strolled up to the microphone. Roxanne couldn't abide the stuck-up cow, but she had to admit that Jazz did a great impersonation of Patsy Cline. 'I Fall To Pieces'. It was one of Roxanne's special favourites. The girl sang it well, with a catch in her voice in all the appropriate places.

'That was really lovely,' Henry commented, clapping enthusiastically.

Roxanne stared at her husband in surprise. It was rare for Henry to get so carried away by a country and western number.

'I'll get us another drink,' he said and, leaning over to the Herrings, asked them what they were having.

This was another first for Henry tonight, Roxanne contemplated. She was always having to remind him of his manners when they were sharing a table with Hubert and Lillian. Hubert was his work colleague when all was said and done.

The young man from America climbed on to the stage next. He borrowed a guitar from the regular guitarist and settled himself on a stool to play. It was a piece unfamiliar to Roxanne but, to judge by the loud applause, it was a very popular choice.

Gentle, romantic – he seemed to be directing the words at Erin. Roxanne watched them both intently, almost feeling the deep surge of emotion the singer was arousing in her usually reticent daughter's soul. She looked at Henry. He, too, was transfixed watching Erin – stopped in his tracks as he was about to cross the room, a tray of drinks in his hands. Roxanne saw her chance to ask Hubert Herring if he knew anything about the wonder drug that everyone was raving about. It might be that Calum could do with a dose of it.

Nudging Hubert on the arm, she said, 'Mind if I asks you summat? It's a bit of a medical question, like. Seeing as how you works at the hospital, I thought you might know.'

'What's wrong with asking your hubby?' his wife, Lillian, suggested, staring at Roxanne with interest.

'Nothing at all. I'd rather ask Hubert here; that's all,' replied Roxanne.

'Fire ahead,' he nodded. Both of them were

looking at her closely now.

'How would anyone go about getting hold of that stuff they'm prescribing for impotence these days? I wondered if you could tell me.'

Husband and wife exchanged knowing looks, then they both glanced across at Henry.

'It ain't nothing *personal*,' Roxanne assured them hastily. 'It's just somebody was asking me about it – that's all.'

'You must mean Viagra. You gets it from your doctor,' Hubert laughed. 'But I don't know nothing about how good it is,' he added. 'I ain't ready for it yet, myself.'

'Oh, blimey – hark at 'e,' exclaimed Lillian, cackling in amusement. Her voice rang out into the hushed atmosphere, and people nearby asked her to shush. 'He'd like everyone to think he's as virile as them Gladiators you sees on the bloomin' telly,' she continued in a whisper loud enough for others to hear.

Roxanne turned her attention back to the stage. She became aware of the haunting, romantic song being sung by the man whose treacle-dark eyes were staring into those of her pretty blonde daughter. Erin looked prettier than ever tonight, she thought. The pale blue ribbon with which she'd tied back her hair matched the colour of her eyes exactly, and the long-sleeved, pale blue and white gingham frock suited her colouring a treat.

Henry, Roxanne saw, still hadn't moved – he had an expression on his face that she'd never seen before. Well, she thought, perhaps she had seen it *once* before. She remembered the incident well. They'd been on their way home from a holiday in Devon and stopped off for a picnic on Exmoor. Erin was only about four or five years old and a poisonous snake had slithered out of the bracken and almost bitten her leg. Almost, but not quite, for Henry had dived on it like a flash, flinging it back into the undergrowth with his bare hand.

Fancy remembering such a daft thing as that, Roxanne chided herself now. Whatever had the snake incident got to do with anything that was happening at the moment?

The song ended, and Erin brought Tyler over to sit with them. Roxanne invited him to Sunday dinner the next day, an invitation he gladly accepted. Erin seemed pleased that she'd asked him. The only person not so delighted was Henry who remained po-faced for the whole of the rest of the evening. Too bad, Henry, Roxanne felt like saying. He'd always been critical of her for making too much fuss of their daughter – now it was *his* turn to act like a broody, possessive hen.

Chapter Twenty-four

Tyler Sinclair, having spent the day at his parents' home in Burnham, was on his way back to Fuzzy Cove where he'd arranged to meet Erin and Jazz in the pub. He passed the bungalow at Upalong where Erin had told him Caitlin had lived until recently, though Erin wasn't able to say where she was now. Tyler had a strong suspicion his wife had started a relationship with the man who'd been driving her to and from work each day. If she wasn't actually living with him, then it was a safe bet the guy would know where she was.

Tyler parked the Megane in the car park at the back of the Smuggler's Retreat and went inside for a drink. Perched on a stool at the bar some five minutes later, he was drawn into conversation by the man sitting next to him – a rather unpleasant-looking, elderly guy who was grumbling to all and sundry about a business rival who, according to him, was fast running him into bankruptcy.

'Young bloody upstart,' the man complained. 'It oughtn't to be allowed.'

'You ain't never still on about Rex Carpenter, be you, Adge? God blimey, why don't you give it a rest?' one of the other customers interjected.

'I'd be surprised if 'e even got planning permission to turn that land into a market garden,' the man went on regardless. 'That there land on Hooper's Hill's good grazing land ... what have happened to all them sheep what used to graze up there?'

'All gone for mutton, over to Sheep Fair at Priddy,' the same man told him.

'Yeah, well, I'll tell thee, mate, it's summat I'm going to be looking into – I'll bet the bugger's got no rights to be using that land for commercial purposes.'

The name Hooper's Hill had rung a bell with Tyler. 'If you don't mind my asking, what do you know about this Carpenter? The man who's taking your trade away?' he asked the unpleasant swarthy one.

The man frowned at Tyler suspiciously. He took another swig of his cider without saying a word.

'Do you know anything about him personally?' Tyler persisted. 'Whether he lives alone, or whether he's married, or what?'

'Why d'you wanna know?' answered the man, still glaring at Tyler suspiciously.

'Because I've an idea he's stolen my wife and I intend to, ever so slightly, reshape his face for him,' Tyler said.

The man shook Tyler by the hand. 'Put it there, boy,' he said. 'I'll be glad to tell you anything you want to know about young Rex Carpenter,' and he went on to do just that, even confirming Tyler's suspicion that the man did have a woman living with him.

When he'd finished – which included furnishing Tyler with an address, and directions to get to it – Tyler treated the old guy to another flagon of rough and bought himself another beer. He'd pay a visit to Carpenter's home the first moment he could, to suss out the territory, he decided.

Tyler was about to tuck into his next pint when he heard a commotion in the pub doorway. A short, dumpy woman with frizzy grey hair and a distraught look on her face was standing in the entrance, holding a tiny dog in her arms.

'Oh, Adge...' the woman was wailing. 'It's terrible bad news I got to tell you.'

'What in the name of pity is it, Min?' Adge spluttered.

'It's our little Floss – she's having pups. When she ran away that time, I took her to the vet's, just to be on the safe side. He said I was to bring her back if she started swellin' up. She did; so I have ... and, ooh, Arthur – she's due to whelp in two weeks' time, he says.'

'You never said a word to me,' her husband exclaimed.

'I didn't want to tell you, 'cos I knew you'd go flipping mad ... and you will.'

'I should say I bloody will. And whose bloody dog is it what's responsible for 'er condition; that's what I'd like to know?'

His wife looked at him worriedly. 'I asked if 'twere too late to do an abortion, but the vet said it were. It'd be against his ethics to do it now. I wa'n't so sure about that, I said. It ain't like a human being, after all.'

'It had better not be that mongrel of Rusty MacPherson's, that's all I can say,' Adge Fletcher replied angrily. Taking the dog from her, he hustled his wife away.

By the time he was due to meet Erin and Jazz at seven thirty, Tyler had consumed a good deal more beer than he'd intended. He was proud of himself for staying off the hard stuff, though. There'd be plenty of opportunity to catch up on *that* when he returned to the States in two days' time.

Jazz was the first to appear. Erin had been held up at work, she told him, and would be joining them just as soon as she could.

'And where's your other friend, Holly?' Tyler enquired.

'Home, all cosy and cuddled up with her Guy, I dare say,' Jazz replied.

'Lucky Guy,' observed Tyler. 'He should think himself very lucky, that dude.'

'He does,' Jazz assured him. 'They absolutely adore one another, those two.'

'She's an altogether tasty girl! Those bright red curls, and—'

'Yeah, all right, don't get too carried away. You sound just like my brother. He used to rave over her, too.'

'She didn't reciprocate, though?'

'No, she never did. I can't think why. He's exceptionally dishy, my bruv.'

'Unusual to hear a gal say that.'

'Perhaps it is. Here's Erin. Hi, love.'

Jazz moved along the bench to let Erin sit next to Tyler.

'We were just saying, Erin,' Jazz said, 'my brother Dominic was really smitten with Holly, wasn't he?'

Erin looked startled. 'Yes, I suppose he was. So what's brought *this* subject up?'

'Tyler was asking about Holly and Guy. They're not only joined at the hip, those two, but just about everywhere else that it's possible to imagine, I told him.'

Tyler frowned. 'The mind boggles,' he said.

'Indeed it does,' said Jazz, 'but I'm telling you, it's the truth.'

'Where is he now – your brother?'

'In Uganda, working for ActionAid,' Jazz said.

Turning to Erin, she went on, 'My sister Georgia's getting married in December. I'm to be a bridesmaid ... me, and Stefanie Madison, my mother's idea of a very *naice* young lady. It'll be quite an occasion. Mirabel's running round like a headless chicken already.'

'Will you be coming back to see us before then?' asked Erin.

Jazz nodded, 'Hopefully.'

She explained to Tyler. 'I'm off to university on Saturday. Warwick, you know. Not Oxford like my father and brother Giles, much to their disgust.'

Erin hesitated, and then said, 'Dominic trained at King's College School of Medicine, in London, didn't he?'

'Fancy you remembering that!' exclaimed Jazz. 'Yeah – and so did Tom, of course.'

'Who's Tom?' Tyler wondered.

'Jazz's boyfriend,' said Erin.

'In my ma and pa's eyes, I guess he is,' Jazz said, her ebony gaze fixed dreamily upon Barry Buckley, who was deep in conversation with a couple of regulars at the bar. 'Tom's going to be flat-sharing with Giles at his bijou pad in Clifton village this winter. Jolly for them, I say,' she went on.

'The *posh* part of Bristol, eh?' Tyler observed.

'Yeah, the great ponce. I hope he and Tom will be very happy together – though Tom's a much nicer person than him, I have to say.'

Tyler told them about the rumpus earlier, when Minnie Fletcher had given Adge the news about their pet.

'He's threatening to do all sorts to the owner of the dog that's put her in the family way,' Tyler laughed.

Erin said nothing; she wondered how long it would take Adge Fletcher to find out that it was Gyp. She was glad now she'd told no one except the MacPhersons how she'd found them running loose together.

'Do either of you know where Rex Carpenter lives?' Tyler asked suddenly.

'No ... no idea,' Erin replied. She was relieved she didn't know; it was probably something connected with Tyler's obsessive relationship with Caitlin. His possessiveness where *she* was concerned was the one aspect about Tyler's personality that bothered Erin somewhat.

'Haven't a clue,' Jazz agreed. 'I know he lives in a caravan, but I couldn't tell you where it is. Why?' she asked as an afterthought.

'Just testing – that's all,' said Tyler. You couldn't trust women any further than you could throw them. 'Anyone want more drinks?' he enquired.

'Don't bother about me. There's something I need to discuss with Barry.' Jazz wandered away, leaving Tyler and Erin to themselves.

'It's a lovely night. Let's go for a drive; we've only got two more nights together,' he told Erin.

It was indeed a beautiful evening, and not at all cold. When they reached a suitable place, Tyler lay his jacket on the ground and pulled her down beside him. In the last few days he'd made plenty of progress with Little-Miss-Perfect and, after a brief fumble in her knickers, he unzipped his chinos and moved up and down on top of her, to gain his satisfaction without actually touching her body. He intended to keep her on the boil – her instincts aroused – so that when he came back in December, she'd be gagging to have him fuck her for real.

The next day, armed with information he'd obtained from Fletcher, Tyler made his way by foot along the short winding trail towards the small caravan site where Rex Carpenter had his home. He needed to do a quick recce of the place while the owner was out. He peeped through the windows of the van to familiarise himself with the layout. He planned to give Caitlin and the boyfriend one almighty scare before he departed for America. Soon, his sweet little wife would be history; he was going to put in for a divorce, citing her adultery. He mustn't forget to call in at the estate agent's later today to put the house at Worle on the market, he thought.

Quarter to six the following morning; leaves were falling thick and fast in the woods around the caravan site as Tyler stopped his car a short distance away. The mobile homes were well spaced out, each surrounded by its own small garden, and none of them overlooked the other. The two bedroom windows of Rex Carpenter's van were in full view of the track, he'd already discovered – just right for what he had in mind. Sitting quite still in the early morning's hush, he let his anger wash over him for a moment. No one did the dirty on Tyler Sinclair and got away with it, he reflected quietly.

The sound of birdsong was all around ... a dampish smell of rotting foliage came into his car and, as he peered through the branches, towards the van, a grey squirrel shot up a tall pine tree nearby. Tyler accidentally moved his hand on the steering wheel and the squirrel bolted, dropping the nut it had been holding in its paws. Tyler had had no intention of startling the animal, though he had no such scruples about startling his wife and her boyfriend.

Wham ... wham ... the flying rocks found their targets, exactly as Tyler had planned. Pressing hard down on the throttle, he sped off along the looping track back to where it joined with the road. As he passed through the village of Fuzzy Cove, the church clock was striking six. Ten minutes later he was back on the motorway, continuing his journey to London.

Caitlin had jumped awake the moment she heard the crash coming from Rex's room. A moment later, the glass in her own bedroom window caved in, and an enormous boulder landed on the floor by her bed. Sick with terror, she peered through the gaping hole and saw the taillights of a car disappearing into the trees.

She looked back into the room and saw that the boulder had missed her cat's basket by inches. There were shards of broken glass all over her eiderdown.

'Are you all right?' she heard Rex call. His voice sounded shocked and faraway. He pushed open her bedroom door and came inside.

'Oh, Rex,' she exclaimed. His head was running with blood; there was blood all over his arm and hand. She sat on the bed, looking silently at him; words had deserted her for the moment.

'You're all right … no damage there?' Rex said, his concerned eyes examining her for any sign of injury.

'No, thank God I was out of range. The boulder shot clear over my bed,' Caitlin replied.

He nodded. 'I'd better take a look outside.'

'Wait – I'm coming with you.' Caitlin took her dressing gown off the door and slipped it on. 'He'll be long gone by now, though,' she told him.

'No need for three guesses as to who it was,' Rex answered quietly.

'No, no need at all,' Caitlin agreed.

It was typical of her husband, she knew. Just the sort of thing that Tyler would think was clever.

'Well, I hope that's made *him* feel better, because I know what it's done to me. I knew I hated him before but now I'd like to kill him,' she said.

She followed Rex into the vestibule and waited while he opened the front door and looked out. As she'd anticipated, there was nothing unusual to be seen.

'Will you call the police?' she asked.

'I shall report it to the police,' Rex said, 'so that when and if he ever comes back, they'll have been put on notice.'

'Angie told me Tyler was flying back to America today; his plane's due to leave at eleven o'clock this morning. American Airlines … we can confirm it if we like. Make sure he's on the passenger list.'

'How did Angie know that?'

'Someone told Holly, I believe, and Angie

wanted me to know.'

'We've got *some* friends in the camp then,' Rex replied, holding his hand to his brow to stem the flow of blood.

'Shut that front door, and come inside,' Caitlin told him, 'I want to look at that head.'

Leading the way into the living room, she switched on the gas fire and settled him on to the couch. 'I'll get some hot water. Before we do anything else, we must get you tidied up.'

She came back a moment later with a bowl of warm water. Parting his brown curls, she examined his head carefully. They were only surface cuts, she was relieved to see, but the bleeding from his scalp was trickling down all round his forehead.

'You're going to need to see a doctor just to make sure there's no glass in these cuts,' she said. 'In the meantime, I've torn up one of your towels. Hold still while I wrap it round, and then I'll get us a nice cup of tea. A little brandy in it won't go amiss. Do you have any?'

'There's a drop in the kitchen, I think.'

'Then let's get well and truly sloshed, shall we?'

She smiled, and Rex was lost. He loved the way her sweet mouth curved over those pearly white teeth.

'Look at you ... you're so beautiful,' he groaned. 'How could the swine want to harm a hair on that lovely head?'

'He could, and he did,' Caitlin told him. 'And while we're at it – in my book he's not fit to breathe the same air as you.'

'Come here.' She moved to sit with him on the

couch and, wrapping her arms round him, pulled him towards her so that his bandaged head was resting on her breast.

'I think I love you,' she murmured quietly. 'I really have to give you a kiss.'

Rex looked up and beheld her beautiful face. He'd been holding her at arm's length for so long now, it had almost become a habit. Now, though, she was in his arms, and hugging him tightly too. It was reciprocal, and he'd never dreamed it could possibly be. Not someone so positively, gorgeously attractive as *her* – he must be the luckiest man alive!

'You are the most gorgeous woman in the whole wide world, and I can't believe this is happening to me,' he exclaimed.

'And how could anyone in their right mind be mean to you?' she whispered. 'You're the kindest, most caring man I've ever known.'

She undid the tie of her dressing gown and let it slip to the floor. Next, she pulled the knee-length tee-shirt she wore as a nightie over her head, and Rex found himself staring, as though mesmerised, at her two pert breasts with the hard peachy nipples surrounded by two golden haloes.

Her bright tawny hair was falling all over his face now as she knelt beside him; he could feel it tickling his neck. Nothing in his life before had had the power to arouse him the way that Caitlin did. He'd known it from the first time he set eyes on her – the day she opened the door at Josh Berry's bungalow and beckoned him inside. He was glad now that he hadn't had sex with Angie, though they'd come very near to it that one time.

Most especially not Angie, he thought; he counted her as a very special friend.

Together now, he and Caitlin made love. It was over in less than a minute, it seemed to him, but the second time they took it more slowly, and the bonding between them was everything Rex had imagined it would be: like recognising, and meeting, another half of yourself, he thought.

Their idyll was interrupted by the need to telephone the surgery for an appointment. And Caitlin had to ring Angie to let her know what had happened and that she would be late. Angie, after questioning Caitlin briefly on the circumstances of the attack, told her to take her time and recover. She would arrange for Josh and Daisy to take care of Evie for the day, she assured her.

'I feel a fraud,' Caitlin confessed to Rex, as eventually they were sitting cuddled together, eating toast and marmalade, and drinking tea from the fresh pot she'd made. 'Here we are ... nothing drastically wrong with us ... there can't be, otherwise we wouldn't have been able to make love.'

'I would have made love to you, even at the point of death,' Rex vowed.

'Well, I'm very glad that wasn't an option,' Caitlin declared, 'but don't forget, you've a doctor's appointment in an hour's time'

'And *you're* coming with me. I'm not letting you out of my sight from now on. Not until we know for sure that nutcase is back in California to stay.'

Caitlin frowned, and a pang of fear ran through

her. A shadow clouded the exquisite gold of her eyes as she said, 'I never want to see him again, Rex. I want to stay here with you, if you'll have me. Live here for always with you.'

'And I want you to, for ever and ever. I'll keep you safe from now on. He'll never catch me unawares again. If ever he comes back to England, we'll make sure we're on our guard.'

'Good.' Caitlin leaned over and snuggled her face into his neck.

'I'd better measure up those windows and board them over for now,' Rex said, 'And then we'll go on down to the surgery. And as for you you're to follow in my footsteps, every step that I take.'

After Angie hung up the phone she found herself wondering about Tyler Sinclair, and the way he'd come after Caitlin; eaten up with jealousy because she and Rex seemed to be getting on really well together. The miracle was that he'd only thrown a rock. What if he'd had a gun instead?

Jealousy was such a destructive force and she was ashamed to think that she, too, had wished Caitlin and Rex weren't as close as it was apparent to everyone they had become. The fact that they'd found happiness together didn't detract anything from her own relationship with Rex. He wasn't at all in love with her, and neither was she with him – it was as simple as *that*, Angie told herself.

It was good that Caitlin and Rex had found one another; who knew what the future held for them

393

now? They might even have a child of their own one day. For heaven's sake, don't be so blasted ungenerous, Angie rebuked herself. Then she dialled Daisy's number and explained the position to her. Hearing Daisy's sympathetic words on their behalf, she was resolved to be far more understanding towards Rex and Caitlin in the future.

The Cavalier was parked just off the road, in a turning in front of a five-barred gate, leading to a field filled with sweetcorn. Calum dipped into the bucket of Miss Millie's fried chicken and, pulling out a succulent thigh, popped it into his mouth. He and Marlene were in his car, respectable again now that they had their clothes on. As far as he knew there was no law against eating Miss Millie's chicken and chips in a car, though there was a law against what they'd been doing half an hour earlier. If a policeman had taken the trouble to shine his torch through the misted-up glass of Calum's old banger, he would have seen enough to fill his black book, Calum was sure.

It was the last time he would be doing it with Marlene Trimble. They were agreed the affair had reached the end of the road. There was no more mileage left in it for either of them. Calum had never had a problem performing with Marlene Trimble, his manhood having never let him down. Even when he was sidetracked by remembering his love for Suzi, the thought of her doing it with her yuppie-type lover always got him so wound up, he never had the slightest trouble rising to the occasion.

He finished the last of his Tango drink and, taking Marlene's empty can from her, squeezed her hand affectionately. 'So long, kid. Take care of yourself,' he told her. 'We'll be in touch some time.'

He took her back to where she'd parked her red Fiesta and, as she was driving away, gave her a friendly wave. Then, following her out of the Gordano service station, he headed down the lane leading to Fuzzy Cove. It wasn't yet turning-out time at the Smuggler's, he remembered – he might have time for a quickie.

Entering the pub with five minutes to go, he greeted the burly blond barman. 'Wotcha, Barry. Make mine a pint of the usual, please.'

'My gawd, Rusty – you're cutting it fine,' Barry said, reaching up for a mug.

Calum wasn't best pleased to have Jacko sidle up to him and offer to pay for his drink. Calum let him go ahead; the snidey bugger was still angling for an invitation to join him and Starkey on their next expedition to France.

'Know anybody what wants a load of logs?' Jacko asked, as Calum took a sip from the pint glass.

It was the first drop of alcohol to pass his lips all evening, and he was well ready to enjoy it. A bit of nooky in the back of the car, he thought, followed by chicken and chips, and now a pint of Courage Best. It had rounded the evening off nicely. He took a deep swig of beer, then, wiping the froth from his mouth, looked into Jacko's slitty, hooded eyes.

'Logs?' he repeated. 'Logs, is it now? Whatever happened to the Iceberg frozen products?'

'*Logs.*' Jacko nodded. 'Lovely, steady-burning apple wood. Know anybody what's got a wood-burnin' stove, Rust?'

'As a matter of fact, I do,' replied Calum.

Josh Berry had had one fitted only a few months ago. After ascertaining the price that Jacko was asking, Calum agreed he would make some enquiries.

Chapter Twenty-five

The telephone through in the living room rang for a while and then stopped. Just as well, Angie thought as she attended to Betty Tinker's request for a book of first-class stamps, because she didn't have the time to answer it. She wondered where Caitlin was. She hadn't said she was going out but, there again, Angie had been so busy in the shop for the last two hours, she probably wouldn't have noticed if Caitlin *had* popped in to tell her where she was going.

Business had picked up so well recently that Angie was beginning to think she'd need another pair of hands to help her out during the busier part of the day. Thanks to Holly's brilliant plan for expansion, one of the innovations they'd introduced was a rack of quality greetings cards, and she was now looking into the possibility of adding an extension in the adjoining storeroom.

With Christmas only a couple of months off, Angie planned to sell not only the seasonal greetings cards, but calendars, tinsels and other necessary baubles, not to mention all the extra confectionery. The ideas were neverending and, although Holly intended to stay on at her job, where the pay was good, several hours of her time each week was taken up with helping Angie with the books.

Angie took the customer's money and popped it into the till. 'Thank you very much, Betty,' she said, handing the woman her purchases in a white plastic carrier.

'You ought to have your name printed on these and then I'd be doing some advertising for you as I walked through the village,' Betty Tinker remarked.

'That's something we're looking into,' Angie assured her. Then she had a sudden thought. 'Has your Leanne got a job yet?' She knew Betty's granddaughter had been looking for work. 'I'd like someone to help out here for a few hours each day; I wonder if she'd be interested?'

'Oh, Angie, that would be splendid,' Betty said. 'She's planning to take a college course next year. It would tide her over till then.'

Angie smiled. 'Ask her to call in and see me after seven this evening, all right?'

That settled, and with the shop miraculously free of customers for a moment, Angie lifted the receiver and pressed the code to find out who'd been ringing. It was Daisy, she discovered; she dialled the number quickly.

Daisy had phoned to tell her that her sister-in-law, Vinnie, had arrived from Scotland, with her son Stuart. They'd travelled south yesterday and spent the previous night in London with Stuart's elder daughter, Nicole, which was the reason they were early.

'I've a problem, though,' Daisy continued. 'I've only got the one spare room. That's fine for Vinnie ... but...'

Angie cut her short. 'Nowhere for her son?'

'That's just what I was about to say,' Daisy replied.

'How long's he planning on staying?' asked Angie.

'Only the one night,' said Daisy. 'He wants to get away first thing in the morning. The thought occurred to me, now that Holly's gone, perhaps you'd put him up.'

'Calum's taken over Holly's room now, Mum. I wouldn't want to ask him to move out, not the way he's feeling.'

'He's still upset about his boat, I suppose,' Daisy said.

'You could say that,' agreed Angie. 'Though he's talking of getting some money together by the end of the month to buy another one.'

'I don't like the sound of this man he's becoming so involved with – nor that Jackson fellow.'

'I agree, Mum, but Calum's adamant it's the last time he'll be getting mixed up with either of them.'

'Let's hope you're right; I don't trust that Jacko an inch. Did you know our Cal's talked Josh into buying a load of firewood from him? Let's hope it's not a disaster, like the ice cream job lot!'

'I don't see what can go wrong with logs, do you? At least they won't melt all over the place.'

'So can I tell Stuart he can spend the night on the bed-settee in your living room?' asked Daisy. 'Josh's sofas are only two-seaters; he'd be mighty uncomfortable trying to lie on them.'

'It depends how tall he is,' Angie laughed. 'They'd be all right for a dwarf.'

'Oh, my lord – he's over six foot,' exclaimed Daisy. 'A big, strong ferryboat skipper, sailing the Western Isles.'

'Goodness,' chuckled Angie, 'I really *am* impressed! No seriously, send him down any time you like. He can dump off his stuff, and then he's free to go wherever he wants. I'll be too tied up here to do more than show him through to our living quarters.'

'I expect he'd like to see Calum at some stage. It must be all of twenty years since they last met.'

'Cal's gone out fishing on the Glues' boat. I'm not sure when he'll be back.'

'Never mind. Josh and I will call in on our way to the Albatross tonight to introduce you to Vinnie. The landlord there's catering for our wedding reception.'

'Heck – it isn't long now, is it? Are you feeling scared?'

'Certainly not scared about marrying Josh. Just a few collywobbles with regards to the preparations.'

'Who's going to give you away?' Angie asked.

'Calum, as long as he behaves himself.'

'It would have been Curt,' Angie said.

'It would,' replied Daisy thoughtfully, then her voice brightened. 'It's only the registry office, though, love – not like a church. We'll have a blessing in the church at some later date. Let's just see what turns up, eh?'

'Of course.'

They said their goodbyes and Angie hung up the phone. She knew by Daisy's remark that she was still clinging to the hope that Curt was somewhere alive and would one day return. Angie dismissed the idea from her mind. Not to think about it at all was easier than dwelling on what-might-have-been, or building hopes and getting kicked in the teeth when nothing ever came of it. So, I'm going to be entertaining a visitor tonight, she mused. She hoped he wouldn't be too late making his exit in the morning – Saturday was always a busy day for her in the shop.

At seven that evening, Angie was engaged in sorting out delivery orders for the following day when the shop bell rang. She emerged from the storeroom and, unfastening the bolts and catches, opened the door.

Stuart Hamilton Forsyth beamed her a friendly smile. 'You were expecting me?' he said.

'I certainly am, if you're who I think you are,' she replied.

'I'm Stuart,' he said, holding out his hand in greeting. 'Aunt Daisy's sent me down to see you.'

Angie accepted his handshake. There was no mistaking the MacPherson resemblance, she thought, her glance taking in the profusion of reddish hairs on his wrist below the sleeve of his pale denim shirt.

'And I'm Angie, Curtis's wife,' she said. 'I'm very pleased to meet you.'

She perused his face and as they exchanged glances, Angie saw that his eyes were exactly the same colour as his shirt.

She invited him to follow her through to the living room where her sons were watching a Simpsons video. Evie lay on the floor between them, propped all around with pillows. Fast approaching her sixth month, she'd grown inquisitive and liked to see what was going on.

'Here's the gang,' Angie said. 'Jake Luke this is Stuart – your father's cousin.'

'Are you our uncle?' enquired Luke solemnly.

'Don't be daft,' exclaimed Jake. 'If he's Dad's *cousin*, how can he be our uncle?'

'You're very welcome to call me Uncle,' Stuart told them. 'On the other hand, plain Stuart will do nicely.'

Angie scooped the baby into her arms, and watched the three of them talking. Her lovely boys, she thought. Small, compared to Stuart but, to judge by the size of their feet and their broadening shoulders, they'd be shooting up fairly fast in the next year or two.

'There – aren't you a fine couple of lads,' Stuart told them. 'Your dad would be very proud of you.' He glanced at Angie, as if to assess her reaction. 'You didn't mind me saying that, did you?'

'No. Why should I? It's the truth,' she replied.

'It's just that I rather wondered whether it might be an insensitive thing to say ... insensitive

401

to *you*, that is. Though I know I never mind it when people compare my two girls' looks to that of their mother. She was a very pretty lady.'

Angie nodded, without answering. She'd forgotten he was widowed. So darn full of her own troubles and woes, she'd paid hardly any heed when Daisy, some months ago, had told her she'd received a letter from Vinnie telling her that Stuart's wife had died.

'I'm just going to bath the baby,' she said, breaking the uneasy silence that had crept in between them. 'I don't know what your plans are for tonight, but Calum ought to be back very soon.' She paused, feeling the need to explain. 'He lives here, you know, since he split up with his long-time partner. They've got two little girls; I keep wishing they'd get back together again. It seems such a darned waste.'

Stuart nodded. 'I know exactly what you mean. Life's too short to be depriving those wee lasses of a mother *and* a dad. Aunt Daisy was saying the same thing just now.'

'Perhaps you might get the chance to talk some sense into the silly man,' Angie said.

'I don't expect to be with him for long. I'll have to be getting away first thing tomorrow.'

'But you won't ...' She stopped, not knowing what to say. Would he think her presumptuous, she wondered, if she gave him the impression she wanted him to stay? *She didn't,* of course, and she didn't want him to think that she did. 'In that case, you won't see much of Calum.'

Angie turned and went upstairs. Only a few hours earlier she'd been hoping he'd push off early, so what was different now? It was no business of hers what Stuart Forsyth chose to do with his life, she reminded herself. She had enough complications as it was, trying to run her own.

Calum waved goodnight to Figgis, who'd finished work for the day and was tying up his dinghy, all ready for the off. As Calum prepared to carry his catch ashore, his thoughts turned to the sorry subject of his present financial position. Matters were still at a standstill on the insurance front, concerning *Solitude,* and would be, he knew, until the police had exhausted their enquiries. The good thing was, it shouldn't take anywhere near as long for Angie to receive the compensation for *Green Pepperoni.* She'd paid the insurance premium on the due date, and the company's loss adjuster, having investigated, had decided she was in no way responsible for the fire. Police suspicion had at last fallen on Leonard Snook. He'd confessed to trespass and to causing the conflagration by draping an article of clothing over the top of the propane gas heater. Following his appearance at a local magistrate's court, where he'd been let off with a fine, he was now living in a dosshouse in Bristol, the divorce judge having awarded full equity in his home to his former wife.

Calum's main goal now was to raise enough cash to buy the fifteen-foot cabin cruiser he'd been sailing on today. *Sticking Point* belonged to Dexy Glue's father, Charlie, who, due to ill health, was no longer able to go fishing. Calum was banking on persuading Angie to loan him the necessary five thousand pounds from the money she ought soon to be receiving. He'd be able to pay her back as soon as his claim for the loss of *Solitude* was sorted.

He wasn't grumbling; he'd had an excellent day's fishing. All the other local fishermen had gone after cod but Calum had chosen to fish in the deep channels in Minehead Bay where he'd come upon a sizeable shoal of blonde rays. All the cute little blondies a man could want, and many more besides! He intended to give half his catch to the Glues, which was the least he could do after the old man's generous loan of *Sticking Point.*

Struggling beneath the weight of a square crate filled to the brim with blondies, Calum ascended the flight of stone steps for the third and final time. Dusk was settling fast, and a stiff breeze blowing in from the river brought the stench of mud with it. With Gyp at his heels, Calum crossed the green to the far side, where he'd left his car. As he was loading the crate into the boot, he glanced up to see Adge Fletcher scowling at him from across the roof of the Cavalier. He was carrying a shotgun.

'Thik bloody hound ... I'm a 'gonna kill that bugger dead as a doornail,' Fletcher shouted, pointing the nozzle at Calum's dog.

'Over my dead body,' yelled Calum.

'Yeah – if that's what it takes.' Adge Fletcher lifted the gun and fired a round of pellets at Gyp, missing him by inches.

Calling Gyp to heel, Calum took off, running

as fast as he could back towards the harbour. Taking advantage of the fast-gathering gloom, he made a dash for some outbuildings, where he knew there'd be places to hide.

He and the dog huddled behind a stack of wooden packing boxes for well over fifteen minutes, gradually recovering their breath. There was no sign of Fletcher in all that time so, cautiously, Calum emerged and looked outside the building, whispering to Gyp to follow. But he'd underestimated the older man's cunning. As they neared the harbour, Fletcher had crept up silently from behind and aimed the gun at Gyp. He fired another burst, and the dog yelped in pain. Calum made a grab for the gun to try and wrench it from Fletcher's hand.

As they struggled, the gun went off, firing into the air. Calum – startled – missed his footing, and toppled over the jetty wall. His leg hit the iron ladder; he heard the crack of snapping bone, then he lay on the ledge in the dark for what seemed like an eternity, with Gyp whimpering by the side of him. There were men still out there fishing the Channel, he reminded himself. They'd have to come back within the hour, or risk being stranded all night. After they'd landed, they would have to come ashore by way of the steps or else climb the ladder near to where Calum lay.

The pain was excruciating and, from time to time, he slipped into unconsciousness. In between he remembered the forthcoming trip to France – the bounteous reward which was going to be his when he'd delivered the goods into the hands of Starkey's appointed receiver. What was the contraband to be this time, he wondered. The trip now seemed to bear all the hallmarks of a drug-smuggling heist. He'd been shocked when Starkey confided in him only the other day that he'd done similar deals with Curtis in the past.

Up until this moment, Calum had successfully blocked the knowledge from his mind. Now, though, he was in no state to care one way or the other. None of it mattered any more, he told himself – he was up shit creek without a paddle. The only trip that Calum MacPherson would be making in the foreseeable future was into a hospital operating theatre.

A week later, Calum was able to make it to his mother's and Josh's wedding, on crutches, his leg in plaster from knee to foot. Three nasty breaks, the surgeon had said, one to the ankle and two to the tibia above. Suzi, driving the Cavalier, took him and their daughters to the registry office in Bristol. Lucie was bubbling over with excitement, telling everyone there she had a dog. She didn't have one yet but, as Suzi had explained to Calum several days before, she soon *would* be getting one.

Adge Fletcher had agreed to let Suzi have Flossie's pup on condition Calum agreed not to bring charges relating to the gun attack. In exchange, he promised to retract his threat to sue Calum for the cost of the poodle's emergency caesarean operation. The puppy's birth had almost caused the death of its mother and, once it had been weaned, Fletcher never wanted to set eyes on it ever again. It was the spitting image of Calum's dog and he hated having to look at it. Still not two weeks old, the male pup was already as big as its mother, according to Minnie. She was depending on Suzi to give it a good home and in the meantime – despite her husband's opposition – she was lavishing lots of tender loving care on it.

Suzi's live-in lover, John, aggrieved and upset by her sympathies and good deeds on Calum's behalf, had decided to move out of her life; their relationship had been slowly deteriorating for several weeks. Since the accident, Calum had been filled with remorse for all the trouble he'd caused and, with Gyp in her potting shed in the back garden, recuperating from a few superficial shotgun wounds to his right hindquarters, it had seemed to Suzi an appropriate time to ask Calum to come back to live.

Josh and Daisy had invited the four members of the Fletcher family to their wedding. As Daisy reminded Calum when he'd threatened to stay away in protest, Josh's first wife, Rhoda, was Minnie Fletcher's sister. Any argy-bargy between Adge and Calum had absolutely nothing to do with Josh.

Holly and Guy made a surprise announcement during the party in the evening. They walked hand-in-hand on to the dance floor and, shyly but proudly, said they wanted everyone to know they were engaged. They weren't planning to marry for a long time yet, but they envied Daisy and Josh their honeymoon, leaving for Southampton early the next morning to join the first leg of a Mediterranean cruise. 'We want one just as nice at that,' Holly joked.

'I thought you were going to Italy to visit Guy's grandparents,' observed Daisy.

'We are! That's why,' Holly agreed.

Angie was sitting with Vinnie, and Vinnie's granddaughters, Nicole and Beth. The announcement came as no surprise to her; she and Holly had discussed the matter thoroughly in the course of the last few weeks. Holly *was* very young, she had to admit, but Angie was pleased her daughter had made such a suitable choice. Her main concern tonight had been to find a reliable babysitter for Evie – one that she could trust. That worry had been resolved. Leanne Tinker, who was now working part-time at the shop, had offered to stay and look after her.

The disco was nowhere near as deafening as lots of discos that Angie had been to, with a mix of popular ballads as well as the usual, raunchier numbers. Angie liked the fast ones best because then she could get out on the floor and strut her stuff like all the others, and not have to sit back bemoaning her lack of a special partner.

Luke, bless his heart, had danced with her a few minutes ago. Then Jake, taking his lead, had done the same. What nice companions they would make for some lucky girls in the future, Angie had told herself proudly.

If only *she* was as nice as them. She wasn't though ... she was a jealous, envious cow. When she'd walked into the room tonight and seen Caitlin, wrapped in the arms of Rex Carpenter, wafting around the floor in her creamy chiffon dress, looking like a floating cloud, she'd been overcome by the same feelings of unreasonable jealousy as the first time she'd seen them together. She really had no idea why. Caitlin was one of the nicest people she knew, while Rex remained the same trustworthy friend he'd always been. Angie had always thought he resembled Tom Hanks but, tonight, he seemed to possess the charisma of a *dozen* movie stars, so much in love he was with Caitlin, and she with him.

There was Suzi, too, Angie mused. Suzi had let her hair down, quite literally. No longer tucked up in that severe bun, but falling loose around her pretty, heart-shaped face. She'd just returned from taking Lucie and Emma to their other grandma's for the night, and now she was sitting with Calum again, attending to his every need. Angie hesitated to read too much into the situation, but they certainly looked to be close again. Whether he would cast her aside when his leg came out of plaster, Angie didn't dare to hazard a guess. If he did, then he would deserve all the sadness and loneliness coming to him.

Still absorbed in all this, she became aware of someone standing watching her and looked up to see Stuart waving his hand in front of her face. 'I'd like to know what's going on in that pretty little head of yours,' he said.

He'd changed out of the navy-blue suit he'd worn to the wedding, she saw, and was wearing the denim shirt that he'd had on the first time they met. His light red hair was almost blond, she noticed, now that she had a chance to study it more closely. Strawberry blond, she guessed, was the name that best described it.

'I was wondering if you'd like to dance. I've just whizzed back from the station in two minutes flat, hoping you'll do me the honour.'

Angie remembered Vinnie had said that he'd arranged to take Beth to Bristol to catch a train connecting with the overnight sleeper to Glasgow. The girl was due to sit an examination first thing on Monday morning and wanted to get in some revision beforehand.

Angie rose to her feet, and Stuart took her into his arms. They danced the next dance, and almost all the other dances for the remainder of the evening. My own special partner, Angie thought – though, like Cinderella and her prince, they would be going their own separate ways after the clock struck midnight.

The next morning Angie spent in the kitchen, roasting a Sunday dinner for herself, the children and Vinnie too. Lamb, with new potatoes and mint sauce. She wanted it to be an extra specially nice meal today. Josh and Daisy had left for Southampton by car after an early breakfast and, as Angie had already asked Vinnie to join her for lunch, it was a simple matter to extend the invitation to Stuart

Stuart, she learned, had spent the night at a guest house in Clevedon with Nicole and her boyfriend, Martin. Nicole and Martin were to have lunch at the Smuggler's with Holly and Guy before setting off for London. Stuart and Vinnie planned to spend another night at the bungalow and leave for Oban first thing the following morning.

Stuart did justice to the lunch that Angie had spent the morning preparing. As he handed her his empty plate, he bowed formally and said with a grin, 'That was very acceptable, ma'am. Very acceptable indeed.' Suzi and Calum had asked him over to Portmills for the afternoon and he did not delay long before making his farewell. When he'd gone, Angie and Vinnie settled down for a chat.

Evie, well used to Vinnie now, treated her like a second granny and was hardly any bother at all. Vinnie had brought some photos of her daughter's family in Canada to show Angie. They spent a while looking at them, as well as some others which Angie produced. By five o'clock it was almost dark so Angie pulled the curtains together and switched on the light. She turned on the gas fire, too; the dull, dreary weather was creating an illusion of chilliness in the living room.

Her sons had gone to Peter Goodyear's house to play video games. Their dearest wish was to have a computer of their own, but they'd accepted the fact there was no money for one. *Perhaps one day,* she told herself ... and, with any luck, a car for her. Not that a car was *too* important right now; Daisy never minded Angie using hers. It was standing in the garage at Cedar Keys, waiting to be collected.

It was six by the time Stuart arrived back from Portmills, just time enough for Angie to hitch a ride to Upalong before her baby's bedtime.

The evening was dark, and the drizzling rain made the visibility poor as Stuart negotiated the twisting, uphill lane. When they reached the bungalow, he left the car on the grass verge while he got out to open the gates. Designed to open inwards, when Stuart pushed against them, he was surprised to find they wouldn't budge.

'What the...?' He turned, quite startled, and beckoned Angie over.

Angie handed the baby to Vinnie and went to take a look. There was an enormous pile of sawn-up logs filling the driveway immediately behind the gate.

'The bloody fool ... it's Jacko!' She wanted to laugh hysterically. Another prize botch-up by Jacko, she thought – the same sort of thing as the raspberry ripple catastrophe.

'Well, we'll have to shift this lot if you're to get the car out,' said Stuart and, climbing over the metal gates, he then helped Angie over behind him.

'I'll stay in the dry with the bairn,' Vinnie said. Switching on the car radio, she settled down in the front passenger seat with Evie on her lap.

Stuart and Angie began shifting the logs, throwing them onto Josh's neatly mown front lawn. 'I'll get the kids to help tidy up before Josh and Daisy get back,' Angie assured him.

The steady drizzle turned into a heavy downpour as, with rain drenching their heads and faces, they made enough room for Angie to reverse the car out into the lane. As soon as she'd done so, she took the baby from Vinnie, and fastened her into the baby seat that Daisy kept permanently in the Metro.

Stuart called out to her cheerfully as she started

to pull away, 'Take care now ... mind how you go. I'll see you when I see you, I guess.' Suddenly, he stepped forward, and banged his fist on the car roof. Angie wound down the window and regarded him curiously.

'I really enjoyed this time with you, Angeline MacPherson,' he said. He put out his hand and touched her nose. 'You've got a raindrop glistening here ... that's OK – it's gone now.'

Angie's stomach turned cartwheels inside her; her heart was beating like a hammer. Shyly, she pushed back a wet black curl that had flopped on to her brow. She looked at him looking at her. 'I feel like a drowned rat,' she said. 'I can't wait to get home to have a nice bath.'

Why on earth had she said *that*, she wondered. It sounded as though she was anxious to get rid of him, and she was anything but that.

'You look in great shape – and thanks for everything. I really mean that.' Stuart raised his right hand in a wave.

Angie released the handbrake and moved away, leaving him standing there all alone in the rain. Unexpectedly, an incredible sadness welled up inside her. She felt empty; bereft; terribly lonely somehow. There was nothing she could do to stop the tears from flowing like twin rivers down her cheeks.

Chapter Twenty-six

Hallowe'en; exactly a year since Curt's disappearance. In the evening, Jake and Luke went out trick or treating with their mates, just as they'd always done. Angie, although she'd been feeling somewhat despondent all day, didn't allow her personal grief to rub off on them by making a great issue of the date. Encouraged by the gift company rep, she'd set out for sale a display of witches' hats, cardboard black cats, plastic pumpkins, and spooky masks. There were profits to be made, and she couldn't afford not to make them.

Holly and Guy, on their way to a party, called in to see her during the evening. Holly was a little reluctant to leave Angie on her own, but Angie persuaded her she would be all right, that she would actually prefer to be by herself to think.

'Not *too* deeply, eh, Mum?' Holly said, eyeing her mother doubtfully.

'No, just going over all the things that have happened in the past twelve months. There's so many *nice* things, when I turn them over in my mind. Evie for one, of course.'

'Of course.'

Angie waited on the doorstep with Holly while Guy went round to the back of the shop to fetch the car. Holly was wearing a smart new black trouser suit and she complimented her daughter on her chic appearance.

Holly nodded. 'Thanks. I was saying, Mum, last Hallowe'en I didn't even have a boyfriend, and here's me and Guy engaged! There's Gran married to Josh – and *you've* got the shop. That's something you'd never expected, isn't it? All it needs is for Calum and Suzi to get back together, permanently, and everyone will be happy.'

'Mmm, *everyone*,' Angie agreed.

'I'm sorry – that was heartless of me. Well, if it makes you feel any better, I've got a feeling that Dad isn't dead. Though where he's been gone to all this time, I can't for the life of me imagine.'

'I'd be living in a fool's paradise if I went on believing he'd come walking through this door any minute.' Angie patted her daughter's smart, black-trousered bottom. 'Off you go now ... here's Guy with the car.'

Holly's expression lightened suddenly. 'And here are my two brothers coming up the road. Good, so now you'll have some company for the evening, Mumsie dearest.'

Towards the end of the evening, as Angie was placing the tablecloth on the kitchen table ready for breakfast the next day, she thought again about their conversation. Both Holly *and* Daisy had said they believed that Curtis would return one day. Angie didn't hold out much hope of *that* happening. She went to secure the bolts, top and bottom, on the back door, and turned off the kitchen light, ready to go upstairs to bed. Now they no longer had Gyp to protect the household with his warning bark, she was being doubly careful with security.

It was almost half past eleven, way after her normal bedtime, by the time she climbed the stairs. She and the boys had been watching a film on television, a Hallowe'en thriller which she had allowed them to stay up to see. After she'd hustled them into the bathroom to clean their teeth, she went into her own room and climbed into the big feather bed. Tilting the lamp to one side, to protect the baby's face from its glare, she opened the novel she'd been reading the previous night and scanned the page where she'd left off.

Suddenly the telephone rang downstairs. Angie's heart leapt with alarm as she jumped quickly out of bed. It *had* to be bad news. Only if it was a call of some importance would anyone disturb her at this time of night. *Curtis* was her immediate thought, yet she wasn't at all sure how she'd react if it was him after all this time. He'd been gone too long; it would be like welcoming a stranger back into her life. Apprehensively, she lifted the receiver to her ear.

'Sorry I'm calling so late, but it's me, Stuart.'

The relief caused Angie to sit down heavily at the bottom of the stairs.

'I've just got in from work. I've been thinking about you on the drive home,' he said. 'I'm sorry if I've woken you up but I wouldn't have been able to sleep unless I checked to see you were all right.'

All sorts of emotions went racing through her, the strongest, most overwhelming, being one of happiness – at the sheer pleasure of hearing Stuart's voice again.

'I know it's a traumatic time for you. I

416

remember you telling me it was last Hallowe'en when Curtis disappeared.'

'I must admit, I *was* feeling a little low earlier this evening,' she said. 'Holly and Guy called in on their way to a party and I didn't want to spoil their enjoyment. I told them I was fine; I was counting my blessings, and not even thinking of anything else.'

'I wish I was there with you. We had a good time the other night, didn't we?'

'We really did. I've never danced for so long in all my life.' Angie paused. 'Curt wasn't *that* keen on dancing,' she added quietly.

'Ellen was, but not necessarily with me,' answered Stuart. 'Anyway, we must look to the future now, lass. I've been talking it over with my mother, and she thinks I should invite you to Scotland for Hogmanay.'

'To *Scotland?*' repeated Angie. 'It sounds such a long way away.'

He laughed. 'It is from Cornwall, where you hail from, but it's not really all that far. If I buy you a ticket, you can catch a plane direct from Bristol to Glasgow.'

'Seriously? You *mean* it?'

'I'm *very* serious.'

'Gosh, Stuart, I don't know what to say.'

'All you have to say is *yes.*'

'Yes, well ... I'd love to, but...'

'If you don't want to leave the baby, you're welcome to bring her, too. And Luke and Jake, if it bothers you leaving them behind. My mother's got plenty of room in her house and she loves having children around. She misses my sister's

417

kids in Canada like nobody's business.'

'I know. She said when she was showing me their photos.'

'So say you'll come. I'd love to see you again.'

She hesitated. 'Yes, OK. I'll do my very best.'

'You *will* come. Say you *will* come ... *please*.'

'I was just wondering about the shop. However, I'm sure we'll manage somehow.'

'Good, I'll get us tickets for the Hogmanay supper at the local hotel and golf club. It's a really smart place, so make sure you bring your best bib and tucker.'

'I'll do that.'

There seemed nothing more to say. Angie went back to bed feeling deliciously happy. For the first time in a whole year, she was beginning to feel like her old self again. Better, in fact, than her old self – more like the way she'd felt at seventeen, when she was Angeline Prosser, living in Polzeath with her aunts Bridget and Norah in their cottage near the sea.

The water in the Bay of Naples was sparkling like vintage champagne beneath the bluest of azure skies. The contrast with November in England, where the weather was almost certainly dismal and dull, was quite unbelievable, Holly thought. She and Guy were spending the first week of their holiday in Sorrento at a smart hotel; next week they would be staying with his grand-parents at their small apartment on the outskirts of the town.

From the balcony of the old-fashioned hotel, Holly looked down at the jetty, at the line-up of cars, trucks and bikes waiting to board the ferry for Capri. A group of men on the back of a bright green lorry were lifting a container with a crane, preparing to hoist it across to the boat. They were singing as they worked – a quartet of cheerful tenors! Holly noticed to her surprise that one of the group had hair as red as hers. When the sun touched upon it, it gleamed like burnished copper.

She turned away and looked across to the Isle of Capri, solid and rounded, rising from the sea. The day before she and Guy had been there on a sightseeing trip. They had taken a bus to the very top, and looked out over the bay to where Vesuvius scowled back at them threateningly. Wisps of cobwebby vapour danced over its smouldering summit and, down in the foothills, the ruins of Pompeii were still visible as a permanent reminder of what the volcano could, and still might, do. Holly glanced at it again now, and shuddered.

Suddenly, she felt an overwhelming desire to see the red-headed man close up. She called out to Guy to tell him she was going to take a short walk.

'What now, this very minute?' he said, half-asleep. 'I thought you wanted to have a siesta before we catch the train to Naples.'

'You don't need to come, Guy. I won't be long, I promise.'

Holly needed to check for herself that the image she'd seen was a figment of her imagination ... that the auburn-haired man wasn't her *dad*.

Slightly reluctant, Guy moved off the bed. 'I'll come,' he said. But, by the time he'd dressed and they'd walked down the winding path to the quayside, the boat and the bright green truck had gone.

'Damn,' she said.

Guy, sensing her disappointment, asked, 'What was all that about, love?'

She shook her head. 'Nothing, I guess.'

It was too very private even to tell *him*, but Holly found herself looking out for the red-haired man all throughout the rest of her stay in Italy.

With Christmas only three days away, Barry Buckley and his staff had decorated the interior of the Smuggler's Retreat in a truly seasonal manner. An enormous fir tree dominated one corner of the lounge bar, while a log fire blazed away in the old stone grate. Tyler, from his seat near the window, was watching out for Erin to arrive. He intended to run out and meet her, and they would hit the road, pronto. Take a drive into the countryside to find another pub where he'd be less likely to run into anyone he knew, in particular Caitlin and or the guy she was living with. Tyler had come to England principally to spend Christmas with his family, and he also had some important things he wanted to discuss with Erin.

Tyler and Erin had been gone an hour when Caitlin and Rex came in. The bar area was so crowded that they found themselves sharing a table with the Merediths. As Caitlin squeezed into the vacant space next to Henry, she thought she detected a slight coolness on the part of Roxanne. Henry, though, seemed pleased to see her, and soon began asking questions about her life in California.

'That's all he ever goes on about,' said Roxanne disparagingly, 'blooming Yankee-land. I'll be glad when he buggers off to the damn place and gets it out of his system.'

She dipped into her red suede handbag and took out a pack of Rothman's, lighting one up with a small silver lighter. She took a few puffs and edged along the seat until she was almost sitting on Rex's lap. 'How's it going, Rex, my love?' Her foxy brown eyes perused him closely – flirtatiously, Caitlin thought. Without waiting for Rex to answer, Roxanne remarked to Caitlin, 'I see your ex is back over yere again.'

'Yes, so I've heard,' Caitlin said.

'Mmm?' Roxanne arched her pencilled eyebrows and, patting her beehive hairstyle into place at the back, added, 'You ain't in close touch with him then no more?'

'Not in *close* touch, but I do keep a track of his movements. We're in the process of selling a house, so I have to know roughly where he might be.'

Roxanne's next remark was pitched at Rex. 'You two living together, I hear.'

'That's not something I'm prepared to discuss, Roxanne,' he countered, beaming her back a warm smile so that she couldn't accuse him of being unfriendly.

Roxanne batted her mascaraed eyelids coyly

421

and fiddled with the gaudy gilt clasp on her bag. She eyed Rex a trifle uncertainly, but said nothing more.

'Is there any chance you might go back to the States to live?' Henry enquired of Caitlin.

Caitlin glanced at Rex and shook her head decisively. 'I wouldn't think so ... no, most definitely not,' she said.

Henry saw the look of love that passed between the two of them, and he knew there was no chance of this warm, nice, woman ever returning to Tyler Sinclair. Until this moment, he had nursed a wild hope that she might. If only Roxanne wasn't so smitten with the wretched bloke, he thought, but Roxanne always did have a soft spot for any passably good-looking man. Even at this moment, she was doing her best to attract the very fellow Henry had just seen exchange the most wondrous of love-looks with a woman he so obviously adored.

Henry was jolted from his introspection when Caitlin confided quietly, 'I wish you could warn your daughter, Henry. That's if it's not already too late.'

He glanced at Roxanne, who had a bad habit of misinterpreting a harmless little tête-à-tête. Fortunately, she was still busy ogling Rex, and hadn't seen Caitlin whispering to him.

'I might as well have saved my breath,' Henry replied in a low voice. 'They're off out together every waking moment.' He shook his head frustratedly. 'It's especially difficult when her mother thinks the sun shines out of the blasted man's backside.'

Caitlin took a sip of her lager and lime. 'That's what you're up against, I'm afraid. He can charm the birds from off the trees when he sets a mind to it.'

'He'll *have* to be going back to the USA soon, though, won't he?'

Caitlin recognised a certain desperation in Henry's voice. 'Of course he will,' she said kindly. 'The group are booked to do a number of important gigs over the next six months.'

'You know – that's somewhere I've always wanted to go, America. I'd like to hear all about it from you one day but, in the circumstances...' Henry shrugged his shoulders.

'Perhaps one day when it's all sorted out, we'll have a good old get-together. You, your wife, and Rex and me,' Caitlin told him.

Later, at home, when Henry and Roxanne were drinking their bedtime cups of cocoa, Henry tried again to drum some sense into his wife's stupid head. As usual, she wasn't the least bit interested in his point of view.

'Of course she'd say that,' she snorted angrily. 'They don't get on – Tyler told you that the day he come yere to dinner. He didn't even know she was having a babby when she left 'un, and come on back to England.'

'And why was that, I wonder? What on earth would have made her do *that?*'

''Cos she wanted to be home with her mum and dad, instead of staying out there, at her husband's side, where she knew very well she belonged.'

'She's not shown much sign of wanting her

423

mum and dad since she's been living in Fuzzy Cove then – not as I've heard, anyway.'

'It just goes to show the girl don't know what she *do* blinking want.'

Henry looked at Roxanne sadly, admitting defeat to himself. Even now, while they were having this conversation, their daughter was out there somewhere ... in that man's car ... getting up to who knew what. Henry dreaded to think what seductive techniques the slimy devil was playing on Erin, his sweet vulnerable girl. He could only hope that when Christmas was over, the perisher would return from whence he came and Erin would see him for what he was: the scum of the earth; a manipulative, scheming skunk.

In the week since Jazz had come home from university, she'd seen her father's mood deteriorate until he seemed to be in a more or less permanent strop. The slightest remark she made to him invariably resulted in the grumpiest of replies.

'What's up with Pa?' she asked her mother, who was rushing around the place like a scalded cat, with her elder daughter's wedding due to take place in five days' time. Jazz thought Mirabel's face was like a raincloud – threatening to pour at any minute.

'I really can't discuss it, Jasmine. You must ask him for yourself. Ooh, goodness...' She shuddered. 'I suppose you're going to *have* to know sooner or later.'

'Know *what?* What is it with this family? You're

424

hiding something from me, and I want to know what.'

'Oh, dear. Why isn't Dominic coming over for the wedding?' Mirabel complained, changing the subject completely.

'Because he's in bloody Africa, and his term of duty doesn't finish until the end of March,' snapped Jazz, feeling her own patience slipping away fast.

'If he could see Stefanie now that she's all grown up, I'm sure he would realise what a suitable wife she'd make for an up-and-coming medical specialist.'

'Dom's not a medical specialist, Ma, and for all we know, he's got no ambition to be one. I've heard him say he wants to be a GP in due course of time.'

'But now he's talking of staying in Africa for good. He says so in his latest letter. I'm sure it's something to do with the girl at the shop becoming engaged – the one with the carrot-red hair.'

'Oh, well, that's his decision, Ma. I guess Dom knows what he wants.'

'Perhaps you're right. But goodness me – I'd always believed *Giles* to be the sensible one, the sort of son that I and your father had always dreamed of having.'

Jazz snorted dismissively. 'He's as pompous and stuffy as father already, and he's only half his age.'

'We never imagined he'd grow up to be such a wretched disappointment. Even your father never suspected a thing and he's a *man* ... a

Queen's Counsel ... rubbing shoulders with different people every day of his working life.'

'What *are* you waffling on about?' Jazz asked.

Mirabel Stone was busy pairing up some newly cleaned curtains, ready for rehanging in the drawing room. 'Oh, well – you might as well know,' she said, sinking into a sea of oyster-pink silk on the Axminster-carpeted floor. She screwed up her mouth in distaste. 'Giles is *living* with your friend, Tom.'

'I know,' said Jazz. 'Of course I bloody know. He was my boyfriend, wasn't he?'

'I wish you wouldn't use *language*, Jasmine. It sounds so terribly common.'

'I don't give a flying fuck what it sounds like – just tell me what's happened to Giles.'

'He and Tom are ... you know ... gay,' her mother managed to splutter.

'Holy cow!' exclaimed Jazz. 'Well, no wonder old Tom made sure he kept his dicky tucked safely out of sight whenever I spent the night at his pad.'

'You did what? You actually stayed there with him?'

'Yes, and for all the reaction my presence stirred up in him, I should have twigged the truth months ago. Bloody hell. Well, it just goes to show, eh? I'm not surprised Pa's got his knickers in a twist. How *will* he hold his head up at the Wig and Pen club when word gets around that his son, the up-and-coming junior barrister, is as crooked as a flipping corkscrew?'

The day after Boxing Day was Georgia Stone's

wedding day. Erin had received an invitation, but wasn't going to be there. Tyler had made that decision for her and, although Holly and Jazz knew that this was probably so, Erin wasn't prepared to discuss it with them, even though they were her best friends. It was Jazz's fault, anyway, that she'd become so tied up with Tyler. If she hadn't said that Dominic intended to stay in Uganda for good, Erin would never even have looked at any other man.

Now that she'd started to build a new life for herself, she had to do what was best for *her*, she thought. It was a sit-down banquet, anyway, and the very last thing Erin felt like doing was eating a whacking great meal. She'd been experiencing some of her old eating problems lately, though she had no idea why that should be. Her job at the old people's home was running as smoothly as ever. No one there ever hassled her to do something she didn't want, and yet, for some unknown reason, she'd felt recently as though she was under a great deal of pressure.

It couldn't possibly be related to her relationship with Tyler, she reasoned. He was so gentle and thoughtful; all he ever did was show her how much he cared for her. He was on good terms with her mother too and, as Erin knew, Roxanne wasn't the easiest of people to get along with. It troubled her somewhat that Henry hadn't taken to Tyler as well as she would have liked him to. But that was her father's hard luck. He was seriously missing out by adopting this negative attitude towards her boyfriend. Tyler could have introduced him to all manner of people, and taken him to all those places of interest he wanted to see.

Tyler and she were making love regularly now, usually in the back of his car, or in some hidden hollow of the woods, when the weather allowed. Tonight they planned to sleep in comfort, in Erin's parents' double bed. Roxanne had announced that she would be spending the night with Myrna, at Clapton-in-Gordano, and Henry, Erin knew, was working nights this week. Neither would be making an appearance before seven the next morning and, by then, Tyler should be well on his way back to Burnham-on-Sea.

In the wee small hours, however, when Erin and Tyler were well in the land of slumber, Henry, having suffered an attack of severe pain to his right shoulder reaching all the way down to his oesophagus, was being checked over by the hospital emergency doctor. The medic, diagnosing the pain as a bout of acute indigestion, promptly instructed a nurse to contact Henry's wife to come and take him home.

For probably the first time ever, Roxanne *was* sleeping where she had told Henry she'd be. As soon as she got the news, she took a taxi to the hospital. She had no intention of bringing Henry home until she'd had a word with the casualty officer. Hospitals, as she well knew, were always chucking people out before they were fit enough to leave. She'd heard all the horror stories imaginable from Myrna; the village surgery was *rife* with tales of disaster.

After her chat with Henry's doctor, who put her mind at rest, Roxanne guided her spouse into

428

another taxi for the ten-minute ride home. She managed to get him up the stairs – a hard task in itself, as he was still doubled up with pain. When she threw open the bedroom door, she wasn't best pleased to find Erin and Tyler asleep in the marital bed. When she ordered them from the room, she was even more dismayed to see that they didn't have a stitch of clothes on between them.

The presence of a stranger in their bed necessitated Roxanne changing the bedclothes to make it hygienic for Henry to sleep in. He looked so very ill, it seemed to her there was a strong chance she might need to call in another doctor before morning. After she'd got Henry settled, she went downstairs to check for herself that Tyler had left the house. Seeing no sign of him, she hurried back up to Erin's room to make sure that she was back in her own bed – and *alone*. Erin looked to be asleep, Roxanne thought, though she might well have been feigning it. Roxanne was hesitant to create a scene just now, for fear of the effect it might have on Henry.

Early the next morning, Henry, though still wobbly, was on his feet again. He'd been in no condition in the middle of the night to kick up a fuss about Erin and Tyler using their double bed. He more than made up for it now, however, shouting at Erin as he'd never shouted at her before. He made it clear she was to have nothing more to do with the man or she would find herself out on her ear.

Erin immediately leapt to Tyler's defence but, to Henry's astonishment, Roxanne actually sided with *him*. She came down on their daughter like a ton of bricks, her anger fuelled by the fear she'd experienced at the thought of his sudden demise. It wasn't in Roxanne's nature to sit calmly by and watch her husband driven into an early grave by some two-bit Yankee-doodle, she declared.

When Erin returned from work that night, they presented her with an ultimatum. Either she stopped seeing Tyler, or she would have to take up the matron's offer of a residential post at The Conifers. The move would enhance her career greatly, her employer had said. She'd be able to train as an official care worker, with certificates to show for it. Erin made all the noises she knew her mother and father wanted to hear, and then went out to meet Tyler, as they'd arranged by telephone that morning.

The following day, Erin packed her bags, telling her parents she was moving into The Conifers, and Tyler would be driving her there. Two days later on New Year's Eve Roxanne received a telephone call from The Conifers wanting to know if Erin had recovered from the flu. Matron had assumed that she'd fallen victim to the virulent bug that had rampaged through the home and knocked most of her staff for six.

By that time, Erin and Tyler were a world away from The Conifers nursing home and Fuzzy Cove. They were basking on a beach near the Holiday Inn at San Diego, lapping up the warm Californian sunshine. Tyler would be joining the rest of his group in three days' time when Persimmon Sorbet would be entertaining the members of a swish country club in the hills beyond Santa Barbara. Two weeks later, they were booked to appear at an exclusive new nightclub, where many of the Hollywood movie stars liked to dine.

Apart from a little homesickness, Erin was in her seventh heaven. Tyler had promised her she'd be living in the lap of luxury if she returned with him to America. She had absolutely no complaints. Everything he'd told her that night, snuggled up in the back of his car on the coast road to Clevedon, had very definitely come to pass.

Chapter Twenty-seven

Stuart was waiting for Angie when she arrived at Glasgow Airport the day before New Year's Eve. She was first off the plane and it was several minutes before she noticed him; he was leaning over a barrier rail, his back towards her, scanning the slow straggle of incoming passengers. The soft brown leather jacket he was wearing suited his light auburn hair and fair skin a treat, she thought. Her heart did a little flip; it wasn't her imagination ... she really did fancy this man.

She came up behind him and tapped him on the shoulder. Surprised, he swivelled around.

'Hi, Stuart,' she said.

'*Angie*. Where did you spring from?' he exclaimed.

'From Bristol Airport – direct flight through to

Glasgow, Scotland, just like the man said.'

'I meant...' Stuart shook his head. 'Here – let me look at you.'

Angie felt good in the new camel-coloured coat that Daisy and Josh had given her for Christmas. Around her neck, she wore a paisley silk scarf in shades of beige, rust and green – a present from her boys, though she guessed that Daisy had had some say in the choice.

'You look really great,' he said.

'For a middle-aged mother of four!'

'Nothing like a middle-aged mother of four. If you're fishing for compliments, don't bother. I'm already well prejudiced on your behalf, ma'am.'

Angie followed him out to the car park, and they were soon headed north in the direction of Oban. The route was a spectacular one, winding through snow-covered glens and hillsides, with breathtaking glimpses of ice-capped mountains away in the far distance. The day was cold; the cobalt blue sky cheerless, with curious white clouds floating like strands of ribbon along the horizon. After they'd travelled an hour or so, their arrival at a service station gave them the chance to relax face to face. They both tucked into spicy chilli con carne then coffee afterwards, with an enormous Danish pastry each.

Darkness had fallen by the time they reached the coast. The trees and buildings along the way were transformed into sinister shapes, half hidden in the night shadows. To the right of the road they passed a stretch of water and the ruins of a castle, whose black outline reminded Angie of the *House of Horror* movies that the twins always pestered her to be allowed to watch on television.

'That castle looks as if it's growing out of the lake,' she remarked to Stuart.

'It's a *loch* actually, though only a small wee one,' he said.

'Oh...' Angie was impressed. She'd had her first glimpse of a real Scottish loch! There seemed nothing more to say.

Vinnie was standing on the doorstep waiting for them when they arrived. Stuart had phoned her from the service station to tell her they'd already eaten. In spite of this, however, she insisted on serving them a bowlful of her delicious homemade tomato soup, and crusty bread, warm from the oven.

The moment he'd finished eating, Stuart made his farewells and set off for his own home, ten miles further north. Beth was home from university, he'd explained, though she'd be joining a group of friends the following morning to go skiing in the Cairngorms. He would drop her off at the bus station, he'd said, and then pick up Angie to take her sightseeing.

'So Daisy was happy to look after the bairn,' Vinnie remarked to Angie when Stuart had gone. 'I didn't think she'd mind. Evie's a bonny-natured little thing.'

Angie nodded. 'Mum seemed to really *want* me to come, and Holly and Guy have moved into Mariner's Cottage, temporarily, so I'd no need to uproot the boys. There's any amount of people mucking in as far as the shop's concerned. Caitlin, Leanne, Rex. Even Calum's said he'll lend a hand if necessary.'

'How's his leg now? Is he out of plaster yet?'

'He is, and it seems to be healing well. It's almost three months since his accident.'

Angie went on to tell Vinnie that Calum expected soon to be working for Kevin Buttercup, who was opening a small shop on the harbour at Fuzzy Cove, selling fishing tackle. Kevin had had a win on the lottery, she explained. Not a big one, but ample for his requirements.

'Och, that's good news! I remember the lad well and he seemed a really decent sort. Fishing tackle, eh? That's something Calum shouldn't have any trouble selling.' She sighed. 'Let's hope he behaves himself from now on, if only for Daisy's sake.'

'Suzi's, too,' Angie said. 'They're back together again, and even talking of getting spliced.'

Vinnie told her that Nicole had telephoned to say that she'd arranged a hair appointment for Angie. 'It's at the salon where Nicole trained before she moved to London,' Vinnie remarked proudly.

'Great.' Angie was well pleased. With the lovely new dress she'd bought to wear to the party, a smart hairdo was all she needed to feel especially well turned out.

That night she slept soundly in the quietude of Vinnie's solidly built house. She awoke early the next morning and, springing out of bed, went to the window eager to look out. The sea was nearer than she'd expected it to be. On the other side of the coast road that ran along in front of the house, the wild Atlantic rollers were crashing on

434

to the rocky shoreline. The sky was laden with the threat of snow but Angie's spirits soared upwards, like a bird into a summer sky.

The sight and sound of the ocean always had this effect on her and, although she'd never visited this part of the world before, she felt completely at home. A thought occurred to her. It might not be just the presence of the sea creating this enormous buzz of pleasure right now. The butterflies fluttering around in her tummy might well be connected to a special *someone* who'd be arriving soon to spirit her away in his car.

Stuart arrived just before nine, surprising his mother who hadn't expected him for another hour. He first took Angie for a stroll round the harbour. There, they wandered into a manufacturers' showroom full of Caithness glass and quality china selling at knockdown prices. Even on her low budget, Angie was able to buy a jade and blue paperweight for Holly, and for Daisy and Josh a set of four cut-glass brandy goblets.

Outside, they found a bench where they sat for a while, gazing out to sea and talking. Angie found herself telling Stuart things she'd never told anyone else. She discussed with him the sense of complete abandonment and loneliness she sometimes felt if she mulled too deeply over Curt's disappearance. He sympathised, saying he knew just what it was like.

When their conversation paused, Stuart suggested they went for a drive, and it crossed Angie's mind that he might be planning to take her to his home ... *the place where he'd lived all those years with his wife!* The pang of dismay she felt echoed the jealousy she'd experienced when she realised Caitlin and Rex were going steady. God – I *can't* be jealous of a dead woman, can I? she questioned in disbelief.

Unexpectedly, Stuart announced, 'We'll turn round and go back now, I think. Mum's expecting us for lunch at one o'clock.' He turned to Angie and smiled. 'And I'll have to get away early, in order to spruce myself up for tonight.'

In the early afternoon, after Stuart left, Angie and Vinnie settled down for a cosy chat. Vinnie would be seeing in the New Year at the local British Legion club, she said, with friends that she'd known all her life. She didn't expect to be back until the early hours of morning, but Stuart had a key, so if he and Angie were home before her, they could let themselves in.

Angie was ready and waiting when Stuart arrived to pick her up. She felt exceptionally glamorous in the floaty red dress that Holly had helped her choose. The soft puckers in the fitted bodice emphasised the curves of her breasts, and the knee-length skirt was full, swirling and gracefully feminine. With the sheerest of sheer dark tights, and her best black, mock-suede shoes, she was confident she looked her best. She was more than pleased, too, with the cut and blow-dry that Nicole's friend, Helen, had given her.

At the last minute, she applied a dash of Tendre Poison to her wrists and behind her ears, then, sliding her arms into the silk-lined sleeves of the coat that Vinnie had loaned her, she was ready – collywobbles and all – for the evening to begin.

It was Vinnie who'd decided that the camel-coloured coat didn't go well with a red dress and black accessories. Inviting Angie to follow her upstairs, she'd taken from her wardrobe a black woollen coat with a mock fur collar. It was fabulous – luxuriously full, timeless in fashion – though Angie suspected that Vinnie had probably had it for ages. When Angie tried it on she found that it fitted perfectly and, although Vinnie wasn't the most huggable of people, she'd nonetheless given her a huge one.

The road Stuart took out of town trailed the sea for several miles before curving suddenly inland. Some minutes later, they drove past the loch and the castle that Angie had pointed out to Stuart the previous evening. She remembered how relaxed she'd been in his company then, yet now she was stuck to think of a single word to say. The tension between them hung like a heavy mesh fence; not exactly *unpleasant,* she thought, just unfathomable, and rather mysterious.

The hotel, when they reached it, possessed ornate entrance gates that opened on to a long driveway leading to the imposing, castle-like building. Inside the entrance was a baronial hall, resplendent with antlered deer heads, and a welcoming fire burning in an enormous stone grate. There were people milling around everywhere and waiters weaving in and out, bearing silver salvers that held champagne flutes sparkling with buck's fizz. Angie glanced at her programme, and saw that after the six-course dinner, the evening's entertainment included a ceilidh band, a pipe band with Scottish dancers, and then disco dancing into the wee small hours.

Stuart introduced her to some of his friends; to Angie's relief, they welcomed her most warmly.

'We're so pleased he's found someone special to bring,' one woman said, taking her to one side while Stuart was talking to a group of men.

'He hasn't been to a Hogmanay party for at least three years,' said her companion, a friendly-looking girl with freckles on her nose and face.

'Was his wife ill that long?' enquired Angie curiously.

'Och, no.' The freckle-faced woman shook her head. 'Perhaps I shouldn't be telling you this, but he and Ellen had been separated for more than four years when she died. She was away, living with another man, you know.'

'*Some other man*,' remarked her friend, sneering. 'When she took ill, it was Stuart she turned to. *Stuart*, who visited her in hospital, and even took her home during the time she was in remission.'

'I had no idea...'

Angie was surprised that Vinnie – if not Stuart – hadn't told her about it. When Stuart joined her again, she couldn't resist saying to him, 'This is the first time you've been to a New Year's party for several years, I'm told.'

His clear blue eyes remained steady on her face as he explained, 'I came on my own once, and hated every minute of it. Everyone seemed to be here with someone else. It was the loneliest place on earth to be.'

'Your wife wasn't with you then?' Angie asked.

Stuart's eyes dulled with the pain of remembrance, and she wanted to put out her hand and touch his, tell him it was all right now. It would never happen to him again – not if she had any say in it.

'No,' he said, 'I'd planned to tell you tonight, on the way home. She left me, and...'

'It's all right. I know a bit about it. The girl in the gold...' Angie indicated with her hand.

'*Judy.*' Stuart let out a sigh. 'I'm glad it was Jude who told you. She and Andy are two of my closest friends.'

'I was wondering why your mum hadn't said anything.'

'Because I told her not to. I didn't want people asking me about it.'

'Don't say any more if you don't want to.'

'At least not tonight, eh?' Stuart said quietly.

Later in the evening, the DJ took the microphone and announced there would be a short interlude while the thirsty entertainers took a well-earned rest. He invited everyone to join in for thirty minutes of disco dancing. The first note of a song drifted out from the amplifier. They looked at each other and grinned fit to bust.

'I know this is corny, but we've just *got* to do it,' Stuart said, as the sound of Chris de Burgh's 'Lady in Red' filled the stately ballroom.

'It was inevitable they'd play this,' he whispered when he and Angie were dancing. '*Inevitable* you're wearing this dress. Inevitable that I'm feeling so shook-up and trembly, like a laddie out on my first real date.'

A throb of excitement pulsed through her veins; it felt similar to the shot of morphine they'd given her in hospital when she'd had a minor operation.

'Lady in Red' was followed by Eric Clapton's 'Wonderful Tonight', and then Bryan Adams succeeded by Phil Collins: all of Angie's special favourites. From now on, whenever she heard them, they would remind her of this magical night here in a fairytale castle in Scotland, dancing cheek to cheek with a man she was lusting after like she would never have believed possible.

As the last stroke of midnight chimed coloured balloons, released from the ceiling, came floating down on their heads. Stuart caught a red one for her, and she a blue one for him. They looked quickly at each other first and laughed, then pausing, gazed into each other's eyes. Stuart pulled her into his arms, and kissed her lightly on the lips. She responded with fervour, and he, noticing this, kissed her even more passionately.

Angie wound her arms round his neck. The feel of him was familiar to her; it was as if she had known him always. They stood still during the long, long kiss then, reluctantly, Stuart released his hold and she moved slightly away.

The band began to play 'Auld Lang Syne'. People were forming circles, criss-crossing their arms and grabbing the hand of the person next to them. Stuart and Angie slipped in among them and joined in singing the traditional ballad. As the last poignant notes subsided, they sauntered back to the table where they'd left their party poppers and whistles. Donning paper hats, they joined in throwing streamers at all the other guests.

It was after three when the party finally wound down, and they emerged into the cold night. The car park, they saw, had been buried beneath several inches of snow. Stuart held her hand all the way back to town while the snow continued to fall thick and fast. Again, they made the journey in silence but this time it was a comfortable silence, broken only when Stuart commented on some passing happening: a car stuck in a snowbank; another skidding on the icy road surface.

Vinnie was waiting up for them back at the house. Stuart gave her a hug and a New Year's kiss; then, after he'd planted a quick peck on Angie's cheek, he hurried out into the cold icy night and drove swiftly away.

Angie watched him go, her thoughts in turmoil. She couldn't wait to get to bed, to be alone to think things over. There was no way that he could be as excited as she was, she reasoned, or he'd never have disappeared so quickly. Tomorrow was another day, though, and Stuart had told her he would be taking her somewhere special, a stretch of coast where his friends had a holiday cottage. Although the house was closed for the winter, he really wanted her to see the beach.

'I'll bet it's lovely there in the summer,' she'd said, thinking how cold it would be right now.

'In summer, it's paradise; I'll give you that,' he'd replied. 'But when a place is really special – summer or winter – nothing alters the way you feel about it.'

They'd fallen silent after that, leaving Angie to ponder his words. She felt exactly the same herself about Cornwall, she realised.

Angie and Vinnie were having breakfast the

following morning when Daisy phoned to wish them a happy New Year. It was no use their ringing Mariner's Cottage, she said – she'd tried a minute ago, and been unable to rouse a living soul. Holly had given a party which had lasted all night, she told Angie, though most of the people there she'd never even heard of before. Daisy had however spoken earlier to Caitlin, who'd told her that two of Guy's sisters had been at the party with their other brother, Vince. They'd been having a whale of a time until midnight, when their father turned up and whisked them away home to Hotwells.

'Not in a coach made from a *pumpkin?*' said Angie, laughing.

'No a black Fiat car, was what Caitlin said.'

'I'll bet Holly didn't think much of that,' remarked Angie, remembering her daughter's strong views about women's lib.

'Angry? She was spitting *nails.*'

'And my boys? Did they last out until the bitter end?' Angie hoped her innocent lads had been spared from seeing anything they shouldn't have.

'Caitlin made certain they were tucked up in bed by the time she and Rex left the party at two,' Daisy assured her.

'Good,' said Angie, relieved. 'And Evie? I hope *she's* not giving you and Josh too much bother.'

'Good Lord, no – he adores her. Every little girl would benefit from having a father figure like Josh.'

There was no hint of sadness in Daisy's voice when she told Angie this. Angie hoped it meant that her mother-in-law had at last accepted the

442

fact that Curt might have met with an accident, and be lying dead somewhere. It was only a few months ago that Daisy had been carried away by Holly's story about a man she'd seen in Italy who happened to have ginger hair. The possibility of it being Curtis had caused Daisy's imagination to work overtime for quite some while, but Angie had never once supposed that it was him. For one thing, he'd always hated hot sunny places. She certainly had never been able to drag him to one, even to go on holiday.

Stuart duly arrived as promised and, as they were setting off, he handed Angie a small parcel done up in festive paper and tied with tinselly ribbon.

'A belated Christmas present,' he murmured, concentrating his gaze on the wing mirror, ready to pull away.

Inside the wrapping paper was a green and blue tartan wool scarf. Angie slipped it round her neck, tucking the ends into the lapels of her coat.

'That was sweet of you,' she said shyly. She hadn't thought to buy him a Christmas gift.

Stuart nodded. 'Good! You're going to need it where we're going, I can tell you.'

They drove through the snowy landscape, talking mostly of mundane matters, but the tension between them was nowhere as marked as it had been the previous night. Twenty minutes into their journey, Stuart turned off the road on to a track through a forest of tall fir trees. They followed it for about a mile until it ran out into a small parking area alongside a white clapboard house.

'This is it,' Stuart said. 'My friend's cottage.'

He held open the car door against the force of the icy north wind, and assisted Angie to step out.

The wind was so cold she could hardly move. As the icy blast hit her face she laughed, visualising stalactites six inches long forming on the end of her nose. The laugh seemed to freeze on her face, and she closed her mouth quickly lest it might never shut again. She pulled the tartan scarf up so that it covered her nose, breathing in the newness of its smell.

Stuart draped his arm round her shoulders and, braving the elements together they ventured on to the beach. The frozen, snow-covered sand scrunched under their feet as they walked.

'Isn't it grand? Isn't it canny?' he cried and, picking up a smooth, round pebble, hurled it out into the waves.

Angie picked up another, shiny and black, with lacy frost patterns all over its smooth surface. 'I shall keep this for a paperweight,' she said. 'It might not be as pretty as the one I've got for Holly but...'

Her voice trailed off, and she thought, it'll be a lovely reminder of this place. It was unlikely she would ever come here again.

Stuart brushed the snow and sand from a piece of driftwood the size of her shoe and gave it her. 'Bit big for a paperweight, I grant you,' he said, 'but it'll make a wonderful doorstop.'

They turned round and hurried back to the car, glad to climb inside for protection. They drove back to the main road, stopping off at a fast food restaurant where their lunch was rounded off with succulent pancakes, filled with cherries and whipped cream.

They drove around for another hour, talking and listening to his tapes, the music setting the mood for what they both had in mind. At last Stuart took Angie home to the little stone cottage where he'd lived alone since his daughter, Beth, went away to university at Stirling.

Before his early morning drive to Oban, he'd lighted a fire in the grate, and now, with the help of a few sticks and a couple of logs, he coaxed the dull embers back to life.

'I'll make us some tea,' he said, going out to his tiny back kitchen to fill a kettle with water.

Angie followed, wanting to explore his home ... see where he lived ... store it up in her memory for when she was back at Fuzzy Cove and this would only be a dream.

Sensing her presence, Stuart turned round. Still holding the kettle, he said quietly, 'Please don't look at me like that, Angelina.'

She didn't reply. Her voice seemed to have become jammed in her throat, allowing no sound to come out.

'Oh, Angie...' He let out a harsh moan. 'Come here, I want you so very much.'

She went into his arms as if drawn by witchcraft. The attraction she'd felt for him since the first day they met was mutual, she knew that now for sure.

'Shall we go upstairs?' he said. 'Or shall I fetch some covers and lay them on the floor, here in front of the fire?'

'Here.' Angie nodded, her fingers clutching his jumper sleeve as if they had a mind of their own and were reluctant to let him go.

When he returned he was carrying an eiderdown which he spread on the floor. Holding out his hand, he pulled Angie down beside him. His lips found hers and without pausing from kissing he undid his buttons and stripped off to his neat cotton boxer shorts. Neat they might be, and designed for modesty, yet Angie could see that his manhood was on the point of thrusting through the front opening.

I've never made love to anyone else but Curt, she thought, and then everything but Stuart vanished from her mind. This was the here and now. This man – the man she fancied so strongly – wanted *her* every bit as much as she did him.

Stuart's lovemaking was infinitely more tender than anything she'd ever experienced. His hands caressed her body as, cupping and fondling her breasts, he kissed each one gently in turn, in a sweet succession of movement.

Now his hand was between her thighs, parting the soft flesh so that Angie must open her legs to him. She could hardly wait to have his fingers enter that secret part of her, that incredibly private place that belonged only to *her*. She groped beneath the waistband of his shorts, trying to ease them down. First, though, she must remove the obstacle that was stopping her from doing so. Taking his penis gently between her fingers, she helped him to wriggle out of his underpants.

Now he was naked; lying on top of her – eyes of

pale denim piercing deep into her soul. He kissed her again, light little kisses at first, then swiftly becoming more passionate.

'What is it with you, Angie MacPherson?' he groaned. 'You're driving me out of my mind.'

He rolled back on to his side and, with the palms of his hands, explored her nakedness again. His fingers touched her intimately and she lay quite still, hardly daring to breathe for fear of missing a second of the beautiful sensations he was bringing to life deep within her body.

'Stuart, Stuart,' she gasped, pulling him on top of her, and not a moment too soon. His silent eruption burst inside her and the whole universe fell to pieces. Shockwaves reverberated throughout the lengths and depths of her body, reaching out to touch her every extremity. Nothing else existed then for Angie ... only the two of them. They lay very still, locked in love, for several more minutes. Then slowly, very slowly, she began her return to the land of the living.

'That was out of this world,' she breathed. 'Even my fingertips are tingling.'

'Good, eh? It certainly was for *me*. It was over far too quickly, though. I shall be coming back for second helpings, I promise you, before we head back for Oban.'

'I've never done that before, except–'

'Shss...' He teased her mouth gently with his tongue.

'It was never like *that*,' she whispered. 'It's as though you've cast a spell over me.'

'You, too, Angeline, my angel – you've put the voodoo touch on me all right. We'll have to work

447

something out. I've *got* to see you again.'

Her eyes were wondrous pools of hazel green. He wanted to dive into their unexplored depths, share with her everything that made her *Angie*. Suddenly he thought, What if Curtis comes back? Which one of us would she choose?

Dismissing the unthinkable from his mind, he entered her body a second time, pressing kisses on her eager lips with burning repetition, while Angie, all inhibitions gone, wrapped her legs around his waist and held him tightly to her.

She felt his explosion as he came inside her, but was content to lie perfectly still this time. Afterwards – all passion spent – they lay naked in front of the glowing fire, warm, toasted, each of them done to a perfect turn.

Chapter Twenty-eight

The golden afternoon gave way to glorious evening and in turn to spectacular night, but Henry was in no mood to appreciate the sight of a dark velvet sky, with a myriad stars twinkling over the desert highway, and the silvery half-moon suspended up there with them, like a scene from a Disney animated cartoon. Nothing seemed to stay *still* in this great vast country of America. Itchy, lively – even the stars had a certain rhythm of movement, and he couldn't afford to let all this distract his concentration from the task that lay ahead.

Sitting on a Greyhound bus bound for San Francisco, Henry thought back over his journey since leaving the UK and arriving at Los Angeles airport two days before. How consistently it seemed that the bus stations here and at home were always to be found in the seedier part of town. It instilled the need for a certain wariness, a sort of half-glancing over one's shoulder as you approached your point of departure. However, now that he was safely settled aboard, he could feel himself beginning to unwind.

Of all the places in the world that Tyler could have brought Henry's daughter to, it had to be this one, he thought, this *magic* place, the mecca of all his dreams. In any other circumstances, Henry would have enjoyed the experience; but not tonight – nor at any time in the foreseeable future. He must seek out Erin, rescue her if she needed rescuing, and take her home. Henry was pretty sure she needed it. According to Caitlin, Tyler Sinclair had a severe drink problem. When he was on the hard stuff, an entirely different Tyler took over: hard-boiled and utterly ruthless.

Henry sighed. What a way to spend his Easter vacation! The very place he'd most wanted to visit, and all he'd seen of his Eldorado so far were the interiors of a handful of recording studios in downtown LA.

Having had no luck at finding Tyler in any of them, he'd called into a theatrical booking agency, where a helpful clerk had furnished him with details of Persimmon Sorbet's future venues. They were booked to do a gig three days from now at Marin County, across the Golden

Gate Bridge from San Francisco, the young woman had told him. She'd pricked up her ears at the band's name. 'Wowee ... hey, I really dig those guys,' she'd said.

Peering out into the darkness, Henry saw an overhead road sign for Salinas showing the turn-off to Monterey. So much for his dream of visiting Cannery Row, he thought. It was the book of that name that had first whetted his appetite to learn more about this part of the great USA.

When he arrived at San Francisco he booked into a small hotel near the waterfront, and put through a call to his wife in England. He'd worked out it was mid-afternoon in Fuzzy Cove, and dialled the number of the betting shop. Roxanne, when she answered, sounded worried. She told him that Holly MacPherson had received a letter from Erin, posted over a month ago from the town of Pasadena. Erin hadn't told her much in the letter apparently, but what she had said had given Holly cause for alarm. She strongly suspected Erin was experiencing her eating problems again.

However Roxanne provided Henry with one small glimmer of hope. Caitlin had given her the address of the motel where Tyler often stayed when the group was performing in San Francisco. He'd sometimes left Caitlin there on her own, and she'd suggested to Roxanne that he might do the same with Erin. Henry didn't hold out a lot of hope on that score. In his opinion, the madman was far more likely to want Erin with him when he went out of town. There was always the chance, too, Henry realised, that Erin hadn't recognised him yet for the rat he was, and would actually *want* to be with him.

Henry went to take a look at the motel Roxanne had mentioned. When he checked with the receptionist there, he found that although Tyler wasn't booked in at the present time, he was indeed a regular guest. There was nothing for Henry to do but sit and wait out the next couple of days. It was a short walk to Fisherman's Wharf from his hotel, and he spent some of the time there watching the seals that Caitlin had told him about. He was tempted by the prospect of a ferry trip over to the island of Alcatraz, too, but decided that in his present unsettled mood he wouldn't be able to devote his full attention to its fascinating history.

Dominic Stone was back in England, having returned from Africa several months earlier than expected. After his working companion, Marcus, had left, things hadn't been the same and, when his own contract camc up for renewal the following month, he decided to pack the job in, return to England, and apply for a residency in a hospital in the Bristol area.

Ever since Jazz had written to tell him that Holly and Guy were engaged and living together, he'd realised there was no point in his waiting in hope for her, though he trusted that he and Holly could still be friends. It was to her that he turned when he first got back to Fuzzy Cove – there *was* nobody else. Jazz was away at Warwick, and Erin, he discovered, had gone to the States with a

451

bloke he had never even heard of.

Dominic had been pleasantly surprised to discover that Holly's boyfriend, Guy, wasn't at all the Continental smoothie that he first thought he might be. They'd since struck up a reasonably good friendship, been to a couple of football matches together, and downed a few beers in the bar of the Smuggler's Retreat.

One evening the three of them were having a quiet drink when Holly surprised Dominic by confiding how much Erin had always fancied him. She'd only taken up with the other fellow, Holly said, because she'd been convinced that Dominic was never coming back.

The more Dominic thought about it, the more he wished someone had told him that before. He was particularly annoyed with Jazz, who'd put him off when he'd suggested inviting Erin to spend a weekend with him when he was about to finish his stint in Gloucester. Dominic had always thought Erin a really sweet girl and that all she needed was someone who would look after her properly. He'd been an idiot to listen to Jasmine – *she*, who'd messed up her own life by falling in love with a man more than twice her age when she was still only a kid at school.

From where he sat he could see his sister right now, perched on a bar stool and engaged in close conversation with the burly blond barman, Barry. If their body language was anything to go by, they'd resumed their close relationship. If they weren't lovers already, then it wouldn't be long before they were. Dominic would bet a fiver on it!

Rex was far happier selling his fresh fruit and vegetables from a proper shop and had cut down his delivery round to three days a week instead of six. Angie had gone to Scotland to stay with her Aunt Vinnie for the Easter break, having left Caitlin and himself to run the shop. This time she'd taken Evie with her, and the boys were staying alternately with their grandparents at Cedar Keys, or at their own home here at Mariner's Cottage.

Rex wished that Angie would go away more often. In fact, he had it in mind to ask her – if the time should ever come when she felt she'd had enough of the retail trade – whether she'd consider renting the business to him, with a view to his buying her out.

He was pleased that Calum showed no interest in taking over the family business. They'd talked about it only recently, and Calum had said how much he enjoyed working in Kevin Buttercup's shop. It was gratifying to be able to use his wide knowledge of fishing, to sell and demonstrate different types of equipment to the beginners and old hands alike who frequented the shop. Calum was at long last getting his act together, it seemed to Rex. He was nothing at all like the Jack-the-Lad he'd forever been renowned as.

Luke was curled up on the sofa alongside Daisy, while Jake was at the table helping Josh to solve the *Mail on Sunday* crossword puzzle.

Jake, reading aloud, quoted, 'Thirty-one across "Georgia plantation in the novel *Gone With The Wind*".'

"Tara,' answered Daisy, quick as a flash.

'Gran! Grandad's supposed to say it,' Jake wailed.

'Sorry,' Daisy said.

Since Evie had started lisping the word Danda, the boys had taken to calling Josh Grandad, too. Daisy was really pleased about that.

Josh waved the pen at Jake. 'Right, Jake ... here's one for you. "A member of the cattle tribe also called a buffalo" – five letters.'

'Easy-peasy,' yelled Jake. 'Bison. What's the next one, Grandad?'

Luke was more interested in hearing all about Daisy's heart surgery. He asked her, 'Was it really scary?'

'Not too scary, love' she said. 'I was awake all the time, watching. It was quite interesting really.'

'You mean you *watched* while they were putting that thing in your heart?' Luke said, cringing away from her.

'In my artery, actually, Luke. It was scary in a way, but most of the other patients had to have their chests cut open. At least my little Stent spared me from having *that*.'

'So, when you go through one of those X-ray machines that they have at airports, will it set the machine off buzzing?'

Daisy laughed. 'I asked the doctor that one, Luke. It's made of stainless steel, he said, and won't have any effect.'

When Daisy was tucking him into bed later that night, Luke reached up and hugged her tightly. 'I love you, Gran,' he murmured quietly, 'I hope that little metal thing never falls out of your heart.'

'I wonder if it *really is* your Vinnie who's the main attraction in Scotland?' said Josh thoughtfully, when he and Daisy were in their own bed, preparing to go to sleep.

His comment set Daisy wondering, too. The thought had crossed her mind when she'd watched Angie and Stuart dancing together at the disco on the evening of her wedding.

'Would it bother you, love?' Josh asked.

She hesitated. 'No, but...'

'Go on,' he prompted.

'Well ... what if?'

'But they're much too young to spend the rest of their lives on their own, Dais. He's a widower, and Angie, she's, well ... as you know.'

'I suppose so. But what about the man that Holly saw in Sorrento?'

'Daisy, darling, you're clutching at straws, and so is Holly, too.'

Daisy snuggled into the crook of Josh's arm. 'Mmm – yes. I guess the poor love does need a nice cuddle now and then.'

'That's the way to look at it, my sweet. Come here and give me a kiss goodnight.'

'*Don't* ... I'm warning you, Emma, stop teasing that dog.'

Emma was pulling the puppy's tail, jealous because it was Lucie's pet and not hers. 'It's not fair,' she grumbled.

'But Lucie's big enough to take Barney for

walks, Emma. You're not; he'd pull you over.'

Suzi looked at Calum, who was sitting by the fire in his easy chair, Gyp at his feet. Tongue in cheek, she added, 'Which is the only reason we wanted Daddy back here, as you girls know. The puppy needs a firm hand if it's to turn out as obedient a dog as Gyp.'

Gyp's ears pricked up and, whining quietly, fixed Suzi with a deep, poignant stare.

'You're the greatest, I know, Gyppy boy,' she said. 'You don't have to look at me like that.'

'And Barney Boko's *second* best,' Lucie added, dancing into the room, wearing red tap-dancing shoes and a frilly pink tutu. Lucie had named the pup Barney, after her favourite TV character, but her daddy had added the Boko, which had stuck.

'What a bunch,' Suzi said, looking fondly at the three of them.

'I want a titten,' pleaded Emma, doing her best to pronounce *kitten*.

'Oh, I'm buggered,' Calum said.

Suzi smoothed his ginger hair fondly. 'You won't mind, will you, Cal, but we saw an advert for some in the newspaper shop, and I told her we might go and take a look at them.'

'*Me* – a titten, Daddy. Lucie can keep Barney for her very own.'

'Come you here, you little hussy,' said Calum, pulling Emma on to his knee. 'Look at them eyes,' he said to Suzi. 'Rusty topknot, like the rest of us, but this one's mooners are the colour of treacle taffey.'

'Makes a change, eh?' teased Suzi. 'Can't have it all your own way.'

'I'll make sure the next 'un gets eyes like mine. MacPherson strain's got to be stronger than Glue's.'

'What next one?' Suzi ignored the *got to be*.

'The next 'un I'm going to plant in you,' Calum said. 'After we gets married.'

'Married? Can I be a bridesmaid, Dad?' Lucie tap-danced across the room and landed in Calum's lap, pushing her younger sister aside.

'Me, too,' clamoured Emma, 'I'll be a bridesmaid first I think, and then I'll have a titten.'

'A titten first, *I* rather think,' Suzi told her.

'I don't know about *that*. The sooner we do it, the better,' said Calum. 'By the time we gets our blue-eyed son, we wants to be respectably spliced.'

'I can't believe what I'm hearing, but I'll take you up on that kind offer before you change your mind,' Suzi agreed.

A few days later Calum drove out to Lulsgate to meet Angie and Evie off the Glasgow plane. When they were settled in the Cavalier, with Evie strapped into Emma's car seat, he told Angie about his and Suzi's plans for getting wed.

'You'd better be serious this time, Cal,' she told him sternly.

'Too true I'm bloody serious! I've made my mistakes – you knows that better than anybody, Ange. There's not many gets a second chance like what Suzi's giving me now.'

'I believe you, Calum. Just don't let them down again; that's all I'm saying to you.'

'I'd be mental if I did. I'll never forget the day when I stood beneath that bloody tree in the pourin' rain, thinking I'd lost them all for good.'

'Just as long as you always remember how awful it was without them.'

Calum pressed the button to start his Clapton tape, a permanent fixture in his car. He sang along to 'Lay Down Sally', substituting the name Suzi for Sally.

'This've kept me going, listening to this. It's her and me's special song,' he said.

'Flip it over on to the other side after, Cal, please. I, too, have a vested interest in this tape. "Wonderful Tonight". It's got a special meaning for me. Stuart and I danced to it on New Year's Eve.'

'*Stuart?* Bloody hell, Ange. I thought 'twere Aunt Lavinia you was off up to Scotland visiting – not our bloody Stuart.'

'Shss, Cal. I'm listening to the words. You haven't got 'Lady in Red' by Chris de Burgh, by any chance, have you?'

'No, I bloody ain't.' He still sounded shocked.

'You don't mind, do you, Calum?' Angie said cautiously.

'Mind? Course I don't mind. Only what would happen if?'

She knew what he meant. 'Stuart and I didn't plan for this to happen,' she said. 'We'd just have to cross that bridge if it ever arose.'

'You be happy, my lover. Life's much too short to sit alone and mope. I should know. I've been an expert at that.'

When the song finished, Calum switched off

the tape. 'Do our mother know?' he said.

Angie shook her head. 'She has no reason to, not yet. Please don't tell her, will you?'

'I shan't breathe a word to a living soul ... you knows me better than that, Angie-babe.'

'That's why I'm trusting you with my secret now. Auntie Vinnie guessed, of course, but I've asked her to keep it to herself a while longer.' She paused. 'I love him, Cal, It's a completely different sort of love from the one I felt for Curt. We're absolutely crazy about each other.'

'Then you go for it, gal. Do what's best for you.'

'It's not quite as simple as that. There's no way I'll get together with Stuart permanently, or anything, until I know for sure what's happened to Curt.'

'Then you might be in for a bloody long wait.'

'So be it then, Cal – there's nothing else I can do.'

Calum paused, then said, 'There's still no news on the insurance front. I never realised it'd take so long when I asked you for that loan.'

'It's OK. You've got your boat, and I've got your IOU.'

'Trust me, Ange. I won't let you down. Even if I got to sell *Sticking Point*, you'll get your money back.'

'If ever I'm desperate, I'll let you know. In the meantime, the shop's beginning to show a profit, and I've got the balance of the compensation for *Pepperoni* tucked away safely in the bank.'

As Calum pulled into the driveway at Cedar Keys, Angie's sons came rushing out to meet her.

'Here they are, Gran. Here's Mum, and Evie,'

shouted Jake. He opened the car door and lifted his sister out. 'Let's get you indoors, I want to see how fast you can crawl,' he said, while Evie gurgled her delight at seeing him.

'She's almost walking now, Jake,' Angie said. 'She's been walking round the furniture at Auntie Vinnie's house.'

'At Stuart's, too,' Calum whispered quietly in her ear. 'If that kid could speak, what a tale she'd tell! I hope you covered her eyes when you and old Stewpot was at it on the rug.'

'Calum, you're shocking. How did you know it was on the rug?' Angie gave him a clip round the back of the neck.

'Don't worry. Your secret's safe with me.' Calum's eyes twinkled as he added, 'I've gone all respectable, Angie-babe – it makes a pleasant change to see *you* doing summat you didn't ought to be doin'.'

Tyler had thought he'd found in Erin the girl he'd been looking for all his life – a nice gentle girl, as pliable as Caitlin had been in the early days of their marriage. In your dreams, pal, he was telling himself, for once again the fairy story had ended badly. Erin was a mental case, pure and simple and, what was more, she was physically incapable of eating like a normal human being. Tyler fixed his hard dark eyes on her from across the cheap motel table, and launched into a tirade of complaint.

'All that shit about wanting to please me ... you're just like that other cow. When I think of the mega-crap I took from her about *me* being responsible for her losing a baby, it makes me want to spit. You're all the same, the lot of you. Women! I've had it up to my goddamned eyeballs, I can tell you.'

He leaned across the table and Erin flinched away, biting hard on her bottom lip to stop herself from crying. She couldn't halt the tears from flowing, though. The sight of them inflamed Tyler's anger more, and he raised his fist as if to hit her.

'You're all a bunch of bloody liars. Admit it – *you're* a liar.'

'Just leave me alone!' Erin rushed into the bedroom and curled up on the bed, shoving her fist into her mouth to stop from sobbing out loud.

'Say *I'm a liar,*' demanded Tyler, standing in the doorway and raising his hand threateningly.

'I ... I'm a liar,' she said slowly.

'That's right, I'm a bloody liar,' he mocked. 'I pretend to eat, then I stick my fingers down my throat and sick it all up again.'

Like a zombie, Erin repeated the words. She *was* a liar, of course. Back home in Fuzzy Cove, she used to lie to her mum and dad – her *darling* mum and dad.

'Leave me alone, Tyler, *please. I* want my mum.' Her crying was becoming louder and it was driving him crazy ... *nuts.*

'Your mother's an old slapper and you're a bloody liar, just like t'other one was. There's women gets killed in car crashes or blown up by bombs, yet still their babies survive. How could she have said I murdered ours, just 'cos I gave her one small poke in the belly?'

Erin knew just what had set him off. He'd received a letter from Caitlin's solicitor; it had been waiting at the motel when they arrived back the previous night. Ever since, he'd been hitting the bottle steadily, blaming her and Caitlin for all his woes. They hadn't moved out of the room; Tyler never needed food when he was drinking heavily and, as for her, food was the last thing that Erin wanted. She'd hardly had a morsel to eat for days.

'I thought that *you* were different, darling,' he said as he advanced towards her. Erin's throat had constricted into a tight band of fear. She struggled, but he yanked her off the bed by her hair. 'We're going to watch a movie, honey,' he said. 'And *you* are going to enjoy it.'

Still gripping her hair, he led her into the main room and, sitting her down on the couch in front of the television, fed one of his special X-certificate tapes into the video.

Would he do what he always did, *after* or *during*, Erin wondered fearfully. She prayed to stay strong enough to endure the next couple of hours. She'd try to blank her mind out – think of her mother and father in England. Of Holly, Jazz and herself together ... the Three Witches of Fuzzy Cove as the men in the Bluebird Café had always called them.

Caitlin, resting on the caravan couch, tickled the cat's dusky ears, and tried to concentrate on TV. Her thoughts were with Henry Meredith in America, trying to locate his daughter. She'd called in to see Roxanne the previous evening and found her in a dreadful state, and not at all the hard-boiled person that Caitlin had always thought her to be. Caitlin had remembered that Lisa, wife of Damian the keyboard player, would be certain to know where Erin was. Lisa would help Henry find her, Caitlin was sure of that.

Roxanne had been grateful for the information and, as the conversation had warmed, Caitlin had confided in her that she thought she might be pregnant. The rough-and-ready woman had gathered her into her arms, half smothering her in her vast, highly perfumed bosom. 'I'm so pleased for you,' she'd said. 'You'll be all right this time, with Rex to look after you, my blossom. He's nothing like that awful bugger what you was married to.'

Later at home, when Caitlin confessed to Rex that she'd given away their secret, he'd reminded her that Myrna Duffy was Roxanne's sister; it was Myrna who'd taken Caitlin's urine sample at the surgery for testing. It wouldn't be long before the whole village knew about it, he said, so they might as well start the ball rolling with Roxanne.

What a small world it was, here in Fuzzy Cove, Caitlin thought; yet she'd never felt so completely surrounded by friends.

Rex, she knew, was particularly pleased about the baby. His ex-wife, Delphine, was still making it difficult for him to have a normal relationship with their boy and girl and, in fact, refused to allow them to come anywhere near Caitlin. When they were older and able to make up their own minds, they would realise how much their father loved them, Caitlin reasoned. It was because Delphine was impossible to live with that Rex had been forced to move out of the house originally. The wisdom of Solomon was what was required in situations like this, Rex often said. In the meantime, he'd have this new little baby to nurture and love. And *it* would have the nicest, most caring man in all the world for its father. This child was heaven-blessed.

Caitlin was looking forward to having her nephews, Ryan and Sam, to stay this weekend, while their parents went hill-climbing in the Peak District. The boys would find it tremendous fun living in a trailer in the woods, as Caitlin did. She was most content living there with Rex, and it was a well-known fact that contentment in a mother helped to build a healthy happy baby.

The sea fret drifting in from the Bay formed droplets of moisture on the jacaranda leaves; they were plopping on Henry's head like intermittent raindrops as he stood on the sidewalk, waiting for Lisa to show up. He moved away from under the trees and, glancing at his watch, saw that it was almost three o'clock. She should be arriving any minute now.

Lisa had told him over the phone that the group were rehearsing all afternoon at a studio in Pacific Heights, and she would call in there first to make certain Tyler was with them. After that, she'd come on down to the waterfront to pick Henry up. She'd told him where to wait.

A moment later Lisa appeared. Little and dark, walking briskly, she was exactly as she'd described herself over the telephone. They made their introductions, and Henry followed her to where she'd parked her car. Within minutes they were driving through the hilly streets of the city, bound for the motel at the end of the Van Ness line where she'd warned Erin to be packed and ready to leave.

Two hours later Henry and Erin were seated aboard a USAir flight, bound for Los Angeles and then British Airways and home. The following day Erin was once more safe, back in her mother's arms. There were assorted bruises – lash stripes across her lower back and legs – to be attended to, but Roxanne's concerns prompted a visit from Dr Chadwick, who soon reassured them that the angry-looking lacerations were not serious medically.

Erin had begged Lisa not to tell Damian about the beatings that Tyler had given her. If the other members of the group fired him from the band, he'd almost certainly lose his permit to work in the States and *that*, Erin made clear, was the last thing that she wanted to happen.

Chapter Twenty-nine

It was a sunny morning in June, and children were searching for crabs on the rugged shore off Strumble Head on the Pembrokeshire coast of West Wales. Between the rocks, they came across a length of white planking with the letters *'itude'* painted on it in black. Their parents reported the find to the local coastguards who realised it could be the first evidence of a shipwreck. Further along the coast, another portion of the plank was found.

Computerised records showed that a sailing dinghy registered in the name *Solitude* and owned by Calum MacPherson, of Portmills, Bristol, had been reported missing eighteen months before. The Avon and Somerset police force was contacted and Calum duly notified. Marine insurers arranged for salvage experts to search the surrounding coastal waters for the hull of the dinghy.

On the first weekend in July, Henry and Roxanne went away for a two-night break in a smart four-star hotel in the Quantocks. Their relationship was back on track again, now that Henry had exchanged his job on the hospital switchboard for a nine-to-five clerical position in the X-ray Department.

'Come yere, you lovely hunk of man,' Roxanne pulled Henry towards her, almost suffocating him beneath the feather duvet. Henry wasn't complaining. She no longer saw him as a five-foot weakling; he was her new John Wayne, or whichever cowboy turned her on at the time.

'There's one thing for sure – *you* don't need no Viagra,' she remarked, after their second successful session of lovemaking since their arrival at the hotel earlier that day.

'Not with *you* I don't, my love,' Henry chuckled. Rolling on to his back, he said,

'Whatever made you ask that pillock, Herring, about Viagra, Rox? He and Lillian seemed to think it was *me* that needed it.'

'I know ... I'm sorry about that.' Roxanne paused, and, picking her words carefully, said, 'I'd heard that Rusty Mac was having a bit of trouble in that department. You know how he's always brought his problems to me – even though I'm not the least bit interested in his sex life.'

'I'd never have guessed that *he* had any trouble in that department, Roxanne.'

'No, nor me,' she agreed.

'You do realise that Hubert works in the morgue,' said Henry. 'I wouldn't think the people he deals with are in any state to be bothered about their lack of an erection.'

Roxanne remained silent as she mulled this remark over.

'They call them *stiffs*, I know,' said Henry, 'but I'm pretty sure that *that* part of the body is one of the first to stop firing on all cylinders.'

'Oh, blimey – then let's make the most of it while we can, my treasure.' Roxanne snuggled in closer to him again.

'Let me tell you all about the trip to the Grand Canyon we'll be taking this autumn. If you're a very good girl, we might throw in Las Vegas, too.'

'Can't wait, my cocker,' purred Roxanne, adding thoughtfully, 'It's a damn good job our Erin's settled and back at work, or I wouldn't never have bin able to enjoy meself anywhere.'

'And she's taking her training quite seriously this time, too,' Henry remarked.

'D'you reckon she'll land up marrying Dominic

Stone? He do seem ever so nice.'

'He is, indeed – a doctor, no less – and he appears to be really fond of her.'

Henry reflected upon the change in his daughter since her return from America. It seemed a contradictory thing, but the experience had actually made Erin a stronger person. She was eating sensibly again, and looked a different girl altogether from the poor bedraggled child he'd brought back to England on that overnight flight from LA.

Henry was pleased to notice that Erin's taste in clothing had improved, too. She was no longer going around in brown boots and black tights, and the long sleeves she'd always insisted on wearing were meant to cover up nothing more than her skinny arms. Henry dreaded to think what he'd mentally accused his daughter of trying to hide.

She'd proudly shown him the skimpy white dress that she'd bought to wear tonight. She and Holly, Dominic and Guy, were off to the Night Owl nightclub in Bristol to celebrate the anniversary of Holly's and Guy's first meeting.

'Rather them than me,' Henry murmured as he cuddled into his wife's ample frame. This, to his mind, was a far better way of spending a Saturday night than gallivanting off to some noisy nightclub in the city, or to the country and western nights where Roxanne used to drag him.

Angie was taking it easy on Sunday afternoon – the boys were out playing, and Evie was amusing herself with her building blocks on the living-room floor. Since Calum had told her about the wreckage found on the Pembrokeshire beach, Angie had been bracing herself for bad news. She hoped when it came she'd be brave enough to cope. She was halfway prepared, though. Unlike her daughter and mother-in-law, Angie had pretty much given up hope of ever finding Curt alive. She was sure he would never have stayed away, or stayed silent for so long, if he was.

In the quiet of the afternoon, she thought about Curt's last goodbye. He'd been in such good spirits, kissing her warmly, and leaving her in no doubt of his feelings for her. Though neither of them knew it then, she'd been two months pregnant with Evie. That probably accounted for the snappy way she'd spoken to him that day. She regretted it now, but thankfully Curt had seemed to bear her no ill-will.

When she heard the shop bell ring it seemed the continuation of the premonition. Angie was hardly surprised to find Suzi and Calum, and two police officers, waiting there to speak to her. They followed her through to the living room, where she sank down on to the settee, preparing herself for the worst.

Solitude's hull had been located and raised from the sea bed more or less intact, the police constable explained. There were signs that she'd been rammed by another vessel – some foreign remnants of grey paint had been found on her caved-in port side.

Calum squeezed Angie's hand. His dark sapphire eyes were sombre when he said, 'They've found a body, Ange.'

'I'm afraid so, Mrs MacPherson. A man – probably in his forties,' the policewoman confirmed. 'There were serious head injuries, most likely sustained during the collision.' She paused. 'The body is at the coroner's office at Milford Haven, awaiting an autopsy, and pathological reports,' she added.

'Identification?' Angie whispered to Calum fearfully.

'I'll handle that,' Calum said. 'No need to worry yourself about anything like that.'

Calum did, indeed, handle *everything* for her. After the police officers had left, he went next door to break the news to Holly, then sped off to Upalong to tell his mother and Josh.

There was pandemonium in Mariner's Cottage when Holly burst in on Angie a few moments later. She'd so pinned her hopes on finding her father alive that her grief was simply unquenchable.

Angie was relieved the boys were out, though she was aware she'd have to break the news to them that their father was dead the moment they returned. In comforting her daughter, though, Angie was in some small measure able to find her own strength. But she still dreaded the moment she'd have to face Daisy. If Holly was this distressed, how would she find it in her to comfort Curt's mother? She was glad now that she'd cooled it with Stuart the last time she'd spoken to him. Their affair was an added complication.

That night Angie tossed and turned in bed, going through in her mind the scenario of Curt's last minutes before the boat went down. He had been a ghost on the edge of her life for so long now, unclear in outline, always disappearing into the mist on a boat with sails ahoist. Now she knew the dream had been real. The ship *had* sunk and her very worst nightmares had come true.

Tormented by why it had happened, it crossed her mind that perhaps Calum had been involved with something he ought not to have been. *Solitude* was *his* boat, after all. There seemed no point casting blame, though; it wouldn't bring Curtis back. If Calum was in any way responsible for the tragedy, then he would have to live with that knowledge.

In Angie's mind, there was no way on earth that Curt would have been so dishonest or stupid as to smuggle absolutely anything into the country, apart from the occasional bottle of booze he sometimes presented her with, and the odd carton of cigarettes that the other men had given him in exchange for some fish that he'd caught. 'No chance,' she'd assured the police officers when they asked. They'd condescendingly said they would take her word for it; there'd been no suggestion of anything illegal on board when they'd searched the wreck of the sailing ship.

Angie's thoughts turned again to Stuart. When she'd parted from him at Easter, she'd told him that she needed some time to herself. She was scared at the speed with which their love affair had taken off. Like a bush fire, it had gone too far, too fast. They'd had to involve Vinnie in their secret, but she couldn't tell Daisy or Holly about it – they'd both still been banking on the hope that Curt was alive.

By the time morning came, Angie had made up her mind. As soon as the funeral and all the rest of the formalities were over, she would go to visit her aunts in Polzeath. She and the children would go down by coach and stay for the whole of August. Caitlin and Rex would be only too happy to move into Mariner's Cottage and take care of the shop, she knew.

Angie was seriously considering taking Rex up on his offer to buy her out. Until she'd become involved with Stuart, she would never have dreamed of handing over the reins to someone else so soon. The shop had been her life and salvation in the early days of Curt's disappearance, but now she was eager to make the break and move on with her life.

Stuart phoned her the next morning to say he'd be coming down to Fuzzy Cove right away. He appreciated that he'd have to stay in the background, he assured her, but Curtis *was* his first cousin; no one would think it strange that he'd want to be there. His mother would follow by train in a day or so's time. Josh had told him there was room for them both at Cedar Keys now that Daisy had bought a folding bed.

On the day before her husband's funeral, Angie and Stuart went for a walk up over the hill at Upalong. When they reached the summit they crossed the road and walked a little way along the cliff path that overlooked the Channel, where it washed the shores of Kilkenny Bay. Sheltered from prying eyes by a cluster of hawthorns, Stuart stopped and took her into his arms. He reassured her that everything would be all right again one day. He was even prepared to give up his job and look for a similar one in the West Country if that was what it would take for them to be together.

'I promise I won't rush you, but I can't let you go,' he said. He rested his cheek on Angie's brow, and they stood together, rocking gently to and fro in complete empathy with one another.

She told him she was taking the children to Cornwall for the school holidays. 'After that, you and I will have to get together to decide what we're going to do in the future ... where you might work ... and where we're going to live.' She looked deeply into Stuart's eyes, and said, 'As long as it's not too great a distance from the sea.'

He smiled. 'Not much chance of that happening. I'm a ferry boat skipper, remember? That's the job I'm trained for, and it's what I like to do.' He traced her brow lightly with his finger. 'I'll leave you alone for now then, eh? Stay away for as long as you want me to ... for as long as it takes, my angel.'

On Saturday, a few days later, when Stuart had arranged to go off by himself to catch up with some necessary errands, Angie contacted Calum to ask him if he'd like to join her in a picnic on the beach. The weather was warm and sunny, and she wanted to keep her promise to take his little girls with Evie, who had just started to walk. Suzi was spending the day helping her mother, Dorothy, at the Bluebird Café while Dexy was away on holiday.

Kilkenny Bay had been a favourite haunt of

theirs when Curt was alive, Angie recalled. They'd spent many happy hours there as a family – Curt playing football or cricket with his sons, while she and Holly, having selected a patch of soft ground and covering it with a blanket, liked to relax in the sunshine and read, have a doze, or chat.

While Lucie and Emma were introducing Evie to their secret rock pools, Calum and Angie opened cans of lager and began discussing the events of the past week, and the months which preceded them. She told him what suggestions Stuart had made for their future and Calum was full of encouragement.

'Go for it,' Angie,' he enthused. 'He's a sound bloke, and if he's willing to turn his life upside down with getting a new job, and all that, he must be serious and not just spouting a lot of hot air.'

'But what on earth will Holly and Daisy think? They're both still in a dreadful state,' she said worriedly.

'That's because they never wanted to face the truth – they was searching up blind alleys, trying to deny the fact that our Curt could have met with an accident and been drowned. You and me, Ange, we always knew he would never have gone away and left you and the kids. It wasn't in him to do a thing like that.'

Angie rose to her feet and sauntered down to the water's edge, where a container ship, with Japanese logo, was heading off into the wide grey estuary. Its engines were chugging cheerfully and rhythmically; it sounded happy to be going home.

Calum went over to Angie, waiting for her to speak. He was sure there was more she wanted to say to him.

'Calum, please tell me something,' she said after a while. 'Curt wasn't involved in anything bad, was he? The police sort of suggested that he might be, though they admitted they had absolutely no proof of anything like that – either on the day he was drowned, or in any part of his past life.'

He didn't reply straight away, then, slipping an arm round her waist, he asked quietly, 'And how did that make you feel, Ange?'

'Angry, bloody angry, Cal. Curt's the father of my children, and I know he'd never do anything like that.'

Calum hesitated a moment, then he told her, 'You've a perfect right to feel angry. Curt was straight as a die – the brains of the family – not a dopey bugger like I.'

'You're not dopey; you're my best mate. Say you always will be, Cal.'

'You, Angie-babe, deserve to be happy, so go and be happy with Stewpot the brave, though, personally, I've got a job to understand a word he says. Och, aye, the noo.'

Calum put an end to the seriousness of the conversation, the same way that he always did. Acting the clown came easy to him; he'd been doing it ever since primary school when he'd once caused Roxanne Cox to wet her knickers in the classroom from laughing so much.

As Angie set about preparing the picnic meal, Calum remained deep in thought. There was no point dwelling on what might or might not have happened out there in the Channel almost two long years ago, he told himself. It might be that Starkey knew a thing or two about certain events, but if that was so, he'd be duty-bound to keep the knowledge to himself.

Calum most certainly didn't want to know. Better to let matters remain as they are, he thought – to delve too deeply into things could cause a lot of unnecessary grief and pain and Curtis's loved ones had already suffered enough.

You might just as well start digging into the reasons why they named this place after a town in the middle of Ireland, Calum mused. Lore would have it that it was all tied up with a smuggling racket which had taken place more than three hundred years ago. The legitimate import in those days was pigs; the contraband, more likely than not, Irish whiskey. It was ancient history now, though, and there weren't many people who ever gave it a thought. They were all too busy getting on with their own lives.

Calum glanced over at the three little girls, still busy poking sticks and throwing the odd pebble into the rock pool.

'Would you look at that babby there,' he murmured aloud. She was the spitting image of her dad – you'd recognise that copper topknot a mile away. It would be a terrible thing to have Curt's image tarnished in her eyes – not to mention Holly's and the twins.

The children were coming towards him now; his daughters helping Evie to walk on the uneven shingle. As usual, Emma was fussing unnecessarily, causing the little one to become increasingly angry.

Calum called out to her. "Hoy there, Em – leave the little 'un bide. Can't you see she don't want you picking her up? She's trying her best to walk on her own.'

His brother's child had a temper like fury – Calum had heard her screeching from some long distance away. It would serve her in good stead in the future, he thought. A chip off the old block, like her sister, Holly ... he couldn't see anything or anyone easily crushing *that* independent spirit.

The day he was due to go back to Scotland, Stuart called in on Angie to say goodbye. He eyed the large pile of garments she was ironing a trifle dubiously. 'Looks like you're ready to take off very soon,' he said.

Angie nodded. 'That's right. We'll be leaving as soon as we can.'

Stuart's voice was wistful when he said, 'So – we'll be in touch again in September then?'

'Mmm ... I guess so.' She continued with her ironing and didn't look up.

'Och – it's only a short hop from Bristol to Glasgow. Or haven't I told you that before?'

'You have indeed,' she said, 'Many times. And didn't I set out to prove that it was?'

She suddenly recalled their loving times in Scotland and, immediately, everything became clear. 'Stuart,' she said, 'getting back to what we were talking about the other day up on the cliff path overlooking the bay, the day before the funeral. About ... you know ... where we might live.'

'Aye, I remember, and you said not too far away from the sea.'

'Well ... I think I can say in all truth, I'd be willing to give your homeland a go.'

'You mean you would come with me to Scotland?'

'If you think it's a good idea.'

Stuart's face broke into an enormous grin. 'Angeline MacPherson ... what can I say? I think it's an altogether *brilliant* idea.'

This Large Print Book for the partially sighted, who cannot read normal print, is published under the auspices of

THE ULVERSCROFT FOUNDATION

MD

A.V.

SL

J